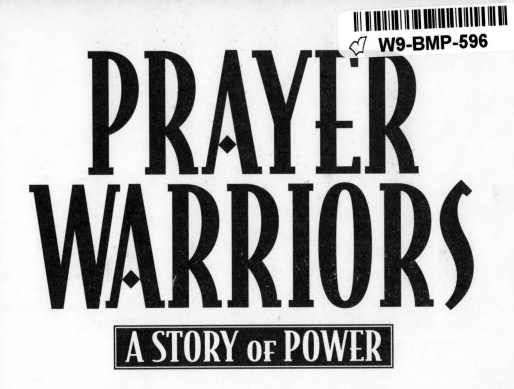

PRAYER WARRIORS

A STORY OF POWER

CELESTE PERRINO WALKER

Pacific Press®Publishing Association
Nampa, Idaho
Oshawa, Ontario, Canada

Edited by Jerry D. Thomas
Designed by Dennis Ferree
Cover illustration by Brian Fox

Copyright © 1997 by
Pacific Press® Publishing Association
Printed in the United States of America
All Rights Reserved

Walker, Celeste perrino
    Prayer warriors : a story of power / Celeste perrino Walker.
        p.   cm.
    ISBN 0-8163-1359-8 (pbk. : alk. paper)
    I. Title
    PS3573.A42525P7
    813'.54—dc20   96-21113
                                                            CIP

00 01 02 • 5 4 3

This book is lovingly dedicated to
my parents,
Peter and Adrienne Perrino,
who taught me
to love reading.

Just look what you did!

ACKNOWLEDGMENTS

I would like to thank the following people without whose help this book might never have been written:

Glen Robinson—A great cheerleader who was excited about the book before it was even written and who encouraged me through the rough initial stages of submission. You were right; it did need a few less characters.

The folk at Ultralight Aviation for sending me specs and photos of the ultralight I was writing about.

My dad—for finding me information about river blindness and Africa via computer.

Chuck Huenergardt—a pilot I met in cyberspace, for his advice on the sequences leading up to the plane crash and the technolingo I would have had to make up otherwise. :)

Rich Edison—for reading the entire manuscript (he was the only one who dared) and for giving me a truly valuable critique as well as medical advice for my characters. Also, for constantly repeating the four words a writer loves best, "Give me more pages!"

My husband, Rob—for sharing me with my computer, without complaint . . . well, mostly. And for believing that I could do it, when I wasn't even sure myself. And also for listening patiently while I worked out various story lines . . . now aren't you glad you did?

My son, Joshua—for giving up Mommy for a little while so I could work. It wasn't easy for me either, sweetie.

And last, but by no means least, my editor, Jerry D. Thomas, for putting up with me again. This makes three, doesn't it? You are truly a brave man.

CAST OF CHARACTERS

Billie Jo Raynard: Billie Jo's husband, Jimmy, was injured in a logging accident which left him in a coma. Doctors do not hold out much hope for him. Billie Jo cares for him at home with the help of a visiting nurse. She has two children, Cassidy (4) and Dallas (18 months).

Jimmy Raynard: Billie Jo's husband. A logger. In a coma.

Helen Raynard: Billie Jo's mother-in-law. A very controlling person. She dislikes Billie Jo. She would like to take over Jimmy's care and resents any "interference" by Billie Jo.

Leah Moreau: Billie Jo's friend.

Angel:
    Jewel
Demon:
    Nog

Ethel Bennington: Crippled by arthritis, Ethel is assisted during the day by a visiting nurse. People call all the time to give her prayer requests, and Ethel prays for them all during the day. The visiting nurse records each one in a notebook.

Cindi Trahan: Ethel Bennington and Jimmy Raynard's visiting nurse. Cindi and her husband, Marc, have been praying for a baby, but they remain childless.

Marc Trahan: Cindi's husband.

Russell Duffy: Sells medical supplies. Attends the same church as Cindi and Marc.

Julia Duffy: Russell's pregnant teenage daughter. Julia is considering an abortion.

Ray Vargas: Julia's boyfriend and the father of her baby. A rowdy character, he nevertheless loves Julia and wants what's best for her.

Pastor Hendricks: Pastor of the church they all attend.

Angels:

    Supervising angel: Reissa

    Shania

    Recording angel: Michel

    Calum

    Gaye

Demons:

    Sparn

    Rafe

Don Germaine: Very bitter. Very opinionated. Very outspoken. He ran a clinic in Rwanda and was trapped there during the war. Cannot get over the things he experienced. Has recently been assigned a new clinic outpost just outside of Niamey.

Nwibe Okeke: Native African man who contracted river blindness. Is led around by a stick held by his son, Marcus. His wife passed away a few years previously. He works at the clinic doing anything he is capable of.

Marcus Okeke: Nwibe's son.

Wahabi Okeke: Bartender in Niamey. Brother of Nwibe.

Shay Beauregard: Young Cajun girl from Louisiana. Impressed to enter a mission field after graduating from college with a degree in nursing.

Toby O'Connell: Nurse from the United States. Madly in love with her husband, Davy. They enjoy flying their Cessna airplane and fixing up their house in Boston.

Davy O'Connell: Toby's husband. Madly in love with her too.

Angels:

> Julian (Don)
>
> Gaius (Shay)
>
> Lileah (Toby)
>
> Jes (Davy)

Demons:

> Merck (Don)
>
> Jezeel (Shay)
>
> Lucien (Toby)

Lyle Ryan: A double amputee as the result of a car accident the night of graduation from high school. Lyle is bitter about the accident and angry at God. Has become a hermit.

Berniece Kendall: Her husband Peter suffered a massive heart attack that caused the accident, which claimed his life and resulted in Lyle's amputation. She lives just up and across the road from him. Thinks about Lyle occasionally, but tries not to. Not sure whatever happened to him.

Calla Kendall: Berniece's niece who comes to live with her while she's attending college. Loves just about any kind of sport.

Angel:

> Shelan

Demon:

> Warg

Also:

Archangel: Noble

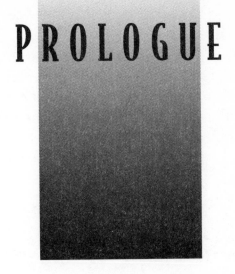

PROLOGUE

The sun crept over the tops of the pine trees lining the long, winding driveway. A massive house slowly took on more detail as the warmth of the sun caressed it. Three stories high, the porch was supported by pillars as thick as a man's waist, the lawn immense and immaculately landscaped, the windows dark except for one. Hunched over in the window, the figure of an aged woman gradually took shape. A careful observer, looking up from the yard, might have noticed a warm glow surrounding the figure.

Her silver hair wrapped neatly in a bun, her gnarled hands clasped tightly in prayer, the old woman's lips moved soundlessly until she felt the warmth of the sun begin to shine through the window. Watery blue eyes fluttered open as her wrinkled face was made younger by a smile that could not be squelched by age or pain. Joyfully she absorbed the scene in the heavens.

A kaleidoscope of color painted the horizon. The reds and oranges of the sunrise bled together to create a still more vibrant shade, and wisps of gray clouds, like fissures in the firmament, divided the color into one giant plate of stained glass.

"Glory to God in the highest and peace to His people on earth!"

the old woman shouted with abandon. Gone were thoughts of the pain that had woken her early that morning. Instead, she was filled with the majesty of the King of heaven.

"Hallelujah!" she cried, lifting her crippled hands up and clapping them together with joy, heedless of the fiery pain in her joints.

Around the old woman, scores of angels congregated. One, a recording angel, paused in his duties long enough to smile at the uncensured joy of the old woman. The rest, commissioned to bring the constant requests of the old woman to the throne of heaven, bustled back and forth, kept continually busy by her prayers that seemingly never ceased.

The tallest of the angels sat beside the old woman, with one arm resting protectively around her thin shoulders. From this angel radiated a glow that lighted up the room. Although she couldn't see them, the old woman herself seemed to sense the presence of the angels and thanked God for them many times in her prayers.

Studying the old woman's face intently, the angel seemed satisfied that she was ready to return to her prayers, having drunk in the beauty of the sunrise. "There is to be a new mission clinic in Africa," the angel informed her. "But, they will need much help. The doctor who is to be sent is well-beloved by you, but the things he has suffered are not known to anyone.

"He will begin a struggle that will threaten his spiritual life.

He needs your prayers. He will also need a staff. There is a great need for workers. Pray that there will be those who desire to enter the mission field. Ease and plenty have made them comfortable and few now care to go. Pray that they will see their work in terms of eternal value.

"And continue to remember those who have been irreparably injured," the angel urged gently.

At those words, the old woman looked down at her own useless hands, a thoughtful expression on her face. She attempted to flex the crooked fingers, but they refused to budge. A wry smile tugged at the corners of her mouth.

"Keep in mind also that you cannot know the will of the Master. But that in everything, He wants what is for your best good . . ." The angel's voice trailed off sadly before she began again in a whisper, pain lacing her words. "Even when it does not seem so to you," she finished.

The angel went on, not speaking so much to the old woman now as simply freeing her own mind. "There is so much you cannot understand in your humanity. You are so preoccupied with life, with living, that you forget the war raging all around you. You must not forget!" she stressed, her features animated, her voice charged with excitement and urgency. "Take up your arms and fight. Fight as you've never fought before. This battle belongs to the Lord. He has already overcome. He will give you strength. He will be your armor and your shield. So, fight, warrior of prayer, fight."

The angel finished, glancing down at her charge who had already bent her head to begin praying again. Her rush of satisfaction was short-lived. It withered in the knowledge of how few of these warriors there were. While the enemy raged in battle, the troops were content to tend to their own affairs, not even realizing that the battle extended to their own homes, their own lives.

Somehow, they must be awakened. And with each of these

faithful ones, it would begin. The angel squeezed the old woman's shoulders and bowed her head, praying as well. The glow around them intensified until it was too bright to look at.

Demons, who had been waiting on the perimeter for their chance at this steadfast one, slunk away one by one. The last to remain spit venomously and uttered a curse in their direction before he, too, disappeared in search of easier prey.

CHAPTER

Billie Jo Raynard stumbled down the hallway, drawn by the sound of the baby's cry. Soft moonlight shone in the window, providing enough illumination to help her avoid stepping on Cass's stuffed horse left lying in the middle of the floor. When she pushed open the door of the kids' room, Cass looked up drowsily and mumbled something in her sleep before burrowing back under her covers.

Eighteen-month-old Dallas stopped crying when he saw her and reached his arms out to her over the top of his crib. "Mama, baba," he demanded.

Billie Jo gathered him up in her arms and carried him back to her bedroom. As she laid him on the big queen-sized bed she used to share with Jimmy, she was struck again by how empty it was. Until six months ago, she'd had to cram herself between Jimmy's giant slumbering form and Dallas' tiny body, elbowing for leverage. Back then she used to wish for a bigger bed. Now she wished for a fuller one.

She set Dallas down in the warm spot she'd just vacated and put a pillow on the other side of him so he wouldn't roll off the bed. Lifting her shirt, she fumbled with the snap of her bra. Dallas searched eagerly for her nipple and latched on, sucking contentedly.

Billie Jo sank onto her pillow and drifted off into the world of half awake and half asleep reserved exclusively for nursing mothers and their nightly vigils. She mentally oriented herself. In the morning it would be Tuesday. Tuesday. Cass had a doctor's appointment. That meant Helen would be coming over to watch Jimmy. And groceries. She had to get groceries. They were out of almost everything.

Her thoughts paused long enough for her to switch Dallas to the other side. She wound a finger in one of his silky, soft curls. He really needed a haircut, but it would be his first, and she kept putting it off. It was something she had hoped to share with Jimmy. Now . . .

"Face it," she thought for the thousandth time since she'd brought Jimmy home from the hospital, "Doctors don't know everything. God knows everything. Maybe it's God's will that Jimmy gets better."

"Maybe it isn't," her negative side argued back.

"Please, Lord," she begged silently, as tears squeezed through her shut eyelids. "Please let Jimmy get well again. His kids need him. I need him. Please, Lord. I know I said for better or for worse, but I'm not sure I can take it if it gets much worse."

Dallas pulled away from her and smacked his lips. His eyes were half closed, a good sign that he intended to go right back to sleep. Billie Jo carried him back to his room and laid him gently in his crib. She covered him up and softly kissed his forehead. He stirred but didn't waken, a faint smile on his lips.

Before going back to bed, she made her way quietly to the living room to check on Jimmy. He lay on the cot she'd set up, sleeping peacefully. Just looking at him, a person might never guess there was anything wrong with him. All the external injuries—the broken ribs, the lacerations, and everything else had healed. Everything but his brain.

She ran a hand beneath him and groaned when she felt it was soaked. Almost mechanically, she pulled out a fresh set of sheets, a towel, and another johnny to dress him in. Jimmy was a big man, and Billie Jo struggled to roll him over as the nurses showed her, changing one side of the bed first, then rolling him back to change the other side, careful not to let the clean sheets get wet by touching the others.

Two unseen beings, occupying the living room with Billie Jo, watched her with interest. One stood at least seven feet tall and was garbed in an almost blinding white light. His skin seemed to be of highly polished bronze, his features well chiseled, a peaceful and sympathetic expression on his face. Graceful wings fanned the air behind him as he concentrated on his charge. He bent over to lay an encouraging hand on Billie Jo's shoulder.

"Aw, leave her alone, why don't you?" his companion spat as he crowded in by Billie Jo's elbow. "She'll be mine in the end. Why waste your time?"

The angel turned slightly, his brilliance making the demon squint and shuffle off to the side to avoid coming in direct contact with it.

"No soul is a waste of time, Nog. Even you should know that," chided the angel.

The demon scowled. Although they had once shared the same beautiful heavenly courts, the once proud, majestic being, after participating in the perpetuation of sin for thousands of years, retained none of his former beauty.

The noble brow of the angel, which indicated a great intellect, was narrow on the demon, housing a scheming and twisted mind. His eyes, once clear and bright, were sunken deep into their sockets. A close look made Jewel turn quickly away. Black as an abyss, the eyes of the demon were cunning and shrewd. All the collective pain caused, felt, and experienced since the fall of Adam reflected out of those evil eyes.

Stoop-shouldered, Nog barely reached Jewel's chin. His skin, unlike Jewel's, hung loosely around his frame, like that of a cancer patient in the advanced stage of the disease. Wings that were created gossamer, shining, and graceful hung limp and tired from his back like an inky shadow, absorbing whatever light fell on them but refusing to release it. Saggy skin and a weak chin belied Nog's inner resourcefulness, making him appear old and worn out.

But Jewel wasn't fooled by appearances. Nog was desperate. All the demons were desperate. Ever since the Great Prince, Jesus, had conquered death and provided a way of escape for all who believed, Satan, the great deceiver, had redoubled his efforts to take down as many with him as possible when it was all over. Each one lost was a victory for the demons. And each one saved caused rejoicing throughout all heaven.

When the bed was changed and a thick towel placed beneath Jimmy's hips to absorb the next accident, Billie Jo pulled off his sopping johnny and put the clean one on him. As she struggled to pull his arm free of the wet johnny, it flung out, knocking her back. She lay pinned beneath the weight of his arm, trying to catch her breath. She wondered idly how long it would take for Jimmy's arm to shrivel up when the muscles "atrophied" like the doctors said.

With a grunt, she pushed his arm aside and finished dressing him. He looked so peaceful, as though any moment he would open his eyes and say, "Hey there, darlin'. Come give me some sugar."

She smiled at the thought and without thinking, she bent down and kissed him on the mouth, the scratchiness of his beard bringing back memories stilled by the cool, unresponsive lips. Billie Jo laid her head on Jimmy's chest for a moment and listened to the rhythmic thumping of his heart.

"I love you, Jimmy Raynard. Wake up."

Kneeling beside the cot, she took one of Jimmy's big hands in her own. A feeling of desperation welled up inside. Yes, she loved Jimmy. So much that her heart nearly burst with it, but physically and mentally, she was exhausted from taking care of him. Would he ever be well? Would life ever return to "normal"? Sometimes Billie Jo wondered if she remembered what normal felt like.

Tight bands constricted around her chest. The sensation of smothering was almost overwhelming. Her whole body cried out for peace, for normalcy, for what they had before the accident.

"It'll never be any better than this," Nog growled, hovering near Billie Jo's elbow like a dark shadow. He'd been in the same position now for six months, badgering her and heaping discouragement on her. She was bound to break. It was only a matter of time. "In fact, it might get much worse. Jimmy might die. Or maybe he'll just stay like this and you'll have to take care of him and your kids for the rest of your life. How would you like that?"

Nog belched without bothering to excuse himself. He was toying with her now. "You know, suicide is an attractive alternative. Just slip into the sweet peace of death. A few little pills. You won't even feel a thing."

Billie Jo shook her head as if she was trying to clear cobwebs. Where did that thought come from? Suicide? Her? Well, she had to admit that sometimes the thought was enticing. But, where would that leave Cassidy and Dallas? Billie Jo shook her head again, this time more firmly. No. Never.

Nog slunk glumly around her to the other elbow. Too far. He'd pushed her a little too far. But, he hadn't been able to help himself. Sometimes these types went for the suicide out when the pressure became unbearable. He'd bide his time. He hadn't lost yet.

"But, you will," Jewel informed him as though reading Nog's thoughts. "Her faith is strong and she is a fighter. She won't easily buy into your worn out old line."

Nog snarled, crowding in closer. "Want to bet? Just let her push herself through a few more months with little or no sleep, and we'll see what her judgment is like then. I'll nudge her over the edge as easily as that." He snapped his long, gnarled fingers in emphasis, and Jewel shuddered.

Billie Jo bowed her head. "Dear Lord, it's just You and me here in the middle of the night again. I can't remember the last time I slept through the night in one piece. Must have been before Cass came. Anyway, here I am again. Me and Jimmy. Lord, he needs You so much. Ever since he fell out of that tree, he just, well, you know, Lord. The doctors say he's a vegetable, but I don't believe that," Billie Jo added quickly. "I know my Jimmy is still in this body somewhere, Lord. Please help him get out. Heal his mind the way You healed his body. Help him come back to me and the kids."

Nog yelped as if he'd touched something hot and retreated to the other side of the room where he glowered at Jewel, who placed a wing protectively around Billie Jo's shoulder. The usual brightness of the angel intensified as he joined his own prayer to Billie Jo's. The molten glow that surrounded him spread to encompass her as well. The brightness shone like liquid fire, shimmering and fluid. Almost immediately, Billie Jo's shoulders relaxed, and a smile touched her lips.

Billie Jo felt peace flow through her like a warm, comforting wave. Maybe life would never be normal again, but, at least, God would never abandon her. He would always be right there by her side, strengthening her for whatever came next.

"Thank You, Lord," she murmured. Lips still moving in prayer, she snuggled her cheek on Jimmy's hand and drifted off to sleep, keeping the night watch.

Lyle Ryan watched his girlfriend Kara's hair as she turned. It was like slow motion on TV. Light filtered through the blond waves, making it look like a waterfall of pure sunshine. Kara's hair was what first caught Lyle's attention.

She smiled at him and raised one eyebrow, as if asking what he was thinking. Her teeth were startlingly white against her tan. Lyle wondered, not for the first time, which he appreciated more, her beauty or her personality.

"Lyle, man of the hour, have a cold one."

An icy, wet can, pressed into his hand, brought Lyle back to the present. As though it were being brought up to speed, he was suddenly conscious of the music blaring in the background. The song was *Wind Beneath My Wings*, their class song.

Shelan tried to focus Lyle's attention on the beer in his hand. "You don't want that, Lyle," she urged. "It will pollute your body and your mind. It will impair your judgment. Stand up for yourself. Say you don't want it."

Lyle stared stupidly at the can in his hand. He reached out a hand to stop Kevin. "I don't want a beer," he said, trying to give it back.

"Sissy," Warg hissed. His cruel, piercing eyes watched Lyle carefully, sizing him up, determining what would hurt him the most. "What kind of a man are you, can't drink a beer? One little old beer. Ain't gonna hurt you. Big, bad football player. Maybe you ought to be a cheerleader instead."

Kevin turned toward Lyle, his face registering surprise. "It's all right, Lyle, there's plenty more. Drink up. This is your party."

Lyle shook his head, his face flushing. "No, thanks, but I don't want any." Lyle was conscious of the stares of his classmates. He heard snickering in the corner but couldn't tell if it was about him or some private joke. He was uncomfortably aware of Kara looking on, a puzzled expression on her face.

"Your girl's gonna find herself a real man, wimp," Warg smirked. "Drink it."

"Real men don't have to rely on artificial substances to prove their manhood," Shelan insisted, more to Warg than to Lyle. *"Strength of character. That is what women admire."*

"Oh, what do you know about it?" Warg demanded.

Lyle pressed the can firmly back into Kevin's hand. "I don't want it," he repeated. He felt his face flush during the awkward pause that followed. Then, as if on cue, conversation started up again and people turned away from him. Lyle let out a long breath, unaware that he'd been holding it. He turned to find Kara at his elbow.

"Should we put the beer in a champagne glass?" she asked, her voice laced with sarcasm. "After all, we are supposed to be celebrating."

Lyle ignored the tone in her voice, noticing for the first time that she held a beer can herself. He felt a wave of shock ripple through him. He hadn't known that she drank alcohol. He tried to take the can from her hand.

"Come on, Kara. You don't want that stuff. It's bad for you."

She pulled away from him angrily. "Give me that," she snarled. "Don't drink if you don't want to, but don't tell me what to do. Think you're so smart. Doesn't give you the right to run my life. I'm not your wife."

"Not yet," Lyle murmured sadly as he watched her stalk away, her back rigid and unyielding. "Maybe not ever."

This party was turning into a nightmare. He shook himself sternly. *Just because you're not drinking and everyone else is doesn't mean that you can't enjoy yourself. This is your party. Everyone is here because of you. Go have fun.*

Fortifying himself with his own pep talk, Lyle pasted on a smile, joined in the first conversation he intercepted, and ran with it.

"Mrs. Cobb was definitely more difficult than Mr. Fields. Don't you agree, Pam?" Joey was asking.

Pam shrugged and curled a lip in disdain. "I don't know. I never rated them on a scale of one to ten. Why don't we ask the expert, our valedictorian. What do you think, Lyle?"

Lyle grinned. Here was a question he could field. "Mrs. Cobb hands down," he agreed. Joey smiled and washed down a slug of beer. "Of course, the real slave driver was Coach Ellis."

Joey groaned. "I don't know how you put up with him, man. I had him for P.E., and that was enough. What a rush. I never used so much deodorant in my life as I did in that class."

Pam rolled her eyes and moved off to join a more feminine conversation. Joey chuckled and jerked his head in her direction. "She said Yes," he confided.

Lyle felt his mouth drop open. Joey and Pam? Married? He forced himself to say something he didn't feel. "Hey, that's great! Congratulations! When's the big day?"

Joey accepted a slap on the shoulder. "In the fall. So, while you're off at college making touchdowns, we'll be making babies."

"You want kids?" Lyle asked, stunned. "Already?"

"Why wait?" Joey asked. "I love kids. I want dozens."

"That's great," Lyle stammered. "Really great. I'm happy for you." He started to move off and lose himself in the crowd, but Joey stopped him with a hand on his shoulder.

"Hey, Lyle, congratulations on the scholarship. Really, I mean it. You worked hard for that, man. You earned it. I want to see you in the Super Bowl someday."

"I'll be there," Lyle promised. He scanned the crowd for Kara and saw her talking to Derek Elliott, captain of the hockey team. She flipped her hair back over one shoulder and smiled. Lyle heard her giggle all the way across the crowd.

Anger coursed through him. What was she doing? Making him pay for what she perceived as weakness?

In the end, he left early, chased away from his own party by his jealousy. He drove toward his house, gaining speed as he went. Slamming the car into fourth, he stomped on the pedal. The car, his late father's prize mustang, surged ahead, the engine more than capable of keeping up with Lyle's anger.

"Come on, Sissy boy," Warg berated him. *"You can go faster than that, can't you?"* His big frame was crunched up in the front seat beside Lyle. He leaned closer. *"Not scared, are you?"*

Lyle punched the pedal closer to the floor. Mad, that's what he was. As he watched the needle leap across the speedometer, he felt a faint satisfaction take the edge off his fury.

"Lyle, please," Shelan begged from the back seat. *"Slow down. You're only hurting yourself. It would be so easy to lose control of this car. What are you gaining from driving recklessly? It doesn't do anything to glorify your Master."*

Lyle picked his foot up off the accelerator and relaxed into the seat as the car slowed down. All of a sudden, he felt childish. He squinted out at the road. It was twilight, and his eyes were playing tricks on him. On the road ahead he could see the silken waves of Kara's hair. In his ear he heard her high-pitched giggle as she smiled up at Derek.

Then the flash of blond hair became the dying sun glinting off the windshield of a car careening wildly out of control. Kara's high-pitched giggle melted into the scream of metal twisting and scraping on the pavement.

Desperately, Lyle yanked the steering wheel over, trying to avoid the oncoming vehicle and sending his car into a skid. Too late, he over-corrected and sat helplessly as the other vehicle plowed headlong into his car. His mouth opened in a soundless scream.

When he woke up, he was drenched in sweat and shaking all over. He knew what woke him even before he was completely awake. It was always the same dream. It always ended the same way. And always, he couldn't scream.

Lyle heaved himself up in bed and squirmed into his wheel-chair. Blood pounded angrily in his ears and throbbed in his temples. Having no other outlet, he pounded viciously on the arms of his chair while hot, angry tears coursed down his cheeks.

It was always the same. Even after six years, he couldn't shake the memory of that night. The night that ruined his life and his career. The night his life officially ended. Absently, his hands slid down his thighs, stopping where his pajama bottoms lay flat against the chair, just above where his knees should have been. His fingers jerked back as if he'd touched something distasteful.

He wheeled his chair over to the window and after a struggle, pushed it open. The warm spring air caressed his flushed face. Spring was always the worst. Everything about it reminded him of the hopes he'd held at graduation. The closer it got to June, the worse the nightmares would get until he was finally a complete insomniac, trying to avoid having to sleep at all. Already he could see dark circles under his eyes when he forced himself to face the mirror, which he avoided whenever possible.

The God who had felt so close to him at graduation, when his future looked so rosy and promising, seemed to have retreated to some unreachable place since the accident. Not that Lyle had tried approaching Him much beyond an occasional angry fist raised toward heaven, accompanied by a hoarse wail of, "Why did You do this to me?"

Mostly, Lyle preferred to believe that God had abandoned him, maybe that He didn't even exist. It was much easier than believing that God had allowed this to happen to him, or worse, that God had done this to him for some reason.

Shelan sighed heavily. "That's not true. You know that's not true," she said, but she knew Lyle could hardly hear her. He had guarded his bitterness and anger for so long now that they blocked out her voice. It was like a faint whisper filtering through the trees.

"When are you going to give up, you useless angel?" Warg snarled. "I am growing tired of your ceaseless optimism. Don't you have someone else you can irritate? This one is mine, all mine."

Shelan drew herself up, glorious wings fanning the air gen-

tly behind her. "He is not lost. There are some praying for him still."

Warg's harsh laugh grated in her ears as she bowed her head. It was true. Someone did still remember Lyle in prayer. If only he would look up and remember God. If only he would listen to her. Just once more.

Don Germaine stared vaguely out the window of the plane and tried to still the trembling of his hands by clasping them fiercely in his lap. The buzz of voices around him penetrated his thoughts, and he looked around briefly. He tried to distract himself by eavesdropping on snatches of conversation he picked up around him.

A girl laughed, her head thrown back, her eyes sparkling. He envied her easy, carefree attitude. How long had it been since he'd felt that way? College, maybe? No, too earnest to be carefree. Back then he'd been out to cure the world single-handedly. Well, he and God, anyway.

He smiled wryly as he remembered his self-righteous attitude toward his classmates and, eventually, his colleagues. Not that he'd changed much. That was why, while friends he'd graduated with and worked with side by side had gone on to six-figure incomes and beautiful houses, he still lived out of a suitcase and ran his clinic from a hut that more closely resembled an abandoned shack than a hospital.

He leaned his head back against the seat and closed his eyes, but it was no use. His brain filled in the dark space with images he couldn't bear to remember. Quickly, he opened his eyes again.

"Sir? Sir?" The soft voice at first seemed to be a hazy part of Don Germaine's own thoughts. But the cackle of the pilot's welcoming comments brought him back to the present.

"Sir? It's time to put on your seatbelt." The flight attendant smiled at him, a polite, firm smile that didn't leave room for argument. She pointed to the "seatbelt" light that was already on as she strapped herself into "takeoff" position, her seat facing the rear of the DC-10.

"Sorry." Don fumbled awkwardly for the belt, snapping it into place. He rubbed his temples. It felt as though steel bands were tightening around his skull and his stomach was warming up for those funny maneuvers that always made him wish he'd skipped lunch.

"Flying bothers you?" the flight attendant asked. Her sympathy seemed more like something she wore than something she felt. She reminded him of some nurses he'd worked with in the States. All business, no compassion.

"Always has," he replied irritably.

She smiled again, a shallow, mirthless smile, and Don found himself wondering if people who knew her thought it was as aggravating as he was beginning to find it. "Are you traveling for business?" she asked.

Why don't you go bother someone else? he thought. Out loud he said, "Something like that. I'm going to run a medical clinic in Niger, Africa."

"Oh." Something in the way she said it and the neatly arched eyebrows led him to believe that she was sorry she asked. Probably one of those types that was afraid to get her hands dirty helping someone out. "Well, good luck to you, then."

"You've got her now," Merck observed. *"Go on, make her squirm a little."* He was so sure that Don would follow his suggestion that he didn't even bother to look up from where he

was studying the scenery below as the plane gently lifted into the air.

Don couldn't resist. As the flight attendant rose from her seat and turned to leave, he caught her wrist. "You know, it might help me to talk until we get settled into the air."

Annoyance crept behind her eyes. She removed her wrist from his grasp. "I really couldn't . . ."

"Oh, come on. You asked where I was going. I'll tell you."

Don's eyes flickered to her name tag. Diane. She looked like a Diane. Tall and thin, her jet black hair framed a face as white as marble. "I'll tell you all about it in detail, Diane," he promised. She flinched at the sound of her name but didn't sit down.

"Well, what?" she asked finally.

"The worst thing in these clinics is the pathetic lack of medicines or dressings. And equipment? Forget it. I've amputated limbs with my pocketknife, using no anesthetic."

Diane squirmed uncomfortably at the words "no anesthetic."

"Now, I'm no dentist, but pulling teeth is really interesting. Why don't you sit down and let me tell you about it?"

Diane gripped the back of the chair next to Don, her knuckles white. "I'm sorry, but I have work to do. Please excuse me."

As she fled up the aisle, Don chuckled. "Weak stomach. Too bad."

"Yeah, yeah," Merck mocked sarcastically. "You're a master in the fine art of queasiness. What else is new?" He leaned back in the seat and tapped his long, bony fingers together. "Now, the real master of disaster is, well, you know." He pointed up.

As if Merck had taken his scrawny finger and actually tilted Don's chin, Don found himself staring at the ceiling of the plane, instantly sober. The grin faded from his lips as haunting images from the nightmare he'd endured in Rwanda passed before him. A toddler sitting forlornly beside the corpse of his mother, trying to nurse. A man completely gutted and beheaded. A pile of children, beaten to death with clubs.

Shaking hands reached up to rub his eyes, as if he could rub the images away. He would give anything to blot them from his mind.

"Where were You?" he groaned. "Where were You? How could You let this happen?" He shot an accusing glance at the ceiling as if God might suddenly materialize there and answer his charge.

"He was right there in the middle of the suffering," Julian reminded Don gently. "You know that—in here." He placed his strong hand over Don's chest. Unconsciously, Don squirmed beneath his touch and looked away, unwilling to listen to the voice of the angel.

"Sure He was right in the middle of it," Merck agreed, a nasty smile revealing black and broken teeth. "He was right in the middle of it because He caused it." Merck's voice rose to a shriek, but it failed to provoke the kind of response he hoped for from the angel. Julian regarded Merck sorrowfully.

"Aw, keep your eyes in your head, worthless," Merck muttered, needled. "You know I'm right."

Julian refused to be baited. Instead, he turned his attention to Don. "You know that there will come a time when Jesus will come back and there will be no more suffering. Hold on to that hope. Don't let the deceiver gain a foothold in your heart with his discouragement," Julian begged.

"Too late for that," Merck smirked. He leaned closer to Don but was careful to stay outside the ring of light projected by the angel. "Isn't it?"

Don's trembling fingers made their way to the collar of his shirt, which he loosened. The air in this bird was so thin. Maybe it was the temperature. Did they have to keep it so hot? He wiped perspiration from his forehead. What was he doing here anyway, letting them send him to another little hick outpost clinic? He had been happy where he was until . . .

"I won't," he muttered determinedly. "I won't think about it."

Think about something else. The new clinic in Niger. There

was a school, the clinic, a tiny, but thriving, agricultural program, and a small mission compound. That was it. Oh, and one double-place ultralight.

"A what?" he remembered asking Dorsey, the project coordinator at Operation C.A.R.E. headquarters.

"It's a two-seater ultralight. You know, like a plane, only a lot more open."

"I don't get it. What am I supposed to do with it?"

"Beats me," Dorsey replied. "Far as I know, no one has ever used it for anything except hanging the laundry on. Some rich guy spent three months at the compound building the thing. I think it was some sort of therapy for him."

"Yeah? Well, I wish he'd thought building an X-ray machine was therapeutic," Don replied. "Sheesh. What was that guy thinking of? Why not spend the money on something we could actually use?"

"You've got a nurse, a brand new graduate, coming over from the States. I don't know when she'll be coming, but it will be soon," Dorsey informed him. "She's not going to have a clue, Germaine, so treat her nice, huh?"

"Great," Don groaned. "Just what I need. A nurse still wet behind the ears. Why don't you just let me train some of the locals?"

Dorsey shrugged. "You've got some locals on your staff. This girl wanted to come. Don't sweat it. You need the help. Believe me."

The plane window Don was staring out of disappeared and in its place he could see Dorsey's face, etched in pain and guilt. "Listen, Don, I'm really sorry about what happened back there in Rwanda. I don't know. I keep asking myself, was it our fault? Did we ask you to do too much? Did we make it impossible for you to get out in time? I just don't know, but man, I'm really sorry. I can't imagine how it must have been."

"Then be thankful," Don replied shortly. "Look, Dorsey, I don't want to talk about this right now. Maybe later, huh?"

At the time, Don couldn't quite place the look Dorsey had given him. Now he wondered if it had been pity. "Yeah, sure, whatever you say. Hey, you let us know if you need anything out there. Anything at all."

"Right," Don agreed. "Just as long as it doesn't cost any money, right?"

Dorsey laughed. "I always said you were the smart one, Germaine."

Don rested his head back on the seat and closed his eyes. These memories were getting him nowhere. Maybe if he tried hard enough, he could just go to sleep, and when he woke up, he'd be there.

CHAPTER 2

Davy O'Connell buzzed his secretary as he flipped through his Rolodex. The way her voice came out of the machine, Davy sometimes, mostly when he was bored, liked to imagine that she was actually inside the thing.

"Yes?" she asked. She sounded annoyed.

"Jen? Would you do me a huge favor, please?"

She let out her breath in a blast that made the machine crackle. "That's why they pay me the big bucks, Davy. Don't you know that?" she joked, the tension in her voice gone.

"So, that's the reason," Davy teased. "Listen, Jen, I need a dozen roses for Toby . . . the big anniversary, you know. Five years. Wow! I can hardly believe it myself. Hey, make that two dozen roses. Heck, make it five dozen. That will really impress her."

"Five . . . dozen . . . roses?" Jen's voice quavered. "Lucky lady. Any special color?"

"Red," Davy replied, pulling a card from the Rolodex and giving it a twirl. "My love is like a red, red rose. Or something like that."

"Is that what you want the card to say?"

"You know me better than that," Davy chided. "I'll get the card myself."

"So, that all?"

"Thanks, Jen, you're a real jewel."

"Yeah, yeah. Remember that next secretaries' day, would you? I could use a few roses myself."

Davy flicked the Rolodex card in his hand with one finger. Killington Ski Area in beautiful, scenic, snowy Vermont. Just the thing for two people madly in love looking for a place to spend a quiet, long, romantic weekend. His eyes wandered to a snapshot of Toby floating out of the sky during her first sky dive. He smiled at the photo as he lifted the receiver of his phone and dialed the number. Boy, would she be surprised.

"Don't take the plane, Davy," Jes pleaded. "Please don't take the plane. The enemy has plans to hurt you, to destroy you. Listen, please."

Davy, adept for many years at ignoring his angel's pleas, nevertheless couldn't shake a feeling of uneasiness as he waited for someone on the other end to pick up the phone.

Why should the thought of flying suddenly bother him? He and Toby flew their Cessna 182 all the time. A nice flight to Vermont for a romantic weekend was just the thing. Still . . .

Shay Beauregard stared at the blinking cursor on the computer terminal in front of her and frowned. It was hard to believe that this was the last time she'd be writing a patient note as a student nurse. The next time she sat at a hospital computer, she would be a registered nurse.

Her hand wandered unconsciously to a long black curl that had worked its way out from under her nurse's cap. She wound it around her finger as she played with the words in her head. The trouble with writing patient notes was that they were so boring, just the plain facts. Shay was always trying to liven them up, and that's where she got in trouble with her nursing instructor.

A call bell above her head began to buzz incessantly, like the annoying chirp of a cricket hiding under the furniture. Shay forced herself back to the present with a sigh. The notes would have to wait until later. She hurried down the hall, wrinkling her nose at the strong smell of antiseptic. The lunch trays would be up soon. That would hide it a little.

The light above room 202 blinked at her, reminding her to hurry. As she entered the room, little Sara Beth sat up quickly and smiled at her from the white expanse of her bed. With her pointy chin and big blue eyes, she reminded Shay of a pixie. Blond hair fell in tangled wisps around her face. Shay made a mental note to make sure that Sara Beth's hair got washed later.

"And what can I do for you, bright eyes?" she asked, stooping over the bed to fluff Sara Beth's pillows. The action had become unconscious, just like her nursing instructor had predicted.

"Can I have some apple juice?" Sara Beth asked, cocking her head to one side. For an instant, in her look, Shay remembered something from her past. Something she'd almost forgotten. Then it was gone, and she couldn't recall it.

Her forehead creased as she tried to bring the vague image back, but it was lost in the misty depths of her subconscious. She quickly returned Sara Beth's smile and rumpled her messy hair. "I don't see why not. Give me your glass."

As she took the glass and headed for the nurses' station to fill it, she played the incident back in her memory, hoping to bring back the thought she'd had and then lost. It was something in the way Sara Beth tilted her head . . . something.

Suddenly, she remembered. It was a look exactly like the one Deniece had given her once when they were little. It had happened one day when they were playing in a vacant lot. Playing horses. That was before they'd gotten interested in dolls . . . and boys.

The memory came back so fresh that Shay could almost smell the stunted grass and see the green stains on her palms. She was on her hands and knees, scooting around the lot. Deniece was right behind her, pretending to neigh and buck. They were supposed to be wild horses in a roundup.

"Whee, whee," Deniece whinnied, bucking back and forth. She reared up, her hands pawing the air in front of her like the stallions they'd seen in the movies. She slammed down onto the grass and bolted in the opposite direction. Shay reared and followed her.

One minute they were racing toward the opposite end of the lawn, the next Deniece was crumpled up in a heap crying. Shay was at her side in an instant.

"What is it? What's wrong?" she asked fearfully. Her eyes darted around the lot, searching frantically for the cause of Deniece's sudden outburst. If Deniece got hurt, they were going to be in big trouble.

"My knee," Deniece wailed, clutching her knee to her chest, blood oozing out between her fingers.

"Is it broke?" Shay asked. What did you do for a broke knee?

"I cut it!" Deniece howled and made faces as Shay pried her fingers off her knee. There was lots of blood making it impossible to see the cut. Shay grabbed Deniece firmly around the wrist.

"Come on. We've got to go in the house so I can fix you up." Deniece limped along beside her, bawling as Shay steered her down the block to her house. From the open bathroom window she could see the sitter out in the backyard hanging clothes, her back turned to them. She was thankful that her father wasn't home from work yet. Shay directed Deniece to the toilet and told her to sit down. She dug around in the cabinet for something to put on Deniece's knee.

"This is going to sting," she said as she prepared to pour hydrogen peroxide on Deniece's cut. Dad always said that, and it was always true. Deniece gritted her teeth but only whimpered piteously as Shay watched the peroxide foam up. She swabbed at Deniece's knee with some toilet paper and got off most of the blood. What was left was a tiny cut. Hardly worth bandaging, she assured Deniece.

Still, better to be safe. Shay found some of the antibiotic ointment her father used whenever she had a cut and hunted for a Band-Aid. "Hold still," she demanded as Deniece wriggled and whined. "This part isn't going to hurt."

"Says you," Deniece sniffed, wiping at her grimy face with an equally grimy hand, her tears smudging the dirt into muddy streaks.

Shay sat back on her heels to admire her work. "There. Just like new." That's when Deniece had given her 'the look,' half gratitude, half admiration.

That moment sealed her fate. *I'm going to be a nurse*, she remembered thinking. *And I am a nurse*, she thought as she smiled at the memory and put the apple juice back in the refrigerator.

Deniece had been her first best friend, the partner she chose for every game, the one she passed top secret notes to. They were joined at the hip. They baby-sat together (two for the price of one) and always double-dated.

Shay smiled ruefully. Not much had changed since those days. Except maybe their priorities. Now, instead of glossy pictures of muscled stallions hanging on their walls, dreams of romantic husbands and curly-headed babies intruded on even their busiest moments.

A sudden feeling of sadness gripped Shay so hard she thought for a minute she'd have to sit down. For months now, ever since she first made the decision to go to Africa as a missionary, she'd been forcing herself not to think of the people she was leaving behind.

Dad said he was proud of her and threatened to go himself if she didn't. But she could see in his eyes how lonely he would be after she was gone. Maybe it would be different if Mom were alive.

Deniece was another story. One day she was happy for Shay, the next she was swamped in depression. It didn't help that she was up for a promotion in her job. Shay half believed that if she wasn't, she might just pack up altogether and join her. Of course, how much use would an African mission have for a commodities trader?

She forced the thoughts away as she approached Sara Beth's room with her apple juice. Sara Beth sat with her hands folded on her lap waiting patiently.

"Here you go, sweetheart." Shay handed her the glass and sat casually on the edge of her bed. Sara Beth sipped the apple juice primly, pausing every now and then to smile at Shay as if they shared a secret.

"Do you have any kids?" Sara Beth asked curiously.

Shay laughed. "Not yet. I've got to get a husband first."

"You don't look too bad," Sara Beth observed. "Can't you get anyone to marry you?"

Shay choked on a laugh that almost exploded from her lips. "I don't know," she gasped. "I haven't tried yet."

"Well, don't give up. I believe in you."

"Thank you, sweetie. I'll remember that."

"Then will you have some kids?" Sara Beth persisted.

"I hope so," Shay said, maybe a little too fervently. "Why?"

"Because I want to play with them."

"I think you'd get bored waiting for them to grow up." Shay leaned toward Sara Beth and lowered her voice conspiratorially. "But, I'll tell you what. I get out at three o'clock. After I go home and change, I'll come back and play a game with you. How's that?"

Sara Beth's eyes lighted up. "You mean it?" she squealed.

"I mean it," Shay promised.

Besides, Shay reasoned, coming back later would put off leaving the hospital for good just a little longer. Not that she didn't want to leave, it was just that, well, leaving the safety and help of instructors and launching off on your own was just a tiny bit scary.

Gaius laid one large strong hand on Shay's shoulder and one on Sara Beth's head in a sort of benediction. "But, think of how many Sara Beth's there will be to comfort and encourage and take care of. Your tender heart will be such a blessing to God's least ones in that desolate clinic in Africa." Gaius's countenance glowed even brighter. He lifted his face up as if seeing right through the ceiling of the small hospital room.

When he spoke again, his voice was low and throaty. "It thrills me to accompany you on God's mission. You will do fine."

She tried to ignore the part of her that insisted that it was also very exciting. For some reason, that part of her had been speaking loud and clear lately. It was almost unnerving.

For four years she'd been planning on a well-paying career in surgical nursing and then BLAM! All of a sudden, that unreasonable part of her began yearning for the unknown, the unexplored, the uncertain. The feeling of compassion that welled up inside her every time she pictured herself a modern Florence Nightingale, in a hospital in Africa helping her mother's people, her ancestors, was almost unbearable. It was that feeling that caused her to throw all caution to the wind. She was going to Africa, no matter what.

As she returned home to get changed, she strained to think of some kind of game that Sara Beth would enjoy. She rummaged through her old toy box looking for something that would strike her fancy. Finally, she settled on a puzzle of kittens all tangled up with a ball of string.

When she arrived back at the hospital, she found Sara Beth alone in her room. She held up the puzzle and watched the little girl's eyes get animated.

"Kitties!" Sara Beth squealed.

Shay dumped the contents on the bedside table. "We've got to hurry. Your folks will be here in a half hour or so."

"They're not coming," Sara Beth informed her, avoiding Shay's eyes.

"Oh?" Shay tried not to sound surprised.

"They've got a dinner or something."

Shay struggled with the anger that engulfed her. How could any parent leave a child alone in a hospital room and go out to dinner? She scooted her chair protectively closer to Sara Beth.

"You mean I've got you all to myself?"

Sara Beth giggled. "You want me?"

"I sure do," Shay said. "Someday, when I have a little girl all my own, I want her to be just like you."

Sara Beth looked at her sideways. "You mean it?"

Shay nodded. Someday she would, too. Her house would be stuffed with kids and echo with laughter. There would be big family picnics, camp-outs, canoe trips, hiking trips. They'd have a blast, she and her husband and their four children, maybe five.

Then she flushed a little self-consciously. Of course, it would help if she found a husband first.

CHAPTER 3

Cindi Trahan pulled off the road and immediately slowed down to a crawl as she drove up the winding driveway. A slight breeze blew wisps of early morning fog across her path, making it difficult to see. She was always extra careful because any one of Ethel Bennington's six cats could be running around. Cindi let them out every night, and they wouldn't come in until she spooned cat food into their bowls later on.

She pulled up to the house, a huge, stately, old rattletrap, much too big for one severely handicapped person to live in. Cutting the engine, a frown wrinkled her forehead as she noticed a light on in the old woman's bedroom. Must be she'd had a bad night. Cindi didn't waste any time getting her bag of nursing supplies from the trunk and running lightly up the stairs to the side door. Using her key, she let herself in.

One of the cats squeezed in behind her before she could close the door. It rubbed up against her legs. Absently, she looked down to see which one it was. Pumpkin. She scooped the cat up and brought it into Ethel's room, knowing she'd appreciate the diversion if she was as bad off as Cindi expected she would be.

She entered Ethel's room and found her sitting up in bed, lopsidedly propped up on an abundance of pillows, hands folded in her lap, lips moving soundlessly. Her eyes were closed and by the serene expression on her face, Cindi would never guess just looking at her that she was in terrible pain.

The group of angels surrounding Ethel Bennington's bed parted to make room for Cindi when she opened the door to come in. Several had their arms wrapped around Ethel, one held the old woman's hand. Reissa, who stood half a head taller and was a little brighter than her companions, smiled with joy at the sight of Ethel's faithful nurse and friend. Unseen, she approached Cindi, laying an urgent hand on her shoulder.

"Quickly, she suffers much."

Cindi walked over to Ethel's bed and laid her hand gently on her arm. After a few seconds, the old woman's lips stopped moving, and she opened her eyes. A watery blue, they were dull with pain. Ethel tried to smile but winced with the effort.

"Is it real bad, love?" Cindi asked, setting the cat on the bed and reaching for the glass of water and pain pills she'd left on Ethel's nightstand before leaving the previous evening. She placed the painkillers in Ethel's mouth and held the glass of water while Ethel took a grateful swallow.

"I don't understand, Ethel, why didn't you take the painkillers yourself if it was that bad?" She waited until the old woman had finished drinking before replacing the cup on the nightstand. To her amazement, Ethel chuckled, her gnarled hands stroking the soft fur of the cat on her lap as it purred deeply.

"Honey child, the apostle Paul suffered with a thorn in the flesh, what's a little arthritis?"

Cindi snorted good-naturedly. "I don't believe the apostle Paul was as old as you are, Ethel. There's nothing wrong with taking painkillers when you need them, you know. There's no weakness in that." While she talked, she fluffed Ethel's pillows and straightened her up in the bed. "Now, tell me, what would you like this morning for breakfast?"

Ethel's crooked, crippled hands reached out to grasp Cindi's. The skin felt paper thin; deep blue veins stood out like roads on a relief map. "Man cannot live on bread alone," she quoted. "Sit with me for a minute, and we'll have a season of prayer first, before you start the day."

Smiling, Cindi sank onto the edge of the bed, carefully holding Ethel's frail hand in her own strong one. Ethel's "seasons of prayer" began from the moment she awoke until she closed her eyes in sleep for the night. Cindi bowed her head as Ethel's shaky voice began to pray.

As Ethel prayed, the angels sang out, their voices combining to surpass the most glorious combination of musical instruments ever devised by man. Their heartsong filled the room with praise to the Master as the two women prayed, one a strong saint seasoned by many battles with the adversary, the other earnest and youthful, learning the power of praise and prayer.

Suddenly, amidst the angels a bright light began to glow, growing stronger and stronger. Sheer happiness reflected on the countenances of the angels, and the faces of Ethel and Cindi shone with the peace imparted by the Master's Spirit as He filled the room like a warm blanket wrapping them in love directly from the throne of heaven.

Sunlight was streaming in the window by the time "amen" rolled off Ethel's tongue and Cindi lifted her head and opened her eyes. The entire room seemed bathed in an aura of peace and love. Outside, the fog had been burned off by the strong rays of the sun. Much like prayer burns away the fogginess in our lives, Cindi mused as she set about to prepare breakfast for Ethel.

Although she asked every morning, the menu never varied. Lumpy oatmeal, whole wheat toast, a piece of fruit, and a hard-boiled egg made up Ethel's breakfast each day. The only thing that ever changed was the type of fruit. Generally, Ethel preferred whatever was in season. This morning it was a red apple, which Cindi picked right off a tree outside the kitchen window and shined on the hem of her shirt.

Cindi set the breakfast tray down on the bedstand and opened the window before settling herself in a chair beside the bed to take notes while she helped Ethel feed herself. Ethel offered a simple grace before allowing Cindi to place a spoonful of oatmeal in her mouth.

While Ethel chewed, Cindi flipped open the cover of the notebook that Ethel cheerfully called her prayer journal. The book wasn't so much a journal of Ethel's own prayers as it was a collection of prayer requests called in from literally all over the country. There were so many that Ethel had finally asked Cindi to begin keeping track of them all in a notebook so that she wouldn't forget any, although the old woman's mind was so keen that she often remembered requests that Cindi inadvertently skipped.

"Today," Cindi began, referring to the notebook, "we have a request from Mr. Duffy for his daughter, Julia. He's worried about her and thinks there might be some problem with her boyfriend, Ray."

Ethel nodded, listening intently. "This is a new one, isn't it?"

"Yes, he called last night just before I left, so I jotted it down." She checked the name off on the list and continued on. "Oh, and Mrs. Gladden called to say that her prayer request for healing for her brother's pneumonia was answered. He's out of the hospital and back to work."

"Praise the Lord," Ethel exclaimed, a smile lighting her face. "Isn't He wonderful?"

Cindi smiled. "He certainly is."

She continued down the list, alternately checking off names in between feeding Ethel the rest of her breakfast. When she finished, it would be time for a sponge bath and back rub. And then Ethel would begin praying through the requests while Cindi did the housework and prepared lunch. Later, she'd check in on another patient, Jimmy Raynard, while she was out running errands. Cindi felt joy well up in her heart as she considered the day ahead. How blessed she was to have such a wonderful job.

When Billie Jo awoke, light streamed in the tattered drapes of the living room and spilled onto the floor. A thump, followed by a whispered instruction in the other room, caught her attention and brought her fully awake. She struggled to sit up and chased a loose strand of hair off her forehead.

"Cass?" Her voice was hoarse and heavy with sleep. "Cassidy, what's going on?"

The girl peered around the partition that divided the kitchen from the living room. Her big brown eyes were wide and innocent. "Nothin', Momma. Just thought I'd get Dallas an' me somethin' ta eat. Made you some too."

Billie Jo pushed herself up off the floor, massaging a crick in her neck. Slowly, the thoughts came back. She'd fallen asleep sitting on the floor with her cheek resting on Jimmy's hand. And there was something else. Peace, a feeling of peace.

She smiled as she remembered it and paused to bow her head in a quick prayer before heading for the kitchen to see what Cassidy had been doing.

Nog slunk to a corner of the room and chewed his long, filthy nails as he watched Jewel accompany Billie Jo into the kitchen. His eyes narrowed slyly as he contemplated his offense. So, she was feeling peaceful, eh? Nothing would so completely shatter that feeling as a visit from her mother-in-law.

Helen wasn't supposed to drop by until later. Billie Jo had told her around ten o'clock. That way she could have Jimmy changed, the kids' dressed, and the breakfast dishes done so that Helen would have nothing much to harp on. But, if Helen were to come early . . .

Nog didn't even leave enough time to completely finish the thought. He knew exactly what would happen and didn't waste any time. In the twinkling of an eye, he would be at Helen's side. Persuading her to come ahead of schedule would be one of the easiest tasks of the day.

As Billie Jo rounded the corner of the kitchen, her eyes took in the mess all over the floor, countertop, and Dallas' small face. Cassidy appeared to have used every available dish making "something ta eat." Dallas had a thick layer of blackberry jam spread all over his face, hair, and T-shirt. Two toasts lay face down on the floor swimming in a puddle of orange juice. Three bowls of cereal were set out on the kitchen table, and by the looks of the soggy cereal they contained had been among the first items Cassidy prepared for breakfast. A trail of milk led from the refrigerator all the way to the table with a gap now and then where Cassidy or Dallas had tramped through it.

Cassidy's eyes hadn't left her mother's face from the moment she entered the room, and Billie Jo was careful not to let her daughter read her mind. "Any toast for me?" she asked with forced cheerfulness as she scooped Dallas up and received a sweet, sticky kiss.

Cassidy's answering smile was filled with relief and pleasure. "Do you want any jam on that, Momma?" she asked solicitously. "No butter, though, ain't that right?"

"Jam, no butter," Billie Jo agreed, purposely overlooking Cass's grammatical slip, although the realization made her squirm. Ever since the accident, she'd been letting Cass get away with things that she wouldn't have stood for before. Sure, she felt bad when she saw Cass just staring at Jimmy and sometimes cuddled up on the cot beside him telling him about something that happened to her that day, but that didn't excuse her behavior sometimes.

"I'll deal with that later," she told herself again. "I've got enough to worry about right now."

She let Cass lead her to a chair at the table and get her two slices of somewhat burnt toast liberally smeared with some of her own blackberry jam. The jam she had just finished putting up the day before . . . Billie Jo blinked back tears. No use thinking about that. She pulled Cassidy into the crook of her arm and nearly crushed Dallas on her lap with the force of her embrace.

"Thank you, sweetheart," she said gruffly. Dallas let out a howl of protest that forced her to release her grip on the two of them. She smiled for Cassidy and blew a raspberry on Dallas' cheek, sending him into a peal of laughter. "You know what? I'm going to let this cool off a little while I get Daddy changed. Then I'll have breakfast with you both. How's that?"

"Well, don't let it get too cold, Momma," Cassidy instructed. "It's s'posed to be eaten hot, you know. Tastes best that way."

"It sure does, honey," Billie Jo agreed, "but Daddy really needs to be changed first. And you're next," she informed Dallas, her fingers searching for the ticklish spot under his arm. His laughter was interrupted by a knock on the door.

Startled, Billie Jo glanced at her watch. Too early to be the visiting nurse. And much too early to be Helen. A shiver chased down her spine as she set Dallas on the floor and went to answer the door.

Helen Raynard was never one to wait on the doorstep, and she forced her way in just as soon as Billie Jo cracked the door open. "You're early, Mother," Billie Jo stammered, shrinking under the scrutiny Helen applied to the house and the children. She watched as her mother-in-law's eyes widened at the sight of the kitchen and the kids.

Ignoring Billie Jo altogether, Helen walked briskly up to the side of the cot and smiled down at her son. "Hello, Jimmy, darling. How are you this morning? It's beautiful out, dear. Father sends his love, and he said to tell you that Inco stock shot up three points, and don't you wish now you'd bought some when he told you to?"

Helen laughed a shallow laugh, and Billie Jo cringed when Helen swept a hand beneath the sheet to see if Jimmy was dry. She pulled it out with a gasp of disbelief and turned to Billie Jo, acknowledging her presence in the room for the first time since she'd entered it.

"Haven't you changed Jimmy's bedding yet this morning?" The question was innocent enough, but her tone was laden with accusation. Billie Jo blushed with shame beneath it.

"Momma was just gonna do that," Cassidy piped up, not at all intimidated by her grandmother.

Helen fixed her with a tolerant smile. "Honey, you don't have to cover up for your Momma's negligence."

Billie Jo watched Cassidy's eyebrows waggle, puzzled as she tried to place "negligence" into a familiar context. She laid a protective hand on Cass's shoulder. "I was," she admitted, not because she felt that Helen would believe her, but because she had to say it out loud for her own sanity.

"Likely story," Nog chortled, leaning so close to Helen's tall frame that his breath blasted her cheek. "She leaves him like this half the day. Go ahead, ask her. If she's got any guts, she'll admit it and tell you the truth."

Helen's eyes narrowed suspiciously. "Just how long were you planning to leave my Jimmy this way?" she demanded. The way she stressed "my" made Billie Jo squirm. It had taken years for Helen to recede into the background of their married lives. Now, in six short months, here she was at the helm again. Would she never let go?

"You know she's just trying to antagonize you. You don't have

to give in to her. Remember, a gentle answer turns away wrath, but a harsh word stirs up anger," Jewel reminded her. "Be strong." He raised his wings as if to protect her from the onslaught, but Billie Jo shrugged angrily away from him.

"I should have known when Jimmy married you that you'd amount to nothing. Why, look around." Helen spread her hands wide enough to encompass the entire small house. "The kitchen is disastrous, the children are filthy, and my son lies here in a puddle of his own urine. And you, what monumental tasks have occupied you this morning that you couldn't take a few minutes to straighten up your house and take care of your helpless husband?"

For one instant, only one, Billie Jo was struck speechless. It would have been better, she realized upon later reflection, if she could have remained that way. "Who are you to come into my house and berate me?" she asked in a voice that shook with emotion. "My husband, my children, and my house are none of your concern."

Helen arched one perfectly groomed eyebrow. "Is that so? May I remind you that *you* asked me to come here this morning. Cassidy has a doctor's appointment that," she glanced at her watch, "you will be late for if you don't get moving."

Billie Jo's lower lip trembled with anger as she bit back the harsh words that stung her tongue. "I . . . I'm sorry, Helen," she whispered hoarsely. "I didn't realize it was so late. I haven't had much sleep lately."

As she spoke, Billie Jo picked absently at some lint on her bathrobe. She despised herself for giving in to Helen's bullying, but if she wanted to make that doctor's appointment and pick up some groceries to restock their dwindling supplies, then she was forced to rely on Helen to help her out.

"Come on, Cass," she mumbled. "We've got to get dressed so we can get you to the doctor's on time."

The entire time she cleaned up the children and got them

both dressed, Billie Jo was aware of Helen loudly complaining to Jimmy as she changed his sheets and fussed around his bed arranging things and fluffing his pillows. As angry as she was with Helen, Billie Jo realized that she was more shamed for having been caught the way she was. Helen was right. She *should* have seen to Jimmy first thing.

"That's right, you miserable sinner," Nog was quick to agree. "There's no reason you couldn't have gotten up early and had breakfast waiting for the children when they got up. Your poor, helpless husband should have been all changed by then and the house straightened up. You're so incredibly lazy! What a slug."

Nog stole a glance at Jewel and smirked. "See? I told you. She's pathetic. So easily stirred up, so easily influenced."

"And the peace of God, which transcends all understanding, will guard your hearts and your minds in Christ Jesus," Jewel quoted back to him, more for Billie Jo's benefit than for Nog's. But Billie Jo wasn't listening to him.

"Too late now," she muttered as she bundled the children into their winter coats. "Tomorrow will be different though. I promise, Lord." She shot a pleading look heavenward. Surely God could understand the tiredness that throbbed through her whole being. Surely God could forgive her for this slip in her Christian duty. Billie Jo was sure that He could, still she couldn't stop wondering what would happen if He couldn't.

"We'll be back soon," she promised Helen, unable to meet her mother-in-law's steely gaze.

"Don't worry about anything," Helen replied with false sweetness. "I'll have the whole place clean as a new penny by the time you get back. I won't be sitting around burning good daylight doing nothing."

Billie Jo herded the kids out the door and closed it behind her with a sigh. She paused for a moment on the threshold, squeezing her eyes tight against the tears that threatened to flow unchecked.

"Somethin' the matter, Momma?" Cass asked, a worried frown wrinkling her smooth forehead.

Billie Jo forced a smile. "Nothing that can't be fixed, honey. Let's go. We're going to be late if we don't hurry."

Jes looked around the table, a concerned expression on her usually serene face. Seated before her were some of the Master's most loyal servants. Jes smoothed her shining robe and folded her hands on her lap so they wouldn't betray her nervousness.

"I have heard them plotting. The one called Lucien admits proudly that he is planning to harm David and Toby O'Connell."

"I, too, have heard his threats," Lileah agreed, her eyes flitting from one familiar face to the other. "Jes is right. Lucien plans to kill David. Toby can't stand up to this kind of test."

"Is there anyone who cares for them? Anyone who prays for them?" Reissa asked earnestly. Jes knew her kind eyes would see the answer before she even had time to respond.

A quick shake of her head was all she managed. "No. They do not even seem to care for their own souls. And no one prays for them."

"If Toby relies on Him, the Master will see her through even this trial," Reissa said.

"I know," Lileah replied quietly. "But, Toby hasn't listened to me for a long time now. I do not believe that she will begin now. She will blame the Master. Her heart is not in a place where it will see this as something to turn her toward the king-

dom. She is too strong, too self-reliant. And she loves this man more than anything in this life. To destroy him will destroy her. The risk is too great. She could be lost forever."

Talk quieted as Noble, an archangel, entered the room. A full foot taller than any of the other occupants of the room, Noble nevertheless presented himself in a singularly humble fashion. His face still glowed from his encounter with the Master, a serene smile touched his lips. The angels leaned forward in a body to hear what the Master had had to say.

The roar of the little Cessna filled Toby's ears as she smiled happily at Davy. He grinned back, looking boyish, she thought, as he leaned forward in the seat and tapped on the instrument panel.

"Problem?" she asked, not really worried.

Davy shook his head. "Not unless you've changed your mind about going."

"Not on your life," Toby shot back quickly. "This was such a great idea, Davy." Her eyes sparkled mischievously. "And those roses. What are you going to do on our twenty-fifth anniversary?"

"Go broke!" Davy laughed. "But, you're worth it, angel." Davy leaned toward Toby and kissed her. She tried to melt against him, but he pushed her gently back into her seat. "Let's get to the hotel first. Somebody's got to fly this thing."

Toby clung to his neck, her fingers twisting in his thick black hair. "I love you, Davy. You know that?" She buried her face in the flannel of his shirt.

It was his lucky shirt, the one he always wore when they went flying. According to Davy, it was the one he was wearing when he did his first solo flight. Which accounted for the fact that it was a little small on him, Toby reasoned.

She traced the grim line of his mouth and sat back in her own seat. "Something the matter?"

Beyond the window of the plane rolled miles of choppy white mountains dotted with trees. There was a shadow over the landscape and at first Toby thought there was something blocking the sun, then she remembered that in the mountains the sun went down early. It was getting close to sundown.

"Want me to fly for a while? You get some rest. We should be there soon. I'll let you know . . ." her voice trailed off in a whisper as she caught a look of utter panic cross Davy's face.

"What is it?" she hissed, unable to tear her eyes from his face. "Tell me!" she demanded. "What's wrong?"

"There's a break in the oil line," Davy yelled as if she were ten feet away instead of two. "The pressure is dropping fast."

"We've got to get down!" Toby shrieked, looking wildly out the window, weighing their options. "Where can we take the plane down?"

"We can't," Davy shouted impatiently, desperately. "There's nothing flat. Too many trees. I don't know. Maybe over there farther, on the other side of that slope. It looks a little clearer over there."

Toby's reply whistled off into nothing as the reality that had occurred to Davy moments before became clear. She gripped the edge of the seat. Her knuckles white, her stomach churning.

She had a wild impulse to grab the controls out of Davy's hands and lower the plane herself. She fought it, knowing it would be the wrong thing to do. If there was no place to land, then there was just no place. It was then she noticed how rough the engine sounded. Why hadn't she noticed it before?

"How close is the ski area? How close is the airport?" Toby heard her voice, but it sounded like a stranger.

"Close," Davy admitted. "But we're not going to make it. I can hold on and see if I can't find a clearing before the engine seizes up. But I want you to jump now."

Toby stared at him blankly, afraid that maybe he was losing his mind, or maybe she was, maybe they both were. "What do you mean? We're barely high enough, and besides, we don't carry a chute on the plane."

"Look under the gear back there," Davy instructed, between white lips clenched tight. "I threw yours on. I don't know why, just this feeling. I don't know why," he repeated.

Toby dug under the rucksacks and suitcases, locating her old parachute. The one she bought back when she learned how to sky-dive.

"Put it on, hurry," Davy urged. "I want you out of here before we lose too much altitude."

Toby strapped on the parachute, checking and rechecking the straps almost mechanically, as if her life did not depend on their condition. Davy nodded at her.

"Hurry, get set up. When I signal you, jump."

Toby gripped the edge of the seat, knuckles white. "No," she said firmly. "I won't go without you."

Davy turned to look at her, his eyes meeting hers for the first time. Toby was sure he could see the panic in hers and, she hoped, the determination not to leave him. A light smile touched his lips but didn't quite climb up to his eyes. "Well, now, we'd really be in a sorry predicament if I jumped, too, since I don't have a chute. Look," he pointed out the cockpit window. "See those trees? The wings are loaded with fuel, but if I can line up between them and take the wings off I think I can land the plane without it exploding on impact from the crash landing. But, I don't want to have to worry about getting the two of us out of the plane after that. So, jump already."

"But what if something happens?" Toby asked, her voice a whisper that could barely be heard above the plane's engine.

"Nothing will happen," Davy insisted. "Don't you have any faith in me?"

Toby threw her arms around his neck and squeezed hard. "I love you, Davy," she said, her voice choking off as tears slipped down her cheeks and onto his lucky shirt.

"I love you, too, angel," Davy replied.

Toby tried to kiss him, hoping it wouldn't be the last time, but he pushed her away. "Go! Now! I'll see you on the ground."

It wasn't the first time Toby had jumped from a plane; still, the only thing that kept racing through her mind as she floated to the ground was that this was not going to end well. Not well at all.

She landed feet first in a large drift, but was yanked out by the force of her parachute catching a gust of wind. She settled even softer in a clearing, and her chute floated gently onto the branches of a tree. Toby looked up, searching the darkening sky for the familiar form of their Cessna.

"Land! Land!" she shrieked at the little plane as if Davy could hear her. "What are you waiting for?"

In an instant, as if in slow motion, she watched as the plane wobbled a little before it aligned itself with two trees. While Toby observed the scene with the absent detachment of someone watching their own surgery under local anesthesia, one fact became startlingly clear. From her vantage point higher up the mountain, Toby could see what Davy couldn't. The trees he was lining up with weren't side by side.

The plane hit the closest tree, on the left, first. With a tortured scream of metal, clear even to Toby, the wing was wrenched off, but the forward thrust of the plane flung it around the tree until the other wing connected with the tree on the right. Flames shot up into the sky as the mangled airplane disappeared from Toby's view and tumbled down to the ground.

Toby sank to her knees in the snow. "No!" she screamed hysterically, reason fleeing before her overwhelming grief. "No! No! No!" Before her eyes black dots danced on the snow and among the trees, obscuring the thick cloud of smoke that wound its way into the sky from somewhere below her on the mountain.

Something was strangling her. Its hot, oppressive presence crushing her breath. Mercifully, she yielded to it and sank quietly into a heap on the snow.

Noble glanced at each of the angels, encouraging them with a look, before he spoke.

"The Master has said that the man will live," Noble informed the assembled group, his voice melodious and haunting like the sound of panpipes. It hovered in the air even after he finished speaking. "But his memory will be taken from him."

No word was spoken as the angels nodded in silent agreement. The judgment was fair. David and Toby O'Connell would have their chance to be drawn closer to God if they so chose. Or . . .

Jes sat long after the others had returned to their work. A firm hand on her shoulder brought her mind back to the present. "Come," Lileah said gently. "There is work for us."

CHAPTER 4

The leaves of the weeping willow rustled around Lyle as he sat beneath its drooping branches, hidden completely as if enveloped in a shroud. He could see out, but no one could see him. From his vantage point beneath the tree he could watch life pass by but not be a part of it, which was just the way he liked it.

Intermittently, the wind picked up, causing the boughs to sigh and moan deeply as if the tree itself was in mourning. The sound matched his mood perfectly, though at the moment, exhaustion had claimed him. Head nodding onto his chest, his fingers relaxed, and the pen he held dropped onto the sketch pad in his lap and rolled off, falling to the grass.

Shelan watched Lyle sleep, with a look of compassion on her face. Night after night, Warg had tortured the boy with nightmares about the accident. Last night Lyle had kept a silent vigil by his window, refusing to give in to sleep, determined to spend one night without reliving the horror of twisted steel and screams that had ended his dreams.

Tender feelings of sympathy swept over Shelan as she moved her position a little and laid one protective wing across Lyle's drooping shoulder. His blond hair was long, ragged, and could stand a washing. Haggard lines drawn in his face made him look older than he was. Dressed in his deceased father's clothes, which were outdated even when the man had worn them, it was easy to see why people who bothered to wonder thought that Lyle was an old man.

The musical sound of laughter caught Shelan's attention, and she looked out across and slightly down the street. Berniece Kendall was standing in her doorway, hands on her hips, a delighted smile on her face. Parked in the road in front of her house was a battered up old Chevette, stuffed almost to overflowing, covered with stickers and rust. A lithe girl with honey-colored hair jumped out of the car laughing and raced up the walk to throw her arms around the older woman.

"Aunt Berniece! I'm so glad to see you!"

"Oh, Calla! Look at you! Why, your mom said I'd hardly recognize you! You've gotten so tall. Let me help you move your things in, and then we'll have some lemonade out on the porch." Berniece circled the girl's slim waist with one arm as they walked back toward the car. "Are you excited about starting college?"

Calla grinned. "I'm not sure. I'm so juiced about moving out here in the first place. Besides, I've got a few months to get used to the idea. Thank you so much for letting me stay with you."

Berniece stopped and faced the girl, putting her hands on Calla's shoulders. "Now, you know it's my pleasure, honey. I've been so lonely rattling around in that old, empty house since Uncle Peter . . . well, you know. I just get kinda lonely sometimes. I'm so glad to have the company."

The bantering across the street continued as Berniece and Calla lugged her bags into the house and took out of Calla's car what looked like enough sports equipment to outfit an entire gym class. Shelan turned to Lyle and studied his face. What a difference that spark of life across the street could make in his *life. But, they would be finished unpacking the car before Lyle woke up. Unless . . .*

With one powerful stroke of her graceful wing, Shelan caused a breeze to kick up, upsetting Lyle's ink bottle and sending his pen nibs pattering like hail onto the sketch pad in his lap. Lyle's head jerked up, and he looked around with wild eyes, struggling out of the bonds of sleep. When he saw the ink spoiling his picture and soaking into his sketch pad, he cursed and began to wipe at it futilely, using the corner of his shirt.

Calla's laugh, when Lyle heard it, startled him. He looked up suddenly, a wave of fear coursing through him, heart beating wildly. Was someone laughing at him? Through the long strands of the weeping willow, he caught a glimpse of activity across the street. The laughter seemed to be coming from that direction. He brushed a few branches out of the way, trying to get a better look. What he saw took his breath away.

Calla was struggling with a violin case, blond hair cascading into her eyes. She brushed it back carelessly with one hand and finally freed the violin. Grabbing a pair of inline skates and slinging them over her back with her free hand, she wrestled an enormous suitcase out of the back of the little, old, banged-up car, half dragging and half carrying it up the walkway.

She stopped at the bottom of the steps and sank onto the suitcase, panting and out of breath. Suddenly, she lifted her arms up and threw her head back, eyes closed, soaking up the dwindling sunshine that bathed her in a kind of glow making it seem as though she was lighted up from the inside. She breathed deeply as if trying to capture every scent borne on the wind and lock it into her memory.

Questions tore through Lyle's mind like racehorses. Who was she? Where did she come from? What was going on? Was she moving in?

He watched as Berniece appeared on the doorstep and regarded her niece with a fond look. "Don't tell me you're worn out already?"

Calla jumped up and renewed her struggle with the luggage. "Not a chance. I won't rest tonight until I'm all settled in."

Warg reappeared and assessed the situation with shrewd eyes, taking in the hopeful look on Shelan's face as she watched Lyle drinking in the scene across the road. Warg's breath hissed out in annoyance, and he leaned over Lyle's chair, twisted lips inches from Lyle's ear.

"You remember Berniece Kendall, don't you? Peter's wife? Peter, whose heart attack caused this . . ." Warg laid a hand on Lyle's leg, just above the site of the amputation. Lyle squirmed in his chair, his concentration broken. A flush of anger crept up his face at the thought, and his hands clenched into fists, pounding on the arms of his chair.

Warg leaned back, a smug smile crossing his face. "That's better. Wouldn't want to forget something like that, would we?"

Lyle's face crumpled in agony and behind his tortured eyes, Shelan could see images of the accident flash past in quick succession. Strangled gurgles escaped from his lips as sobs choked up from deep inside his chest. All thoughts of Calla were forgotten as waves of pain from the past crashed over him, and he gave himself up to drown in them.

"Lyle," Shelan begged. "Please, don't do this to yourself. Fight this. You can overcome. All you have to do is ask for help from the Spirit, and this depression can't take over your life this way. Pray, Lyle. Pray like you have never prayed before."

Warg chuckled. Soon he would be joined by other demons who would form a virtually unpenetrable blanket surrounding Lyle, making him feel as though he would smother beneath it. Shelan took one last look at the despair etched on Lyle's face before she decided that there was only one thing she could do. Unwilling to let one more instant pass before acting, she disappeared before Warg even missed her.

Prayer Warriors

Dust choked up in a wind that spun it into a tiny tornado-like sculpture and whipped it across the desolate landscape. Shay watched numbly as it danced away. There had to be more dust in Africa than anyplace else in the world, she thought glumly. Already she felt as though she'd chewed her way through miles of it from Niamey to the mission in Niger.

She heaved a sigh and wriggled into a more comfortable position perched up on her luggage as the sun beat down on her. Children played some kind of game that reminded her of soccer, with a ball that looked as if it was made out of leaves, pausing now and then to point at her and whisper curiously.

Loneliness threatened to overcome her as she waited there. Not only had her flight been long and rough, but it didn't appear that she had even been expected at the mission once she had arrived.

"Dr. Germaine said nothing about a nurse coming today," a kindly, but firm, woman told her when she had arrived at the mission.

"But, I'm with Operation C.A.R.E.," Shay had objected as images of being shuttled off in humiliation back to the States on the back of some farmer's oxen cart flooded through her head. "Mr. Dorsey said that he spoke with Dr. Germaine, that he knew I was coming. I don't understand what the problem is."

"Neither do I," the woman countered, leveling Shay with an

open, appraising look. "But, if you'll wait until Dr. Germaine returns, I'm sure we can clear this all up swiftly and in short order."

"When will that be?" Shay heard herself ask in a small voice.

"That, I do not know," the woman answered. "But, you are welcome to make yourself comfortable and wait." Her face softened at the droop in Shay's shoulders and the air of despair that surrounded her. "It shouldn't be too long now. He went to visit the chief's son in the next village."

That had been three hours ago and sitting outside the clinic on her lumpy luggage was losing any appeal that it held in the first place.

"Well, at least he had a good excuse," Shay muttered to herself. "I mean, the chief is important. If his son is sick, I guess you really hop to it." She allowed herself to imagine Dr. Germaine returning just as this torturous sun began to set, apologizing profusely for her wait and showing her to her quarters where she could soak in a nice long bath and try to forget everything that had happened since she'd left her father and Deniece at the airport in Baton Rouge what seemed like years ago. The image was so satisfying that she almost found herself smiling for the first time all day. Almost. If it hadn't been for that sun . . .

"Aren't there any clouds in this place?" she grumbled, shielding her eyes from the unrelenting glare.

"Not too many during a drought such as this one," a deep voice answered as a shadow fell across her, bringing on a sudden chill that had nothing to do with the temperature.

Shay turned slowly, her eyes rising from the hem of a wrinkled, flowing, tunic-style white robe up a full six feet to the sightless face smiling kindly down at her. She swallowed hard and struggled to get to her feet. The man before her held a long, polished pole, not like the canes carried by blind people used in the States. Strong ebony fingers wrapped around the pole as it rested in the dirt at her feet, and he leaned on it slightly as he spoke to her.

"You must be the nurse we were told about," he observed. "Welcome to Niger mission."

Shay swallowed hard and licked her lips, tasting the salt of her own sweat mixed with another layer of the infernal dust. "Uh, thank you, but how . . . how did you know? I mean, nobody seems to be expecting me."

The man chuckled, a low sound that bubbled up from inside his chest and lighted up his face, despite the blank whiteness of his eyes. "We are not often visited by people from the United States who are not expected, madame."

"How did you know I was from . . ." Shay began before stopping herself as she realized what she was saying.

"You want to know how I knew you were from the United States when I can't see?" the man said, finishing her thought. Shay was glad he couldn't see the blush that burned her cheeks. "First of all, there is your accent, and if not for that, the way you smell . . . airline food, expensive soap . . . or perfume? and besides," a grin split his face, "Akueke told me that you were here waiting for Dr. Germaine."

Shay's mouth, which had dropped open, closed with a snap as she realized what he was saying. "So," she returned unable to keep the smile out of her voice, "what you're saying then is that you cheated?"

The man shrugged. "If that's what you call it, then yes, I guess so." He stuck out one hand. "Nwibe Okeke," he said.

Shay took his hand, marvelling how smooth and strong it felt as he shook hers. "I'm Shay Beauregard," she said smiling, and added, "recently from the States. And it is perfume, by the way. It's called . . ."

"Slow Dance," Nwibe finished.

Shay stepped back and appraised him with increasing respect. "You're good at this. Should I ask how you knew that?"

Nwibe shrugged, smiling. "You aren't the first visitor we have had from civilization," he explained, jerking his head in the general direction of Niamey, from which she had so recently come. He motioned one hand to encompass the desolate land before her. "Besides, the school teacher often has Marcus fetch her some when we make the trip to Niamey."

Shay nodded knowingly. "I see," she said, even though the details remained hazy. The conversation was starting to confuse her as she became aware of a vague pounding somewhere behind her eyes. She stretched out a hand to steady herself on one of the corrugated steel walls of the clinic.

"Madame?"

Through the haze of black dots that suddenly appeared in front of her eyes, Shay was aware of the concerned face of her new friend floating disjointedly in front of her. Why was she so cold? She shivered as she watched the black dots converge into a solid curtain, and an incessant buzzing began in her head.

"Marcus!" a voice boomed. "Come here, boy! Quickly!"

A sea of hands buoyed her along gently, patting her softly to the accompaniment of low, murmuring voices. Heat and cold alternately penetrated the thick fog that had settled so heavily around her. Shay heard her own voice moaning in her throat.

"Madame? Madame?"

Shay thrashed back and forth on the hard, uneven surface where she lay. Would that voice never shut up? A sudden, sharp, choking, burning sensation raced up her nasal passages as she tried to draw in a breath. Gagging, she felt herself struggling unwillingly out of the fog. When her eyelids fluttered open, the first face she saw was not only unfamiliar, it was scowling at her.

"Where am I?" she asked thickly, trying to force her tongue away from the roof of her mouth.

"A touch of heatstroke, probably combined with stress and flighty female hormones," the man said, talking to an area above and to the right of her head. "Just what I need, a kid nurse who faints under the first rays of the sun. Like I've got time to baby someone who's not dying."

Shay struggled onto her elbows. "What are you talking about?" she demanded. "Where am I? What's going on?"

The man swung his full attention on her for the first time, fierce gray eyes seeming to pierce her soul. Shay squirmed uneasily beneath his gaze. "Why don't you go home?" he asked. "You don't belong here, and if you can't see that now, you will soon. So why don't you save us all some trouble and just take your little bags and head back to the States?"

Shay sank weakly back onto the cot where she lay, tears stinging her eyes. "Are you telling me I have to go home?" she asked, her voice as small as a five-year-old being chastised by a parent.

"No, I can't do that unless you really mess up," the man said, unwrapping a stethoscope from around his neck and laying it on a crude wooden table beside him. "But I am strongly suggesting it."

Shay stared at the ceiling above her, pointedly avoiding his eyes. "Then, I'm not going," she said.

"What?"

She glanced at him quickly, pleased to see the surprise in his voice registered on his face. "I said I'm not leaving," she repeated, a little more determined this time. "Dr. Germaine," she added deliberately.

The man shrugged his shoulders before getting up and turning his back on her. "Suit yourself." He headed for the door, then stopped and turned back, adding as if in afterthought, "*If you think you're up to it*, there are some instruments to clean before supper."

He was out the door before Shay could struggle into a sitting position. "Why . . . I . . . ." she sputtered. A gentle hand on her shoulder restrained her. She turned to see Nwibe stationed by her side. Next to him a small boy watched her, eyes as wide and dark as pools of India ink.

"Rest, Madame," Nwibe instructed.

The kindness in his voice brought tears to Shay's eyes. "What happened to me?" she asked.

"You've had a long day," Nwibe explained. "And you spent too much time in the sun."

"Sunstroke," Shay groaned, striking her forehead with the heel of her hand. "How could I be so stupid?"

"It is understandable," Nwibe said. "You are not familiar with our climate, and you have had a lot on your mind."

"Apparently too much," Shay agreed, sarcasm in her voice. She heaved a sigh and jerked her head in the direction in which Dr. Germaine had disappeared. "Why was he so miserable?"

Nwibe shrugged. "Dr. Germaine has had a lot on his mind, also, Madame."

Shay's eyebrows shot up, and her lips twisted into a wry smile. "Catchy, is it? And please don't call me Madame. It makes me feel old. Call me Shay. OK?"

Nwibe smiled and nodded.

She pushed herself up and swung her legs over the side of the bed despite the pressure of Nwibe's hand on her shoulder urging her to lay back down. She held her head in her hands until the throbbing lessened enough to allow her to survey her surroundings. "Would you be kind enough to show me where the equipment is that Dr. Germaine needs cleaned? And where is the autoclave?"

Nwibe shook his head. "You are a stubborn woman," he observed.

"Thank you," Shay responded. "That's the nicest thing anyone has said to me since I arrived."

Three hours later, when the clinic was as spotless as she could make it, she followed the sounds of voices coming from the main compound of the mission. People who she assumed comprised the staff of the mission were gathered around a rough table, clearing up the remains of the evening meal. Dr. Germaine turned and regarded her with feigned surprise.

"Why, Miss Beauregard," he said, greeting her as if they were old friends. "Join us, please."

"No, thank you," Shay replied flatly. "I'd like to know where you want me to sleep, or should I just dig out a little hollow in the sand outside the clinic and sleep there?"

Dr. Germaine laughed hollowly. "Of course not, of course not." He turned to the boy Shay recognized as Nwibe's son, who was seated beside his father. "Marcus, would you please show Miss Beauregard where her room is? You can put her in the same room the last nurse stayed in. You know, the one who lasted two weeks." He looked at her pointedly as Marcus jumped up from the table and ran around to stand beside her.

"Don't worry, Doctor," Shay replied sarcastically. "I won't make any decorating changes until I've been here longer than that."

Marcus slipped his hand into hers and tugged, urging her to follow him. She let the boy tow her along through the dark interior hallway of the compound until they reached a room on the far side. Marcus pushed open the door and motioned for her to go in.

She staggered through the door, surprised to see her luggage set out and her bed made up. A candle threw a soft glow around the room. She shuffled over to the bed and sank onto it gratefully. Lifting one hand, she motioned wearily around the room. "Who did all this?" she asked. "Was it your father?"

Marcus shook his head. "Not my father. It was Dr. Germaine."

Shay stared at him in disbelief. "You're kidding?!" At the puzzled look on his face, she elaborated. "Lying? Are you lying to me?"

Marcus shook his head fiercely. "No, Madame Shay. Lying is not right. Lying is a sin. I do not lie."

"I'm sorry," Shay said apologetically. "I didn't mean that. It's just that this is so unexpected after what happened today."

"Madame Shay? May I go now?"

Shay tried to shake the fatigue from her head. She looked up at Marcus, her eyes blurry. "I'm sorry. Yes, Marcus. You can go. Thank you so much."

Eyes lighting up from the appreciation, Marcus backed out the door and closed it softly behind him, leaving Shay alone with the candlelight and the darkness. Groaning, she let herself fall back onto the bed and watched the light from the candle flame shift over the ceiling. All visions of a hot bath disintegrated as images from the day swirled through her head as if she was reliving every moment in fast forward. Racing on, they blurred together, sending her finally spinning off into a fitful sleep.

Toby awoke, chilled to the bone. The setting sun was dropping faster than the New Year's apple in Times Square. Trailing up into the sky from somewhere below her was a thin film of smoke.

The plane!

Suddenly everything came rushing back. Davy was in the plane. She had to get to the plane. She rose jerkily to her feet and staggered three paces before being yanked back by the lines attaching her to the parachute. Angrily she fumbled with them, taking twice as long to undo them in her haste. Her fingers throbbed deeply with pain from the cold, but she barely noticed them.

Finally free of the chute, she waded through the snow, sinking in up to her hips in spots. Tears of frustration stung her eyes and froze almost immediately as they trickled down her cheeks. The cold air made her cough as she sucked it in, her lungs pumping as if she was running a marathon.

Half falling, half crawling, she found herself suddenly on a trail packed down by snowmobile tracks. It went in the opposite direction from where she believed the plane was. She hesitated for a moment, wondering if since the going was quicker she'd be better off following it to see if it led to someone who could help her.

Her indecision caused a feeling of panic to wash over her. There was no time to think here! Davy's life could hang in the balance.

"Oh, God, help me!" she wailed between lips blue from the cold. The name seemed so unfamiliar that her tongue stumbled over it. What right had she to call on God for help? But, what choice did she have? "Where do I go?"

Lileah was at Toby's side in an instant. "Toby, listen to me, you must follow the path of the snowmobile. There is help waiting for you at the end. You will never make it to where Davy is. Not in this snow, not this late at night. It will be futile, and he will die before help arrives unless you find it soon."

Lucien scowled. "That's a crock," he spat. "Be a hero, O'Connell. Go find your husband. Don't listen to her. Do it your way."

Toby looked around frantically. She took one hesitating step in the direction of the plane and then stopped and cocked her head as if listening for something just barely out of hearing range.

"You asked for God's help," Lileah reminded her gently. "Now go, and I will guide you. Go now! There is not a moment to lose."

Toby's head snapped up. There was no way she could make it to the plane in this snow. She had to take a chance and go for help. Running as quickly as she could, she began descending the snowmobile path. No time to think. No time to question. Just time to listen and hope the conviction she felt in her heart was God's answer to her prayer.

"*You're never going to make it, O'Connell,*" Lucien jeered. "*You're too slow, you're too tired, you're just not good enough. By the time you find help, Davy will be barbecued beyond belief. Either that or maybe he's dead already. Have you thought of that? Maybe you're killing yourself here for nothing. Why don't you slow down? Take a rest? It probably won't make any difference in the end, anyway.*"

"*Come on, Toby, you can do it,*" Lileah encouraged. "*They that wait upon the Lord will run and not grow weary, they will walk and not faint . . .*"

Toby sobbed with every breath that choked in and out of her mouth. A Bible verse was playing over and over in her mind like a broken record. Now, why was she remembering that at a time like this? It was the oddest thing. She wondered if she'd memorized it sometime in the past, maybe when she was going to church.

Above her head the sky had darkened enough to produce a few stars, and the moon hung low over the mountains. Every time Toby's breath passed her lips, it spewed out into a foggy cloud in front of her, reminding her that the temperature had dropped even more. The snowmobile path in front of her was lighted by a shaft of moonlight that exaggerated the shadow of every bump and crevice in the hard-packed snow.

How long she had been staggering down the mountain, Toby couldn't guess. It seemed like forever. Her lungs burned from the force of the cold air rushing in and out of them. Her body was numb, and she couldn't remember the last time she had felt anything at all in her fingers and feet. Confused by shock, direction, and darkness, she had long since lost track of the smoke ascending from the plane.

The rhythm of the Bible verse repeating in her head was the beat to which she moved, planting one foot after the other. Occasionally, her mind would wander, and she found herself thinking of silly things like the first time she'd had homemade ice cream and the time she and Davy had gone jogging in New York City, and as a joke, he'd thrown her into the Hudson Bay and then jumped in after her.

Toby found herself smiling stiffly at that thought. She tried hard to bring up more of the memory, but she couldn't. That was when she realized that she was no longer moving. She shook her head groggily. Why wasn't she moving? It was hard to locate her body parts by feel because many of them were numb. She moved her head from one side to the other and realized that she was sprawled out face first in the snow, apparently having tripped. But how long had she been lying there?

She pushed herself up onto her knees and located the moon. It hadn't changed position much since the last time she remembered looking at it. Chest heaving from exertion, Toby knelt in the snow, willing herself to get onto her feet.

"Please, God, help me," Toby cried again. This time Toby had the feeling that she was calling on a friend. One whom she hadn't seen in a long time but a friend who cared about her. "Please help me."

Lileah placed a wing around Toby and with her strong arms helped her onto her feet. Keeping one arm around Toby's waist, Lileah supported her as she continued down the mountain. "He will call upon me and I will answer him," Lileah quoted, comfortingly. "I will be with him in trouble. I will deliver him and honor him."

Toby felt new energy surge through her tired body. A feeling of peace settled over her like a blanket, warming her mind, if not her body. Before she knew it, Toby found herself murmuring a prayer for Davy's safety too.

When she became aware of the voices, she had a feeling that she'd been hearing them for awhile and that they just hadn't registered. But, suddenly they were as clear as if the person speaking was standing right in front of her. The voices were carrying easily through the thin winter air, but from where?

"Right, Carl, I'll check that carburetor before I leave. What's 'at? D'you say something?"

"Help me!" Toby screamed, but when the sound left her throat, it was little more than a hoarse whisper. "I'm over here! Help me!!"

"Carl? D'you hear that?" Toby heard snow crunching beneath the feet of the speaker. "Hello? Somebody out there?"

Toby licked her lips and swallowed hard before trying again. "Help me!"

A different voice answered this time. "Someone is out there. I could swear they said 'help' or 'here'. Hello? Is someone there?"

Desperate, Toby looked around frantically. There had to be some way to communicate with them. Who knew how far away they were, and she couldn't get her voice to carry far enough.

Lileah laid one arm across Toby's shoulder and pointed to a large branch lying in the snow. "Toby, listen to me. Take that branch and hit the trunk of that tree. Tap out S.O.S. so the men can hear you and find you."

"Oh, like that's really going to help," Lucien snorted derisively. "A little dramatic, aren't we? Come on, why don't you just take the branch and use it like a dowsing tool to find help."

Lileah spread one wing around Toby like a shield to ward off the words of the demon. "Go on, Toby. Take the branch."

Toby stared at the branch for a full minute before the thought sank in enough for her to act on it. Stumbling to the branch, she picked it up and whacked it feebly against the trunk of a nearby tree. Summoning the remainder of her energy, she swung again and again. Three quick taps, three long, three quick. Every time the branch connected with the tree trunk, Toby felt as though her arms were going to pop right out of the sockets.

"What the . . . ?" the first man's voice said.

"That's an S.O.S.," Carl replied. "Come on. Somebody *is* in trouble."

Toby stared dully at the tree and wondered if she had the energy to try again. She began to draw the branch back, but her arm was stopped by a firm hand. Her fingers loosened, letting the branch drop to the snow as she turned to look into the face of her rescuer.

"Help me," she whispered. "Help me."

"It's OK. You'll be all right now. We'll help you." The man's face looked odd frosted over by moonlight. He had a beard, and his eyes were kind with laugh lines deeply etched around the corners. His companion was a tall, thin man with a red ski cap pulled tightly over his head. Hands stuffed into his pockets, he hung back, unsure of what to make of her.

Toby sagged in the man's strong arms, feeling as though all strength had suddenly left her. Safe, she was safe.

"Ma'am? Ma'am? What happened to you?"

The man's voice penetrated her thoughts, reminding her that while she may be safe, Davy wasn't.

"Davy," she gasped, suddenly stiffening up in the man's arms and pulling away. "Davy. Please help Davy. My husband. The plane. Went down. Up there." She motioned up the mountain behind her and was vaguely aware of the men exchanging incredulous looks.

"Ma'am? Are you saying that a plane went down on the mountain?" The man's voice took on a professional quality, the kind Toby recognized from her training as an intensive care nurse.

She nodded her head up and down and tried to detach herself mentally from being overwhelmed by the exhaustion threatening to overtake her body. "Yes, my husband, our plane, it went down up the mountain somewhere. I followed this path down. Please, you have to help him."

The man supporting her turned to his friend. "Mike, get back to the warming hut. Radio the police, the ambulance, and see if you can get anybody from the ski patrol. Tell them what she said. I'll be there as soon as I can."

Mike nodded and turned, the crunching of his rapid steps through the snow quickly fading. Carl took off his mittens and pulled them gently over Toby's blue hands. Then he removed his coat and placed it around her shaking shoulders.

"It's going to be all right," he said. "We'll get some people up there to find your husband, and we'll get you right down to the hospital. Can you walk? No, wait."

Before Toby could even respond, Carl lifted her right off her feet and began carrying her through the snow. Toby let her head rest against his chest as the warmth from his jacket seeped into her. His kindness brought tears to her eyes, but before they could even trickle down her cheeks, she was asleep.

CHAPTER 5

Billie Jo stared with red-rimmed eyes at the ring in her tea mug. She swallowed past the lump in her throat and listened to the sounds of Cassidy and Dallas playing in the other room with her friend Leah's children. Leah sat across from her, reaching out to squeeze her hand sympathetically every now and then.

"I don't know what to do, Leah." Billie Jo's voice was barely a raspy whisper. She shook her head, tears splattering onto the table like raindrops. "Everything is so hard now. I just don't know how much more I can take. Before Jimmy died . . ." Billie Jo stopped abruptly, her face draining of all color.

"Did you hear what I just said?" she gasped.

"You said everything is hard now," Leah repeated.

"I said before Jimmy died." Her voice dropped lower than before. "Leah, Jimmy isn't dead. Why'd I say he was?" She sat back, her eyes open wide with the revelation. "I think of him as though he's dead. Don't I?" she demanded, as if Leah was privy to her thoughts. "Oh, Leah, I'm scared. What if it's some kind of bad sign? Me thinking of him like he was dead already."

Leah shook her head, testing her tea gingerly. "Don't be thinkin' like that, Billie Jo, that ain't the way it is, and you know it. 'Sides, there's no such thing as bad signs, you know that. Everythin' is in the hands of God, and things that happen, well, them's just coincidence or something. It sure don't mean that Jimmy's gonna die just 'cause the thought crossed your mind."

Tears trickled down Billie Jo's cheeks, and she stared at the tabletop. "I miss him so much. I miss the way he used to come home smelling of woodchips and gasoline. I miss the way he used to look deep into my eyes like he could read my thoughts or something. I miss the way he used to hold my hand. He was so strong, so gentle . . ." Her voice breaking, Billie Jo buried her face in her hands, shoulders shaking with gentle sobs.

"Momma?" Cassidy rounded the corner and came to an abrupt halt, seeing her mother crying.

"It's OK, child," Billie Jo heard Leah say. "Your momma's just letting out some of the sad. It'll be OK. Go play with the other kids for awhile like a good girl, huh? Thanks, baby."

Billie Jo wiped her eyes with the heels of her hands, sniffling as Leah handed her a tissue. She tried on a weak smile, but it felt fake. "I'm sorry to unload all of this on you," she apologized.

Leah squeezed Billie Jo's hand hard. "Don't you never be sorry for such as that. What are friends for if they can't comfort each other when one of 'ems feeling badly? But, Billie Jo, you can't just go on feeling bad. You've got to get your strength from somewhere. You need to be prayin'. You need to be prayin' like you never prayed 'afore in your life."

Billie Jo nodded. "I know it. I pray a lot. And the other night, when I was praying by Jimmy's side, I felt this sense of peace just flow over me. But you're right. I need to be praying now like never before. Not just for me to have the strength to go through this, but for Jimmy to be healed, and if not healed, then . . ." Her voice faltered. "Then, what? That's what I need to know."

Leah clasped Billie Jo's hands in both of her own. Her palms felt rough and somehow comforting as her hands encircled Billie Jo's. She bowed her head, and Billie Jo followed her lead.

"Lord," she prayed, "we know that you ain't deserted Billie Jo nor Jimmy, Lord. What plan You got for Jimmy we don't know, but we trust him in Your hands. Heal his mind if'n it's Your will. Be with Billie Jo and the kids. Help 'em get through this tough time. Send Your holy angels to watch over 'em and keep 'em safe."

As Leah prayed on, her voice sincere, her prayer simple, Jewel spread his wings around the two women accompanied by Leah's guardian angel, Michel. Bowing their heads, the two angels joined their prayers to ones ascending from the two women seated at the table. As they prayed, other angels began gathering around the table, joining their prayers until there was a steady, strong stream of prayer flowing up to heaven.

Nog slunk around glaring at the group, avoiding the intense light broadcast by the angels. Distressed by the turn of events, he paced back and forth, hurling insults at the angels who didn't even acknowledge his existence. Finally, he could stand it no longer and fled from the room to find a place not inhabited by the host of heaven.

When Billie Jo looked across the table at Leah a half hour later, she knew that the hope reflected in Leah's eyes had settled deep into her own heart. The situation hadn't changed, but her outlook had. Impulsively, she leaned forward and threw her arms around her friend, hugging her hard.

"I'm so glad you came today."

Leah returned Billie Jo's hug and stroked her hair comfortingly. "So am I. You know you can always call me if you get to feelin' depressed again. You know that, don't you? Cain't go taking all this load on your own shoulders." She stood up from the table, suddenly businesslike. "Now, point me to the vacuum, and I'll help you get this place right straightened up before I go."

Billie Jo started to protest, but seeing the determined look on Leah's face, she swallowed it and meekly pointed to the closet where she kept the old broken-down vacuum that Jimmy's mother had passed on when it became too decrepit for her to use anymore. Leah marched over to the closet and came back brandishing the vacuum and shouting a rallying cry to the troops in the living room. In short order, she had the kids dusting, straightening, and washing dishes. Billie Jo picked up a dish towel to dry the dishes, but Leah handed her a Bible and directed her into the living room where Dallas was playing on the floor beside Jimmy's cot.

"You go right on in there now and take a load off. Set yourself right down and read Jimmy some of the psalms. Weren't them his favorites? Betcha he's pining to hear 'em."

Billie Jo sank gratefully onto the sofa, surrounded by an unseen circle of angels. Opening the worn Bible, she began with Jimmy's favorite psalm. Her voice was strong with faith in the promises of God. "He who dwells in the shelter of the Most High will rest in the shadow of the Almighty. I will say of the Lord, 'He is my refuge and my fortress, my God, in whom I trust. . . .' "

The summer had passed quickly, and still Shelan had failed to penetrate the grasp of the demons upon Lyle. Warg's success had gathered more demons who had ceased roaming the earth and had begun congregating around the little house on Chestnut Lane. Depression, dark and foreboding, hung so thick in the air that Shelan wasn't able to get an untainted breath.

Lyle spent most days beneath the boughs of the willow tree or in front of his window that overlooked the street, keeping a close eye on Calla Kendall. He knew her routine so well that he set his alarm clock by it when she went out in the morning for a jog, just so he could catch a glimpse of her as she passed by, and he didn't go to bed at night until he saw her light go out.

His sketch pad was filled with sketches of Calla running, skating, playing her violin, and sitting on the steps daydreaming. There were hundreds. And, lately, he had taken to writing poetry about her. Dark, passionate poetry that Shelan shuddered to look at.

She watched him now, standing a safe distance from where he sat, surrounded by demons who were happily filling his mind. Shelan shook her head sadly. Beside her, Noble wore a concerned look as he watched the antics of the demons and Lyle's apparent helplessness in resisting them. Like a drop of crystal, a tear slid down his cheek.

"You will not be able to pierce their influence over him right now, Shelan," Noble said finally. "He does not want you to help him. He is enjoying this . . . this . . . orgy of grief and depression he's feeling. The only chance you have to reach him is through someone who will pray for him. Is there such a person?"

Shelan thought immediately of Berniece Kendall. The woman had prayed faithfully for Lyle every day since the accident, though she didn't really know what had happened to him. "Yes, there is one. The wife of the man whose heart attack caused Lyle's accident prays for him still. Though her prayers are non-specific.

"A few months ago I approached her, suggesting a visit. I thought it might help to jog Lyle out of his self-centeredness. She considered it, even prayed about it. I thought she would go, but she didn't. That was months ago."

Noble nodded thoughtfully. "What I suggest is this. Go to the woman. Give her a burden to pray for his salvation earnestly, as if his very life depends on it." He took one last, tearful look at the assembly of demons. "Because it does."

Lyle breathed sluggishly under the blanket of depression that hung heavily over him. It was as tangible as the fog that wove lazily through the air. Seemed like he was always depressed lately. Usually the feeling went away some after the date of the accident passed, but this year he hadn't been able to shake it, for some reason. And actually, he didn't really care.

The depression had become a friend, of sorts. He could wallow in self-pity, and there was no one to answer to for it. His mother had long since begun to lose her grip on sanity. Most of the time she existed in her own little world, sometimes calling him by his father's name. But she still managed to handle everyday life pretty well.

His Aunt Melanie came by each week to take his mom grocery shopping, and most weeks she came back with enough ingredients to make meals that were fairly well-balanced. There had been a few times when he'd found odd things like peanut butter in his tomato soup or mayonnaise on top of his pudding in place of whipped cream.

It was hard to think of life being good. Especially when he compared it to where he had hoped his life would be at this point. And then the anger came, surging within him like an unending fountain. It seemed the more he expressed it, the more came to replace it.

Lyle dug his fingers into his hair, grabbing it and shaking his head in misery. He was so absorbed in his own thoughts that when the gentle melody finally reached his consciousness, at first he thought it was coming from inside his head, like some beautiful long-forgotten tune from childhood.

The hauntingly sweet voice of a violin threaded through the damp fog. Lyle strained to catch every pensive note. At last he recognized the piece. It was Bach's *Jesu, Joy of Man's Desiring*. A song his mother used to be asked to sing every Christmas at their little church. It was one of his favorites.

Strange, he mused, that he didn't remember hearing it for years. Now it wound around his heart, provoking memories of happier times that brought an unconscious smile to his lips. All the warmth and security he'd experienced growing up rushed over him like a wave, bringing tears of sadness as well as joy.

The music faded away as the song ended, and Lyle slowly became aware once more of his surroundings. The silence that encompassed him was unbearable. Tentatively, he began to whistle the notes of the song. Barely audible at first, he gained confidence as the song once more mingled with the fog, and he filled his lungs with air, his whistle as sweet as a songbird.

He was halfway through the song when he caught sight of Calla jogging. Her steps were slow, her expression puzzled as she looked around, trying to find the source of the whistling. Lyle almost skipped a beat but realized that the fog and the tree would hide his identity as well as his location. Finally, Calla picked up her pace, shrugging her shoulders slightly.

Lyle chuckled to himself. She'd noticed him after all. It hadn't been much, and she didn't know it was him, but she'd been listening to him. To him. Worthless, weak, crippled Lyle Ryan.

Shelan shook her head. "Oh, Lyle, you're not any of those things. You're a beautiful son of God. A prince, infinitely precious in His sight. You must realize that. I must help you realize that."

CHAPTER 6

Gaius gazed down with love at his charge while she slept, his wings spread out over the humble cot where she lay as if they were a canopy of protection from the day ahead. Exhaustion showed on Shay's face, even relaxed as it was by sleep. Every tired line reflected one more act of kindness, one extra mile she had walked since arriving. At this rate, the girl would wear herself out before the year was spent. It was something that worried Gaius at times.

She was on a crusade—a crusade to improve all Africa, or at least this one little part. A born "fixer," Gaius watched as Shay pushed herself to the limits to minister to the afflicted at the mission. And all the while, her mind explored ways to comfort the one man who would prefer that she didn't exist.

Shay opened her eyes as the morning sun filtered through the haze of dust that always seemed to be hanging in the air no matter what time of day it was. She rolled over on her side and cracked her eyes at the alarm clock on the rickety little wooden stand next to her cot. Eight o'clock in the morning. She'd overslept!

Jumping out of bed, she raced wildly for her suitcase, only to get tangled in the sheets and sprawl face first onto the floor. What a way to start the day. She pulled her permanently wrinkled clothes out of the suitcase and put them on as fast as she could.

Around her the room hadn't changed much in the month since she'd arrived. Small changes, maybe . . . curtains on the window, made from a blouse that survived the trip but not the first day of work, some artwork courtesy of Marcus, who had adoringly attached himself to her, and local crafts she'd received from thankful patients.

Yes, in a month's time she'd really come a long way and made many new friends. Everyone at the mission compound looked at her with respect. Everyone, that is, except Dr. Don Germaine. Shay let out an unconscious huff of indignation. Well, she'd see about that.

It hadn't taken her too long to realize that the hard-to-please doctor protected a very broken heart beneath a coarse and irritating exterior designed to keep anyone from seeing it. It hadn't taken long to realize this, because the very first night she'd spent at the mission, she'd woken up in the middle of the night to the sound of agonized groaning coming from somewhere on the compound.

Disoriented and terrified, she'd cowered on her cot, clutching a sheet that was soaked with her own perspiration. Finally, she'd gotten up enough courage to creep out into the hallway. The sound came from down the hall. Only a shaft of moonlight penetrated the darkness. She stopped counting the number of times she almost bolted back to her room in terror before she stopped in front of the last door on the right.

The moans had long since increased in volume and were mixed with heart-wrenching sobs. Someone was in terrible pain. And whoever it was was on the other side of that door.

Shay licked her lips. Hesitantly her hand reached out to knock on the door. But before her knuckles could connect with the wood, a firm, warm palm encircled her hand, stopping her. Her knees wobbled weakly as she staggered a few panicked paces away from the door. Seconds before a piercing scream bolted from her lips, a quiet voice stopped her.

"Please do not do that. You will only embarrass him."

Slowly Nwibe's shape separated from the general darkness. "But, but, I don't understand. Who, who . . . why?" Shay's tongue tripped, her heart pounding fiercely as raw fear coursed through her.

Nwibe's soft chuckle took the edge off her fear. "It is the doctor who is having a nightmare. This is not the first time. He wants to be left alone."

"Why?" Shay whispered. "I mean, why is he having a nightmare?"

"Rwanda," Nwibe replied simply. "I thought perhaps you would wake up and investigate. It will be OK. I will walk you back to your room. Try to sleep. He will awaken soon, and all will be quiet again."

As they walked along, Nwibe moved so independently that Shay could almost believe that he could see. "How did you . . . I mean, if you can't see, then how did you find my hand in the dark to stop me from knocking?"

"You forget, it is always dark for me," he reminded her. "There are many ways to see without eyes. I "felt" you there and the breeze as you raised your hand." He shrugged. "It is hard to explain."

Since that day, Shay often marveled at how the tall, reserved African "saw" things. At times she was convinced that he saw more than she did. When she had questions or felt awkward working in the primitive conditions, Nwibe stepped in, helping her over the problem before blending once more into the background of the clinic where he performed whatever chores his hands could find, no matter how menial.

Shay decided to forego breakfast. Instead, she ran lightly across the courtyard to the clinic. Dr. Germaine was bent over a baby who had been admitted the day before, due to malnutrition. The baby's obviously pregnant and malnourished mother stood patiently beside the bed waiting for the doctor's comments. Marcus was seated at his father's feet as the two inventoried supplies which had come in on the last shipment from Operation C.A.R.E. headquarters.

"Quite the lady of leisure this morning, Miss Beauregard," Dr. Germaine said, without even glancing up.

Shay stiffened and took her place beside him as he continued to examine the patient. The sharp retort forming on her lips died as the memory of his sobs echoed in her head. Instead, she smiled. "Miss me, did you, Doctor?"

Out of the corner of her eye, she caught Nwibe ducking his head to hide a look of amusement. Dr. Germaine ignored her, turning to the baby's mother and leading her gently to a chair by his desk. While Shay busied herself tending to the infant, Dr. Germaine explained the child's condition in simple terms to the mother before sending her over to the mission compound with strict instructions to see Akueke for a nourishing meal and whatever supplies she felt they could spare.

Shay deftly changed the baby and propped him up on her shoulder, rocking back and forth to quiet him as she went over the case of each patient with Dr. Germaine. She'd had a hard time adjusting to the lack of computers at first, but what was even harder for her to deal with was Dr. Germaine's almost total dearth of medical documentation.

He'd laughed in her face when she even suggested it. "These people come in here to be treated for malnourishment, dysentery, cuts, bites, and diseases, and you want me to keep a record of when they eat, drink, and sleep?"

Still, Shay felt much better following the practices she'd learned at school. She'd developed her own system of nursing notes, crude though they were. Eventually, she felt sure, she could prove their worth to Dr. Germaine. Until then, she was entirely responsible for keeping them updated by herself.

Juggling the baby and a pen and paper, she copied down the status of each patient in the little clinic as Dr. Germaine related anything new that had transpired since she'd gotten off duty the evening before. When he was finished, he ran one hand through his dark, unruly hair and rubbed the other over the shadow of beard stubble on his face.

"How long have you been here, Doctor?" Shay asked, concerned by the dark circles under his eyes. "Why don't you go rest? I can handle things."

Germaine snorted. "I'll believe that when I see it. First, you could try being here on time. Or would you prefer that I send someone to give you a wake-up call each morning? Maybe deliver breakfast in bed so you wouldn't have to inconvenience yourself by showing up to eat it with the rest of us."

Shay swallowed hard as tears stung her eyes. "I'm sorry I was late. I overslept. My alarm didn't go off."

"Yeah, well, don't let it get to be a habit, huh?" Standing abruptly, he nearly bumped into her as he staggered out of the building leaving Shay staring after him, hurt and perplexed.

Merck watched Don make his way to the compound. The nightmares he had supplied the night before had kept Don up the entire evening, sweating and shaking in his bed as memories from Rwanda had bombarded him with increasing force. Finally, he'd given up trying to fend them off and gone to the clinic, desperate for the company of others, even though they were sleeping. Just the soft breath of the baby on his cheek as he rocked her had comforted him. Now he was undoubtedly headed to his room to sleep, and Merck felt free to hang around and see what other types of mischief he could stir up.

Jezeel joined him as the two studied the situation. Many angels were about as the direct result of prayer cover from the United States. The demons' division leader, Sparn, or as they liked to call him behind his back, Sparn the Terrible, was un-

der direct orders from Satan himself to cut off the prayer link from the States. Accompanied by Merck's efforts to bring down Don Germaine, there was a very good opportunity to discredit Operation C.A.R.E. by association and severely hamper or shut down many of their outreach projects.

As they understood it, the leader of the prayer link was a very feeble old woman whose time was almost up anyway. As Satan sarcastically put it, "not too much trouble for such a mighty leader as Sparn." Well, as any demon could plainly see, the angels were still thick, as a testament to Sparn's miserable failure so far.

"He's been here since two this morning," Nwibe supplied the answer to her question before she even asked it. "He's just tired, that's all. Don't take it to heart."

Merck jabbed Jezeel with one bony elbow. The demon hissed at him and spat a slimy string of foul-smelling liquid past Merck's shoulder. Merck ignored the message and pointed to Shay. "We could start there. A little misunderstanding could go a long way, don't you think?" He smiled, revealing a set of extremely dirty, jagged teeth.

Shay shrugged off the uneasiness that Dr. Germaine's words had left her with. "No," she smiled. "I won't. How are you two this morning?" she asked, a mischievous glint in her eye as she shook her finger at Marcus. "I hope you read that book I gave you last night. I want a full report."

The boy stared at the floor of the clinic, and his father seemed suddenly aloof. "The pictures are very nice," Marcus ventured finally, not glancing up to meet the puzzled look in Shay's eyes.

"Yes," she replied slowly. "There are very nice pictures in the book. But, did you like the story?"

"Don't answer her, boy," Merck warned. "You know your father is too proud to admit that you can't read, because it's his fault. Let her think what she wants, but don't let her know you can't read."

Jezeel cackled with glee. "That's right. Don't look at her either."

Gaius watched the exchange from Shay's side, where he had been marveling at the beautiful baby she was taking care of, while sorrowfully contemplating the condition the human race had fallen into.

Marcus shifted nervously and rubbed his fingers over the smooth wood of the pole he used to guide his father with. Not speaking, he rolled it back and forth between his palms. Nwibe refrained from looking her way as well, and Shay felt a sudden wave of shame and regret wash over her. Maybe they were offended by the story in the book. Why hadn't she thought of that in the first place?

She mentally kicked herself as she turned from them and continued to care for the baby, biting her lip in consternation. When would she ever learn to think before she acted?

"That's right," Jezeel harassed her. "Can't you see what you've done? You've insulted them. And after they've been so nice to you and helped you out so much. That was really low."

"Things are not always as they seem," Gaius reminded Shay. "You are new here. It is possible that you inadvertently offended Nwibe, or maybe you are misinterpreting him. Why don't you talk to him and clear the air?"

Shay spun back to face Nwibe, heart pounding in fear but convicted that she needed to settle the matter before it went any further. "Did the story offend you?" she blurted out.

Nwibe stopped what he was doing and looked up, his sightless eyes turned in the direction her voice had come from. It was a long time before he spoke. When he did, his words were accompanied by a heavy sigh. "Marcus cannot read the story."

Shay's lower lip trembled, and she caught it between her teeth as tears stung her eyes. "You mean that you won't let him read it because I gave it to him?"

Nwibe held up both hands. "No, no, that is not it at all. Marcus cannot read the story because he cannot read."

Shay laughed in relief. "He can't read? He can't read?" At the look of shame on Nwibe's face, her laughter stopped abruptly. "Why, he's at least ten. And there's a school here." Slowly it dawned on her that Marcus was never *in* school. He was always with his father.

Throughout the previous month, Shay had come to understand a little about the relationship between the man and his son. Ever since Nwibe had contracted river blindness when Marcus was only three years old, the boy had acted as a kind of "seeing eye" child, leading his father around by the long pole that was always with either one or the other of them. Worn smooth by use, it was stronger than any umbilical cord, binding Marcus to his father for life.

Because he was constantly needed by his father, the boy had no time for ordinary activities like school. Something that, Shay suddenly realized, Nwibe felt very guilty about. She walked over and stood in front of them, chucking Marcus under the chin.

"Hey, did you know that I can read?" she asked Marcus. The boy looked up, his dark eyes pools of sadness. "And do you know, I bet that I can even teach you how to read." The glimmer of hope that suddenly lighted Marcus's face was promptly squelched by his father.

"We have no time for things that are nonessential," Nwibe said proudly. "Marcus has no need to learn how to read."

Shay winked at the boy, not willing to give up that easily. "Who says reading is nonessential? Why, I would say that reading is very essential. Wouldn't you, Marcus?"

The boy looked up at his father and then at Shay before nodding vigorously. "You needn't think that you are fooling me, you two," Nwibe informed them. Suddenly he chuckled. "You are a stubborn woman," he said. "But he cannot go to school."

Shay raised her eyebrows. "Who said anything about school? Yet?"

Toby felt as though she'd stared at the marbled walls of the waiting room of the Intensive Care Unit at the Rutland Regional Medical Center for years instead of days. Wearing clothes a few sizes too large, generously loaned to her by Carl's wife, DeeDee, when rescue personnel informed her that her luggage had gone up with the rest of the plane, she looked like a child who had gotten into her mother's closet to play dress-up. Her brown hair hung in uncombed wisps around her face, which was pale and drawn from lack of sleep.

She shifted position where she was curled up on the chair in the waiting room. A good sign that she'd been there too long, she mused, was that she had figured out a rotation schedule for her body so that her limbs wouldn't fall asleep from the awkward positions enforced upon her by the singularly uncomfortable chair. Resting her chin on one bandaged hand, she stared out the window onto the part of the city below that she could see while her mind wandered, reconstructing the events of the past few days, ever since the plane crash.

"We never saw anything like it," she remembered one incredulous member of the rescue team say. "That plane was twisted worse than any pretzel I ever saw. By the time we got there, it was just a flaming torch lighting up the sky like some kind of roman candle. We were sure no one could have survived that crash. But there he was, leaning up against a tree, hardly a scratch on him, either. Like some big hand had lifted him right out of the plane and set him up against that tree."

Hardly a scratch on him.

But, unconscious.

Toby sighed. And still unconscious. And doctors weren't sure why, although many had ventured guesses, the most probable being trauma to the head, suffered during the crash. A CAT scan showed no abnormalities except a tiny bit of swelling that the doctor's dismissed out of hand.

"What do doctors know anyway?" Lucien snickered inso-lently. *"Probably the swelling will get worse. You know I'm right. You're a nurse, O'Connell. You know what swelling on the brain could mean. Bad news, really bad news. And there's nothing anybody can do except wait. Wait and wait. Aren't you getting tired of waiting? Why don't you go back home? Give up. Davy'd understand when he wakes up. IF he wakes up."*

Toby shuddered as her mind morbidly wandered down bleak corridors into a future she didn't even want to consider. One without Davy. She shook herself as a feeling of depression settled over her with a chill.

"Toby, remember that night on the mountain? You called out to God to help you?" Lileah reminded her gently. *"God is still here, Toby. He can still help you. All you have to do is ask. Why don't you ask Him, Toby? Why don't you ask Him to help you?"*

Toby recalled the night she'd been on the mountain. She thought about the request for help, squeezed out of her by des-peration. Still, there had been that feeling of peace, of assurance that had followed that prayer, as unorthodox as it was. She felt a little like praying again. She looked around self-consciously. The only other person in the waiting room was an elderly man, asleep with his head thrown back, his mouth hanging open as he snored loudly.

"God? Um, I was just thinking, well, that is, I wondered." Toby stopped and tried to collect her thoughts.

"You call that praying?" Lucien sneered. "That's pathetic. Why bother? You don't even know how to do it right."

"Toby, you're doing fine," Lileah encouraged. "Remember, the Master wants you to approach the throne of grace with confidence, so that you may receive mercy and find grace to help you in your time of need."

"Um, God, I need help. Well, that is, Davy needs help. Could You . . . uh, would You . . ."

"Mrs. O'Connell?"

The voice startled her. Toby looked up, blushing with embarrassment. A nurse stood before her, and suddenly a wave of panic swept over her. Davy! "Yes? Is something wrong?"

The face of the nurse in front of her was smiling pleasantly. Toby recognized her as one of the friendlier nurses on the day shift. "Mrs. O'Connell? I have good news. Your husband has regained consciousness. Doctor Nesbith is with him right now, but after he leaves, you should be permitted in to see him for just a few minutes. We don't want him to get tired out."

Toby leapt out of the chair, sobs choking in her throat. "Davy! Oh, Davy! Thank You, God!" She raced past the nurse toward the room where Davy was. Not even pausing at the closed door, she wrenched it open. Dr. Nesbith looked up, irritation registering on his face.

"Mrs. O'Connell, please, would you wait outside until I've finished examining your husband?"

Davy's dark hair, always unruly, framed a face that was paler than Toby had ever seen it. His blue eyes were striking, but vacant. He looked up at her, a puzzled expression on his face. Putting one hand on his temple, he squeezed his eyes shut. "That light. Oh, it hurts."

Toby reached out quickly, brushing the switch off. Dr. Nesbith frowned at her. "Mrs. O'Connell, please, I need the light at the moment. I'll be through shortly. Now, if you'll please go wait until I come out to talk to you."

"I'm not going anywhere," Toby said stubbornly. "Not until I can talk to Davy. Davy? Honey? How do you feel?"

Davy opened his eyes slowly and looked at her as if he was seeing her for the first time. His forehead wrinkled in concentration. Finally his breath whispered out between his lips. "I'm sorry. Do I know you?"

Toby didn't realize that her mouth was gaping until she tried to swallow and found it impossible. She approached Davy's bed hesitantly. "Honey? You remember me. It's Toby." She reached out and took one of his hands, squeezing it in her own, trying to ignore Dr. Nesbith's pitying look. "Davy? Baby? It's Toby," she sobbed.

Davy pulled his hand away from her. "I'm sorry. I don't remember you."

"Mrs. O'Connell? Please, would you wait outside?" Dr. Nesbith nodded to the nurse who had followed Toby into the room. "Joann? Please bring Mrs. O'Connell outside for a few minutes, would you? I'll be right out."

Toby allowed herself to be led out into the hallway by Joann's kind, but firm, grip on her elbow. Her breathing raced as she began to hyperventilate. She was vaguely aware of Joann calling to Dr. Nesbith and then someone placing an oxygen mask over her nose and mouth until her breathing slowed finally and returned to normal.

Dr. Nesbith sat down in a chair beside her, his face sober. "Mrs. O'Connell, you already know that your husband has experienced some memory loss as a result of the crash. Now, he just woke up, so obviously, we don't know how extensive it is or how permanent."

At the word *permanent*, Toby flinched and reached for the oxygen mask again. Dr. Nesbith patted her arm sympathetically. "As soon as we know anything, we'll let you know. Now, I don't want you in there pestering him, plying him with questions to try to jog his memory. But when he's awake, if he feels like visitors, I don't see any reason why you shouldn't go in and talk to him. Seeing you, listening to you, he might begin to remember things. We just don't know at this point."

"Can I . . . can I go in and see him now?" Toby asked, sniffing as she wiped one hand across her face, trying to erase the evidence of her tears.

Dr. Nesbith nodded reluctantly. "I suppose so. But, just for a minute."

He turned and walked to the nurse's station as Toby squared her shoulders and walked timidly to Davy's door, knocking lightly. When there was no answer, she pushed it open and let herself in. The tears flowed unchecked when she saw Davy sleeping peacefully. She didn't have the heart to wake him. She just stood there, leaning against the door, crying softly.

Billie Jo drifted in and out of consciousness, vaguely aware of the kids playing. Dallas's shrill baby squeals mingled with Cassidy's little girl giggles as they romped around the living room where Billie Jo had surrendered to exhaustion on the couch. She had the vague conviction that it was late in the day and that something important was supposed to happen, but she couldn't seem to grasp what that was.

Somewhere, someone was knocking on something. It was a loud, persistent knocking that filtered in around the kids' racket. Fighting the clutches of sleep, Billie Jo struggled to wake up and

find out what the knocking was all about. Just before she suc-
cessfully navigated her way to consciousness, a loud crash and a
gasp brought her suddenly, completely awake.

The total chaos that greeted her was too overwhelming to sort
out efficiently. Toys and clothes were scattered over the floor
where Dallas and Cass had been playing. The chair was over-
turned, but Billie Jo saw immediately that it hadn't been the
chair that caused the crash, as it had fallen on a beanbag. The
crash had been the result of one leg of Jimmy's cot caving in.

The other leg, as well, threatened to collapse beneath Jimmy's
weight as gravity slid him toward the floor. The metal leg groaned
and bowed. Standing in the doorway, staring aghast at the scene
in front of her but too shocked to move, was Helen, who had
finally used her key to come in when no one answered her knock.

Billie Jo jumped up before she even realized that she intended
to. Using strength she didn't know she possessed, she grasped
the end of the cot and pulled it level. A swift kick at the errant
leg locked it back into position. Gingerly, she set the cot back
down and tugged Jimmy back into position.

Turning, she faced her mother-in-law as if she were moving in
slow motion. Cassidy wrapped Dallas protectively in her arms,
eyes moving fearfully from her mother to her grandmother. Helen
was shaking all over, her face a livid shade of red. Billie Jo watched
her dispassionately, thinking that any minute now she would
explode just as viciously as Mount St. Helen. A chuckle at the
thought escaped her lips before she could stop it.

"You . . . think . . . this . . . is . . . funny?" Helen demanded,
exaggerating each word, her voice as loud as the foreman in a
sawmill. Veins at her temples bulged and throbbed. Billie Jo
counted the pulses in an attempt to separate herself from the
situation.

*Nog hooted with pleasure, his features twisted with ecstacy
at the fury emanating from Helen. It reached out like a tangible
entity, wrapping around Billie Jo, taunting her to react to it, to*

fight back. "Oooooh," he mocked, grinning wildly. "She's just asking for it, isn't she? Give it to her. Go on, give it to her good. What business is it of hers anyway?"

"The Spirit of God is the Master of your life, Billie Jo," Jewel reminded her gently. *"There is no power greater than His. You do not need to lower yourself to be controlled by this base emotion. You can stay above it. Remember, a soft answer turns away wrath."*

Billie Jo fought to control herself as she felt anger easily matching Helen's well up inside her. "No, I don't think this is funny," she said keeping her voice even. "It was just . . . something that occurred to me was funny. That's all." Her eyes blinked rapidly. *Lord, help me,* she prayed. *She wants to start a fight, and I don't want to give in, but she's got no right to act this way, as if it's all my fault. I've been up half the night all week. I needed the sleep. I couldn't help it . . .*

Helen's eyes narrowed suspiciously. "What are you doing? Your lips are moving."

Billie Jo clamped her mouth shut. "Were they? I was just praying, that's all."

"Hrmph," Helen muttered. "Why don't you pray for some initiative as long as you're going to bother God. Ask Him for some motivation, too, while you're at it."

The light surrounding Jewel flared as Billie Jo prayed. It spread to include Billie Jo, shielding her from the intended sting of Helen's attack and infusing her with peace and calm. "Remember where she's coming from," Jewel reminded Billie Jo. *"She's had a hard life, and the Master loves her as He loves you. And He has asked you to love each other the way He loves you. He'll help you do that."*

Billie Jo bit her lip. It was understandable that Helen was upset, she reasoned. After all, it must seem very negligent to her since she didn't know everything that had led up to this state of utter confusion she'd walked into. And right now was not the time to try to explain it, either. Not with Cassidy and Dallas watching the entire exchange with wide eyes.

"Well, I know God can provide all my needs," Billie Jo replied simply, putting a smile on for the children's benefit. She clapped her hands together. "Now, Cass, if you please, would you help Mommy pick up this room so it will be all clean when the visiting nurse comes? Thank you, baby."

"I like that," Helen muttered, as she took off her coat; finding no place to hang it, she laid it on the kitchen table. "It doesn't matter what the place looks like for me, but for the visiting nurse it's got to look like a palace. Somebody's priorities are a little skewed, if you ask me."

Billie Jo continued praying as she worked her way around the room picking up toys and straightening things. She'd long since learned to tune out Helen's barbs, and they became the unintelligible undertone to which she worked. Though she was unaware of it, as she prayed, the house filled with more and more angels until Nog was again chased out by their presence.

C H A P T E R

7

Toby stood beside the wheelchair that held her entire future—the hunched over form of Davy O'Connell, fully mended. Except where it mattered most. Every time she looked down at him and was met by that puzzled, blank expression, her eyes filled with tears. She gripped the bag they'd given her with some of Davy's things that had been salvaged from the plane.

An orderly wheeled Davy toward the door of the hospital that led outside while Toby shuffled along beside, trying to keep up, offering a mind-numbing chatter to cover the fact that Davy said nothing. Outside, a rental car waited.

Toby tried to help Davy into the car, but he shrugged her off and lowered himself into the passenger side, slamming the door as she stood on the curb fighting back tears. Squaring her shoulders, she stalked around to the driver's side and got in. It was going to be a long ride back to Boston.

Four hours and a short, unintentional detour later, Toby pulled up in their driveway, exhausted mentally, emotionally, and physically. Davy hadn't spoken one word since they'd left the hospital, and she'd been too close to tears to broach a conversation herself. Now he sat there, dumbly staring at the house as if he'd never seen it before.

As if he'd never seen it before.

Well, she reminded herself, he hadn't. At least, this new Davy hadn't. She wondered dully if the new Davy would like all the decorating the old Davy had done to the house since they'd bought it two years ago. It reflected his taste more than hers.

Davy got out of the car slowly and headed up the front walk. Toby stood watching him, a fresh wave of grief washing over her. "We don't use the front door," she called softly. He turned to look at her, but instead of the reminder ringing any bells, annoyance crossed his face. "You always said that only snobs and tax collectors would ever go to the front door." She pointed toward the side of the house. "We always use the side door."

Davy headed across the lawn to the side door while Toby retrieved his belongings and locked up the car. She opened the door for him and stepped inside, turning to him with a weak smile. "Welcome home, Davy."

He brushed past and wandered slowly through the house. *Like an intruder*, Toby thought. *Or like he was a burglar inventorying the place or something, mentally calculating how much everything would bring at an auction*. She shuddered at the thought. Surely something here would jog his memory.

"Where's my room?" Davy asked. It was the first thing she'd heard him say all day, and the sound of his voice startled her.

"*Our* room is upstairs," she corrected him gently, pointing to the circular stair leading to the second floor. "The last room on the left."

As Davy made his way slowly up the staircase, Toby sifted through the pile of mail on the kitchen table. It was as though they'd been gone for a year instead of just two weeks. It would take forever to get through the stack. She sat down gratefully. Just what she needed. A mindless task.

When she finally had all the important stuff separated from the junk mail, Toby made her way upstairs. She met Davy on his way down, a suitcase in each hand.

"Have you got any cash on you?" he asked as she backed down the stairs in front of him, mouth hanging open.

"Cash? What for?" she croaked.

"For a hotel room," Davy replied, his eyes avoiding hers. "I'm not comfortable here. I'm going to go get a room for a few days and try to sort things out."

"You're not comfortable here?" Toby echoed, her voice gaining volume with each syllable. "In your own house? You designed this house! How could you not be comfortable here?"

Davy shrugged. "I don't know. I'm just not. It gives me the creeps. *You* give me the creeps. Always looking at me like you expect something, like you want to see "him" in me. Well, I'm not him. I don't even know who *he* was."

Toby shoved a fist in her mouth to keep from begging him to stay. Tears streaming down her face, she fumbled with her purse and pulled out all the cash she had. On impulse, she took out her credit card and handed it to him. "There, your name is on that too. Use it if you need more money."

Davy's eyes lighted up for the first time since he'd come out of the coma. "Thanks! I'll call you, you know, sometime, and we'll talk. OK?"

Toby didn't move as he pocketed the money, picked up his suitcases, and brushed past her to go out the door. Even after it had slammed behind him and the echo of his footsteps faded, she continued to stand in the middle of the kitchen floor, staring dumbly.

"I'm in shock," she finally whispered to herself. "That's what's happening to me. I'm in shock."

The "shock" lasted three weeks, during which time she lost twenty pounds, her job, and most of her friends. Every time the phone rang, she expected it to be Davy. On the days she mustered enough energy to crawl out of bed, she prowled the streets hoping to catch a glimpse of him. Some days she never even made it out of bed. Ordinary things like brushing her teeth or eating became overwhelming tasks. Even breathing seemed like too much trouble.

The group of demons, camped out at Toby's house, filled the place with the dank stench of depression. Lucien had gathered a multitude around him to prey on the despair Toby was experiencing. Together they goaded her with dark thoughts.

Maybe Davy was dead.

Maybe someone had mugged him.

Maybe he had left the country.

Maybe he wasn't ever coming back.

Maybe she should give up and just end her life.

Toby herself seemed incapable of overpowering the hold the demons had gained or of even shaking their stronghold enough to loosen some of the bonds they'd placed around her. Lileah spent every day guarding the perimeter of the house, waiting anxiously for permission to help Toby, wishing there was even one person who remembered her in prayer. But there was no one, and Toby had not spoken to the One who had rescued her from the woods since Davy opened his eyes again.

The day Noble arrived was like any other day. An air of authority surrounded the angel. Even Lucien stopped what he was doing and approached the pair of angels where they stood outside the house. Inside, Lileah was keenly aware that demons were harassing and taunting Toby, telling her she was worthless and urging her to kill herself.

"What are you doing here?" Lucien spat, eyeing Noble with suspicion. "You can't help her. She doesn't want to be helped, and no one is praying for her, or you'd be in there already. She's so weak she's better off dead anyway. Why prolong it? You know she's going to be ours in the end anyway. She's selfish and obstinate and weak. As we speak, she's thinking about jumping off a bridge. There's nothing you can do for her. Why don't you two just go back and play your harps?" He chuckled.

"Don't worry about a thing. We've got everything under control."

"Toby O'Connell has a strong spirit yet, and she will remember what happened in the woods. It is only a matter of time before she will realize that it is God who helped her and God who can help her again if she will only ask," Lileah said to Noble. "But, these demons have weakened her. If she sees Davy now, I do not know how it will affect her."

"It is time," Noble said. "She will see him today. After that, we will see what happens. We cannot control the lives in our watch. They must live their lives for themselves. Ours is to help them and guide them. Toby O'Connell must live through her life. But there is work for you, Lileah. It will require patience, and you must be ready to act the moment the opportunity arises; the moment she is willing to listen to your voice, you must be there to help her."

Lileah nodded, a solemn expression on her shining face. "I will be there. I will not let her down."

Lucien guffawed, slapping a bony thigh with his long, crooked fingers. "Listen to you two. Think she'll pull out of this nose dive yet, huh? I don't. It's too late for her. Why don't you just give up?"

With his eyes, Noble tracked the form of Toby O'Connell descending the steps of her house. She looked as though she had tumbled out of bed wearing what she'd had on the day before, and Lileah suspected that was probably the case. Her tousled hair had at least three parts, none of them flattering. She wore a pair of jeans and a dirty white T-shirt, with a black jean jacket buttoned up crooked. At least, Lileah noted, she'd managed to find two shoes that matched, and as long as you didn't apply the same rule to her socks, she was doing pretty well.

"She's headed for the water," one of the demons chortled as Toby made her way toward the harbor. "She's going to do it. She's going to jump."

Like a boiling cauldron of evil, the crowd of demons pursued Toby as she walked jerkily toward the Charles River. Lileah and Noble followed along at a distance, not able to penetrate the hold the demons had on Toby without her consent.

Toby shuffled along, each step a supreme effort of will. Part of her wasn't even sure what she was doing out here. Every sound seemed magnified, and the light hurt her eyes. It astounded her that life was continuing despite the fact that she had dropped out of it. She stopped at the docks for a moment, watching the boats, but her attention was on the bridge that spanned the water. She looked at it as though she had never really noticed that it existed until this very moment.

"Hey! Hey, is that you?" A voice yelled.

Toby started and looked around apprehensively, her thoughts interrupted. Davy was waving at her from the deck of a boat tied to a pier. Her heart leapt into her throat. Davy! She lifted a hand and waved back.

"Come on down here, why don't you?" he yelled.

Toby grinned. "Sure, be right there."

She felt the relief course through her body as if it had been a transfusion. Everything was going to be OK. Davy wanted to talk to her. They would straighten everything out, and life would return to normal. It was going to work out.

"Wanna bet?" one of the demons chortled, his tattered wings flapping furiously as he ran to keep up with her and the pack of other demons who followed along. "What do you suppose he's doing on a yacht?"

As Toby walked onto the dock, she wondered idly how Davy had ended up here. He hated boats. Always had. She was still puzzling it over when she reached the side of the boat. Davy leaned on the rail of the deck as he looked down at her.

"Hey, there," he said, a nervous smile on his face. "How are you doing?"

"Oh, fine, fine," Toby replied quickly. "You?"

"Never been better," he said. "At least I don't think so. Anyhow, I've been meaning to call you, but we've been so busy getting the boat ready. We're taking a trip."

Toby was just starting to wonder if the memory loss had caused Davy to slip into referring to himself in the royal "we" when the other half of "we" emerged from below deck and sauntered over to stand beside him, throwing a casual arm around his shoulder. The smile that Davy gave the woman, a tall model-perfect blonde, as he turned and lightly kissed her cheek, was the last thing Toby saw before she blindly spun away and ran down the dock.

"Do it!" Lucien shrieked, clinging to her as she ran. "You saw the bridge. Just jump off, and all your troubles will be over."

Lileah raised her voice to be heard over the cacophony of sound produced by the demons as they jeered Toby toward self-destruction. "Toby, remember the One who saved you in the woods. Turn to Him now, and He will save you."

Toby reeled down the street, arms wrapped around her midriff. When she finally crashed to her knees by the side of the street, stomach heaving violently, she had no idea where she was, and she didn't care.

Russell Duffy sat at the breakfast table, his food untouched, cringing at the retching sounds that easily penetrated the bathroom walls and filled up the little kitchen. Minutes before, his seventeen-year-old daughter Julia's peaked face had taken in the sight of breakfast and turned even whiter before she bolted to the bathroom. And all of a sudden, Russell knew. He knew.

Julia was pregnant.

Why it hadn't hit him before this moment, he couldn't even speculate. Her mother, Meg, had acted just like this when she carried Julia. Russell had even caught a glimpse of Meg's face in Julia's as the nausea swept over her.

He clutched his head in his hands, a low moaning issuing from his lips as he rocked back and forth in his chair. "Dear God, please don't let it be true," he begged, in a whisper.

"It is," Julia said dully as she came back into the kitchen. She drew a ragged breath. "You know, don't you, Daddy?"

Russell looked up at her, pallid and thin, her cheekbones standing out in relief, dark shadows making it appear almost as if she had black eyes. Not trusting his voice, he nodded.

"Well, don't worry about it. I'm going to get an abortion." Julia sounded for all the world as if she was talking about a distasteful, but necessary, trip to the dentist to have a tooth pulled. There was a long pause as what she said registered in Russell's mind.

"*What?* What are you saying?"

Julia's shoulders sagged as if the weight of the world were resting on them. "Ray doesn't want me to have the baby." She rushed on before Russell could say anything. "It doesn't matter anyway, because I can't do it. I'd have to drop out of school, and I'd lose all my friends. How would I take care of a baby? I don't have a job, and I can't expect you to support me and a baby forever. My life would be over before it even starts. I . . . I don't have any choice. Besides," she refused to look up and meet his eyes, which were frantically searching her face. "They told me at the clinic when I called, it's not a baby right now, it's just a blob."

Russell was across the floor almost before he was aware of moving. "Julia, listen to me," he begged, taking her hands in his own. "Think about this. A woman gets pregnant. The baby will be an expense she can't afford; it will be a burden on her life. She goes to the doctor. He says, 'No problem. It isn't really a person yet, a simple procedure, perfectly legal.' She has an abortion.

"Later in life, this same woman's father has a stroke and is paralyzed. He doesn't recognize her, can't talk or control any of his bodily functions. All the nursing homes have waiting lists, and so she must take him into her home for an unspecified period of time. It will be a burden on her and an expense she can't afford.

"She goes to the doctor. He says, 'No problem. He's not really a person anyway, there's this simple little shot which will end his life kindly.' Do you see where I'm headed here?"

Julia swallowed hard, her eyes rimmed with red and swimming with tears. She nodded with quick jerky movements. "Yes, Daddy," she whispered.

"Julia, honey, life is a gift from God. Only He has the right to give it or to take it away. We have to respect that."

"But, Daddy, what am I going to do?" Julia sobbed. "Having a baby would ruin my life!"

Russell wrapped his daughter in his arms, smoothing her cropped black hair absently, his mind scrambling for solutions. "We'll figure something out, baby, OK? We'll figure something out."

Sunlight streamed in Ethel Bennington's window. Gaye sat beside the bed, near the old lady as she prayed, recording every word. Around him a constant flux of activity flowed as

angels came and went, bearing requests to the throne of the Master. Some winged answers all the way across the world in as faraway places as Africa. The room was bathed in an aura of peace and love, which was disturbed suddenly as Cindi Trahan entered the room and sat down in a chair opposite Ethel's bed, waiting for the old woman to pause for a moment in her prayers.

Clinging like a tenacious barnacle to Cindi's side, Gaye recognized Rafe, a demon of despair. Judging from the look on Rafe's face, the demon had experienced a successful morning. He was a particularly powerful demon, prone to gloating over his accomplishments. Gaye realized that Sparn must be getting desperate to send for Rafe. He didn't need to wonder why Rafe was hanging around Cindi rather than Ethel. Cindi was a weaker target and, therefore, would fall sooner. Rafe probably hoped to use her to knock a little spunk out of the old woman on her way down.

"You know, she's been praying for almost a year for you and Marc to have a baby. Don't you think it's about time to give up?" Rafe was hissing in Cindi's ear. "I don't think God wants you to have a baby anyway.

"Or maybe you have some hidden sin you haven't confessed. Did you ever think about that? Maybe that's why your prayers haven't been answered. God doesn't really care if you're happy anyway. I mean, He's up there in heaven, nice and cozy; what does He really care about you? Puny little mortal, nobody cares about you."

Gaye watched as doubt flickered across Cindi's face during Rafe's tirade. She bit her lip, mulling over the doubts Rafe was bombarding her with. Gaye didn't need to have access to her thoughts to know that she was in some part buying into what the demon was saying. Rafe himself sniffed that truth and pulled out all the stops as he continued in full cry.

"If you don't believe me, look at all the prayer requests God *has answered. He sent needed funds to that mission your brother Don runs in Africa, He helped those rescuers to locate that little girl who got lost in the woods just last week, He provided a job for Mr. Simms. I could go on and on! You've got a whole notebook full of answered prayers. What does that tell you?*

"HE DOESN'T CARE ABOUT YOU! That's what it tells you," Rafe cried, hatred for the Master contorting his face. "God is biased. He sits up there in heaven granting this request, denying that one, OUT OF SPITE! He gets a kick out of your pain."

"Stop!" Cindi shouted suddenly, leaping from the chair where she sat, eyes wild. "Stop! In the name of Jesus, get away from me!" Cindi sank onto her knees weeping.

Michel, Ali, and several of the other angels rushed to assist her, their presence, as well as their blinding brilliance, driving the demon away. Rafe shrieked, bolting across the room as if he'd been scorched.

"Don't you ever say "that" name to me," he spat, anger tensing his body. "You puny, worthless, miserable . . ."

Gaye watched as Ethel gazed down on Cindi where she knelt, a serene look of compassion on her face.

"Dear Jesus," Cindi cried, "please send these doubts away from me. Fill my heart with Your love and Your peace. Give me the faith I need to believe that You will answer my prayers in a way that is best for me."

When Cindi's sobs subsided, she rose shakily from her knees. Looking up, she became aware of her surroundings for the first time, seeing Ethel watching her. "I'm sorry, Ethel," she murmured apologetically, "it's just that I had this awful feeling of despair, and it was getting worse. Before I knew what I was doing, I just . . . well, I had to get rid of it."

Ethel smiled gently. "You needn't apologize to me, child. You did the right thing. Don't you remember what Hezekiah, the king of Judah, said when he was threatened by Sennacherib, the king of Assyria, who invaded Judah? He told the people, 'With us is the Lord our God to help us and to fight our battles.' Don't you see? We don't have to fight our battles alone. God will help us."

Cindi sighed weakly. "I know. It's just hard to remember sometimes when we're in the middle of them. But, every time I call on His name and He delivers me, it strengthens my faith."

A wise smile stole over the old woman's face. "And so it should, my dear. So it should."

Cindi crept over to Ethel's bed and sat down tentatively. "Ethel, do you mind if I ask you a question? Do you think it's in God's will for Marc and me to have a child? I mean, we've been praying about it for so long, and Marc and I have been married for ten years. Do you think it's impossible? Or do you think that maybe God just doesn't want us to have children?"

Ethel was silent for a long time, and Cindi was afraid that she would decide not to answer the question. When she finally spoke, her words were deliberate and gentle. "Honey, child, I wouldn't presume to know the will of the Lord. But, there is something I do know. You can be sure that if you wait in His will, and in His time, and if the Lord gives you a child, it will be the best possible thing that can happen. And if not," Ethel shrugged her shoulders, "then perhaps He has something better in mind for you."

Cindi nodded and gently squeezed Ethel's gnarled hands in hers. "Thanks. I needed to hear that. Oh, by the way, Russell Duffy called. That problem with his daughter got worse, and they're going to see the pastor about it. He asked that you pray about the meeting."

"I certainly will," Ethel said. "Have any more requests come in since this morning?"

Cindi shook her head. "No, but I did get a call from my brother Don, and he said to tell you that you could pray over some more supplies anytime, and many thanks for the ones that arrived."

Ethel chuckled. "He's a rascal, your brother." Her face suddenly became pensive. "I feel that he was more affected by his experiences in Rwanda than he will admit, my dear. But I have been praying about that too."

"I think you are probably right," Cindi conceded. "I really wish he'd agreed when I asked him to come back on furlough for a little while. He could have stayed with Marc and me. I know his supervisors at Operation C.A.R.E. wanted him to, but you know Don." Cindi smiled as she thought of her big brother. "He's nothing if not unconventional."

Shelan flew to the side of Berniece Kendall the moment her niece left to go jogging with her boyfriend, Brick Brody. After she watched the young people disappear down the road, Berniece stood for a long moment staring at the house across and just down the street. Usually when she noticed that house, memories of the accident, Peter's heart attack, the whole ordeal at the hospital flooded over her.

Instead, this morning, she was overwhelmed by a desire to pray for Lyle. REALLY pray for him, as if his very life depended on it. She was tempted to brush the urge off. After all, she didn't even know for sure if he lived there, or anywhere, for that matter. For all Berniece Kendall knew, Lyle Ryan was dead.

But . . . there was that still, small voice to consider.

She hadn't ever ignored it yet. So she headed inside as soon as Calla and Brick left and dropped to her knees beside the little wooden table where she did all her Bible study. Words—

insistent, urgent, words—poured out of her as though she were a prayer fountain. She was hardly aware of where they came from.

Lyle wheeled his chair to the window, picked up a cracked pair of binoculars that had belonged to his father, and trained them on the street. Calla Kendall jogged easily down the road, laughing as she smiled up at her jogging partner, Brick Brody.

No, it wasn't smiling, exactly, Lyle thought. *It was more like twinkling. She was twinkling at him.* Lyle's lips twisted in distaste at the very thought of that name. Brick.

Brick was just so sweet. And Brick was just so gorgeous. And Brick was just so polite. And Brick was just so interesting. And Brick was just so Brick. Lyle got sick of hearing Calla tell her aunt about Brick.

"Whoever heard of anyone named Brick anyway?" he muttered. "He looks exactly like a glorified Ken doll," he continued, comforting himself by hearing the words.

Brick easily kept pace with Calla. He was tall and muscular, had shoulders as wide as a refrigerator, and had thick dark hair and a face that might stare out at you from the pages of GQ. Brick was beautiful; therefore, something had to be wrong with him. At least, in Lyle's mind it did. He had wild fantasies about finding out what that something was and confronting Calla with it, whereupon she would immediately send the charlatan from her presence and enthrone Lyle as king of her affections.

Yeah, well, it was a nice daydream.

He set down the binoculars as Calla and Brick ran far enough up the road for some trees to shield them from his view. It would be at least an hour until they got back. He'd heard Calla tell her aunt several times that they jogged eight miles when they went together.

Wheeling swiftly, he rolled across the room to his desk. Pinned on every wall around the room were beautiful, lifelike sketches of Calla. It had taken his mother half the day to get them up just the way he wanted them, and thankfully, she never asked who the subject was or why he wanted them covering nearly all available wall space.

Lyle pulled a worn notebook from one drawer and set it on the desktop. Leaning over it, he drummed his fingers impatiently on the dark wood of the desk, willing words to come to mind. Already he had filled half the notebook with poetry about, or for, Calla. But, for some reason, today there was emptiness in the place where the words came from.

Who was he kidding anyway? Someone as beautiful and vivacious as Calla Kendall could never love someone as misshapen and filled with anger as he was. Not even if she knew he existed. Lyle threw the pen down in frustration and rolled back to the window.

A movement at one of the windows of Calla's house caught his attention. Without really meaning to, he picked up the binoculars and trained them on the window. What he saw sent a shiver down his spine. Berniece Kendall knelt beside a wooden table, her arms raised heavenward, her lips moving frantically, a look of total absorption on her face. All around her, Lyle saw a bright light that made her face shine with the brilliance of it.

He set the binoculars down and sat staring across the street. Why, she was . . . praying. He wondered idly how long it had been since he'd felt like praying. The sight of Berniece immersed in conversation with her heavenly Father gave him a feeling that he slowly realized was heartsickness. A deep yearning filled his whole being. It slid in past the anger that seemed to saturate him. He was so absorbed in the feeling that he barely noticed when tears began to trickle down his cheeks.

"Lyle," Shelan called insistently. *"Can you hear me? The Master misses you. His heart is crying like yours is. Why don't you renew that connection the two of you shared so long ago? Pray, Lyle. Pray."*

Lyle shook his head violently. Pray? Him? He couldn't pray. Too much had happened; he'd slid too far, much too far, for God to reach him now. He was sure that God must hate him for the angry thoughts he'd had, for the horrible words that he'd shouted at his lowest moments. God had to hate him for that.

Shelan's voice clouded with sorrow. "Oh, Lyle, that's not true. He LOVES you. He loves you so much. Won't you come back? Please pray. Pray now." Shelan could sense the presence of the Spirit in the room with them, and she felt a rush of victory.

"Sissy," hissed Warg. "Don't give in to her. What has God ever done for you, boy? He took your legs, destroyed your career, and with it, your life. He might as well have taken your life on the day of the accident as to let you rot here slowly in misery. Don't be a fool. Don't pray to a God like that. He's not worth it."

Lyle bowed his head for a second, but when he looked up, any trace that he might yield to the gentle wooing of the Holy Spirit was gone. His features hardened, almost in defiance of God Himself. As if Lyle was daring God to try to reach him.

Shelan's shoulders sagged. Tears filled her crystal blue eyes as she watched the demons again gather around Lyle. But she refused to give up. The battle was not lost yet. Berniece Kendall had risen from her knees that day with a real burden for Lyle's soul. She would pray for him again. And every time she did, Shelan would be given the opportunity to speak to Lyle's heart.

"Your heavenly Father loves you, Lyle," Shelan said, drawing herself up to her full height. A few of the demons sneered at her, taunting her with failure. She saw Warg watching her warily from the other side of the room.

She knew he wouldn't underestimate his enemy as some of the others did, dismissing the host of heaven without much thought. Warg was too clever for that. Too clever and too suspicious. However, recent victories had left him a trifle smug. He didn't view her progress with Berniece Kendall as a significant threat.

Shelan smiled to herself. No, he didn't think it was worth a second thought. But, he would. And when he did, it would be too late, because Lyle would be out of his grasp.

Toby O'Connell surveyed the town of Niamey owlishly. The setting sun cast rusty orange tones on the landscape that undulated like the sea, rocking beneath her while the surrounding buildings danced wildly. Planting her legs in a wide stance to prevent falling, she turned and staggered back toward Tokoulakoye, a dimly lighted bar.

"Gimme s'more," she slurred. "I can still remember."

The dark face of the African bartender stared back at her passively. "I think, Madame, that you have had enough. I told you once to leave. Yet, here you are again."

Toby clutched her head in her hands and tried to decipher what the man was telling her. But, oh, her head hurt. It was reeling with memories, fresh, painful memories that refused to be buried or numbed even in the alcoholic stupor she'd drunk her way into since leaving the United States a month before.

"Toby," Lileah shouted from her place outside the establishment. Her voice sounded far away, even to her own ears. She was painfully aware that in her intoxicated state Toby couldn't even hear her. Mind altering drugs effectively numbed the conscience and quieted the still, small voice of the Master. Still, she had to try. "Toby, please, I beg of you,

stop. The Master is calling you."

"Ah, leave her alone," Lucien sneered. *"She knows what she's doing. Besides, she's got a right to get smashed. After all, look at what the poor thing has gone through."* He snickered. *"But, that isn't all. Wait until you see what we've got in store for her. If you think she's in bad shape right now, you ain't seen nothing yet."*

"Are you gonna give me s'more booze or what?" she demanded, pounding one fist weakly on the bar.

"GIVE IT TO HER!" Lucien shrieked in the man's ear. *"She'll buy it all night. She'll buy it until she passes out from alcohol poisoning and dies right here in your bar. GIVE IT TO HER! Go on, you'd be doing her a favor, she needs it."*

The man shook his head and continued drying a glass as he watched her, his eyes as dark and unreadable as an abyss. "No, Madame, I am not. And I ask you once again to leave. Please. You are drunk. You are very drunk. Go and sleep it off. There will always be more liquor, you needn't consume it all tonight."

"Thass what you think," Toby hiccuped and took her bearings on the door. The entire floor rocked back and forth as she stepped out. The next instant, it rushed to meet her face. On the way down she glanced off a chair, saved from falling by the strong hands of a white man.

"Yur white," Toby observed.

"So are you," the man returned, assisting her to her feet and dusting her off. Toby struggled to focus on his face, but her eyes refused to cooperate. The face swam in her vision, moving too much for her to figure out what he actually looked like. "However, I have one advantage over you," the man continued. "I am not drunk."

"Thass a dirty lie," Toby snapped. "You are too. If yur not, how come you can't stand up straight?"

The man grinned at her, something Toby had no trouble seeing. And it irritated her. She pulled away from him. "Thank you very mush, but I can manage on my own, if you don' mind."

The man raised his hands in a gesture of surrender. "Suit yourself, Miss. But, watch out. You hear? This is not a safe place for a lady to be wandering around drunk. You never know what could happen. There are many unscrupulous people out there, you know. And if you don't fall victim to one of them, you might fall into one of the uncovered sewers."

Toby reeled out the door of the bar and made her way to the Hotel Moustache, a dirty, but cheap, little hotel where she had rented a room before learning that it served as a brothel with such a rapid turnover rate that the address caused snickers throughout town. Bouncing off the walls as she lurched down the hallway, she finally managed to locate her room and insert her key after several failed tries. She didn't bother to lock it behind her as she took two faltering steps and fell across the bed.

Lucien and the crowd of demons who had pursued Toby from the United States gathered around her bed, singing and dancing in a fevered frenzy. The more Toby allowed her mind to be numbed by the alcohol, the more the demons were able to influence her. Since bringing Davy home, she had been governed by anger and resentment, her life filled with a taste for revenge and programmed for self-destruction.

Above her, the ceiling swam in lazy circles. Waterstained and dirty, the blossoming colors swirled together to create a dizzying pattern. Helplessly, Toby lay there as images and scenes from the last few months plowed through her memory like stubborn freight trains, mowing over everything in their path.

The letter from Davy asking for a divorce came two weeks after she'd seen him on the boat. He was still away on his trip, and while she waited for him to return, she wondered desperately what to do. She considered contesting the divorce, but by the end of the week, she was so angry and irrational that she had decided to give it to him without a fight.

He didn't remember her, he'd made that clear. He didn't want her, obviously. So, why fight it? The real question was, what on earth was she going to do now? She had no job, no husband, no life. The only thing she did have was time. Time and a long-forgotten dream.

"What have you always dreamed of doing, no holds barred?" she'd asked Davy one night shortly after they were married.

"Ummm, I guess what I've always dreamed of doing, ever since I learned to fly, was to go to Africa and be a bush pilot," he'd replied.

And so they'd decided to go together. Like a couple of Indiana Jones adventurers or something, maybe fly for the Peace Corps or some other volunteer project. It had become something to strive for. Their modest little savings account had grown over the years, and they'd talked about it more seriously, but the time hadn't been right in their careers.

But, now . . . was there anything left? It gave Toby a perverse sense of satisfaction to think about fulfilling their dream alone, as if she was cheating Davy out of the pleasure of living through it himself.

It hadn't taken long to formulate a plan. She sold everything that wouldn't fit into two large suitcases. When Davy came back, she told him what she'd done and handed him a check for half of the proceeds. He'd been more than happy about it and wished her luck.

The ceiling came back into focus as her thoughts drifted into the present. And here she was. Here in this stinking little room, drunker than a pirate, headed nowhere and unable to remember much of it. It occurred to her to wonder what was at the end of this road she'd chosen for herself, but as she'd done since leaving, she put off thinking about it until tomorrow.

Tomorrow and sobriety would come soon enough. Then there would be time to think about the future. A little time, anyway, before that first drink kicked in. Then she'd figure out what to do. Until then, she refused to worry about it. Tonight, it was enough to worry that she didn't have the strength or ambition to even remove her boots. Her legs would ache in the morning.

When Toby woke up, the sunlight streaming in through the dirty glass of the curtainless window made her head throb wildly. She lifted one leaden arm and threw it across her face to block out the offending light. Every little sound from the street below was amplified a thousand times and crashed through her head, a fitting accompaniment to the pounding of her heart, which she could clearly hear as the blood whooshed loudly past her eardrums. Her mouth was dry and foul-tasting, and her tongue felt as though someone had knitted a little sweater for it while she slept. She couldn't feel her legs from the knees down.

She strained to remember where she was or what had happened the night before, but all she could recall were flashes. The obstinate bartender, the man at Tokoulakoye's who helped her up—some of the evening's events came back in vague clips. Moaning, she rolled over in an attempt to evade the sun, which began to feel hot on her arm. It would be another scorcher.

Pain exploded in her legs as the blood flow was suddenly renewed. When would she ever remember not to let them drape over the edge of the bed when she crashed? She fumbled with the laces of her boots, every movement making her legs ache even more. She massaged her calves tenderly, wondering which hurt worse, her legs or her head.

When they finally felt serviceable again, she stood up gingerly and made her way to the window, squinting out at the scene below. People were milling around, street vendors already setting up food stalls. From the window, she could see the Kennedy Bridge span the width of the Niger river, which flowed through town like a flat, brown satin ribbon. A few small dugouts paddled against its current while fishermen on the banks untangled their nets.

Beside it, she knew, crocodiles would be slithering in and out of the water. Male launderers used nearby trees on which to spread clothes for drying, and hippos kept sentinel. The flowering trees populating Niamey made it seem almost like a lush garden compared to some of the dusty places in Africa that she had passed through.

Down the street she could see the bar she'd been at the night before. It was already open for business. A drink. That's what she needed.

"Toby, please, no," Lileah pleaded. *"You must remain sober to allow the Spirit to speak to you. There is only one way out of this mess you are in, and that is by calling on the name of the Lord. He will save you. Even you are not far enough gone that He cannot wrap His arms of love around you and keep you from this horrible road you are on. Just believe, Toby. Believe and allow Him to come in. He won't force His way into your heart. You must invite Him."*

Lucien listened passively to Lileah's urgent plea. *"She's not going to listen to you, you know that. Why do you even bother? You might as well give this one up. You aren't going to get her."*

Licking her lips, Toby fumbled awkwardly in the pocket of her jeans to make sure she had her wallet. Not finding it, she searched around on the bed and then the floor, her anxiety increasing with each passing moment. Her fingers probed the dark recesses under the bed but turned up only dust bunnies. Toby forced herself to sit on the edge of the bed and think slowly and rationally.

OK, it had to be here somewhere. Where else could it have gone? Suddenly, the face of the stranger in the bar the night before flashed in front of her eyes.

"This is not a safe place for a lady to be wandering around drunk. You never know what could happen. There are many unscrupulous people out there, you know," he'd said. She remembered the feel of his hands around her waist as he'd helped her up. How easy it had been for him to rob her!

The shrieking of the demons drove Lileah out into the hall-way as they fed off the panic and instant anger that fused through Toby's body. Their howling embodied the most basic instincts, reaching into the ugly depths of the being and grovel-ing there. Lileah couldn't bear to witness it.

Toby's breathing quickened, and she knew she was going to hyperventilate before it even happened. Helplessly, she fell back onto the bed while her lungs pumped rapidly. Her passport, nearly all her money, her identification, her plane tickets, everything had been in her wallet. There was no way to get home and no money to live on until she could get all her documentation re-placed and her tickets reissued.

The money, well . . . there hadn't been too much money. A few traveler's checks that could be refunded, and some small denominations in cash. Most of her money she'd been drawing by wire from her account, and this last batch had been almost gone. She also had a few bucks in her boot in case of emergency. She figured this qualified. She had planned to wire the bank for some more at the next major city.

She thought of the Surete, the head cop shop, where she'd been forced to register on the day of her arrival. Possibly she could get help there, but as she recalled the distinctly hostile faces she'd encountered there, she tended to doubt it.

Maybe the bartender could help her; maybe he knew some-place she could go, something she could do. It was worth a try. By the time her breathing returned to normal, her lips and fin-gertips were tingling. Retrieving a couple dollars from her boots, she put them back on and pushed herself up from the bed. The filth she encountered in the hall made her glad to be outside and making her way across the street on wobbly legs.

Lileah watched Toby enter the bar, sorrow etched on her beau-tiful face. She waited outside the door with several other an-gels. Inside the smoke-filled room, demons circulated with the humans, magnifying existing feelings of worthlessness and anger that were already present. Lileah joined hands with the other angels as they encircled the building, praying earnestly for those inside.

The African bartender regarded her beneath lowered eyebrows as she entered Tokoulakoye, hesitating on the fringes of the room, trying to get up enough courage to say something. She sidled up to the bar and cleared her throat.

"Back so soon, Madame?" he asked, his voice dry and humorless. "I expect you'll be wanting to drink some breakfast?"

Toby smiled nervously. "No, actually, do you remember that man who was in here last night? The one who helped me up?"

The bartender shrugged. "I did not pay strict attention to any guest who was not overly inebriated. I'm sorry that I can't assist you to find your gentleman."

Toby bristled. "He's not my 'gentleman,'" she spat. "He robbed me last night." If she expected any show of sympathy, she was disappointed. "Here," she emphasized. "In your bar. When he helped me up, he helped himself to my wallet. I lost all my money, my passport, my plane tickets. Everything."

The African's face remained impassive. His ebony features broadcast his lack of interest in what she was saying.

"Well?" Toby demanded. "Aren't you going to do anything about it?"

He leaned across the counter until his face was inches from her own. "Madame, what would you have me do? I can allow you to use my telephone to contact whoever you might need to be in touch with regarding your unfortunate situation. But if you are asking me to care that an American woman, who was too intoxicated to stand up straight was possibly robbed by another American who was more enterprising than herself, you are asking too much, because I simply do not care."

Toby stared back at him. "I hate this country," she said vehemently.

The bartender gestured toward the open door. "Then, by all

means, Madame, feel free to leave. There are no bars on our borders and no locks on our door. I'm sure America misses you." He returned to his work behind the counter, pointedly ignoring her.

Toby sagged against the counter in defeat. "What am I going to do?" she moaned. "I've got nowhere to go. It'll take forever to get my stuff replaced in this pitiful excuse for a town. If the people around here moved any slower, they'd be going backward. I just wanna go home."

The African arched one eyebrow. "That is indeed odd, Madame. I could have sworn that home was what you were trying to forget."

Toby glowered at him. The man was getting under her skin. Though lately, she had to admit, that wasn't difficult. "Can I . . . use the phone?" she asked, trying to lace her voice with humility.

He inclined his head toward it, and she let out a grateful breath. An hour later, when she finally had enough of the mess straightened out, she set the receiver down and slumped onto a bar stool. Her fingers drummed out a tuneless rhythm as she stared sightlessly ahead of her. The growling of her stomach reminded her that she hadn't yet eaten and brought her thoughts back to the present.

"I don't suppose you've got anything around here to eat that's free, huh?" she asked the bartender, determined to save as much of her emergency funds as possible. It was more a statement than a question, and she really didn't expect him to answer her. Instead, he wordlessly handed her a banana.

"Thank you," she mumbled, stuffing it unceremoniously into her mouth. She tried to talk around it. "Now can you come up with someplace I can stay for a week, until they can replace my documents?"

The man's face could have been carved from marble. Toby had the feeling that she might just as well ask a rock for water.

"Tell me, Madame," he said finally, "what is it that you do? What is your profession, if you have one?"

Toby straightened up. "I'm a nurse. What of it?"

A light flickered in his eyes, but still he hesitated.

"NO!" Lucien shrieked. "Don't send her to that place! Not that place! Don't help her at all. Let her fend for herself. She got out here with no help. She got robbed with no help. She can find a way out of this predicament all alone."

"I . . . I may know of someplace that can use the services of a nurse for one week. Of course, they probably cannot pay you. But, I am sure that you will find food and a roof over your head for one week."

"Yes?" Toby asked eagerly. "Where's that?"

Lucien paced back and forth in front of the bar growling at the bartender. "Shut up!" he warned, his voice hissing out of his mouth like air leaking from a tire.

The bartender jerked his head in the direction Toby knew to be desert. "There is a little mission several miles from Niamey. I am sure they could use your help until you get your paperwork and leave."

Toby's heart dropped. "A mission? You mean like a church thing?"

"That, Madame, I do not know. The mission is located about fifteen miles outside of town. My brother works there. He contracted river blindness some time ago and has worked there ever since. They are very good to him there."

"Great," Toby muttered. "That's just great. I don't suppose they've got any booze out there?" When she didn't receive a response, she tried again. "Do you think I could take a bottle, you know, on account? Just until my money comes in? I'll pay you, honest."

"I hardly think so, Madame." The slight smile that tugged at the corners of the man's mouth gave him a Mona Lisa look that irritated Toby. However, she was still without directions, and it wouldn't do her any good to make enemies before getting them, so she held her temper in check.

"OK, so, how do I get to this place? When does the bus leave? Or can I just take a cab?"

The bartender's eyes lighted up with glee. "Madame, I am sorry to inform you that you must walk. However, it is possible that if you start walking now, you can be there by nightfall. Especially if you get a ride with a farmer headed in that direction."

Toby groaned. "Walk? Oh, great. That's just fabulous. Sure, walk. Well, can you at least point me in the general direction?"

"That information," he said, staring pointedly at her watch and the gold wedding band on her finger, "will cost you a small price."

The watch was a sacrifice, but Toby realized that she was more than happy to part with the wedding band. An hour later, suitcases as light as she could make them, Toby faced southeast with a resigned air. "If you make it as far as Agadez, you'll know that you passed it," he had laughed.

"By how much?" she'd asked.

"Much too much," he had chortled.

"You'll never make it," Lucien warned. "You'll get lost in the desert, you'll get bit by something horrible, you'll get lost in a dust storm. Besides, even if you did find it, they probably wouldn't want you, and you'd have to come all the way back. Don't go. Stay here. I'm sure they can find you someplace to stay. Go on back and ask him."

"Toby, go to the mission," Lileah countered. "I will help you to reach your destination if you'll only ask the Master for help. There are good people there. They can help you. Don't give up now. Go to the mission."

Toby looked back toward the bar once and sighed. It would be a long, hot walk. She stepped out on her journey, conscious of the fact that she was leaving the greenery of Niamey behind for the dryness of the desert ahead. But, only for a little while, she assured herself. By this time next week, she'd be ensconced in the relative comfort of a bus headed to more civilized destinations. Now, if she could just get through the next seven days, she'd be all set.

Plodding along, the act of putting one foot in front of the other, willing her body along, brought back memories of the night on the mountain. Only this time, instead of extreme cold, she was being forced to endure extreme heat.

She looked up into the sky, scowling at the ball of burning fire that hung there, threatening to consume her with its intensity. "You up there, God?" she asked. "Because if You are, I could sure use some help navigating here. I know this isn't the woods, and no one's life is in danger, but I'd really appreciate it if You could just help me out like You did that time."

Demons scattered like minnows scared by a rock thrown into a pond. Lileah was immediately at Toby's side. "He will be with you," she assured Toby. "He will be with you and guide you every step of the way. Do not be afraid." She walked strongly beside her charge as the demons, cursing their luck, followed along at a distance.

C H A P T E R

Helen was looking at her, disapproval etched on every feature. Billie Jo tried to ignore her piercing, narrow-eyed glare as she mentally went over the checklist in her head.

Safety goggles. Yes.

Work gloves. Yes.

Ear plugs. Yes.

Chain saw. Yes.

Sharpener for the blade and a gas tank. Yes.

She grabbed Jimmy's old jean jacket off the back of the sofa and struggled into it before sitting down and pulling on a pair of work boots. Cassidy stood beside the unusually quiet Dallas, watching Billie Jo with wide, sober eyes. Billie Jo flashed her an encouraging smile, but Cass didn't return it.

"This really is the most idiotic thing I've ever heard of. Honestly!" Helen said. "Why don't you just order the firewood already cut like James and I do? It's so much simpler that way. This is really much too risky. Think of your children. What if something happened to you on top of what happened to Jimmy? Would you want them to go through life without both of their parents?"

Billie Jo cringed at the tears that sprang up suddenly in Cassidy's eyes. She was across the room, wrapping the little girl in a tight embrace before the tears could even spill down Cass's cheeks.

Nog glowered darkly at Billie Jo. "What kind of mother are you anyway? Leaving your kids to go cut wood. You can't cut wood. You're not good at it. You'll have an accident. A bad accident, and then what's going to happen to your kids? Listen to Helen, she knows best." For weeks, Nog had been steadily working on Billie Jo, but instead of growing weaker, she was actually getting stronger. It was maddening.

That miserable friend of hers, Leah, had begun a prayer group, and even though Billie Jo wasn't able to make it most of the time because of Jimmy, the women faithfully prayed for Billie Jo, Jimmy, and the kids. Their prayers had placed a protective wall around Billie Jo that Nog was having a hard time penetrating.

It galled him that what had looked like an easy assignment continued to get harder. It was trying his patience, something he possessed in small supply anyway. He had finally decided that it was about time an "accident" befell Billie Jo. That would most certainly shake her faith if indeed she survived the little "accident" he had planned.

Goading her sense of pride so that she would insist on cutting her own wood had been his first victory. By instilling doubts about her ability to actually carry out the task, he was setting her up for the final stage of his plan. He was pretty sure that Jewel knew something was up, but as far as he could tell, the angel didn't know what his plans were.

Like a cat sizing up a mouse, Nog kept a close and wary eye on the developing circumstances. His chance would come shortly, and when it did, he would be ready. He tried to act nonchalant for Jewel's benefit, but in the end, he knew he'd get the better of the angel.

"Don't you worry about me, baby. I'll be fine. Your daddy taught me how to cut wood." She chucked Cass under the chin and gave her a smile, trying to ignore the churning feelings of mistrust in her gut. "You know that, and Daddy's the best lumberjack in the whole state. Nothing's gonna happen to me."

She gave Cassidy another reassuring squeeze and included Dallas, who tried to wriggle away. "Now, you take care of Dallas and be good for your grandma. Maybe you could read Daddy a story from the Bible. Think so?"

Cassidy grinned. "You know I don't read yet, Momma."

"I know," Billie Jo chuckled. "But you can read him the pictures like you do for Dallas. OK?"

She gave them each a quick kiss and brushed her lips across Jimmy's cool forehead before straightening up to face her mother-in-law. "I'm sure they won't give you any trouble," she said stiffly. "And I would like nothing better than to order my wood already cut," she added in a lower voice. "Except that we need that money for food. Being warm and hungry this winter ain't gonna help us very much. Especially when there's free wood right out back ready and waiting to be cut."

Helen's nose elevated several degrees. "Nonsense. You know James and I are always willing to help out financially. But you're just so pig-headed stubborn you have to do things your own way." She waved her hands in the air. "Well, fine, so be it. But don't expect me to take care of both you *and* Jimmy if you get knocked over the head with a tree trunk."

Billie Jo smiled wryly. "I wouldn't dream of it," she said sweetly. She turned to Cassidy and Dallas before she opened the door to leave. "You two be good, OK?" She blew them kisses. "I love you."

Outside, the cool air was snappy and pungent with the smell of burning leaves. She sucked in a deep breath to clear her head as she climbed into the old beater Chevy that Jimmy used to drive to work. The engine coughed before turning over, then sputtered to life. As she drove down the deeply rutted road to the woodlot in the back, she mulled over what Helen had said.

Sure, Helen and James were always "glad" to help out financially, but only so they could bribe her later on. Billie Jo had learned long ago that whenever they invested their money in anything, they expected returns. If she accepted their money for wood, there would be a payback sooner or later, and she wasn't sure that she could afford the emotional interest she would be forced to pay.

She pulled the truck up to the remnants of last year's wood stack. Only a few logs remained. Jimmy had been going to finish up when . . . Well, it wouldn't do much good to think about that now. Billie Jo slid from the truck and surveyed the forest around her, looking for a likely candidate. An obviously dead tree, just about the right size, beckoned to her.

"That'll be the one," she muttered, popping in her earplugs and pulling on well-worn leather gloves. The chain saw in her hands was heavy. Almost too heavy, she knew. She'd have a hard time limbing with the thing, but she'd have to make do. It roared to life with a belch of smoke.

The power had frightened her at first. It had felt as if the chain saw was alive and operated under its own volition. But once her muscles had grown accustomed to controlling the machine, she'd felt more comfortable. She remembered Jimmy's smile of pleasure and pride the day she had brought her first tree down all by herself.

It had been awhile, she reminded herself as she approached the tree. Better to go slow and play it safe and careful. As the metal teeth of the chain saw dug into the soft flesh of the tree, Billie Jo found herself automatically doing the right things. She hadn't forgotten as much as she thought she had. Moments later, she had sawn a "V" in the trunk and worked the blade into the other side of the tree to fell it.

Nog watched with keen interest as Billie Jo cut into the back side of the tree. The cut was too low. There were so many things that could go wrong when you cut a tree down, he thought to himself. And this was one of them. All he needed to do now was help it along. The top of the tree shook as if in a violent wind.

Nog glanced around and found Jewel watching him intently. The trick would be to "help" the tree without the cursed angel interfering and ruining all his plans. He gauged the worried expression on Billie Jo's face to get his timing just right.

"GET BACK! IT'S FALLING! IT'S GOING TO CLOBBER YOU!" he yelled as loud as he could.

As the trunk wobbled, Billie Jo felt a sense of panic well up inside her. Sometimes when a tree fell, she remembered Jimmy saying, the pressure was so strong that it snapped the trunk in two, causing half of it to shoot out, catching you if you weren't careful. The tree stood, undecided for a moment, then with a decisive sway, it lurched over, crashing through the forest.

With one fierce yank, Nog grabbed the trunk of the tree and heaved it backward toward Billie Jo. It snapped and like a big tinkertoy in the hand of a giant, drove with deadly accuracy at Billie Jo's head.

Too early, she backed up, pulling the blade free. Staggering back, she felt her feet go out from beneath her. As she went down, she watched the tree jerk upward as if it were a puppet in the hands of an angry puppeteer. As the top limbs caught on the branches of neighboring trees, the trunk came straight at her as if in slow motion.

In a swift instant, Jewel was at Billie Jo's side. With one mighty arm, he blocked the fall of the tree, sending it spinning off to the side, where it rolled once before groaning to a rest, the trunk bobbing lazily. Nog hissed as his scheme was ruined and howled in frustration before vanishing from the scene.

When Billie Jo finally realized that she was safe, she found herself sitting bolt upright on the ground, the chain saw still in her hands. Somehow she'd managed to shut it off, but she still held it up in the air as if she were about to cut something. She blinked a few times and questioned what had just taken place.

She'd cut the tree too low in the back. She knew that for certain. The pressure had caused the trunk to splinter like a popsicle stick. When the branches got hung up in the treetops surrounding them, the trunk had jacked out and drove straight for her head as if it were possessed.

Billie Jo set the chain saw down and crawled to her knees, hands trembling. "Thank You, Lord," she said through teeth clenched tightly to keep them from chattering. "Thank You so much for protecting me. And thank You for my guardian angel. I sure know I got one now."

It was a full twenty minutes before Billie Jo was able to climb up to stand on shaky legs and size up the tree that nearly killed her, to figure out where she would start cutting.

The chain saw seemed an extension of herself. As she worked, the pent-up frustration, anger, and fear she had bottled up inside flowed out in the roar and power of the machine. By the time she stopped for a breath, she was dripping in perspiration and panting slightly.

She leaned back against a tree and surveyed her work. A neat line of sawn logs stretched out from her feet to the truck. Now all that remained was to toss them into the truck. Some would have to be split at home. Looking at them, it was hard to imagine that they had nearly cost her her life.

Maybe Helen was right after all. Maybe she should just accept the money and forget this foolishness. Next time she might not be so lucky, and then what? The thought of Cassidy and Dallas growing up with Helen and James was more than she could bear.

She sighed heavily and turned back to her work. She was going to have to make the decision soon, because it wasn't getting any warmer. In her heart, Billie Jo realized that she had already made her decision. It was just going to be mighty hard swallowing that lump of pride in her throat.

Cindi Trahan sat at the kitchen table trying to come up with a menu for the upcoming week. Every now and then, from Ethel's bedroom came the sound of wracking coughs. For three days now Ethel had been sick, and the gloom of it hung over the whole house like an oppressive cloud. People who were usually calling to make prayer requests were now calling to get updates on her condition and to say that *they* were praying for *her*.

On top of the depression she strove to fight off during the day because of Ethel's poor health, Cindi found herself battling it at night too. Each evening she returned to her empty house, which stood as a grim reminder that she continued to be childless despite the prayers of Ethel and others. Why wasn't God answering?

A slight smile touched her lips as she imagined a beautiful baby occupying the spare room that she planned to make into a nursery if there ever was an opportunity. She knew exactly how it would be decorated too. The colors would be pale blues, so pale they would be almost white, with the ceiling painted as if it were a sky at night, the walls as though clouds drifted lazily by. White antique furniture, handed down from her mother's grand-mother, was in storage in the basement, waiting for the chance to grace the beautiful, peaceful, happy room.

Waiting. Just like Cindi and Marc.

They had so much to offer a child, Cindi told herself over and over. Why did God continue to prevent them that blessing? When she saw children, scantily clad, dirty, obviously neglected with parents who didn't want them, it broke her heart. Each time she spoke with her brother Don in Niger, every fiber of her being wanted to take in the orphaned children he told her about. Once it had almost been a reality, but red tape had choked off the possibility and left Cindi more brokenhearted than before.

And so she continued to wait. And wait. And wait.

"But they that wait upon the Lord shall renew their strength; they shall mount up with wings as eagles; they shall run, and not be weary; and they shall walk, and not faint," Reissa reminded Cindi. As the angel spoke the verse, Cindi's face relaxed, the words playing over and over in her head like a comforting melody.

Cindi bowed her head. "I *am* waiting on You, Lord," she whispered. "For I know the plans You have for me, Lord. Plans to prosper me and not to harm me, plans to give me hope and a future. Please give me the strength to wait as long as it takes for You to reveal Your plans for me. Amen."

Angels clustered around Cindi as she prayed. Ali was dispatched immediately to carry the request to the throne of heaven. When she returned, Reissa knew there would be more angels with her. Although Cindi did not know it, the angels were all keenly aware that the wait was almost over and each was eager to watch as the answer to this fervent and often repeated prayer was given. A throb of expectation accompanied their work, and an extra spring was in each step.

She was sitting on the ground outside the clinic when Shay stepped out of the compound into what she fondly called the "furnace." Hunched over into a little ball of misery, she was attended by only one very disinterested man. Beneath her was a steadily growing puddle of blood, and by the looks of her ashen face, Shay guessed it wasn't the only amount she'd lost.

When he caught sight of her, the man smiled broadly as if they were being introduced at a social function. Although he spoke in grand fashion with sweeping gestures as if he had all day to tell a story, Shay didn't understand a word out of his mouth. She turned her attention instead to the girl.

Her pulse was weak, and she was slowly slipping into shock. What amazed Shay even more than the fact that she had lived this long with no medical attention was the shy smile the girl gave her as she scooped her up. Although she was every bit as tall as Shay, she guessed the girl's weight at nearly half as much.

"Doctor Germaine! Emergency!" she bellowed as she turned to kick open the door of the clinic. The man followed behind her uttering what Shay guessed were protests, judging from the tone of his voice. She laid the girl down gently on one of the rough wooden examining tables and began to treat her for shock. Before she was finished, Don burst through the door of the clinic, followed closely by Nwibe, who was running awkwardly behind Marcus.

As Don began an examination, the man who accompanied her babbled quickly, a scowl on his face as he gestured at the girl. Shay turned to Nwibe, who appeared to be listening to the man.

"What's he saying? Do you know what he's saying?"

"He says that he does not want to spend a lot of money to fix this girl. He can give only a small *cadeau*. She is not worth more than that."

Shay interrupted him with a frown. "What's a *cadeau*?"

Nwibe's white eyes rolled in his head as he struggled to come up with a definition for her. "A *cadeau* is a gift, like a payment."

"What does he mean she's not worth more than that?" she demanded, latching on to his flowing sleeve as if she could change what she was afraid he was about to say.

Nwibe's face took on a patient, tolerant look. "She is expendable."

Shay's mouth dropped open in disbelief. "What do you mean expendable? How could he say that about his own daughter?" She turned on the man. "How can you say that about your daughter?" she asked, gesturing at the girl, knowing he couldn't understand her, but too angry to care.

Nwibe laid a steadying hand on her arm, the strong grip of his fingers focusing her attention on him. "She is not his daughter. She is one of his wives."

Shay broke away from his grip and took a step back. Eyes incredulous, she studied the girl on the table. Young, she was so young. Not more than 14, surely, and perhaps younger than that. Dr. Germaine interrupted her thoughts.

"I'm sorry," he interjected sarcastically, "but if you're through with your little chat, I could use some help here." He directed his next question at Nwibe. "Ask him if she was pregnant."

A string of words shot from Nwibe's tongue like bullets. The man nodded, and the exchange continued until Nwibe nodded, satisfied. "Yes, she was carrying a child. Perhaps four or five months. The baby was lost just this morning."

Don grunted. "I'll need to do a pelvic exam to see if she retained any tissue. The bleeding seems to be stopping, but I want to be sure."

Shay helped Don, her hands automatically doing the work required, but her mind still reeled with unbelief. Later, as she sat with Nwibe outside the clinic in the shade listening to him trying to explain the complex issues surrounding the girl's situation, her mind was still unable to take it all in.

"You see," Nwibe began patiently, "you must understand that

in my culture women do all the work. They herd the animals, bear about twelve children, breastfeed each until he's at least two years old, walk for miles to collect firewood and fetch water, pound the *manioc*, cook the food, grow gardens, and take the produce to the market. For a woman alone, it is too much work. Perhaps the kindest thing that could happen to her is that her husband takes three other wives. She needs the help."

Shay shook her head. "That's sick," she sputtered, outraged.

Nwibe shrugged. "That is the way it is. Women are not valued in my culture. I am not proud of this. But it is possible to buy a woman for less than it costs to purchase a plate of noodles and goat meat in a restaurant."

"I thought Niger abolished slavery," Shay exclaimed, as a tidbit she'd read in a guidebook on her way over resurfaced in her mind.

"They did," a deep voice answered her. Don Germaine looked down at her from the doorway of the clinic, his lips twisted into a sneer. "But, women are not considered slaves. When people talk about slavery, they mean the Hausa, a large Nigerian tribe who migrated through parts of West Africa."

Shay lifted her nose several inches in the air. "I think it's ridiculous. Why don't they do something about it?"

"Good for you!" Don jeered. "Out to change the system. Why don't you start with that one in there?" He jerked his thumb toward the clinic behind him before walking away chuckling to himself.

Shay watched him, anger smoldering inside her. "He's making fun of me," she observed. "But, he'll see. The system will never change if you sit around and do nothing."

Nwibe shook his head. "No, it will not, but I urge you to choose your battles wisely. The conditions of women in my country may outrage you, but think before you let that outrage hurt others instead of help them."

He moved away, leaving Shay gaping after him. "You're on his side?" she howled in disbelief. "Why?"

His silence was the only thing that answered her. Finally she jumped up from where she was sitting and went into the clinic to check on the girl. Her husband sat on the other side of the clinic, cross-legged, on the floor. His lips were stuck out in exaggeration of a pout. He acted as if he was sorry the girl would live.

Even Don, who was not prone to being overly impressed with anything, claimed that her recovery was nothing short of a miracle. The bleeding had stopped, and color was just returning to her face. Shay had been pushing fluids on her all day, but now she slept peacefully, wrapped in some of the surprisingly white sheets Akueke was forever washing.

"What is her name?" she asked the husband, making signals with her hands that she hoped would help him to understand her. His eyes followed her hands as his frown deepened. "Her name. What do you call her? Who is she?"

His gaze returned to the floor, but one word escaped his lips. "Madina."

Shay whispered the name while she picked up the girl's hand and held it lightly in her own. "Madina."

"Don't get too attached to her; you've got to give her back, you know." Don's voice, right beside her shoulder, made her jump guiltily. When she turned, she expected to see him smirking at her but, instead, found a compassionate light smoldering deep in his gray eyes and a kindly smile tugging at his lips. She felt a kinship there, whether he would admit it or not, and the love she had begun to feel for him grew by leaps and bounds. For one crazy instant, she even considered giving him a light kiss.

"I know," she sighed. "I wish I could keep her. Or that I could protect her from her life. Why does it have to be so hard?"

Don didn't answer. "You'd be better off distancing yourself from them," he advised her cryptically, his voice taking on a hard edge and she knew he was thinking about Rwanda. "You can't help all of them. We can only do the best we can for the ones we treat."

Shay moved in a step closer to him. "But you can't separate yourself from loving them," she said pointedly, with more meaning in her voice than she intended. "Just because you can't make their lives better forever, or protect them from life, doesn't mean that you can't love them and do the best you can for them."

Don drew a long shuddering breath, his eyes focused far away. "Just be careful," he warned gruffly. "That's all I'm saying. This girl, and the others who will come like her, aren't stray dogs that you can take in and give a good home. When she can walk again, she'll be going home with that man." He pointed to the husband, still hunched up in the corner.

Before she could stop herself, Shay reached out one hand and laid it on Don's arm. He flinched and turned his eyes on her, cold and questioning. "Couldn't we give her a job?" she pleaded. "She could stay here. I'd share my room, if necessary. She could work here and . . ." Her voice picked up volume as it grew in excitement.

Don shook her arm off. "No. No!" he said loudly, causing the girl's husband to jump. "When she's well, she's going home. And that's the end of it. Don't ever ask me anything like that again." The last sentence he spit out between clenched teeth, his fists balled up at his sides. He stalked out of the clinic while Shay stood looking after him, tears stinging her eyes.

She worked in the clinic the rest of the day, not saying much to anyone. Most of her time she spent wrapping bandages and amusing a two-year-old child who had been admitted for malnutrition. When he'd been brought in, Shay had gasped in horror. Though he was two years old, he had the body of a child half his age. She weighed him on the clinic scales and blinked her eyes at the fifteen-pound reading.

Although his stomach was bloated, spindly arms and legs poked out, seeming ridiculously long in proportion. His wrist was barely bigger around than her thumb, and Shay believed she could count every vertebrae in his back as well as every rib. Immediately, Don had her mixing a batch of loa, a high-energy mixture of sugar, oil, and water. The mothers who accompanied the wasted children always raised their eyebrows knowingly when they saw it, and a bit of the anxiety etched on their faces disappeared.

The ones who hadn't received loa at feeding stations set up around the country had heard from others about this stuff. Stories were told about how children, nearly dead, had, in a matter of weeks, become strong enough to live and play. Keeping them that way was the challenge. The boy's mother had told Shay, in rapid-fire French, that she had to bring his sister to a feeding station just a few months ago but that it was no longer there. For this trip, she'd had to travel far from their home, and she was scared.

The little boy, whose name was Jonathon, was too sick to play, his stomach still grossly distended, his movements lacking animation. Shay amused him by blowing up a rubber glove like a balloon and batting it to him. Jonathon followed it intently with his soft brown eyes. A faint smile lighted his face as he watched her. When he tired of the game, Shay stood, bending backwards, to stretch her cramped spine. She wandered over to the doorway of the clinic and stood looking out over the sun-drenched landscape. The sun, an enormous orange ball this time of day, was slowly sinking into the flat bed of the horizon in preparation for a welcome rest.

A movement out on the desert in the direction of Niamey caught Shay's attention. It looked like . . . a person. A person carrying fairly large bags and staggering. She didn't have time to contemplate the portent of this vision, because Nwibe's panicked voice behind her interrupted her thoughts.

"Madame Shay, the girl bleeds," he said.

Shay whirled around and was at the bedside in a moment. "How did you know?" she asked incredulously. For an answer, he lifted a hand; it was covered with blood.

"I came to give her a drink of water, and I could smell the blood," he said tersely.

"Marcus," Shay said curtly, "run and get Doctor Germaine. Tell him there is an emergency." The boy flew to the door and vanished. Shay probed Madina's abdomen, and she let out a low, tortured moan. "Don't worry, the doctor is coming," she murmured soothingly, as she began to treat her for shock a second time that day.

Toby was so relieved when she arrived at the mission compound that she just stood in the middle of the courtyard for a full five minutes trying to comprehend that she was actually there. Feeling as though she carried at least the top inch of the entire fifteen miles of desert sand on her clothes left only one thought uppermost in her mind: a long, hot bath. A man burst out of the low, cement building in front of her, followed by a small boy sprinting to keep up with the man's long strides.

Toby smiled. "Hi! Say, you weren't expecting me, were you? Where can I get a bath?"

The man, tall with dark, unruly hair and fierce gray eyes, didn't spare her a glance. "What do you think this is?" he snarled. "A hotel?"

Without another word, he bounded into a small outbuilding made of cement with a corrugated tin roof.

"Ha!" Lucien whooped. "See? You walked all this way for

nothing! For nothing!" Disgruntled that he'd had to leave the seedy atmosphere of Niamey for the battlefront of the mission, Lucien was in a foul mood. He knew that as wars went, they were losing at the mission, and no one was happy about it, least of all, Sparn, who was in charge of the quickly escalating problem.

Lucien had been quite content to be merely in charge of Toby, seeing that she stayed drunk and didn't question the deeper things in life. To be sure, she was doing an excellent job of careening down the broad path to destruction without his help, and Lucien, well, Lucien had begun to get a little soft.

Now that they had arrived at the mission, the stench of battle was everywhere, and he groaned, knowing they were about to enter the fray. There were angels, scores of angels, all apparently with their hands full. The demons hung around in little morose clumps picking fights and escalating petty grievances where they could, but all in all, they were quite powerless.

"Welcome to the mission," a deep, gravelly voice behind Lucien growled sarcastically. He knew it had to be Sparn, the division leader, before he even turned around to see the demon's impressive and frightening visage before him. "I know what you've heard about this place, but things are about to heat up here," Sparn continued. "We are finally having some success keeping the old prayer warrior in check. Our hope is that her health will not be strong enough to enable her to fight back the sickness consuming her body. She is so old and so weak maybe she will just give up and die."

The old demon's eyes lighted up with a strange and terrifying light at this thought, and even Lucien shifted uncomfortably. So what if the old woman did die? That would be one more soul they had to give up. If she didn't die, maybe they could get her too. It nagged at Lucien that Sparn would be content to lose even one. As for himself, he'd just as soon keep fighting and try to get them all, but fighting from a distance, *where he didn't have to get his hands dirty. Lucien was eager to get away from this one-on-one type surveillance job and into some real battle-planning strategy sessions with other, more powerful demons. That a nice, tidy little promotion was needed to accomplish this was his only problem.*

He began to heave a resigned sigh but stifled it when he realized that Sparn continued to stand next to him. While they were at the mission, Lucien knew he'd be expected to work hard and get dirty like everyone else. But maybe this would be his proving ground. And if Sparn won this battle, he might be in the right frame of mind to begin handing out promotions to those who had served him well. Lucien promptly determined that he would be one who served well. Then, later, he could serve well from a distance.

Through the open door of the little outbuilding, Toby could see a flurry of activity. Miffed, but curious, she followed the man inside but hung back near the entrance.

"Why didn't you call me sooner?" the man was barking at a young girl whose pale face hovered worriedly over an equally young African woman lying on a rough cot. "Weren't you watching her? She must have bled gallons by now! Why did you take so long? There has to be some tissue in the uterus still. I'll have to do a D&C."

Demons tumbled around the table wild with ecstacy at the smell of death that hung there. They fed off the anger of the doctor and the fear and misery of the nurse. With sharp, goading remarks, they lighted the fires of the humans' basest emotions until they burned brightly. But none noticed the silent, dark man who stood off to the side, his hands covered with blood, his head bowed in prayer.

The girl, a nurse, Toby guessed, bit her lip and brushed back long strands of curly black hair that tumbled into her face. Her dark eyes were wide with fear, but she wore a determined look that refused to give in to the man's bullying. Her movements were clumsy, and she couldn't keep pace with his demands.

"Start a pitocin drip," Don commanded as he massaged the girl's uterus. "I need prostaglandin point two five IM."

"Her blood pressure is seventy over forty," Shay murmured tersely as she turned to prepare the needle.

"What I wouldn't give for packed cells to replace this blood loss," Don muttered to no one in particular. "Well, what are you waiting for? An engraved invitation? Hurry up!"

Angels, answering the prayer of the faithful, silent African man, converged on the little room. From him, they formed a circle of light that surrounded the table where the doctor and nurse worked feverishly. When they did, Lileah reached out and joined the circle, drawing Toby with her. "Go," Lileah whispered urgently. "They need you. They need you."

Toby didn't intend to help. And later, when she thought about it, she couldn't figure out what possessed her, but all of a sudden she found herself by the man's side, crowding out the young girl who at first looked annoyed and then relieved. The girl and the African man moved into position like a drill team, supporting the girl's legs.

Anticipating the doctor's demands, Toby readied the instruments he needed, supplying them before he could even ask. He settled into his work with only an occasional grunt of satisfaction. Not once did he look up at her during the entire time he worked feverishly over the girl, and she had an opportunity to study him at close range.

The hands that held the instruments were skilled and steady. His lips were pursed almost into a grimace by the concentrated look on his face. His eyes, a sober and intense gray, never wavered from his work. He was not overly tall, probably under six feet, she guessed, with a bulk that suggested muscles, though the loose clothes he wore made it difficult to determine.

When he finally completed his work, he stepped back with a deep sigh, and for the first time since she'd seen him, his eyes actually settled on her. They were blank at first, and she couldn't guess what was going through his mind. Finally, his brow wrinkled in bewilderment. "Who on earth are you?" he demanded.

"Toby O'Connell," she replied and then answered his unspoken question. "I'm an intensive care nurse from the States."

His shaggy head shook back and forth as he roared. "No! No more nurses from the United States! I said I wanted native nurses. We're training our own nurses. You're going right back where you came from. Just wait until I get a hold of that Dorsey!"

He stormed out of the building leaving Toby staring in astonishment at the spot he'd so recently occupied. Spinning, she ran after him. She had to take giant steps to match his, and when he wouldn't stop to listen to her, she grabbed his arm and dug both heels into the soft dirt. His momentum dragged her several feet before he finally stopped and turned to face her.

"Wait," she panted angrily. "There's been some misunderstanding. No one sent me. A man in Niamey said I might be able to work here for a week until my documents arrived. They were stolen. No one sent me," she repeated.

Don stared at her critically. "You're only staying a week?" he repeated, as if verifying the information. "So what do you want? I can't pay you. We don't have any money."

Toby bristled. "I don't want money. Just a place to sleep and food until I can get out of this stinkin' hole." At the thunderous look on his face, she hastily added, "Niamey, I mean. I . . . I just wanna go back home." She wondered idly why she had even said the last sentence. There was no home to go back to. Still, even "home" was better that what she had at that moment in Africa.

"Yeah, all right, you can stay," Don conceded finally. "For one week. No longer."

Toby smiled in relief, not pausing to wonder what she would have done if he'd refused. "Great." She stooped to pick up her bags and handed them to him. He took them, set them back down on the dirt, and turned to walk into the main compound. Irritated, she grabbed the arm of a small boy who was passing. "Here, you carry these. My arms are killing me."

Marcus took one long look at the dirty white woman in front of him and wordlessly picked up the bags, staggering slightly beneath the load as he set off after Don. Toby shuffled gratefully after him, wondering if you tipped small boys for carrying your bags.

CHAPTER

9

Pastor Hendricks folded his hands in his lap and leaned forward with an expectant air. Seated in his study, which smelled vaguely of old leather and musty carpeting, were his good friend Russell Duffy, his pale and very nervous-looking daughter, Julia, and her boyfriend, Ray Vargas. If Pastor Hendricks felt like shrinking from the pain reflected in the eyes of the three of them, he didn't show it. Instead, he smiled warmly, compassionately, and invited them to share what was on their hearts.

No one spoke. Russell's face twisted as he searched for words, but nothing came out. Ray fastened his eyes securely on the floor. Julia finally blurted out, "I'm pregnant."

"I see," Pastor Hendricks said, and turned his warm eyes on Ray. "Am I to assume that you are the father of Julia's child?"

Ray glanced up and blushed furiously before his eyes sought the floor again. He nodded jerkily. "Yes, sir."

Julia laid a protective hand on Ray's. "It's not his fault. I mean, it's our fault. We didn't mean to, that is, we weren't planning, I mean, it just happened. We were very sorry that it did, and it hasn't happened again since. But, none of that matters now."

"Oh, I disagree, Julia," Pastor Hendricks protested. "I think that the two of you should be commended on several counts. First of all, you realized what you did was wrong. It's very unfortunate that it took place, but that you recognized it was wrong and took steps to ensure it didn't happen again was a very mature thing to do. You should also be commended for looking to your father and me for help. Many young people in your situation compound their problem by seeking abortions and cause themselves unnecessary pain. I'm glad you didn't do that."

Julia squirmed uncomfortably. "I almost did," she whispered.

"But, you didn't," Pastor Hendricks reminded her firmly. "Have you given any thought to what you want to do about the situation?"

"I want to marry her," Ray said, looking up defiantly, eyes flashing for a moment as he shot a sideways glance at Russell, who threw up his hands in frustration.

"How can you marry her? You aren't even out of high school yet! You work part time at a quick stop, for crying out loud, and you live with your parents. How can you support a wife and child?" Russell tried to keep the anger he felt at the situation out of his voice, but he was doing a poor job of it, and Julia shrank closer to Ray, who took her hand in his own and patted it reassuringly.

Pastor Hendricks jumped in to defuse the situation. "There is no reason that Ray and Julia must be married immediately, Russell. And I certainly wouldn't advise marriage just to provide legitimacy for their unborn child. Marriage is not something you enter into because of a mistake." Pastor Hendricks sat back and looked thoughtfully at the trio in front of him. While his outside demeanor was peaceful enough, inside his mind was churning out a hasty prayer for guidance.

Reissa, already present in the room, responded to his prayer almost before he was finished forming the words. "The Master has plans for this child, which will bring glory to His name.

From the evil intended by the deceiver, He has instead a plan for good. Counsel the couple, welcome them into the church family, support them through this difficult time, and they will go on in the strength of the Lord. But their child will not go with them."

A feeling of peace about the situation flowed over Pastor Hendricks. He didn't know why, but he was sure that all would be well. "Ray and Julia," he began finally, "if the two of you truly love each other and are serious about pursuing marriage, I think it would be wise for you to begin premarital counseling." He held his hands up as Russell began to sputter. "I don't believe it would be wise for you to get married at this time. The more time you spend together before marriage, the better off you will be. And there is no rush.

"Marriage counseling will also help you to see if you are suited for each other. During the counseling we can also discuss what you plan on doing after high school, how you intend to support yourselves, and what your goals are. Using that information, I think we can map out a plan for you that will help you reach those goals."

Julia laid a protective hand on her abdomen. "But, what . . . about . . ."

"The baby?" Pastor Hendricks supplied. "It won't be easy, Julia. But I know that God has a plan for this child. That plan may not include you and Ray raising it. That will ultimately be for both of you to decide. But I think that decision is best made after you have had the benefit of some counseling. You obviously do not want to have an abortion, or you would not have come to me. Am I right?"

Julia nodded, tears trickling gently down her cheeks and splashing onto her folded hands. "No, I don't want an abortion. But I'm not sure I'm ready to be a mother either."

Pastor Hendricks smiled gently. "There are other options. We'll explore them as we go along, OK?"

PRAYER WARRIORS

Lyle dragged himself out of bed, his head still thick with sleep. He'd been up late the night before, drawing a picture of Calla playing the violin. It was nearly perfect, and he had been thinking of doing it in oil as well, but it had been too late to consider starting a project of that size. Just as soon as he had seen Calla off on her run, he would drag out the easel and get started.

He wheeled himself over to the window and peered out. A cold early morning fog hung thickly outside the window. He cursed his luck and strained to see through the fog down the street toward Calla's house. He could just make out her shape walking down to the edge of the lawn where it met the road, but she was alone. Usually Brick jogged with her in the morning before they went to class. She was carrying something bulky over her shoulder, and Lyle realized suddenly that it was her inline skates.

He watched as she sat on the edge of the lawn and pulled on her equipment, tying the skates and standing up gingerly. Her breath blew out in little puffs, mingling with the fog. It was getting cold; this might be her last skate of the season. He'd seen her skate enough to know that she was good, but he was a little apprehensive about her skating in such a fog and wondered idly if her aunt knew what she was doing.

She pushed out strongly and slalomed a little as she headed down the road opposite him. Behind the closed window, Lyle didn't even hear the truck coming that suddenly appeared out of nowhere. The driver swerved at the sight of Calla, who was much too far in the middle of the road. Too late, she tried to hug the shoulder. Bouncing off the side of the truck, she was tossed into the ditch like a rag doll being thrown from the hand of a petulant child. The screeching of tires rang in Lyle's ears as he careened madly down the hall and out the door, heedless of the beating his hands were taking to make his chair move that quickly and the jarring that rattled his teeth.

When he reached the street, he saw the truck driver already bent over Calla's prostrate form, his face stricken with shock and fear. "Please, God," Lyle gasped, "if there is a God, let her be alive."

Tears of joy spilled down Shelan's face as she hastened to take Lyle's first prayer to the Master. How she wished he had turned to the Master under different circumstances, but Shelan knew that sometimes the Master allowed difficult circumstances to bring His children back. This was one of those times.

"Is she alive? Is she alive?" Lyle demanded, squirming out of his chair and dragging his torso along the grass down to where the driver was checking the girl over for any signs of life.

The driver turned to face the apparition that was Lyle Ryan as though he was beginning to doubt his own sanity. "She's alive," he said. "But she needs an ambulance. Where can I find a phone?"

Lyle pointed at his house and told the man where he could locate the phone once inside. As the driver sprinted off, Lyle pulled himself closer to Calla. Sitting up awkwardly on the grass, he reached out to stroke her face gently. "It's going to be OK," he whispered. "You're going to be OK." There was blood on her lip and a nasty gash on her forehead that, strangely enough, hadn't begun to bleed.

The man returned and stood shifting anxiously from one foot to the other. "I don't know what to do next," he confessed. "Do you think she'll be OK?"

"Yes," Lyle replied fiercely, willing himself not to even consider any other possibility. "See that house down there?" He pointed at Calla's house. "Her aunt lives there. Would you go tell her what happened?"

Berniece arrived, white-faced and disheveled behind the driver just as the ambulance screamed its way through the fog and pulled up beside the ditch where Calla lay, semicradled in Lyle's arms. In the flurry of frenzied activity that followed, Lyle was pushed outside the circle of action. Within moments, Calla was strapped down and transferred to the interior of the ambulance. Berniece was helped inside, and a police officer arrived to take statements from the driver and Lyle.

When it was all over, only Lyle remained, rooted to the spot where Calla had rested in the ditch, refusing all offers from the officer for assistance in getting back into his chair and going home. Nothing and no one could force him to move from that spot. The officer made one last attempt before shaking his head in bewilderment, climbing into his cruiser and driving slowly away.

Lyle's head sank into his hands, and he rocked back and forth, low moans squeezing out between his lips. His body shook like a leaf, but it was impossible to tell if it was from the cold or from anxiety. The anguish he felt inside compared to nothing he had ever encountered. Before this moment, all the emotions he had experienced had been totally self-centered. Now, every thought was of Calla and her well-being. If she should die . . .

"No!" Lyle said out loud. "No! She can't die." Sobs racked his body as he tried to block out the thought. "God," he wailed, his voice like the sound of a rusty hinge in the wind, "don't let her die. Please don't let her die. I know You're there, and maybe You don't care about me, but please don't let Calla die."

Shelan laid one strong hand on Lyle's shoulder as he prayed, the light from the angel falling softly on him. She wept along with him, partly out of joy that he was at last calling on the name of God, if not for himself, for this girl. And in part, Shelan wept at the distorted picture Lyle had drawn in his own mind of God, that he could believe that God had punished him for some imagined sin by allowing the accident to happen to him.

"Your accident was the result of sin in the world," Shelan whispered, willing the words to take hold in Lyle's mind. "Sin causes death, death by heart attacks, death by accidents, death by disease. God did not cause death. Your life was spared. You have such an opportunity to speak to others of God's grace if you would only look past yourself. Think of the encouragement you could give to people who have lost limbs as you have."

Noble appeared beside Lyle and wrapped his strong wings around both the human and the angel. His beautiful face wore a calm, peaceful look, and Shelan was comforted by the presence of her strong friend. "The Master has said that the girl, Calla, will live. In time, her obedience may give Lyle a clearer picture of the Master. He has begun to pray," Noble observed. "That is good. Keep watching for the opportunity you need to help him to be closer to the Master. Once this crisis has passed, there is every possibility that he will slip back. Expend every energy to ensure that that does not happen."

Shelan nodded, aware that Warg prowled at the perimeter with a score of demons who had been driven off when Lyle began to pray. "Can I not have help?" Shelan asked.

Noble shook his magnificent head. "No, my friend, but there is one other who prays for the girl. When the time comes, if you still feel you need help, ask again." Shelan nodded and watched as Noble folded up his glorious wings and disappeared from her sight.

Billie Jo heard a thump. At least she thought it was a thump. Around her the room tilted crazily and pink fuzzy shapes floated like clouds around the house, or was she outdoors? Wasn't that her father over there by that tree? How could that be? Dad had been dead ever since she was three. Then who?

Suddenly she could see the person clearly. It was an angel. "Wake up," the angel said urgently. "Wake up! Your children are in danger." And then the angel became a dog. It was Gomer, her father's old hound dog. He began howling loudly, and Billie Jo shushed him.

"Gomer, shut up," she tried to say, but no sound came out. She tried again, "Gomer, shut up." But he wouldn't stop. Finally she found her voice and yelled, "Gomer, shut up!" and awoke to find herself sitting on the edge of the couch where she'd collapsed the night before after Cass's nightmare.

"Go home and shut up?" Helen asked incredulously. "Is that any kind of greeting? What's been going on in here anyway?"

Billie Jo blinked stupidly and wondered the same thing. She had an incredible feeling of déjà vu when she realized that Helen had just arrived again and caught her napping. This time the room was only mildly trashed, and Billie Jo was just about to congratulate herself on managing to stay out of trouble, when her eyes alighted on the knife in Dallas's hand and the blood dripping from his finger at the exact moment that Helen saw the same thing. Dallas stared at the blood, too shocked to cry.

"Use it!" Nog snarled victoriously, seeing the sliver of opportunity presented to him and quickly driving a wedge into it. "This is your chance. She's not taking care of those kids. Take them away. That will break her. And once you've got the children, it will only be a matter of time until you can have your precious son moved into your house too. Act! Now!"

"Ah!" Helen gave a little cry of terror and leapt across the room to snatch the knife out of Dallas's hands and wrapped his finger in a dish towel lying on the floor. Cassidy watched them both placidly without saying a word. Helen turned to Billie Jo, a triumphant and cruel look on her face. "That is absolutely the last straw, missy," she hissed. "I have been concerned for some time about the safety of these children under your care. We both know you've been no kind of mother to them. And I shudder to think of how you treat my son in my absence."

Nog chuckled. "Way to go! Let her have it! You've got her where you want her, now take the kids! Take the kids!" Nog was so intent on Billie Jo's destruction, which he pictured as nearly in his grasp, that he didn't pay any attention to the angels grouping around Billie Jo, praying earnestly for her. Had he bothered to take any interest in the angels, he might have seen that victory wouldn't be quite as easy as he imagined it to be.

Helen stood up straighter as a fierce light flashed in her eyes. "Well, I've had it. I'm taking the children home with me. And they will remain with me until you can better care for them."

Billie Jo stared at her mother-in-law, mouth agape while the words sunk in. Helen wanted to take the children away from her. "But you can't do that!" she sputtered angrily. "They're my children; you can't take them away."

"Oh, I see," Helen said, her voice threateningly loaded with sarcasm. "I suppose you'd rather that I report to children's services what I witnessed in this house this morning and on numerous other occasions when you've been too tired or too lazy to care for your own children? I doubt very much they'd give you any opportunity to argue when they came to take the children away."

Cassidy, who didn't really understand what was going on, only that it was making her mother cry, ran across the room, shooting her grandmother a nasty look. "You leave Momma alone," she instructed. "She was awake all night with me keeping the monsters out of the closet."

Helen pasted on a condescending look for Cassidy's benefit.

"Cassidy, sweetheart, your mother and I are just talking. We've decided that you and your little brother are going to come and stay with Grandma and Grandpa for a little while." Helen smiled broadly. "What do you think of that? Would you like that? Grandpa has some nice candy he's been saving, just for you."

Cassidy looked skeptical, but the mention of candy seemed to change her mind. "Come on, Dallas," she said, promptly holding out her hand to her brother. "Grandpa has some candy for us. You wait here, Momma. We'll be right back."

Helen looked at Billie Jo and shrugged her shoulders as if saying, "Well, what can I do now?" and smiled victoriously. Billie Jo fought to maintain her composure. Cassidy had no idea that Helen intended for her to live with them, and right now it would do no good to frighten the child. She needed some time to think about what to do. There had to be a way to fight Helen and win. For the present, they would be OK with Helen.

Jewel laid one firm hand on Billie Jo's shoulder. "Do not lose hope, child. Be strong for your children and be a courageous witness for the God you serve. Do you remember what God said to Moses? "Is the Lord's arm too short? You will now see whether or not what I say will come true for you." Stand firm and claim a victory for the Lord."

"What about Dallas?" Billie Jo asked dully. "He's still nursing."

"I'll bring him when he needs to be nursed," Helen conceded amiably, now that she'd gotten her own way. "And he can spend the nights here for now."

Billie Jo watched them leave, comforted only by the fact that they wouldn't be far away. Dallas looked a little bewildered, but Cassidy was bubbling with excitement at the thought of candy. Billie Jo's head was pounding with a headache that threatened to split it wide open. There had to be something she could do. Something. Her mind clawed at the heavy blanket of weariness that engulfed her.

Sinking to her knees beside Jimmy's cot she grasped one of his big hands tightly in her own and went straight to the top. "Lord," she whispered, "I need...I...we need Your help. You've been with us so far, Lord. You kept Jimmy from getting killed in that tree and I just know You aren't through with him yet. One day he will open his eyes again and we'll be the family You intended from the start, maybe even better now that we've come to rely so heavily on You." Billie Jo paused for a moment and squeezed her eyes tightly shut in an effort to block the tears that threatened to come with a sudden fury.

"But, right now we've got problems. I can't handle this on my own, and Jimmy can't help me either. We need a miracle, Lord. Only a miracle can bring our family back together. I ain't smart, Lord, You know that, but I believe that You will help me if I ask you. And I'm asking. Please help me get our kids back. I know that . . ." A knock on the door interrupted her and for a moment, Billie Jo flushed with irritation before she remembered that it was time for the visiting nurse to stop by.

While she prayed, Jewel dispatched several angels to bring Billie Jo's request to the Master's throne. The remaining angels formed a supportive wall around Billie Jo, much to the displeasure of several demons who had hung around after Nog's departure to see if they could make any headway before he returned. Whispering among themselves, two decided to issue taunts from a safe distance.

"God isn't in the miracle business anymore, haven't you heard?" one called. "He's gone bankrupt."

"That number is busy," the other taunted. "Try again later."

Soon the remaining demons joined in, becoming bolder as they banded together to discourage Billie Jo.

Pushing herself up from her knees, Billie Jo crossed to the door and opened it to admit Cindi Trahan, who smiled warmly in greeting. "Hello, Billie Jo . . ."

Billie Jo dropped her eyes to the floor, but not before Cindi could see that she'd been crying. Great, this was all she needed, sympathy from a near total stranger. She let her hair fall into her face as she shuffled over to the couch and sat down to watch while Cindi took care of Jimmy, hoping with all her might that Cindi wouldn't say anything.

Peering through the curtain of her hair she watched Cindi hook up the nutritional feeding supplement given to Jimmy through the PEG tube in his stomach. She checked his skin for ulcers and moved his limbs through range of motion exercises, working in silence with only an occasional compassionate look in Billie Jo's direction. When she was through, she walked quietly over and sat down beside Billie Jo, placing an arm around her shoulders. Billie Jo stiffened.

"Don't talk to her," the demons chanted, gaining momentum, heartened by the presence of Rafe, who had accompanied Cindi. "Don't listen to her. She doesn't care about you. Send her on home." Urged on by Rafe's maniacal ravings, they made quick little advances, trying to gain a strategic position of offense, but with the increased amount of angels since Cindi's arrival, their cacophonous shrieks could barely be heard, and they were powerless against the forces of heaven.

"Can I do anything to help?" Cindi asked sympathetically.

Billie Jo tried to catch the sudden sob that exploded from her throat, but she was too late. Leaning against Cindi, she wept bitterly. "Nobody can help me now, but God," she cried. "He's all I got left. My mother-in-law took my kids 'cause she said I wasn't taking care of them proper. And I can't do anything to get them back or she'll take me to court . . . 'cause . . ." Billie Jo shot a defensive look at Cindi as if challenging her to say anything. "Well, I've been so tired taking care of Jimmy and the kids, I fall asleep sometimes, and Dallas, why, he climbed up in the cupboard, got a knife, and cut himself. Helen caught him."

Billie Jo stopped, partially because she didn't have anything left to say and partially because she was overcome by a fresh wave of sobbing. She wasn't sure what to expect. Would Cindi rise up in fury at the injustice done against her? Would she promise to help Billie Jo get her kids back? Would she laugh at Billie Jo?

Cindi took Billie Jo's hands in her own. "You know," she said quietly. "I really admire you. You're a strong person, Billie Jo."

Billie Jo raised incredulous eyes to Cindi's face. "Me? I'm nothin' special," she protested. "I'm just doing what I have to do, that's all." She sighed heavily. "And I don't even do that very well."

Cindi smiled. "Would you like me to pray with you?" When Billie Jo nodded, Cindi bowed her head and prayed a simple prayer asking God for strength for Billie Jo and healing for Jimmy. She spoke to God as a friend and yet, in her voice, Billie Jo could detect an awe, as if she were in the presence of a king or the president of the United States.

"What if God don't answer my prayers?" Billie Jo asked when Cindi had finished praying. "What am I gonna do? I've gotta get my kids back."

"You know, I ask that question a lot myself," Cindi replied as she stood to leave. "And do you know what I think? If I really believe that God is my friend, then I'll believe that He is with me in everything that I go through and that He'll give me His power in my life to not just suffer through my circumstances, but *to be victorious and overcome them*. He promises to do that."

Billie Jo sat in thoughtful silence for a moment. Then she nodded and offered Cindi a shy smile. "I guess that makes sense," she agreed. "Thank you."

Cindi gave Billie Jo a firm hug before she left. "I'll put you on the prayer chain, Billie Jo," she promised. "Every day one of my patients, Ethel Bennington, prays for people on her prayer list, and many other people pray for them too. It's like a giant prayer chain that extends, well, practically around the world."

Rafe remained after the other demons scattered before the

massive army of angels who now occupied the house. "I wouldn't count on the prayer chain too much, if I were you," he sneered at Jewel. "The mighty prayer warrior is on her way down, and once she's gone, that chain will snap . . . like that." He snapped two of his bony fingers together with a loud crack for emphasis and smiled, showing blackened teeth. The sunken pits beneath his cheeks stood out in sharp relief as his mouth opened in a soundless laugh. "Just like that."

Billie Jo waited until Cindi had pulled away from the house, her headlights poking jerkily ahead of her as she made her way back up the bumpy surface of the frozen driveway. Then she closed the door and turned to face what she perceived to be an empty house. And yet, it didn't *feel* empty. It felt full of something. Peace, maybe. Whatever it was, Billie Jo could sense the terrible tension and fear melt away that had gripped her since Helen had taken the children.

CHAPTER 10

The demons were having a feast, and Sparn wandered among them accepting their congratulations and patting a bony shoulder here and there with a gnarled hand. He shook his ratty wings out and straightened up, throwing back his own shoulders, pride in every purposeful step.

He had done this with his own hands. He had used the situation at the mission to his advantage, nourishing hatred and jealousy in the hearts of the staff at the mission. Since Toby's arrival, the battle had taken a decided turn in their favor. A turn which had not gone unnoticed by his superiors.

"Lucien," Sparn barked. "Where is Lucien?"

Lucien sprang before Sparn from his constant position near his elbow, though Sparn seldom noticed him there. "Here I am, sir. Can I do something for you?"

Sparn laid a hand on his chest and gazed at Lucien from watery blue eyes. "It is I who can do something for you. I would like to give you a promotion."

Lucien could hardly keep the excitement from his eyes. "Yes, sir!" Finally, a way out of this miserable hole and on to higher achievements.

"You have carried out your job remarkably well," Sparn said. "The skillful way in which you goad your charge is most admirable. I feel you are deserving of this promotion." He paused for effect before going on. "I want you to be my second-in-command. When I issue the final coup de gras in this war, I want you there to share my glory."

Lucien tried not to show his disappointment. Perhaps there was still a way out of here. Maybe he was just being too hasty. He would bide his time. And when this filthy little war ended, he would prove himself so invaluable that they would be forced to promote him. And not just to second-in-command either. He would be so powerful that they would make Sparn his second-in-command.

His thoughts provided Lucien with so much amusement that he was able to accept the new promotion graciously before asking to be excused, as he had work to do.

"Such dedication," Sparn sighed happily. "It is only a matter of time before the final victory is ours." He let his eyes wander over the mission, picturing what it would look like desolate and leveled by dust storms and neglect. Soon, soon . . .

"You are pompous, arrogant, and self-centered, Doctor!" The words were followed by a string of curses so foul that Shay was actually tempted to cover her ears, as if she thought she might be able to block them out. Toby O'Connell, the nurse who was staying for a week to help them out, brushed by Shay on her way out the clinic door. Dr. Germaine stared after her with what could only be described as poorly disguised admiration, and Shay fought with the jealousy that stabbed her.

She had been here for months, done everything he'd asked, given 150 percent at any job, and was much more pleasant to work with, and yet Dr. Germaine barely acknowledged her existence, let alone acted appreciative. But the dust had barely settled since Toby's arrival, and anyone who observed their fierce verbal battles during which they cut each other to ribbons saw that the woman commanded, and even more amazingly, received respect from the surly doctor. It was almost as if, Shay thought, they were both so filled with hatred and pain that they were grateful to have each other to unleash it on.

"You think deep thoughts for one so young who should be so carefree," Nwibe observed sagely.

Shay had long since given up being astonished at Nwibe's uncanny insight. "Not deep thoughts, my friend, sad ones." Her eyes tracked Dr. Germaine, who finished up with what he was doing and made an excuse to leave the clinic. Probably going to "accidentally" find Toby.

"Why doesn't he like me?" she asked morosely. "I want to help him. I want to comfort him. And he doesn't even know I exist! When he does notice me, it's always to yell at me for doing something wrong or in case I was about to do something wrong."

Shay's brow furrowed darkly as she chased a long strand of hair back behind her ear. "She treats him like dirt, and he actually seems to *like* it. Why is that?"

Nwibe didn't answer for a moment. Just when Shay thought he might have decided not to answer at all, he spoke. "There is much hatred inside the doctor for the things that he saw in Rwanda. He has kept this hatred inside, showing it to no one. With this woman he feels safe, and so he expresses it."

Shay looked at him in disbelief. "How can you say that? What makes her safe? And she's only going to be here for a week. Then what's he going to do?"

"The fact that she will be leaving soon is precisely what makes her a safe receptacle for his anger. Also, because she is not hurt by it." Nwibe laid his hand on her arm. "You could not stand up to that kind of abuse. It would hurt you too much."

Slowly, Shay realized that he was right. With every fiber of her being, she wanted to take Don Germaine into her arms and comfort him, the way you would comfort a small child who fell and scraped his knee. But Don wasn't a small child, and his wounds went much deeper than a scrape. Maybe this was the only way he could deal with the pain he felt.

She stared out the door of the clinic and saw Toby standing on the edge of the compound staring in the direction of Niamey. What was her excuse? She seemed to be filled with the same kind of anger, and yet, supposedly, she was on vacation. Could she be that angry that she'd been robbed?

"No," Lileah said softly, answering Shay's question. "But, there is no possible way you could know the horrible things that have happened in her life. Be tolerant, little sister. Be tolerant and patient. Accept Toby and all her faults the way the Master accepts you. Who knows . . . maybe you will be able to reach her when I have not. You are flesh and blood, a living example of the Master's message. I can only do so much when she refuses to listen to me. But, you . . . you are in front of her all day. You have a week to show her the Master's love."

Shay gulped down a sudden surge of pity for Toby and turned her attention on Marcus, who was drawing designs in the dust on the floor at their feet. She clapped her hands together suddenly, startling him. "OK, Marcus, why don't you spell some words for me . . . how about "Monday"?"

Marcus's eyes lighted up, and he stared up at the ceiling as if the word might be written up there. "M-O-N-D . . . A-Y?" he asked hesitantly.

"Very good," Shay said with a smile. "You are a wonderful speller, Marcus!" Marcus squirmed under the praise. "And that was a pretty hard word. Don't you think so, Nwibe?"

The solemn face, as Shay and Marcus knew, was only for show. "What good this reading and writing will do to put food in the boy's mouth I don't know," Nwibe answered courteously. "But, if it amuses you both, then by all means, do not let me stop you."

Shay winked at Marcus and continued giving him spelling words. When she had first begun to teach Marcus, as she worked around the clinic, she had been afraid that she was aggravating Nwibe, who seemed sober almost to the point of disapproval. But, one day, as she rounded the corner of the clinic, she caught him beneath the shade of a tree, by himself, spelling out the very words she'd given to Marcus that afternoon. She was unsure if he had been aware of her presence, and he had never mentioned it.

Shay was content to let the matter be a mystery, since it told her what she wanted to know, that Nwibe approved of her teaching Marcus to read and write. Soon, she was sure, she could convince him to let the boy go to school.

"Hey! I've got a fun idea," Shay said suddenly. "Let's go on a picnic."

Marcus, who was no stranger to Shay's fun ideas, brightened even more. "Yes, let's go on a picnic!" he shouted. "What's a picnic?"

Shay laughed. "A picnic is when you take your food and go eat out in the country . . . er, desert."

Marcus frowned and asked, "You want to go eat in the desert?" much the same way he might have said, "You want to jump off a cliff?"

Shay caught his hands in hers and gave them a squeeze. "It will be fun, I tell you. We'll pretend that we're picnicking by a lake, and we'll play games. Only," she turned to Nwibe, her forehead wrinkled in concern, "will we have to worry about ants?"

Nwibe's wide smile displayed the whiteness of his teeth to great advantage. "Madame Shay, I do not believe that ants will be a concern."

"Arghh!" Shay made motions as if she were pulling her thick hair out by the roots. "How many times do I have to tell you to drop that "Madame" stuff? You make me feel a hundred years old. Why can't you just call me Shay?"

Nwibe's only answer was a smile.

"Well, then," Shay returned slyly when she had determined

that he wouldn't give in, "shall we go, Mr. Okeke?"

Nwibe's hearty laughter accompanied them out of the clinic. "You are a stubborn woman, Shay Beauregard," Nwibe said.

"I know," Shay said cheerfully as she led the way to locate the others. She had determined to ask Don and Toby if they would like to join the party but fully expected them to decline. Still, she would ask.

Dr. Germaine gave them his full blessing and consent, but begged off. Toby did the same, claiming that she'd had enough of the desert for awhile, and besides, it was her turn to sterilize the instruments. That done, Shay moved on to collect the items necessary for a picnic on the desert, something Akueke thought was absurd. She plainly showed this by her actions as she rolled their food up in a blanket. Shay thanked her politely, almost too politely, hoisted the blanket roll on her shoulder, and led the way out onto the desert. Maybe they were crazy, but they were sure going to have fun.

With his eyes, Don followed the forms of Shay, Nwibe, and Marcus, who looked as though he'd rather be scampering about like an excited puppy than leading his father. Shay undoubtedly noticed the same thing because in the next second she said something to the boy, and the party came to a halt while things were rearranged.

Shay gave Nwibe the guide pole to use as a walking stick. Then she tucked the blanket under one arm and placed the other firmly around Nwibe's waist. Walking this way they set off again, with Marcus bounding ahead in his exuberance to be free. A smile tugged on the corners of Don's mouth. Shay was so carefree, so funloving, so innocent, that it pained him to be around her.

Behind him he heard the sounds of Toby sterilizing the instruments. It was a job that even in the short time she'd been there she already hated, and he could tell that her feelings for it hadn't improved by the sounds she was making as she slammed the equipment around. He turned to her with an irritated sigh.

"Can't you be any quieter than that? You're going to scare all the patients to death."

Toby glowered at him. "Do you want me to do the job, or don't you? I have no reservations about allowing you the distinct honor of doing it yourself, Doctor." The way she said "doctor" made it sound like "Hitler," but Don ignored her tone.

"Suit yourself, then," he snapped. "Look, I have to run into Niamey for some supplies. Do you need anything?"

"Just a passport off this sandtrap," Toby muttered.

"Nothing, then?" Don said breezily. "Fine. I'll be back in a few hours. I'm taking the jeep."

The jeep was Don's nemesis. He hated the thing. It was constantly overheating and had to be babied for the extent of many journeys, which were as infrequent as he could manage to make them.

The drive to Niamey seemed to take forever as he was forced to stop and let the engine cool down numerous times before resuming his trip.

Making his way through the streets, Don's stomach rumbled, reminding him that he had missed lunch. He rummaged around in his pocket and came up with a crumpled dollar bill. Stopping at several street vendors, he filled a bowl with rice, sauce, and vegetables. He dropped onto a small wooden bench and gratefully began to eat after pushing some food aside to later feed the children who hung in the background, not begging but waiting for leftovers from the "kitchen." It was something he had learned from the Nigerians the first time he'd come to Niamey.

After he ate, Don made his way to the Tokoulakoye bar. The interior was dim, and it took several minutes before his eyes adjusted enough to make out the form of the bartender who was wiping down the tables. "Hello, Wahabi," Don said.

"Doctor Germaine," the man exclaimed, joy lighting up his jet-black features. "Welcome! Come sit down and tell me all the news. How is my brother? And Marcus?"

Don hoisted himself up to a seat at the bar while Wahabi poured him a lukewarm soda out of the supply set aside specifically for his favorite patron. "Nwibe is fine," Don replied, taking an appreciative gulp of the soda. "He and Marcus have made a new friend of one of the nurses."

Wahabi's face registered shock, horror, and then sheepishness in quick progression. "Not that she-devil I took pity on, I hope!"

Don laughed. "No, a very sweet Cajun girl from the United States who has been good for them both. Marcus is learning how to read and write. I suspect that Nwibe is learning, too, although the old goat won't admit it."

Wahabi's laughter filled the room. "I am glad for Marcus. When my brother lost his sight from the river blindness, we all thought . . . well, you know the fate of children whose parents become blind. They do not have the opportunity to be children. They must help their parents in order to survive. The child's responsibility to his family is more important than his education . . ." Wahabi's voice became soft and reflective as he added, "or his freedom."

"I know," Don replied. "Marcus is a good boy, and Shay is teaching him well. I even think she has plans to persuade Nwibe to let the boy go to school. But first she has to figure out how he will get around without him during the day. I don't know how they will get along without her when she leaves."

"Leaves?"

Don shrugged. "Her term is only for one year. And then she will return to the States." He barked a short, explosive laugh. "Fortunately, the other one will be gone by the end of the week!"

Wahabi laughed. "Thank you for the warning, my good friend. I will be sure to lock up the bar."

Don spent some more time catching up with Wahabi and debating their favorite topic, African politics, while he tried at intervals to reach his sister Cindi on Wahabi's phone. When he finally was able to get through, the news wasn't good.

"What do you mean Ethel's sick?" he yelled into the receiver, jamming his palm against his free ear to block out the noises from the street that filtered into the bar. Cindi's voice sounded far away and tinny. There was a pause after every few words due to interference in the telecommunications satellite, and Don cursed the distance between them.

"I see, yes, I know. I'm sure you're doing everything possible. Listen, Sis, tell the old warhorse that I'll be praying for her. Would you do that? OK, I'll let you go now. I love you, Cindi. Love to Mom and Dad too. Bye." Don hung up the phone slowly, walked sightlessly past Wahabi and out into the blinding sunshine.

He made his way to the banks of the Niger River without realizing where he was going. He sat down, his actions as slow and painful as if his thirty-five years were multiplied a hundredfold. Ethel, sick? It was unimaginable.

It occurred to him that he'd thought the old lady indestructible. And now, as he came face to face with the fact that she might very well be sick enough to die, he realized how much he depended on her and on her gigantic measure of faith to sustain him in the recent absence of his own faith. As he watched the brown water swirl past, his thoughts flowed with it. Without thinking, he spoke them out loud.

"Lord, You sent me here. I know You did. I felt Your hand on my life from the moment I touched African soil. This is the place for me. This is where You want me to do Your work. I was never cut out to be a doctor in the States, we both know that. And I've always served You willingly and with a grateful heart. Until Rwanda."

Just speaking the word made Don's throat squeeze painfully shut and threatened to block the words that tumbled, unchecked, from his mouth. "What happened? Why did You desert me when I needed You most? When *they* needed You most? They were my friends, my friends! And they were slaughtered, all of them. I cared for their children and anyone else who came to me, hiding us all so we wouldn't be the next victims. The bombings, the mutilation, I can't get away from it."

Don hid his face in his hands as sobs shook his body. All the images that returned to him each night flooded over him, the pain as fresh as if it had all happened the day before. Into these images for the first time came a picture of Jesus, weeping with him.

"Don," He seemed to say, "You can't hide from it. But you can give it all to Me. I have already taken the pain of the entire world on My shoulders and paid the price for the sin which caused it. I can take your pain too."

But, in many ways, the pain was Don's refuge, his hiding place from the things about God that he didn't understand and the things about himself he couldn't face. In the pain, he was safe from confronting himself, his emotions, and growth of any kind. Here, sheltered by the enormous wall of pain, he could hide out indefinitely if he wanted to.

"It is only yourself you are hurting by hiding from the Master," Julian told Don sorrowfully. *"Your fear is holding you captive to Satan's torture. It will only be when you face the problem and allow the Master to fill you with His power that you will be able to overcome the fear and deal with the pain. Will you spend the rest of your life in a prison of your own making when the Master is ready and willing to set you free?"*

"Oh, don't listen to him," Merck sneered. "What does he know? You're safe where you are. Eventually you may even stop having those nightmares. You know, if you do what he says, you'll have all that pain to feel all over again. Are you really sure you want to do that? Think how it will hurt to re-live all that, to come to grips with it. And there are no guaran-tees that you won't feel it again or that you'll be able to forget it. But," he yawned as if the entire conversation was boring to him. "There's no need to decide right now. Why don't you sleep on it? You can think about it more later. What do you say?"

Tired and unwilling to pursue the issue further, Don blocked it from his mind and stood up shakily. He owed Wahabi an apol-ogy for leaving so rudely, and then he needed to head back to the mission. The sun was beginning a rapid descent, and he was suddenly eager to get back and see what Toby had been doing in his absence.

CHAPTER

Russell Duffy watched his daughter Julia as she tried to pull her short black hair into a ponytail, her brow furrowing in concentration as she stared at herself in the living room mirror. Finally, she gave up and brought the sides up instead. Holding it with one hand, she slipped a barrette over it, stuck out her tongue at her image in the mirror, and spun around. When she caught his eyes on her, she smiled.

"Whatcha thinkin', Dad?" she asked, going for her shoes. She settled down on the couch and was just about to bend over to put them on when Russell took them from her hand and began to put them on her feet, just like he had when she was a little girl. When he looked up into her face, he saw that she was crying.

"How are you doing, Julia?" Russell asked. It wasn't a casual inquiry, and Julia didn't shrug it off. She offered him a little smile through her tears.

"I'm doing good, Daddy. Really. The people at church have treated me and Ray so well. We're . . . we're thinking about getting baptized soon." Russell involuntarily squeezed her hand at the news, and she paused to give him a quick hug. "Ray and I want to go to college, and we're talking seriously about getting married after we graduate."

Russell stared in amazement at his daughter. Just a few months ago, Julia had been a scared teenager contemplating a desperate act. Her future held no hope and no prospects. The young woman before him today could hardly be considered the same person. Julia had matured so rapidly it was a little frightening. It saddened him to see that her mistake had robbed her of a certain portion of her childhood and naivete, but at the same time he thanked God daily for the people He had led into her life to help her through it. They had molded her into the person who so impressed him with her strength and maturity.

"I'm so proud of you, honey," Russell said, fighting back tears. A horn beeped outside, and Julia jumped to her feet, clutching her belly with a grimace.

"I won't be able to do that much longer," she laughed, hastily wiping her cheeks. "That will be Ray, Daddy. We're late, so I have to hurry."

Ray and Julia were going on an outing with the youth group at the church. But, when it was over, who knew. Russell tagged after Julia as she grabbed her coat and headed for the door. "When will you be home?" he asked, worry lacing his voice. Julia glanced back and caught the look in his eyes. She came back and stood in front of him, a head shorter than he was. She had the same frank blue eyes her mother had and had never been able to maintain eye contact while telling a lie.

"Don't worry, Daddy," Julia said firmly. "When Ray and I were talking to Pastor Hendricks last week, we made a decision to begin a second virginity. We signed contracts and made the agreement together. But, we'll be home right after the social. I need my baby sleep." With that, Julia gave Russell a light kiss on the cheek and bounded out the doorway to the waiting car. Ray's shadowy figure inside the car waved, and

Russell automatically raised his hand in greeting, letting it drop only after the car backed carefully out of the driveway and pulled slowly away.

"Where are you going, sweetheart?" Mrs. Ryan asked absently as she cracked eggs into a frying pan, heedless of the shell fragments that joined them.

"Just going to visit someone, Mom," Lyle replied, wheeling himself purposefully out of the door.

"Oh, that's nice. Don't play with the neighborhood children too long and be sure you come home before supper. You know how your father hates to take his meals cold."

Lyle didn't pause on his way out the door. "Sure thing, Mom," he called. He knew that as soon as he was out of sight she would forget that he had even left and if she needed him for something would search the whole house looking for him. But he intended to be back long before then.

He pushed the stubborn wheels of his chair resolutely, making his way down the driveway and out onto the road in the direction of Calla Kendall's house. He knew she was home because he'd seen her aunt help her into the house only an hour before. His wheelchair bumped along, shuddering jerkily over small rocks that littered the shoulder of the road. Lyle pushed on, undeterred, until he reached the front door of the house.

Shelan followed the wheelchair, helping Lyle over bumps that shook the wheelchair and jarred his hands unmercifully. She had been waiting for this moment, and once Lyle reached the house safely, Shelan went inside to prepare the way. Seeing Berniece's cat, she caused it to begin to pester Berniece to let it outside. Berniece tried to put the cat off so she could finish fixing dinner, but it was persistent, and she finally picked it up and headed for the front door. When that was accomplished, Shelan went to Calla's room and, with a surge of air from her powerful wing, knocked over a picture of Brick Brody that Calla kept on her bureau, waking her up.

There was no good or easy way to wheel close enough to the door to knock on it. Three cement steps created an insurmountable obstacle. Perplexed, Lyle sat wondering what to do, when suddenly the door opened.

Berniece Kendall held a fluffy doe-colored Burmese cat and had a preoccupied look on her face. As she bent down to set the cat on the steps, her eyes focused on Lyle sitting there in his chair, and she started in surprise.

"Goodness me!" she exclaimed, her hand fluttering up to her chest. She pressed it over her heart as if trying to subdue the rapid beating it had been startled into. In her surprise, she didn't recognize the apparition before her.

"May . . . I . . . help you?" she stammered uncertainly. She peered near-sightedly at Lyle, taking in his face, hard and flushed with exertion, the hair, matted into a tangled mass that hung limply down to his shoulders, and the ratty, outdated clothes. Berniece tried not to gag as the overpowering smell of body odor washed over her. "Aren't you the young man . . ."

Lyle cut her off. "I want to see Calla."

Warg chuckled. "Your good samaritan doesn't seem to want to help the injured man either," he observed. "Couldn't you get him to take a bath before he came over? What a shame. All that way only to be turned back. Oh, well. I win some, you lose more."

Warg squirmed up close to Berniece. "I don't blame you either. I wouldn't let anyone who looked like that into my house to see my beautiful, clean niece. Bad influence, that's what I say. He could be some criminal or something, for all you know. Maybe he wants to get you back because your husband ruined his life. How do you know? Maybe he's even got a gun."

"This is the man you've been praying for," Shelan told Berniece. "He needs your help. Won't you help him?"

Berniece glanced behind her as if weighing her options. "Calla is resting, but I'm sure she would love to see you when she's up and about," she said, tactfully sidestepping Lyle's demand. "I'm sure she'll want to thank you for all your help on the day of the accident."

"I want to see her *now*," Lyle replied evenly.

"Maybe later, when she gets up . . ." Berniece began to say, her voice firm and unyielding as she carefully hid her surprise at seeing him. She found herself wondering if he knew who she was. Who Peter had been.

"Who is it, Aunt Berniece?" Calla's voice called from one of the back bedrooms.

Berniece licked her lips nervously. "It's Lyle Ryan, Calla."

"The one who helped me?" There was surprise and gratitude in the voice. "Would you bring him in? I want to talk to him."

Berniece looked back at Lyle with a faint smile. "There is a ramp you can use in the garage entrance. Peter's brother . . . This way." She opened the garage door and led the way up the ramp, holding the door open for him. Lyle deftly steered the chair down the hallway, following as Berniece headed to Calla's bedroom.

Calla lay back on the pillows, her face white and drawn, making her lips and the flush on her cheeks seem brilliant and almost artificial. The color was reflected in the dozens of red roses covering every available inch of surface space. Calla's hair covered the pillow in golden ripples. She showed no shock at

Lyle's appearance but lifted one hand and waved slightly at him, smiling with her whole face. "They said you saved my life," she said. "Thank you so much."

"I just did what anybody would have done." Lyle could feel himself staring, but he couldn't tear his eyes away. She only smiled more. *She had one of those smiles*, he thought, *that lighted her up from the inside out.* Finally, before it got too awkward, he ripped his eyes away and fastened them on the floor.

"That's not what I heard," she said, her voice soft and full of gratitude. "I heard that if it hadn't been for you, I might have died."

"I don't think so," Lyle said, but in the fleeting second, he allowed his gaze to wander back up to her face. He realized that he hadn't sounded too convincing. As he remembered the accident, the feelings of powerlessness and helplessness washed over him again, twisting his lips into a snarl. He pounded on his thighs. "I couldn't do anything," he cried in anguish. "Nothing but sit there and hold you and pray. That's what I did. Nothing."

Calla reached out and took his hand, and for a single second, Lyle sat stunned while she spoke. "What you did means a lot to me."

Lyle yanked his hand from her grasp as if he had been stung. "Don't . . . I have to . . . my mother is probably looking for me." He spun his chair around so fast he almost knocked over her nightstand. Propelling himself down the hallway, he didn't bother to ask Berniece for assistance as he nudged the side door open and careened down the ramp, clattering and bumping all the way. The door slammed behind him as he sped for home.

Berniece came when she heard the noise and stared after him, mouth hanging open. Calla joined her in the doorway, leaning on the wall for support.

"What do you make of that?" Berniece whispered.

"He's so sad," Calla observed, before her knees buckled.

"Oooh!" Berniece put a strong arm around the girl's waist as Calla sagged against her. "Back to bed!" she ordered. "You know you shouldn't be up yet."

Toby scratched out a few notes on a patient's chart in Shay's crude filing system. She'd backed the girl in the need to keep notes, and Dr. Germaine hadn't objected too much but let them have their way. It surprised Toby, even though she didn't know him too well. She was getting the impression that he didn't let much go by without a fight.

She sighed as she looked around the room. Five days already, but it hardly seemed possible. The days were so busy they seemed to fly by and extend right on into the nights. A few nights she'd slept in the clinic to keep watch over a particularly sick patient, but when there were no critical patients, she learned, the staff slept in the mission compound. Which was fine by her. Already she'd been asked to do way too much hands-on work.

In the States she'd been a supervisor, caring for patients from a distance. Here she was expected to not only do actual nursing work, but also to do the work normally assigned to nursing aides or nurses with lesser degrees. "This is demeaning. I spent a lot of time in school to earn a degree that would provide me with a high-paying career," she once told Dr. Germaine as they changed the bedding of a terminally ill patient.

"And I'm sure the patients appreciate it," he'd replied with false sincerity. "But, my guess is that I went to school a lot longer than you did, and I'm not complaining."

Since then she'd kept her distance as much as she could. She busied herself with passing out medicines and doing treatments, sloughing off as many of the menial duties as she could on Shay. The girl didn't seem to mind, and Toby was almost happy with the arrangement. Except for a little stab of guilt every now and then as she watched Shay in her work, happily interacting with the patients and joking with Nwibe and Marcus. Only she and Don seemed to be on the outside looking in. She shook her head. That was all she needed . . . to start comparing herself with that cretin.

She glanced at her watch and counted out some pain medication for a woman patient who'd had her leg amputated. Each time the woman woke up, she had forgotten that they'd had to amputate her leg. As the fresh realization washed over her each time, Toby felt as though her heart would break. She steeled herself against the feeling this time as she woke Mrs. Akoye for her medication. The woman's eyes opened slowly.

"My leg . . ." Her bony hand crept down the sheet to where it lay flat on the bed. Too high. Just below her knee.

"We had to take the leg, Mrs. Akoye, I'm sorry. Don't you remember? I told you before." Toby's voice lacked any emotion at all, especially sympathy. Don glanced up from the desk. Tears trickled down the woman's face.

"But, my grandchildren," the old lady whispered, not really expecting any comment from Toby and receiving none. "Their parents are dead. I'm all they have left. What am I to do?"

"Take these, Mrs. Akoye, they're for the pain." Toby handed the woman some pills and a glass of water. When she was through, she headed out the door to get a breath of fresh air. Don grabbed her arm and yanked her roughly around until they stood toe to toe outside the clinic.

"Where is your compassion?" he demanded.

Toby's eyes flashed. "I did not come here with a suitcase full, if that's what you mean, Doctor."

"Suitcase?" Don spat. "Suitcase? I'd be happy if you'd managed to cram some into a thimble and use it now and then. The woman lost a leg, not a game of checkers. Maybe you aren't overflowing with compassion and sympathy for these people, but I expect you to pretend that you are from now on."

"I'll pretend just what I . . ." Toby caught herself in time. "Like," she finished simply.

Lileah sighed with relief as she waited for the expletive, and there was none. Maybe Toby had no compassion, as she claimed, but something was happening in her life. Something, Someone, was changing her, even if it was not yet apparent to her or Dr. Germaine.

As she spun around to walk away, Don caught her arm, his long fingers, so skilled at the operating table, digging into the soft flesh under her arm. "You'll do as I like as long as you're working at *my* mission," he said evenly.

Toby's eyebrows shot up in surprise. "Your mission, Doctor? Not God's?" She pulled her arm free and stalked off. It stung where his fingers had bit into her arm, but she didn't rub it. She didn't want him to have the satisfaction of knowing he'd hurt her. She winced. There would be a black-and-blue mark there tomorrow, she knew. But the day after that she'd shake the dust of this place from her boots and be gone. She couldn't wait.

In the hospital where she used to work, they had a name for the lackadaisical, smug attitude of someone who was leaving. They called it "short-timers disease." And Toby had it bad. As the hours crept by and the time for her to leave drew closer, she purposely antagonized Don, picking fights with him over the smallest things.

The day she planned to leave, she had her bags packed and on the steps of the mission before breakfast. Because they were badly in need of help, she'd agreed to stay on until after lunchtime, but one look at Don Germaine that morning, and Toby knew she'd never last that long. His face seemed to have grown older and more surly overnight. Haggard lines she never noticed before were carved into his rugged face, and a sour grimace tugged his lips into a perpetual frown.

"My, my, the goodwill fairy rises from the dead," she quipped sarcastically as he stumbled into the clinic midmorning, his eyes red and bleary. Shay glanced up from her position at the back of the clinic, and her face grew compassionate as she watched Don rub a hand over his face and try to focus on his surroundings.

At Don's elbow, stuck tighter than a blister, was Lucien, a little puffed up with responsibility because Sparn had left him in charge while he went back to the States to take care of the old lady once and for all. He rubbed his hands together glee-fully. "This is going to be a piece of cake," he chortled to him-self.

"Doctor Germaine, you were up so late last night. Why don't you rest awhile longer. We can handle things here," Shay suggested.

"I think not," Toby interjected, bristling. "I don't want to be at this all morning. I agreed to help out, not stay longer. Let's get this work done so I can get out of here."

"Look at her," Lucien said, pointing a long, bony finger at Toby. "She's the cause of all your problems. She's been nothing but trouble since the day she got here. And she'll be nothing but trouble until she leaves. Don't wait for her to go," Lucien urged. "Kick her out!"

Don looked from one to the other, his eyes resting finally on Toby. An unflattering shade of purple crossed his face and the veins on his neck bulged. Patients who could, lifted themselves up onto their elbows to watch the spectacle of the doctor gone mad.

"IF YOU'RE SO HOT TO GET OUT OF HERE, THEN GET OUT!" he shrieked. "I'm sick and tired of your condescending attitude toward my clinic and my patients. The sooner you get out of here, the better I'll like it!"

Toby dropped the instruments she was cleaning. "You want me out? Fine, I'm out. I can't wait to get out of here. This place stinks, this country stinks, and you, Doctor Germaine, stink the worst." With those words, she brushed by him, staggering him slightly as she intentionally bumped him with her shoulder in passing.

Toby grabbed her bags and without a glance backward began walking in the direction of Niamey, thankful at last to be free of the place. And soon she'd be out of Niamey and back home to the States. It did occur to her that there was nothing waiting for her in the States, either, but for the present, she shoved that thought roughly out of her mind. There might be nothing there for her, either, but at least Dr. Germaine wouldn't be there.

CHAPTER 12

Ethel Bennington was lying in bed, a bluish tinge around her lips, her breath wheezing in and out with a rattling sound. She thrashed weakly every now and then, a flush of fever on her face. Angels stood guard around her bedside. Rafe had gathered a few demons together, and they clustered on the outskirts of the room as if waiting for something.

When Sparn arrived, they set up a shriek that set Ethel to thrashing again. A night nurse, employed due to Ethel's deteriorating condition, entered the room and glanced around furtively as if sensing the presence of the demons. She made her way to the side of the bed to check on Ethel.

"How goes the fight?" Sparn asked Rafe, mentally calculating the number of angels present. Glad as he was to be out of the fierce desert climate, he was anxious to return, having left Lucien in charge. He trusted Lucien implicitly with the care of the mission in his absence but felt that he was just a little too enterprising for his own good and certainly for Sparn's. He couldn't help getting the feeling that Lucien wouldn't hesitate to walk all over him to get where he wanted to go.

"Not well so far," Rafe grumbled. "As you can see, they have half the host of heaven here. Or, at least, it seems like it. We haven't been able to do much more than create a feeling of chaos, which seems to affect the old woman. We're hoping to wear her down with persistence, if nothing else."

Sparn shook his head. "Not good enough. There are those of us who are getting desperate. This one must die. And I don't have time to waste gibbering about it or trying to pester her to death." He unsheathed a gleaming sword from his side. "I intend to finish this one off once and for all."

Rafe's eyes widened at the sight of the sword. The edge of the blade seemed to sing in the air as Sparn hefted it, giving it a test swing. "But, how are you going to get past their guard? Look at them in there, they're thicker than fleas on a camel. You wouldn't make it two feet into that room."

"That's where you come in, my devious friend. I want you and these others to cause a distraction. I will slip around by the window, and when you draw their attention away, I will attack." Sparn tested the edge of his sword on Rafe's arm, drawing blood and a yelp of pain from the demon.

Rafe snarled at him. "Well, go then. What are you waiting for?"

Sparn smiled and laughed soundlessly. "What a mighty warrior," he sneered. "Can't stand the sight of blood? We'll have to fix that." Sparn vanished before Rafe could come up with a suitable reply. An icy gale was blowing outside the house, and he wondered idly if it had been manufactured exclusively for him, since the rest of the landscape appeared serene. Through the swirling snow, he could make out a large white car snaking down the driveway. It came to a stop by the house, and three men in dark suits got out of it.

"Ministers," Sparn spat, recognizing the angel guard surrounding the men. At the same instant, he realized what they were planning to do. When people became very sick, they were often anointed with oil, and the ministers and elders prayed for them. This was just the edge that Ethel needed to get well. Sparn knew he had to act fast.

Without waiting for Rafe's signal, he burst into the room. He had a clear shot at Ethel, and he took it, bringing his sword down with such force that he could have cleaved both Ethel and the bed in two had it not been for Reissa's strong arm, which blocked his swing. With a shout of anger and frustration, he turned on the angel, and they grappled together.

Seeing that the plan had gone awry, Rafe led the rest of the demons into the sudden fray. When the three ministers entered, their angel guard had to clear a way for them to reach the bedside where they began the process of prayer and anointing. Sparn and Rafe saw the small bottle of oil at precisely the same time. With corresponding shrieks, they redoubled their efforts, frantically struggling against their angel opponents.

One of the ministers dipped his finger in the oil and reached out his hand to put it on Ethel's forehead just as Sparn managed to break free. With a triumphant shout, he swung his sword once more with all his might.

Before it could complete its arch, a light so bright that even the ministers squinted at it, filled the room. Sparn's sword vanished, and in its place stood Vaidah, an archangel. His sword was bigger and brighter than any in the room. He addressed Ethel in a commanding, compassionate tone.

"Ethel Bennington, the Master has heard the prayers of those who are praying in intercession for you. He has more work for you. Your race is not yet completed. Go on in the strength of the Master."

The minister, a little shaken, but determined, reached out and anointed Ethel's head with the oil. The bright light faded from the ministers' sight, and they finished praying and left. The battle clearly over, Sparn picked himself up from the floor to find that he was injured in scores of places. Without bothering to give any additional orders to Rafe, he slunk *away in defeat.*

Cindi entered Ethel's house the next morning with a sense of dread. Every light was off. The night nurse was asleep at the kitchen table, her head resting on her arms. Cindi hesitantly shook her arm, expecting the worst.

"Is she . . . has she passed away?" she asked when the woman's eyes opened.

The night nurse looked around as if trying to remember just where she was. She smiled slightly. "I must have dozed off. I was reading . . . I'm sorry. What did you say?"

Cindi shook off the irritation that engulfed her. Maybe Ethel meant nothing to this woman, but she was Cindi's friend. She steeled herself against the worst. "Did Mrs. Bennington pass away last night?"

"What?" The night nurse looked shocked. "Pass away? No, why do you say that?"

Cindi looked around. "All the lights are off, and you were asleep." The nurse colored. "Someone is supposed to be with her night and day. If she isn't dead, why aren't you with her?"

The nurse shrugged. "I didn't see the need. Your pastor arrived last night with some other men. They had some kind of ceremony and anointed her head with oil from a bottle. After that, she fell into a very deep sleep. Her fever went down. She hasn't coughed once. I checked on her, but she hasn't budged, and her temperature is normal. I thought she'd be better off if I let her sleep."

"Are you saying she's well?" Cindi asked excitedly.

The nurse smiled. "I wouldn't want to jump to any conclusions, but I do think she's much better. On the road to recovery, if that's what you mean."

Cindi clasped her hands together as tears trickled down her cheeks. "Praise the Lord! That's wonderful!" In her enthusiasm and relief, she grabbed the night nurse and hugged her tightly. "I'm so happy!"

"Yes, I can see that," the nurse said. "I'm going to head on home now. I've got to get my son ready to take the bus. Why don't you give me a call if you need me to come back tonight. But," she smiled. "I have a feeling you won't be needing me anymore."

"Thank you, thank you," Cindi gushed. "I'll certainly call you."

As soon as the woman left, Cindi tiptoed upstairs to Ethel's room. Pushing open the door slightly, she peered in. Ethel lay in a shaft of early morning sunlight. Her face, illuminated by the light, was serene and relaxed, her breathing deep and regular. The ugly flush of fever was gone. Her skin was pale and, Cindi noted with satisfaction, cool to the touch.

Inside the room, all available space was taken by angels, with more coming all the time. Sent as a result of a cacophony of prayers sent up on Ethel's behalf, the number increased each moment. Vaidah, whose tall, shining presence made some of the other angels look small by comparison, guarded the door of the room with a flashing sword. His instructions had been to prevent another attack by Sparn or Rafe.

So far this morning, the demons had kept their distance, but Vaidah knew that it might be only a matter of time. The fall of this mighty prayer warrior played a key part in their plans, and they would not give in so easily. They had only to wait until the moment was right before striking again. And if they did, he would be ready. The forces inside the room were strong, hand-picked by Gabriel himself, and would not fall in a fight.

"Thank You, Lord," Cindi whispered as she shut the door softly and went downstairs to begin the morning routine. Her heart was bursting with gratitude. The feeling was a relief, since lately she had been suffering under a severe depression, her thoughts consumed with images of babies. She fought them as best she could, but on top of Ethel's serious illness, it seemed to be more than she could bear.

When Pastor Hendricks stopped by later to see how Ethel was

doing, she decided to ask him about it. "I just don't understand. Why is God doing this to us? Is it some kind of test or something? If I can prove that I can be content without children, do you think He'll give me one?"

Pastor Hendricks directed Cindi to a seat on the couch. "God doesn't test us in that way," he explained to her. "He knows what's in our hearts better than we do. The theory that He sends us trials to see how much we can bear is skewed. Bad things happen in the world because of sin. God didn't create sin. James tells us that God doesn't tempt anyone.

"Nobody promises us a fair and just existence or a happy life here on earth. Instead, because of sin, we're guaranteed to experience some undeserved suffering. However, God doesn't leave us down here alone to brave it out by ourselves. Instead, He promises that nothing will happen to us that He can't use to benefit us in some way. He works for good in all things. Do you understand?"

Cindi nodded her head. "You're saying that God isn't keeping me from having a baby for some reason. It's because I live in an imperfect world, in an imperfect body. But that if I let Him, God will help me to grow through this experience."

Pastor Hendricks nodded. "That doesn't mean you shouldn't pray for a child. That may be God's will for you. But that shouldn't be the primary focus of your prayer. The primary focus should be on your spiritual growth. Ask God to show you what you can learn from this experience. And He will."

Reissa watched as Cindi showed Pastor Hendricks to the door and then returned to the living room. Cindi stared for a long time out the window as she reflected on his words. Reissa stood close beside her, causing light to envelope her. Cindi didn't cry, and when she finally sank to her knees beside the couch, her face reflected a resolve and a sense of peace.

Reissa could hardly contain her joy. The time was short before the Master would answer her prayer. Although Cindi didn't know it, couldn't even suspect it, her prayer would be answered in a way that would bring glory to God. In the very near future, Cindi would feel the touch of the Master's hand in a way few ever did.

Shay watched in disbelief as Don turned from the doorway after he watched Toby stalk out of the clinic and set off in the direction of Niamey without a backward glance. Face livid and contorted in a grimace of anger, he lashed out at the closest thing to him. Grabbing up a metal bedpan, he threw it against the far wall where it clanged before falling with an equally loud clatter to the floor. "What are you looking at?" he snarled at her open-mouthed gaze.

"Doctor Germaine," Shay returned, attempting to keep her voice level. "Do you think this is appropriate behavior for a hospital?"

"No, I don't think it's appropriate behavior for a hospital," he sneered, mocking her. "But, in case you haven't noticed, THIS IS NOT A HOSPITAL! And no matter what you do, it will never be a hospital. It will always be a god-forsaken hole in the ground where people come only to get patched up, built up, or cut up."

"That sounds like the definition of a hospital to me," Shay said evenly.

The retort Don was prepared to utter died on his lips. He let out a slow breath of defeat, and his shoulders sagged. Suddenly he looked like an old man. Shay felt pity well up in her heart for him. He had been through so much, with no one to comfort him or share his burdens. She made her way to his side and tenderly took his hand. He stared at her in uncomprehending silence.

"This is a very good hospital," Shay said, holding his eyes with her own. There were flecks of green in their depths that she had never seen before. With a little start, she realized she'd never been this close to him. "You've made this hospital what it is. What you can't do is not your fault. You keep berating yourself for things you aren't responsible for. You have to stop that. You are doing all that you can. Can't you be happy with that?"

Don blinked. He seemed unaware that she continued to hold his hand, and he made no attempt to pull it away when she placed her other hand over it and squeezed lightly. "I'm sorry about what happened to you, what you went through in Rwanda. But you have to let go of the past."

"He let it happen," Don whispered, his eyes growing vacant. Shay had the chilling sensation that he was seeing right through her. "He just sat by and let it happen."

"You mean God?" Shay asked, unnerved by the look in his eyes. When he gave no reply, she went on anyway. "If you think that God stood by helplessly while people were being murdered because His hands were tied or He was apathetic, then you don't know Him very well." At the gentle rebuke, Don snapped to attention, his eyes flashing with characteristic anger.

"He didn't stop it," he countered hotly.

"No," Shay agreed, "but He didn't start it either. Bad things happen because of sin, not because of God. What do you expect Him to do? Miraculously shield people from the effects of sin? If He were able to do that, don't you think He would have started with Adam and Eve and prevented the rest? Death is the consequence of sin, not something God uses to bend people to His will or frighten them into obedience. What happened in Rwanda happened because people were following Satan, not because they were following God."

"But my friends, godly people, were murdered!" Don said hoarsely, his face crumbling. "They didn't do anything wrong."

Shay squeezed his hand tighter and patted his head soothingly when it dropped onto her shoulder. She smoothed the curly black hair while soundless sobs racked his body and he shuddered against her. "No, of course not."

Lucien watched the display before him incredulously. Since when did that little wimp stand up to the doctor? What was she blubbering about? She was going to ruin everything he'd spent the morning working toward. And not only that, but Sparn was due any moment. He had returned to the States to close the matter with that pesky old woman who was holding up the works with her confounded prayers, but surely he wouldn't be gone much longer.

And now this.

"What are you thinking of?" Lucien hissed contemptuously. "You're listening to a child! A child!" His voice climbed an octave in his desperation. "What does she know? Nothing. Why, you don't even like her."

Lucien danced an angry little jig while he waited impatiently for Don's response. He didn't have all day. If Don would only reject what this stupid girl was saying, he could salvage the morning enough to present a pleasing picture to Sparn when he came.

Don lifted his head and wiped at his eyes with the back of his hand. "What do you know?" he asked dully. "You're just a kid." He turned and shuffled out of the clinic, as tired and bent as an old man.

Lucien couldn't contain his shout of victory, and his exuberance brought a cluster of demons over to see what all the fuss was about. Lucien watched hurt spread over Shay's face and tears well up in her eyes. "He hates you," he said smugly. "Why don't you go back home? Go on. Go back home where you be-

long. Get some nice job with a fat paycheck every week. Spend a lot of money on yourself. Live it up. But go home."

Shay turned and walked back to the patient she had been caring for. The others turned away to allow her privacy in her grief. They had all been at the clinic long enough to appreciate her kind, gentle way, and it distressed them to see her cry. But most of all, it distressed Nwibe who had listened quietly to the exchange from where he was seated on the floor. Marcus sat silently beside his father, and for awhile, Shay was not even aware of them. She was so wrapped up in her private pain that she did her duties mechanically, her hands doing the work while her mind closed down in response to the pain.

For months she had tried everything she knew to reach Don, to comfort him. She had thought that the love she had for him would eventually break through the darkness that surrounded his life. And when he saw how much she loved him and cared, it would erase the pain of the past. He would realize that he loved her, too, and together they would bring healing to the people of Africa . . . the reformed doctor and the gentle nurse.

"You cannot be his saviour," Nwibe said softly.

Shay jumped. Refusing to look up at Nwibe and afraid that her voice would betray her, she said nothing, but her hands worked faster. Nwibe, however, didn't leave. Instead, he stood as silent and immobile as a statue.

"Only the Lord God can deliver Doctor Germaine from the prison of fear that he is in," Nwibe ventured presently.

"What makes you think he's afraid of anything?" Shay asked, curiosity getting the best of her. She had learned to trust Nwibe's judgment implicitly, but Doctor Germaine? Fear? Nwibe had to be wrong this time.

"The doctor is afraid of himself. He is afraid of learning more about God, which will reveal the deficiency in himself that he cannot face up to," Nwibe explained.

"What deficiency? He's a great doctor," Shay said, trying to shake the feeling that Nwibe's words held some truth.

Nwibe nodded. "Yes, that is true. He is a very good doctor. But he is also a very angry man. He is angry because he would like to package God up in a nice, neat, little box. But, one cannot do that with the Creator of the universe. There are some mysteries that will not be revealed to us in this lifetime."

"So," Shay said, trying to put what Nwibe was saying into a context she could understand easier, "what you're saying is that Doctor Germaine would like to apply scientific principles to God, to dissect Him beneath some kind of spiritual microscope? He wants to pin Him down and figure Him out? And because he can't do that, he's hiding behind his fear, which he's disguising as anger?" When she finished, Shay wasn't even sure she understood what she'd just said.

Nwibe smiled, his teeth startlingly bright against his skin. "Well, I do not have much experience with a microscope, but I believe that is correct. You see, Doctor Germaine is afraid to find out more about God. But I think he will. It will take time though. God is working on him now."

Shay had no doubt that Nwibe was right on that score, and she looked up with admiration at the tall man beside her, realizing for the first time how much she depended on him. *Why*, she thought suddenly, *he's my best friend*. Staggered a little by the revelation, she continued her work in silence. And with Marcus's help, Nwibe pitched in doing as much as he could to help her out.

Shay worked doggedly as she pondered this unusual friendship. She was tired, but the thoughts that flooded her mind in a torrent didn't leave room for exhaustion. If anything, they exhilarated her. Little snatches of images, like pictures in an album, paraded one at a time through her mind. There was Nwibe laughing while she tried to teach him the finer points of singing the blues. Nwibe comforting her after a particularly hard day or a scorching encounter with Don. Nwibe sitting on the steps with her, listening to her count the stars as they appeared in the sky. They marched through her mind in an almost endless procession.

Another thought blindsided her. She would be leaving soon. A stab of pain filled her chest. How could she leave? She'd become so attached to these people, her patients, the staff at the mission. She glanced over at Marcus, who was guiding his father's hand as they washed out bedpans. The boy had come such a long way in such a short time. Why, he was reading and learning the basics of math and other subjects. What would happen to him when she left?

Shay pushed the thought out of her mind. She'd cross that bridge when she got to it. After all, there was some time yet. Anything could happen. Another image popped into her mind and stunned her. In the picture she, Nwibe, and Marcus were boarding a plane for the United States.

"Impossible," she muttered under her breath, and yet, as the day wore on, the image came back several times, and each time it stayed longer and began to seem more possible.

Don came back shortly after he left, but other than a few grunts, he worked in a suffocating silence, his eyes as distant as his thoughts. Every now and then, Shay caught him looking wistfully out the door in the direction of Niamey, and a look she could only describe as regret would cross his face. After a few seconds, he would shake himself and continue on.

For her part, Shay tried to concentrate on what she was doing, but she couldn't help but idly wonder if he missed Toby. He certainly seemed sorry she had left. *I bet if I left, he wouldn't miss me half that much*, she thought viciously as she scrubbed some instruments with much more energy than the task demanded. It irritated her that someone so grating as Toby could occupy a place in his thoughts that she had been trying with great patience and no success to reach for months.

She was beginning to doubt that she'd ever understand what

she'd done wrong. From the first, he'd seemed to dislike her, but she hadn't thought much of it, since dislike was his preferred mode of relating to people. Shay wasn't actually sure she could think of anyone he liked. But, there was something else too. A pain in his eyes when he was around her. She had originally chalked it up to his experiences in Rwanda, but now she wasn't so sure. She was beginning to think that just by virtue of her character, she brought him pain.

Shay shook off the deep thoughts that enveloped her. She was tired, and her mind was beginning to perform sluggishly, as if she was trying to swim through oatmeal. She looked around. The setting sun cast dark shadows around the clinic, but before she could turn on some light, Don's hand clamped down on her shoulder.

"You're dead on your feet. Why don't you go get some rest. You can relieve me at two or so when you get up, and then when I come back on midmorning, you can hit the hay again. How does that sound?"

Shay nodded wearily. She hadn't noticed, but Nwibe and Marcus had already left. One of the native girls who they were training to be a nurse had just arrived, and Shay watched as she began her duties. "Yeah, sure. I'll set my alarm," she said and began to head for the door.

Don's grip on her shoulder tightened. Shay turned to see what he wanted. He opened and closed his mouth a few times in a futile attempt to speak before swallowing hard. "Sleep well, huh?"

Shay mustered all the energy she had left and gave him a weak smile. "I will."

CHAPTER 13

When the anger which had propelled her away from the clinic died down to a sullen smolder, Toby was irritated to find that she wasn't nearly as enthusiastic about leaving as she had thought she would be. Now that her steps were actually carrying her away from the source of her aggravation, she found herself wondering how some of her patients were doing. It was with a supreme effort that she finally managed to occupy her mind with other things.

Niamey seemed to be just as she had left it. After an overly rough trip through the Surete, the head cop shop where everyone entering the city was forced to register, she was finally released. *They let me go*, she thought wryly, *only after I promised that as soon as I got my replacement documents, I was leaving forever*. It was as if the police were beginning to know her.

She smiled slightly when she caught sight of the bartender at Tokoulakoye dodge behind the bar when he caught sight of her. She ducked in the open doorway and made her way to the bar. When he didn't reappear, she drummed her fingers impatiently on the smooth wood of the bar.

"I know you're back there," she informed him. "It's safe to come out. I don't want a drink. Your friends at the mission re-formed me. All I want is the phone. As soon as I get my documents, I'm outta here."

Wahabi slowly came back into view. "And how did you find the mission, Madame?" he said, making no excuse for his avoidance of her.

The first thing to pop into Toby's head at his mention of the mission surprised her. It was something very close to a wave of homesickness. She wanted to say that she had enjoyed it there, in spite of Don Germaine's churlishness. She wanted to say that being there felt strangely like being home. She wanted to say that she missed the people, even her patients, even Don Germaine, and wondered what was happening in her absence. Instead she shrugged and curled a lip in disdain. "I found it dusty, like the rest of this continent. Where's the phone?"

Wahabi sighed deeply and took the phone out from under the bar, sliding it toward her. He watched her with wide, expressive, sensitive eyes, which were as dark and probing as his brother's were hauntingly empty. Before long, she forgot that he was observing her. She listened with mounting rage as the person she finally contacted explained to her that there had been a delay in replacing her documents. It was uncertain at what time in the future they would be ready.

Toby screamed, she threatened, she cursed, but nothing would dissuade the obstinate voice on the other end. After all, documents such as those could not be produced simply out of thin air. One had to wait. These things took time. How much time? No one knew, but certainly it would be soon. The promise was not the least bit comforting. By the time Toby hung up the phone, her face a blotchy purple, the veins in her neck throbbed so hard that she had the distinct impression Wahabi was counting the beats of her heart by watching them.

"No luck?" he asked with sympathy, which Toby wasn't entirely sure was genuine.

She groaned. "A lack of luck doesn't begin to describe the state of my existence." She sagged limply onto the bar and stared morosely in front of her, her eyes vacant and unreadable.

"Well, there is always the mission," Wahabi suggested, more by way of getting rid of her than offering up options.

Toby swung her head around to look at him. "Are you nuts?" she demanded. "I left there under the very worst of circumstances. I'm sure they wouldn't even take me back."

"It seems to me, Madame," Wahabi observed sagely, the bite of sarcasm lacing his voice, "that you have indeed made a habit of leaving places on the very worst of circumstances. Do you intend at some time to change this part of your personality? Because if you do not, there is not a place in the world where you will be welcome."

Toby spared Wahabi a glare that would have made an ordinary man flinch. The bartender was either not phased or a good actor, because he coolly returned the glare with one of his own that insinuated she would be cowardly not to answer the question. Toby bristled. "What do you care, anyway?" she finally blurted out. "At least I won't be here."

"And that consolation, Madame, allows me to sleep peacefully at night." If Wahabi was tempted to smile, he didn't give it away.

Toby sighed in resignation. "You don't like me much, do you?" she asked.

Wahabi registered his surprise at the question by arching one long eyebrow. "Madame, I find your personality grating, your vocabulary offensive, and your attitude abrasive at best. Does that bother you?"

Toby shrugged. Inside, she felt a strange sensation, as if a great fist had taken her stomach and was squeezing it in a vicelike grip. She fought back tears. "No, I guess not. Why should it? Listen, thanks for your help. I hope I don't see you later." She turned and stumbled out of the bar and down the street, walking blindly, not paying attention. She was stopped by a rough hand grabbing her arm just as she was about to step off the road into one of the open sewers which criss-crossed the streets.

"Th-thank you," she stammered. The tall, thin black man who grasped her arm was wearing a turban and spoke to her rapidly in a language Toby guessed was French. He gestured wildly, pointing first at her and then at the sewer. Toby nodded vigorously, trying to convey that she understood the danger and that she would be more careful where she walked.

Avoiding the sewer, she continued on down the street until she grew tired of skirting sewers and dropped with an incredible sense of weariness onto a bench along the street. All around her the street was alive and bustling, but surrounding Toby there seemed to be a circle of silence. She felt strangely detached from her body, as if her head floated just above her shoulders and wasn't connected to it in any way.

In vivid detail, the moments of her life since the day of the plane crash snapped by in quick succession. In sharp detail, she recalled the two times she had faced the unknown and asked for Divine direction. She had the same feeling now. She needed direction.

She couldn't go back to the mission. That was clear. Don had practically kicked her out. And she couldn't stay here either. She didn't have enough money. Surely, the bartender wouldn't help her out again. He'd all but said he hated her. Toby took a deep breath and closed her eyes.

"All right, God. If You're really up there and You know everything, then You can see what a mess my life has become. I'm tired of running, God. And now I have no place to run to. I asked for help from You before, and both times You showed me which way to go. So, I'll ask You again. Where do I go now?"

Eyes closed, Toby waited in what she hoped was a reverent silence, every sense attuned to the answer she trusted to be forthcoming. No thunderbolt flashed across the sky, no hand descended from heaven and pointed the way, no voice boomed forth with instructions. There was just a small voice whispering in her ear.

"Go back to the mission," Lileah said, repeating the Master's command. *"Your place is at the mission. The Master has prepared a place for you there. You are not to worry. Go back and wait on the Lord."*

Toby shook her head and opened her eyes. Slowly the world settled into place. She had the strongest urge to go back to the mission. And what was even stranger was the sense of peace that accompanied it. She had the feeling that if she just went back, everything would work out. And there was something else, the strong sense that she would meet God there.

The day hadn't been going well for Festus, a weak-willed demon who had been charged with following Toby to make sure she didn't go back to the mission. He was to stay with her until Sparn came back to release Lucien from his responsibilities so he could be free to follow her himself. He hadn't wanted the assignment, preferring, instead, his usual job of provoking Marcus's guardian angel. But for some reason, Lucien seemed to think this matter was more important. Personally, Festus thought Lucien was developing quite an attitude and would eventually have to be taken down a peg.

He'd only left Toby for a minute when some other demons from Niamey invited him to torment a few poor souls hanging out in the bar. It was great sport, and he'd lost track of time and Toby. When he finally came upon her again, he thought everything was OK. At least, he thought so, until she got up from the bench along the street and headed in the direction of the mission.

"Where are you going?" he shrieked, his high voice scattering a group of demons near him who were ganging up on a beggar. *"You can't go back there! Don't listen to her."* He shot Lileah a dirty look, but the angel wasn't paying any attention

to him. Her face was more serene than he had ever seen it. Her very peacefulness needled him.

That's when Festus lost control. "Get back here this instant! You won't make it out of the city! I'm warning you!" His words bounced off Toby as if she was made of brick. Incensed by rage, the demon turned on the skulking figure of a man. "See that rich tourist?" he asked, pointing a trembling finger toward Toby. "Rich American. Nobody's looking. No one will catch you. She can spare a few bucks. Rip her off!" The last words tore out of his mouth with the force of a bullet. The man he spoke to, already surrounded by a crowd of wily demons and easily swayed by evil thoughts, sized up Toby carefully and decided that she looked like someone who needed to be relieved of a little pocket change. Walking quickly, he fell into step behind her.

Lileah spotted him at once and knew by the determined light in his eyes what he intended to do. They were approaching an alley. She attempted to herd Toby more toward the middle of the street, but a pedestrian, guided by Festus, jostled Toby back onto the sidewalk and closer to the alley than before.

Before reaching the alley, they would have to pass by the door of the Tokoulakoye. Inside, Wahabi was on the telephone, absorbed in a conversation with a friend who lived far away and did not call often. Lileah caused the line to disconnect just as Toby walked past the door. Wahabi looked up in dismay as the line in his hand went dead, just in time to see Toby tackled by a rough-looking man as she passed in front of the bar just before the alley. It was not the first time someone had been forced into his alley and beaten up.

"Go," Lileah commanded. "She needs your help."

For one second, Wahabi considered letting the obnoxious American get what was coming to her. Then he decided that even though he didn't like her, it was his duty as a man and a native to protect her while she was in his country. He dashed *out the door and into the alley.*

Toby grunted with the force of weight behind the man's rush. It sent her careening into the alley, just past the Tokoulakoye. She glanced off one wall and, carried by her momentum, was thrown up against the opposite one. The rapid succession of events barely gave her time to acknowledge what was happening. Disoriented and bruised, she wasn't quick enough to escape the raised fist that crashed into her face. Her head snapped back, and she lost her balance, collapsing to the litter-strewn ground.

The man, heavyset and coarse, stood over her panting. He shoved her roughly as he searched her pockets. Finding nothing, he kicked her viciously in the ribs. "Where's the money?" he demanded in English that was tainted by an accent Toby couldn't identify. "Where is it?" He pulled out a switchblade and made menacing motions toward her. "If you don't tell me, I'll kill you."

"I haven't got any money!" Toby wailed, paling at the sight of the knife. "God help me! Help me!" she pleaded. At that instant, Wahabi rounded the corner of the alley and dove into the man, knocking him to the ground. The would-be killer scrambled to his feet, slashing at Wahabi before ducking out of the alley and racing off.

Festus howled in fury at the sight of his quarry fleeing. Explaining this to Lucien would be neither fun nor easy. Failure was not something that gave him pleasure. And if Sparn was back, it would be even worse. Festus glared at Lileah, who stood between the demon and Toby and Wahabi. "This isn't over yet, angel," he hissed. "I'll be back."

Wahabi lifted himself into a sitting position and regarded Toby with concern. "Are you OK, Madame?" he asked.

Toby wiped at the trickle of blood that ran down her face from a gash beneath her right eye. "Yes, I think so." She stood hesitantly to her feet and drew in a sharp breath. Her side felt as if it was on fire, probably a broken rib. When Wahabi stood up, she surprised him by throwing an arm around him and giving him an awkward hug. He stiffened, but patted her reassuringly on the shoulder. "You saved my life," she said simply. "Thank you."

"Please, Madame, don't mention it. I was happy to be of assistance. Will Madame be checking into a hotel?" he asked solicitously as he accompanied her out of the alley.

Toby shook her head. "No, I will be going back to the mission."

Wahabi chuckled. "Is that so? Please give my best regards to Doctor Germaine, Nwibe, and Marcus. I'm sure they will be delighted to have you back."

Toby glanced at him sideways. "Now, you don't mean that a bit," she teased.

"You are right," Wahabi agreed, laughing heartily. "I don't. But, you must come in and let me put some ice on your face. You are swelling up like a carcass in the midday sun."

"How poetic," Toby said dryly, as she gingerly touched her face. "And how right. OK, I'll take you up on that offer." She followed him into the bar, where he prepared a cold-compress for her face. "You should have been a doctor," she said, pressing the soothing cold onto her throbbing cheek. "You have a nice bedside manner."

Wahabi inclined his head modestly. "It is nice of you to say so." He indicated the bar with the sweep of his hand. "However, I inherited this bar from my father. I hope that some day I will be able to sell it and do what I would really like to do."

"And what's that?" Toby asked, closing her eyes against the pain.

"Farm," he replied simply.

"Farm?" Toby's eyes flew open in astonishment. "You want to be a farmer? That's your dream?"

"And what's wrong with that?" he asked defensively.

Toby shrugged. "Nothing. Only I would think that you would be able to get enough money by selling this place now to be able to go into farming."

Wahabi shook his head sadly. "Not so. My father gambled heavily during his lifetime, and I have been years paying his debts. Gambling is such a waste. As is drinking."

"You don't drink?" Toby asked. "You own a bar, and you don't drink?"

"No, Madame, I do not. Drinking is an escape from life. I have no desire to escape my life. I only wish to live it to the fullest."

Toby let his words sink in before she said anything. "Yeah? Me too. At least, I think I will. Eventually." She offered him a weak smile, which he returned.

"Why don't you have a drink?" Festus suggested, appearing like a puff of vapor at Toby's elbow. "Bet he'd give you one on the house. You could sure use one after that nasty turn you just took. Just one teeny little drink. Just to steady your nerves. What could be the harm in that?"

Toby licked her lips as she caught sight of the row of bottles behind Wahabi's head. A little rum would go down pretty smooth right about now, even mixed with that warm cola Wahabi kept around. "Could I trouble you for . . ."

"Don't let him trick you," Lileah called from her post by the door of the bar. "He only wants you to begin drinking so that you will keep drinking. That is his goal. In that way, he will prevent you from returning to the mission. Be strong. Do not give in to his temptation."

Toby shook her head. Wahabi was regarding her soberly. "Would it be possible to get . . ." All of a sudden, Toby felt very lightheaded. "Do you have any water?" she gasped finally.

Wahabi poured her a glass and pushed it across the bar toward her. He watched her drink it in gulps so big that some of it spilled down her face. "You should wait until morning to return to the mission," he said. "It will be dark soon, and you are not really up to traveling so far after such an accident."

"I'll be fine," Toby insisted, pushing herself to her feet with a grimace. All she could think of was the drink she wanted, but she was determined not to cave in to her own weakness. "I really should get going though. Thank you so much for all your help. I'll be sure to look you up the next time I'm in Niamey," she called back over her shoulder, half joking.

Outside, Toby got her bearings and began again to walk toward the mission. "OK, God," she whispered toward the canopy of blue overhead. "Let's see if we can make it out of town this time."

CHAPTER

14

Billie Jo hugged her knees to her chest as she rested her chin on her hands. Staring out the big picture window, she watched fat, fluffy snowflakes drift lazily out of the sky. Her whole body ached with a profound sense of grief and loneliness. If she listened hard enough, she could almost hear Cassidy's and Dallas's laughter echoing through the now-silent house.

As she watched, a sudden wind kicked up. The air smoked with snow. A shaft of sunlight pierced the dense shroud, creating a million tiny rainbows, before a cloud obscured the sun again and the wind died down, allowing the snowflakes to resume their gentle downward journey.

Behind her, Jimmy's even breathing marked the passage of hours until the children would come for a visit when Helen stopped by later on. They had been gone a week now, with Helen only bringing them back so Dallas could nurse during the day and then dropping him off at night. Sometimes Billie Jo wouldn't even put him to bed but would hold him fiercely all night long as he slept peacefully in her arms.

He was too little to know what was happening, but Cassidy informed her that he cried a lot and drove Helen nearly to distraction. Cassidy herself looked pale and couldn't understand why she had to remain at her grandparents' house, but she seemed to know that she shouldn't ask about it. Her eyes were ringed by dark circles, which Billie Jo traced sadly during the fleeting times when they were together.

"Don't worry, baby," Billie Jo would whisper in her ear when Helen was out of hearing range. "Everything will work out. It will be fine."

When Cassidy asked how long she had to stay with Helen and James, Billie Jo put her off, saying only that it wouldn't be for long. She insisted that she was working on something. She had a plan. The little girl was satisfied enough by this answer that she returned uncomplaining with her grandmother. The way she bore the situation with silent patience tore at Billie Jo's heart.

The only tangible plan that came to mind was born of desperation. When the void left by the children became so painful that Billie Jo thought she might lose her mind because of it, a thought popped into her head. Why not kidnap the children?

She could run away. Far away where Helen and James couldn't track them down. And then with an almost audible *thunk!* her mind returned to reality. What on earth would she do with Jimmy? How could she flee with two small children and a husband in a coma? It was tempting to think about coming back for Jimmy if he should ever . . . improve. But Billie Jo determined that the thought was ludicrous and put it out of her mind. Instead, she concentrated on what she *could* do.

"I can pray," Billie Jo said out loud to no one in particular. "And I'm doing it."

She sighed deeply and turned away from the window. It would be at least two hours before Helen arrived with the children, and Cindi wasn't going to stop by until suppertime on her way home from her other job. Billie Jo scanned the room around her with a critical eye. With so much extra time on her hands lately, she'd used it to give the house a thorough cleaning. In the back of her mind, she felt that maybe if she could just keep the house spotless and be courteous to Helen when she came, in a week or two, after the novelty of having the children around wore off, Helen would relent and give them back.

Well, that was in the back of her mind, anyway. She didn't place any firm hope in it because, after all, that would be subject to Helen's fickle moods, her dislike of Billie Jo on the whole, and her remarkably stubborn persistence. Billie Jo wasn't about to place her hopes in anything that unstable. Instead, she leaned with her whole weight on the Lord. With Him she knew she would never be disappointed, no matter what happened.

He was her constant companion from the moment she woke up in the morning until her heavy eyelids finally fluttered shut in sleep at night. Billie Jo had made sporadic attempts to read the Bible before, but since Helen had taken the children, she spent nearly every spare moment with her nose buried in its pages. Between her reading and questions she'd asked Cindi, she was beginning to see a difference between "legal" obedience and "joyful" obedience.

When Helen first took the children, Billie Jo's prayers had consisted of asking, begging, cajoling, and demanding that they be returned to her. She could only see one way for God to answer her prayer, and that was what she prayed for. But it felt as if her prayers went about as far as the ceiling before coming back to rest at her feet, unanswered.

Frustrated, Billie Jo had asked for Cindi's advice one day when she came to check on Jimmy. "I just don't understand it," she told Cindi. "I pray and pray, and God doesn't answer my prayer."

Cindi laid a compassionate hand on her arm. "Billie Jo, let me ask you something. Do you trust God?"

Billie Jo opened her mouth to say Yes but hesitated. Did she? She believed in God. She believed that He heard her prayers. She believed that He cared about her. But, trust?

Trust. That involved a whole lot more than belief. That was

like looking out of a ten-story window at the giant inflatable pillow called belief and jumping out of the window. That was trust. The act of jumping. The act of relying on your belief. It was one thing to believe but something else entirely to trust.

"I . . . ah . . . I'm not sure," she faltered, concern etched on her face.

Cindi squeezed her arm gently. "It's OK, Billie Jo. Let me ask you another question. Why do you do what God says?"

Billie Jo shrugged. "Well, you know, 'cause He said to do it."

"And why do you think He told us to do certain things like not lie, not steal, that kind of thing?"

Billie Jo thought for a moment before responding. "It's like when I tell my kids not to touch the hot woodstove, I guess," she said finally. "It'll hurt 'em if they do it."

"Do your kids believe you?"

Billie Jo smiled. "They know the stove is hot. And when they get to doubting me I show them this." Billie Jo shoved her sleeve up and pointed to a fading burn mark on her arm. "I got this loading the stove with wood one day. I tell them that story, and they don't try to touch the stove themselves."

"And God does the same thing with us," Cindi said, enthusiastically. "He tells us that sin is wrong, and if we start thinking it might not be so bad, He points us to the reminders on Jesus' hands and feet from where He was crucified. He reminds us that the consequence of sin is death the way you remind your kids that the consequence of touching the stove is getting burned. Do you understand?"

Billie Jo nodded. "But, what does that have to do with my prayers?" she asked.

"You see," Cindi explained. "At first, we obey just because God said so. Maybe you don't want to. Maybe you don't feel like it. You just do it because He said to do it. And if you stay in that spot, then you will feel like a martyr. And what you will be practicing is a legal obedience. That doesn't honor God. You have to move from legal obedience to joyful obedience.

Cindi's voice got excited as if the concept was something she had just begun to learn and she was eager to share it. "It's the kind of obedience that races through you and becomes a part of you. That's when being obedient becomes joyful. That's when you are obeying because you love God and you trust that He is 'able to do exceedingly abundantly above all that we ask or think, according to the power that works in us.'

"It comes down to trust. Do we trust God to do that? If not, then we are stuck in that legal form of obedience, which will make us miserable on earth and prevent us from really getting to know God and being saved." Cindi drew a deep breath and offered Billie Jo an apologetic smile. "I'm sorry, have I confused you?"

Billie Jo shook her head shyly. "No, I think I get all that. You're saying I got to trust God to do even more for me than I'm asking."

"Exactly," Cindi exclaimed, pleased. "And don't limit God in your prayers by telling Him what to do. He may have something even more wonderful in store for you."

The concept excited Billie Jo's imagination. Something more wonderful than she could imagine. It made sense. After all, this was God. He had all the resources of heaven and earth at His disposal. Why was she tying His hands with her puny human view of the problem and her demands for the solution she had cooked up? If she really believed that God was with her, was helping her, was working for her good in all things, then she had to believe that He would answer her prayer in a way that was best all around, even if she couldn't see why at the moment.

Billie Jo looked down on the sleeping face of her husband. So peaceful. She ran her fingers through his thick, dark hair. It had the same ebony color as Dallas's. Cass had inherited Billie Jo's dirty blonde color. Billie Jo traced the high arch of Jimmy's cheekbones. They seemed set in relief of the rest of his face, his cheeks sunken in below them.

Billie Jo smiled gently. "You need a haircut, darlin'." Before she knew it, she had the scissors out and was clipping the soft black locks. She hummed tunelessly as she worked.

Soon the children would be here. She let herself think about how nice Jimmy would look for their arrival as an excitement built up inside her. Her thoughts raced on through the day. If she hurried, she could finish the doll she was working on for Cassidy before they came back again to bring Dallas for the evening. The weariness she had felt earlier dissipated. She had a lot to do.

Jewel stood beside Billie Jo, his face reflecting the peace of his Creator. Ever since Nog had succeeded in forcing Billie Jo into giving the children over to her mother-in-law, he had been strangely absent from the house. The place was heavily guarded by angels, provided by consistent prayer cover from the re-covering prayer warrior, Ethel Bennington.

Nog was visibly uncomfortable around that many heavenly beings and hid behind taunts and jabs given from a distance that would provide him adequate time to flee. Mostly, he restricted his visits to the times when Helen brought the children over, using the tense moments to provoke quarrels.

Jewel knew that Nog's disappearance had nothing to do with overconfidence. On the contrary, he was reportedly redoubling his efforts with Helen, who was paying more and more attention to him as the days progressed. This concerned Jewel. Certainly, Nog was not giving up, which could only mean that he was making a final thrust to bring Billie Jo down, and using her mother-in-law to do it.

Jewel wondered what the demon had in mind. He had a feeling that it had something to do with the Master's order for a special force of angels to be assigned to this post. Even they did not know why they had been called, but it was certain to be for an exciting reason.

PRAYER WARRIORS

Russell struggled to keep the tears out of his eyes. While the organ played "Shall We Gather at the River," he dabbed at his eyes and sniffed loudly. Even as he watched first Julia and then Ray climb into the baptismal tank and be lowered beneath the water, he could hardly believe that it was happening.

Could that be his daughter, his little girl? That woman with the radiant face gently rounded now from the pregnancy? The beautiful smile that reminded him so much of his late wife? Could this be the little girl who just a year ago was questioning his value system? Questioning God? Wanting a more "exciting" lifestyle?

And Ray. Russell couldn't believe that this was the same young man who used to pick Julia up on his motorcycle, wearing a black leather jacket and bandanna. This was not the same kid who sullenly submitted to Russell's questioning as if it was the Spanish Inquisition. Out of those previously angry eyes now flashed a light of truth and honesty so strong it almost hurt to look at him.

Both Ray and Julia took their commitment to Christianity seriously. So seriously that they had jogged even Russell into a deeper study of the Bible himself. For the first time since his wife died, he didn't wake up every morning asking "why?" He just wished it hadn't taken him so long to become interested in Julia. While he had passed through the various stages of grieving, Julia had gone off to fill her loneliness without benefit of parental concern.

Russell found himself again wondering what would happen to Julia and Ray's baby when it was born. They had discussed the subject at length with Pastor Hendricks and always reached the same conclusion. They were not ready to start a family.

At odd times, when Russell caught Julia staring off in space, her hand absently caressing her distended abdomen, he wondered what she really thought about the baby. Did she not want it because it reminded her of how it came to be? Did she want to start with a fresh slate? Was she frightened of the responsibility? He had asked, in a blundering, fatherly sort of way, but she had hedged around the question. The only thing she said that stuck in his mind later was that she felt God would provide for the baby, but she didn't feel that it was in her future to raise it.

Russell wasn't exactly sure what that left her with. They'd discussed the subject of adoption a few times, but Julia refused to consider giving her baby over into the hands of a stranger, and Ray agreed with her. She wanted to know the people who would be bringing up the baby. And somehow they managed to procrastinate about seeing an adoption agency. The whole thing was getting a little frustrating to him.

"You must be so excited," a voice beside him whispered.

Russell started slightly and looked at the person sitting next to him, whom he'd been unaware of. Cindi Trahan and her husband Marc had spent a considerable amount of time with Julia and Ray, preparing them for baptism. Evenings found them all together studying the Bible at the kitchen table, sometimes playing games or watching movies. They'd become very good friends and talked about every subject under heaven . . . except the coming baby.

Russell grinned. "Excited hardly seems adequate," he whispered back. "I think I'm in shock. I don't believe this is really happening. You know," he continued, "I've decided to recommit my life to the Lord too."

Cindi's smile lighted up her whole face as she laid her hand on his arm. "That's wonderful, Russ. I'm so happy for you."

Cindi nodded her head in Julia's direction. "Have you got that crib put together yet? She'll be needing it soon."

Russell shifted uncomfortably in his pew. The church people had gotten together to give Julia and Ray a shower. Along with many other baby gifts, they'd given the couple a beautiful crib. "I guess I should get to that, huh?" he agreed lamely.

"You know, Marc would be more than happy to come over and help you. What about this weekend? Would that be good? I'll ask him."

Russell clutched at Cindi's hand, which still rested on his arm, before she could turn to Marc. How could he tell her that Julia didn't want the crib set up because she didn't believe that the baby would be coming home with her. "No, Cindi, really, that's OK. I don't need any help."

Cindi made a noise in the back of her throat, which clearly indicated that she thought he was joking. "Yeah, right. Marc will be glad to help. Seriously. Marc?"

Russell squeezed Cindi's hand so tightly that she cried out. "I'm sorry, I didn't mean to . . . that is, you see," Russell lowered his voice so much that he wasn't even sure Cindi could hear him. "The baby won't be coming home, so we don't need to set up the crib."

"You mean Julia and Ray will be getting their own place? Well, they'll still need to set the crib up there."

Russell shook his head. "No, you don't understand. Julia is positive the baby won't be coming home with us at all. Any of us."

Cindi's eyes widened in fear. "The baby is going to . . . die? How do they know that?"

Russell sighed impatiently. "No, no, the baby isn't going to die. Julia and Ray don't want the baby."

Cindi looked at him blankly. "Don't want the baby? How could they not want the baby?"

"No, that isn't what I mean exactly. You see, that's not all there is to it," he explained. "They both want to go to college. They don't feel that they can offer the baby a good life right now."

"So . . . I don't understand. Are they giving the baby up for adoption?"

Russell tried to keep the frustration from his voice. "That's just it. They haven't made any plans to give the baby up either. I don't know what's going to happen. Julia just keeps saying she has a feeling that God will work something out. But I don't know how He'll do that if she sits around doing nothing."

Cindi licked her lips, a look of pure fear on her face. "Russell, do you think Julia would let Marc and me adopt the baby?" she asked tentatively. The way she sat as still as a statue made Russell think she was holding her breath while she waited for his answer.

"You and Marc? Would you? I mean, is that something you'd be interested in?" Russell asked, nearly overwhelmed with surprise.

"Interested in?" Cindi squeaked. "We have been praying for a child for years. This baby could be the answer to our prayers."

Russell sat in stunned silence while her words sank in. "Well, I . . . why I just don't know . . . I will certainly mention this conversation to Julia. Or would you prefer to speak to her yourself?"

"No," Cindi said. "I think you should approach her about it. If it isn't something she would be interested in, I don't think I could keep myself from bursting into tears. Besides, she may not like it that I know about it. I get the impression that you guys have been keeping this under wraps."

Russell sighed with relief. "Yes, we haven't been very open about the situation, because everything is so undecided at the moment. Julia and Ray have made plans to get married as soon as they both graduate from college, but beyond that, everything is up in the air. I appreciate your discretion about the matter."

Cindi nodded. "You can count on it."

Russell rose to his feet as the organist began to play the closing hymn. When Cindi didn't join him, he shot a quick glance downward and found her shaking like a leaf, her head bowed. Marc had his arm around her and was rubbing her back.

Russell sat down again. Uncomfortable, he cleared his throat. "You OK?"

Cindi looked up, her eyes shining with tears. "I'll be fine," she assured him with an attempt at a smile. "It's just the thought of . . . a . . . baby." Her voice caught with sobs in her throat. "I want to be happy about the possibility," she whispered hoarsely. "But, I'm afraid."

Russ patted her back awkwardly, his hand bumping into Marc's. "Don't you worry," he said, a lump in his own throat. "It'll all work out. You'll see."

The three of them continued to sit locked in a hug, rocking slightly in time with the music that swelled around them as the congregation continued to sing. But the few hundred voices in the church were drowned out by the heavenly ones that echoed as thousands of angels sang along with them. Their crystalline voices blended and explored octaves not even known to man. But none sang so loud or so beautifully as Reissa.

Joy and praise welled up in her heart, raising her clear voice above the others.

Lyle sat in quiet anticipation beneath the snow-laden, drooping branches of the weeping willow tree. A clump of snow tumbled down from a leaf above him and plopped onto his forearm. He wiped it away in irritation and concentrated on the little spot between the dangling branches of the weeping willow that gave him a clear view of the road.

Any minute now, Calla would come out of the house to go jogging. She'd begun jogging again the day before, even though Berniece called warnings and protestations after her until she was out of earshot. The only difference between now and before the accident was that she was no longer accompanied by her shadow, Brick Brody. Lyle hadn't seen Brick's car around since shortly after the accident, and he'd been unable to figure out why.

Had they had a fight? Had he dumped her for someone else? Had she dumped him?

Her only jogging partner now was a rather rowdy chocolate labrador retriever who was tickled to be outside and running. He bounded beside her, sometimes jerking her so hard that she dropped the leash and had to chase after him. Lyle had never seen the dog up close, but he seemed harmless enough.

His chair creaked as he leaned forward in anticipation. Calla came down the front steps with the dog on a lead. Berniece trailed them to the edge of the road, clutching a bathrobe around her, her feet stuffed into a pair of old boots so big they had to have belonged to her late husband.

"Calla? Maybe you should go jog at the track. What do you think of that? I'll drive you down."

Calla laughed. "No, Aunt Berniece. I'll be fine. I'll watch for cars. Promise."

She began an easy jog down the street. Berniece watched her fretfully for a few minutes before returning inside, her lips moving as if she was talking to herself. She threw one more worried glance after Calla before she closed the door behind her.

Shelan waited until Calla had begun to pass Lyle's house before she coaxed a gray squirrel out onto the lawn by pointing out a particularly nice nut in plain view on the snow. The little animal chattered anxiously, but tempted by the nut, it bounded across the lawn, not paying particular attention to Calla passing on the road. Calla herself barely gave the squirrel a glance, but her dog took one look and crossed the lawn in a single bound.

The squirrel, having secured the nut in one of its cheek pouches, gave a startled chirp as it saw the big dog bearing down on it and sprang to the nearest tree. Lyle never moved as the squirrel used his chair as a springboard to jump onto the trunk of the willow and scurry to safety where he began to squawk and chatter at the dog in defense of his territory.

Lyle continued to sit perfectly still as the big dog nosed in the branches of the willow, nose snuffling furiously. Paralyzed with fear, he watched the dog stiffen as the hackles rose along its back. Its lips fluttered as if a breeze were blowing, and a low, ominous rumble vibrated out of the animal.

Calla followed him cautiously onto the lawn, looking around nervously as if she was afraid someone might come out and yell at her. "Hershey, come!" she demanded. "Come! What is it? What do you see?"

Calla squinted into the branches of the tree, and Lyle closed his own eyes as if maybe he could hide that way. Her quick intake of breath let him know that he'd been spotted. He opened his eyes to see her smiling hesitantly at him.

"Well, hello!" she said. "What are you doing hiding out under there? Aren't you cold?"

Hershey's growl grew in volume, and Calla grabbed his leash, pulling him back as he strained to get closer to Lyle. Embarrassed at being caught spying on her, Lyle wheeled his chair out from under the tree. "I'm not hiding," he said defensively. "It's where I sit when I want to . . . think."

"Oh," Calla said, her eyebrows lowering suspiciously. "Well, I hope Hershey didn't scare you. He's really just a pussycat. He's more apt to lick you to death than he is to bite you. He does have a pretty impressive growl, though, don't you, Hersh?"

Now that Lyle was out in the open, the big dog was eager to play with him. He jerked Calla behind him as he put his front paws on Lyle's lap, almost knocking his chair over. Long shoe-strings of drool hung from his mouth as he panted heavily, giving Lyle's face a friendly swipe with his pink tongue.

"Get him off me!" Lyle shouted, trying to push the animal away. Hershey mistook the gesture for friendly wrestling and tried to maneuver his back legs onto the chair too. Calla watched with a horrified expression on her face. Her efforts to pull the dog back off Lyle were futile, but probably would have been successful in the long run.

Shelan had other ideas though. She coaxed the squirrel from the tree and shooed him across the lawn directly in back of Lyle's chair. He stopped arrogantly before he had crossed half the distance and sat up on his hind legs to taunt the dog. His tail jerking with each chirp, he insulted Hershey's heritage.

The instant Hershey spotted the squirrel, he gathered himself up like a coiled spring. With one mighty leap, he cleared the chair, pulling Calla behind him. She collided with the chair, and Hershey came to the end of his leash. Like toppling dominoes, Hershey, Lyle, and Calla all found themselves in a pile on the snow as the squirrel chirped one final insult and scurried away.

When Calla looked up, her face was twisted up. Convinced she was in pain, Lyle's anger evaporated as he struggled to extricate himself from the tangle of bodies and metal. A funny, squeaking kind of noise was coming from between her tightly clamped lips.

"Are you OK? Where does it hurt?" Lyle asked, frantically struggling to get Hershey's backside off his arm so he could push himself up into a sitting position.

The squeaking became a howl, and Lyle watched in amazement as Calla rolled on the ground laughing so hard that tears spilled down her face. Lifting herself onto her elbows, she looked at Lyle for a moment and then burst into hysterical laughter again.

As he watched her, a chuckle escaped from his lips before he knew it. Another followed. And then another. Glancing over at Hershey, he saw the dog panting nonchalantly as if this kind of thing happened to him all the time. Before he knew it, Lyle was laughing almost as hard as Calla. Every now and then they'd look at each other and try to stop, and it would start up all over again.

"You . . . look . . . so funny," she gasped weakly, pointing at the snow clinging to his hair.

"Maybe, but that's an incredible odor you've discovered," Lyle said, wrinkling his nose and pointing to her sneaker. Calla's eyes followed his finger.

"*Eeeewww,*" she said and shot an accusing glance at Hershey. "That's *your* fault!" The dog feigned innocence, his tail thumping wildly, slapping Lyle across the face each time. It sent them both into renewed peals of laughter.

Finally Calla pulled herself free and stood up. She righted Lyle's chair and helped him get back into it. Hershey, who decided he'd had enough excitement for the day, curled up into a ball on the snow and dozed off.

"Now he settles down," Calla said in exasperation. "Wouldn't you know." She offered Lyle a hesitant smile. "I'm really sorry about all that. You sure you're OK?"

Lyle nodded. He was more than OK. He felt almost free inside. As if someone had taken the cork off his emotions, allowing him to feel something other than anger. His arms tingled, and he had the feeling deep inside as if he might laugh again.

Calla's eyes narrowed as she studied him. Lyle shifted uncomfortably in his chair, suddenly aware of how he probably looked in a way that he hadn't considered since before the accident. This was, after all, a pretty girl. And he was . . . a mess.

"I know how to cut hair, you know," Calla said matter-of-factly. "In fact, I'm pretty good at it. Would you let me cut yours?"

Lyle stiffened in shock. "Right now?"

Calla stifled a giggle. "No, silly. I'll have to come back tonight after school." She glanced hastily at her watch. "Wow! I'm late. I've got to get going, or I'll be late for school. Tonight then?"

"My mother usually cuts my hair," Lyle hedged uncertainly.

"I'm sure she won't mind," Calla assured him as she dragged Hershey to his feet and began jogging down to the road. "So, is it a date?"

Lyle's heart triple-beated in his chest. *A date!* "OK," he yelled after her. She threw him a parting smile before heading down the street in earnest, Hershey loping along beside her. Lyle continued to stare after her, in dumbfounded amazement. He replayed the morning several times in his head before shaking himself into the present, a sappy smile on his face.

Lyle spent the remainder of the day skulking through the house. He was so jittery that even his mother noticed.

"Will you go sit yourself down and read or something, George?" she asked irritably, calling him by his father's name. She brushed a strand of steel gray hair behind one ear and peered at him through smudged bifocals. "I haven't seen you this jumpy since the day you brought me to the hospital to have the baby." She chuckled for a minute before a frown crossed her lips. "Whatever did happen to that baby, I wonder?"

Lyle sighed heavily. He hated to admit it, but lately it seemed as though his mother was getting worse. She'd always been a little absent-minded, but now it seemed to be an accident if she called him by his right name, and some days she mistook him for a stranger, which was getting more and more dangerous. One night she had attacked him when he went to the kitchen for a drink of water in the middle of the night, convinced he was an intruder.

"I think I'll go lie down," she mused, heading instead for the kitchen where she began preparing to cook dinner.

Before Lyle could redirect her, he heard the crunch of gravel on the driveway outside, followed by a knock on the door. Pushing the wheels of his chair so hard he almost flipped over, Lyle attempted to reach the door before his mother, but he wasn't fast enough.

"I'm sorry, dear, but I don't want any Girl Scout cookies this year. I have to watch my blood pressure, you know," Mrs. Ryan said, smiling sweetly.

"Oh, I'm not selling Girl Scout cookies," Calla replied. "I'm here to see your son."

"Lyle?" Mrs. Ryan said, a puzzled look crossing her face. "I'm so sorry, but I don't know where Lyle . . ."

"I'm right here, Mom," Lyle interrupted, trying to edge past her to the door. "Come right on in," he told Calla.

"Why, so he is. Lyle, where have you been? I haven't seen you for so long."

Calla edged through the open doorway. The first thing Lyle noticed was that she was dressed up. And she smelled good. Like lilacs. Her hair was done up in some fancy kind of braid, and she had a black backpack slung over one shoulder. She looked expectantly from Lyle to his mother.

"Uh," Lyle stammered, finally realizing that she was waiting for an introduction. "Uh, Calla Kendall, this is my mother, Edyth Ryan."

Calla shook Mrs. Ryan's hand warmly. "It's nice to meet you."

Mrs. Ryan's smile was a little befuddled. "You, too, my dear. Now, if you'll excuse me, I really must finish making dinner." She turned and wandered down the hall to her bedroom.

Calla stared after her in confusion.

Lyle shook his head. "She's getting very mixed up," he explained. "I'm starting to get worried about her." He cleared his throat uncomfortably. "Well, you were going to cut my hair?"

"Oh, yeah." Calla set her pack down on the table and rummaged around inside until she came out with a pair of scissors, a comb, blowdryer, a towel, and some shampoo. "You ready?"

Lyle watched her skeptically as she laid everything out on the kitchen table. "I guess," he said finally, swallowing hard. Somehow he had an idea that this wasn't going to be the kind of haircut his mother usually gave him.

As he watched his wet locks of hair drift to the floor and listened to the quiet snip-snip of the scissors as Calla worked, his suspicions were confirmed. By the time she finished, his whole head felt lighter, as if it was floating. She put some kind of gel in his hair and then started in with the blowdryer.

When she finished, she sprayed his hair with something that smelled like grapes and stepped back to admire her work. Her eyes widened in surprise. "Wow!" she exclaimed, then her forehead creased. "Now we've got to take care of that beard. Want me to? I know how."

"No," he said, panic grabbing hold of him. What had she done to him already? "I can do it."

"All right," she agreed. "Why don't you go shave and take a shower and then we can go."

"Go?" Lyle stared at her blankly. "Go where?"

"To the social. I thought it would be fun. Don't you want to go?"

Lyle felt the now familiar feeling of his head spinning. Things were happening too fast. "I don't know . . . I," Lyle struggled to think of a good excuse, but none came to mind.

"Why don't you come?" Calla urged. "It'll be fun. Besides, there's someone there I want you to meet."

"Who?" Lyle asked, wondering who could possibly be interested in meeting him.

"Well, now, if I told you, it wouldn't be a surprise, would it?"

Calla teased slyly. "Now, hurry up. We don't have much time."

Lyle screwed up his face to make one final protest before he thought better of it and made his way to the bathroom to take a shower and shave, as she had instructed. It had been awhile since he'd shaved last. Sometimes he'd kept it up, and sometimes he'd let his beard grow and grow until he got sick of it. Now the razor was rusty, and he nicked himself several times. Still, the image in the mirror facing him when he was through startled him.

Who was that young stranger?

"That's you, Lyle. That's what you look like with hope in your eyes. Do you see what a difference love can make?" Shelan asked.

"Bah," Warg scoffed. *"That's not love. That's pity. She just wants to help the poor cripple look presentable again. It's like taking in a stray puppy. You'll see. It won't last long, and then she'll be on to the next charity project and forget all about you."*

"With love there must be some trust," Shelan continued. *"Think about that."*

"Yeah," Warg agreed sarcastically. *"Give that little tidbit a lot of thought. Trust. Hah! The only thing you'll ever get out of trusting someone is a broken heart. Take it from me. I know about these things. Look where trusting has gotten you so far. Not a pretty picture, is it?"*

Lyle shook his head as conflicting thoughts assailed him. Part of him wondered why Calla was taking such an interest in him, and the rest of him was afraid to find out why. What if it was pity?

"Stop," he told himself sternly. "This is the best thing that's happened to you in years. Don't mess it up by over analyzing it. Just take it at face value."

"What?" Calla called. "Did you call me?"

Lyle reddened. "No," he said, turning on the water in the tub to drown out any further slips. "Be out in a minute."

He had one last moment of embarrassment coming out of the tub when he realized that it wouldn't do much good to get back into his dirty clothes after taking a bath. "Do you think you could bring me some clean clothes?" he called through the door.

"Sure," Calla answered. "Where would they be?"

He gave her directions to get to his room and waited anxiously until she returned. She cracked the door open and passed the clothes through to him. Lyle reached for them in dismay. She must have dug through his entire dresser to find these. He hadn't worn them since high school.

But he couldn't bring himself to ask her to get different clothes, so he pulled them on. They bagged on him a little, reminding him of how much muscle mass he'd lost since his football days. He smoothed the material of the shirt, memories flooding back in a rush.

"That's right," Warg hissed. *"Remember? It was her uncle's fault. He killed your dreams. He killed your career. He might as well have killed you. Look at yourself. You're a waste of space."*

Shelan hovered protectively over Lyle. "There are other things more important to remember than the hurts and anger of the past. The past is just that. The past. It's gone. Learn from it. Grow and move on."

"Do you remember going to church? Do you remember how you spent time in prison ministry before the accident? Do you remember praying in the early morning, looking out on the blossoming day from your window? Do you remember the time you led a boy to Christ at summer camp? Do you remember things like that, Lyle?"

A smile touched Lyle's lips as he allowed Shelan to pull him along through the good times in his life. He remembered things he hadn't even thought about for years. Playing guitar for the youth group, going on hikes in the summer to Rocky Ridge, singing around a bonfire after a church baseball game. Calla's voice interrupted his reverie.

"Hey, we're going to be late," she called. "You almost ready?"

Lyle gave one more incredulous look at the handsome young man in the mirror before he turned his chair and nudged the door open. "I'm ready," he said.

"Hey, you look like a new person," Calla said approvingly. "See what a haircut can do when the right person does it?" she giggled at her own joke, and Lyle chuckled in spite of himself.

Riding in the car made him dizzy, but he didn't admit it to Calla. The landscape rushed by so rapidly it gave him a headache. He started every time Calla drew close to another car, his hands gripping the sides of the seat until his knuckles turned white.

"You're looking a little pasty," Calla observed. "Do you get motion sick?"

"Not usually," Lyle replied, distracted by the way the town had changed since he'd last seen it. There were shops and people and cars. Everything was so built up. A creepy feeling swept over him, as if he was Rip Van Winkle returning after a long nap. It amazed him that even though he'd dropped out of life, it had continued on without him.

"Well, here we are," Calla said, pulling her beat-up little car to a dramatic stop in the parking lot of Lyle's old high school. A crowd of people were in the parking lot. There were balloons, and someone had even set up a food stand.

"What is this?" Lyle asked, straining to see what was going on.

"I told you. It's a social. There's going to be all kinds of games and events and stuff in the gym. You'll love it. Come on." Calla hopped out of the car. She pulled Lyle's chair out of the backseat and unfolded it. He refused her offer of help and managed to make it from the car to the chair without assistance. Once seated, he gripped the wheels and shot ahead of her, metal rattling as he bumped over the rough surface.

Calla sprinted to catch up with him. "I'll push you if you want," she offered. "I'm stronger than I look."

"No, thanks," Lyle replied tersely. "I can manage."

She held the door open for him and he pushed himself along the familiar corridor to the gymnasium. Adults being towed by children swarmed everywhere. It seemed as if everyone was involved with something. A sack race was taking place on one section of the gym and an egg toss in another, but the thing that caught Lyle's eye was a small boy in a strange looking wheelchair. A tall man stood next to him coaching him, and the boy was doing wheelies as they both laughed.

The chair looked as though it was about to collapse into itself. While Lyle watched, the boy raced it effortlessly around the gym. When he looked up and saw Lyle, he spun over. His bright blue eyes were sparkling beneath a mop of shock-red hair. Freckles congregated around the bridge of his nose, and when he smiled, dimples punctuated his mouth.

"Would you like a turn?" he asked. "It's really fun."

"What is it?" Lyle asked, examining the chair's construction.

"It's a racing chair, silly," the boy replied. "Haven't you ever seen one before? I've been wanting one for a while, and my parents are trying to get one for me. Wanna try it?"

The tall man with auburn hair strolled over, pushing the boy's empty chair. He smiled pleasantly. "Are you going to take it for a spin?" he asked.

"Well . . ." Lyle hesitated. What good would it do? There was no way he could ever afford something like that even if he did like it. On the other hand, it didn't cost anything to try it out.

"Go ahead, Lyle," Calla urged. "Mr. Duffy is the man I wanted you to meet."

Lyle glanced up at the big man. "Why?" he asked bluntly.

Russell laughed heartily. "Why not? I'm a pretty nice guy."

"Yeah, well, what would you care about me?"

Russell sobered instantly. "I care about all God's children, Lyle. And some need more care than others."

"I'm not one of them," Lyle declared stubbornly. "I get by just fine on my own."

Russell passed over the comment smoothly. "Would you like to try out the chair, Lyle?"

Lyle shrugged. "Sure," he said gruffly. "Why not?"

They helped him into the chair and the little boy, Jared, gave him some pointers. Lyle spun the chair uncertainly around the gym. It moved effortlessly beneath his hands. The floor sped by at an almost alarming rate. After the first rush of fear from the speed subsided, Lyle found himself wanting to go faster. He pushed the wheels harder and harder, glorying in the sense of freedom he felt as the chair glided around the outside edge of the gym. He pulled up in front of the others breathless, his face flushed with joy.

"This is really fun," he said enthusiastically. "I felt like I was flying."

"You were flying," Russell said. "You're very fast, Lyle. You could have a future in racing."

Lyle perked up, he could feel his competitive nature stirring in a way it hadn't since the accident. "Racing? What?"

"Wheelchair racing," Russell explained. "It's quite a sport. Some very fine athletes compete in it, so you'd have to work hard, but I think you have a lot of potential."

"Really?"

Calla stepped up beside him as he ran his hands lovingly over the smooth metal of the chair. "You know, Lyle, I was talking to Mr. Duffy, and he says you can buy these chairs on a payment plan."

Lyle squinted up at her and frowned. "Yeah? That's great, but I don't have a job, so I don't have any means of paying."

"There's nothing to prevent you from getting a job," Calla pointed out. "In fact, I happen to know that my bank is looking for a customer service representative."

"So?" Lyle growled sullenly. "I don't have a car. I don't have any experience. I don't have the kind of clothes I would need for a job like that."

"Sounds to me as if you're focusing on the negatives," Russell observed. "Why don't you think about some positives?"

"Like what?" Lyle challenged.

"You're bright. You're capable. You're inventive."

"And you've got friends," Calla interjected. "I could give you a lift. I have to go right by there every day on my way to school."

"You know, Lyle, you can do anything you really set your mind to," Russell said gently.

Lyle's mind whirled as he ran his hands lovingly over the contours of the sleek chair. "What are you guys going to get out of all this?"

Russell threw his head back and laughed. "Why, Miss Kendall," he joked, "we must look pretty shifty."

Lyle smiled in spite of himself. "I'm sorry. I'm just not used to people being nice to me for no reason."

"Oh, we have a reason," Russell admitted. "We try to do unto others as we would like others to do unto us."

"I get it." Lyle nodded with sudden understanding. "You're nice to me because you're Christians. I used to be a Christian."

"What do you mean you used to be?" Calla asked. "Aren't you anymore?"

Lyle gazed at her thoughtfully for a moment. "Why would a good God allow what happened to me?" he asked. "Look at my legs. I was going to college on a football scholarship. If God was so great, He wouldn't have let this happen to me. And if He did, then I don't want anything to do with Him."

Russell's face clouded with sorrow. "You know, Lyle. This is a sin-filled world. Bad things happen to people. But, it's not because God wants it that way. Right now we're living in a place racked with sin and ruled by Satan, but soon we'll be living in heaven where sin will not exist, ruled by God."

"A lot of bad stuff goes on down here because of sin and its consequences," Calla added earnestly. "God won't always bail us out of it, but He will always be with us when we go through it."

"Well, He must be busy then, because He hasn't been with me since the accident," Lyle said.

"He's there," Russell responded. "Maybe you're not looking in the right place."

Lyle glanced up to see if the big man was joking. Convinced that he was indeed serious, he returned his gaze to the floor. That thought hadn't occurred to him before. Maybe he hadn't been looking in the right place. Maybe he shouldn't focus so much on "why" the accident had happened and instead try to find out how God planned to help him and what he could learn spiritually from it.

"This," Shelan said triumphantly, "is what the Master has been trying to tell you. He has never left your side, Lyle. Never. Listen to what they are saying to you. They speak the truth."

"Oh, please!" snorted Warg. "Your legs are the truth. Your chair is the truth. God doesn't care. He never has, and He never will. If nothing else, you should know that by now."

"God loves you, Lyle. That is what I've been trying to tell you all this time. He's right here, waiting for you. All you need to do is ask for His help. Just look for Him, not in the wreckage of your life, but in the hope for your future. He's there, waiting for you."

"Yeah, maybe," he admitted finally. "Can we go back home now?" he asked Calla. "I'm kinda tired.

She nodded. "Sure, if that's what you want."

He raised his eyes to meet Russell's before they left. "Thank you for what you said. I'll think about it."

Russell smiled jovially. "You do that. And let me know when you want me to deliver that chair. It was nice meeting you, Lyle."

"Yeah, you too," Lyle agreed. He let Calla push him back to the car while his mind spun in swift circles. The past twelve hours seemed like a dream. It made his head hurt to think back on all that had happened in that short time span. One thing he was sure of was that he wouldn't sleep well tonight with all that was going through his head. He'd be up half the night sorting through it.

CHAPTER 15

Shay waited for Nwibe to come to the table at the dining hall where all the staff took their meals. Lately, his arrival had caused butterflies in her stomach. She had become keenly aware of his presence no matter where they were. And it had not gone without some kidding on the part of Akueke.

The woman, who was only in her early forties but was so wrinkled that she seemed to be at least eighty, took an inordinate amount of pleasure in the blossoming romance between Shay and Nwibe, mostly because Nwibe seemed to be oblivious to it.

"He notices everything else," Shay complained to the cook one day. "Why can't he see what's right in front of his nose?"

Akueke cackled. "Make no mistake. He knows what is in your heart. If you doubt me, then ask him outright. I do not believe he will deny it. Go on. Ask him."

And so Shay had determined that she would. After all, she was a grown woman. He was a grown man. They were best friends. Surely two adult best friends could discuss something like love. Even if it was their own.

She jumped slightly when Marcus finally led Nwibe into the

room. She pushed the food on her plate around a little more vigorously and tried not to notice. Out of the corner of her eye, she saw Marcus glance at her a few times in the hope of catching her attention, but he was seated far down the long wooden table. It was clear he had something exciting to relate. Finally the boy cleared his throat, ignored protocol, and called down the table to her.

"Madame Shay? I have finished the book you gave me to read," he announced proudly.

Shay momentarily forgot her uneasiness and looked up with a happy smile on her face. "That's wonderful, Marcus. Didn't I tell you reading was wonderful? How did you like the story?"

"I enjoyed the story very much. As did my father. I have been reading it aloud to him each night," he confided.

"Yes, he is even better company than the radio we keep in our room," Nwibe said, by way of ending the conversation. He smiled a little apologetically for Marcus's wagging tongue.

Toby looked over at Marcus and gave him a rare smile. "It's very good to know how to read, Marcus. You should be very proud of yourself."

"Not going to do him much good out here," Don growled, talking around a mouthful of food. "What good's it going to do him?"

Toby flattened him with a hostile glare. "Listen to yourself. Who's the one who is always ragging about getting native help? Do you expect the natives to become doctors and nurses without first learning how to read and write? Decide which side of the issue you stand on, Doctor, or else just sit down."

Don opened his mouth and closed it without saying anything. He continued to apply himself to his meal, with only a murderous look now and then in Toby's direction.

Shay shifted uncomfortably. Ever since the day Toby had returned, she and Don had been at a standoff. There had been no outright fights, but they weren't friends either. For an instant, when Don first glimpsed Toby when she returned, Shay had thought she'd seen relief in his eyes. He had tenderly bandaged her ribs and her face, the grim set of his jaw announcing that if he could get a hold of the scoundrel who had done this, that guy would be plenty sorry. Jealous twinges assaulted Shay when she considered that Don might actually love Toby.

But as the days had gone on, she became convinced that Toby and Don were just too incompatible. A cauldron of anger seemed to seethe inside each of them, waiting to erupt with the unpredictability of a volcano. Oddly, it didn't relieve her to think that they just weren't meant for each other. Instead, she had other things to occupy her mind.

Like Nwibe, for instance. Over the past few months, she had begun to realize that she was in love with the tall African. And yet, she couldn't bring herself to tell him. And it seemed that he carefully avoided giving her a reason to believe that he felt the same way. Whether it was out of stubbornness or for some other reason, Shay could only guess.

Marcus had subsided into a curious kind of silence as he watched the adults around him interacting. He ate solemnly, his wide eyes missing nothing, probably taking in more of the conversation than they would credit him for. Still, he didn't venture anything further, even when he caught and returned the smile Shay gave him.

Shay felt her chest tighten with emotion as she watched the boy. She'd grown so fond of him in the preceding months she just couldn't imagine how she could ever leave him . . . or his father. A wild plan had been circling through her mind lately. At first she had dismissed it as impossible. But the more she thought about it, the more the idea grew in strength.

Throughout the day, she struggled to find a few minutes to talk with Nwibe alone. Rephrasing each sentence in her mind, she knew exactly what she planned to say. She would begin by delicately relating her feelings for him and waiting for a response. When he affirmed them, she would go on to tell him her plan for them in light of her soon-to-be-ending mission term.

It'll be easy, she reassured herself to calm the butterflies that collided frantically in her stomach. But when she found herself alone with Nwibe at the end of the day, she blurted the whole thing out before she could stop herself. "You know," she said, not looking directly at him and not pausing for a breath, "you've become such a special friend to me, and I really care for you a great deal. Actually, I, well, that is, I've come to love you very much, as my friend and more. And Marcus, well, I love Marcus as if he were my own son.

"But you know I have to leave soon. I don't want to go, and I was thinking, why couldn't I just stay here? I mean, I could. There's nothing to prevent me from staying. I mean, it's not like they're likely to force me to return to the States. And I want to stay. I like my work. And, well, what do you think about getting married?" Shay stopped with a suddenness that made her gasp for air.

During the entire time she had been speaking, Nwibe's face had not so much as twitched. For all the reaction she received, Shay was tempted to think he hadn't heard a word she said. Just before the pause became unbearable, a look of supreme compassion spread across his face.

"My wonderful little friend," he began, and at these words Shay's heart sank into the dust at her feet. "I am honored that you would consider me a suitable marriage partner, but I am afraid that what you are suggesting is impossible."

"Because you don't love me?" Shay asked in a small, miserable voice.

"Oh, my, no!" Nwibe exclaimed. "On the contrary, I have found it impossible not to love you. This is a feeling I am unaccustomed to. With Marcus's mother, Alifa, the match was arranged by our families. It was my duty to love her, and I was sad when she died, but I felt nothing of what I feel for you."

"But," Shay protested. "If you love me, then why can't we be married? Is it Marcus? Are you afraid that he wouldn't accept me as his mother?"

"No," Nwibe shook his head. "I have no fear of that. The boy loves you very much too. He will be quite heartbroken when you leave."

"What then?" Shay demanded in exasperation. "Is it because I'm so young?"

Nwibe cocked his head. "That is part of it. You see, my young friend, you have not lived much in this world. How can you be sure which route is best for you to travel? You came to Africa for an experience. Return to America and finish your education in living. Then, when you are sure, if you still wish to return, you will come back."

"That's not the only reason," Shay objected, biting her lip against the tears that threatened to come. "Is it?"

"No," Nwibe replied honestly. "There is too much difference in our cultures. You could never fully accept our way of life here. Maybe for this one year you have found it a novel experience, but if you had to live like this for the rest of your life, you would become restless and want to leave."

"Then come live with me in Louisiana," Shay challenged. "Marcus could attend school. We could get you a guide dog to help you get around. And you could work at a clinic or hospital there."

Nwibe shook his head gently. "No, I would not be happy in America. This is my home, and this is where I will stay."

"You've got everything all figured out, haven't you?" Shay cried. "I don't know why you're being so stubborn about this when it would make us both happy to be together and we could do so much good for the people around us."

"I am preventing you from making a mistake, my friend," he said softly. "I do not want you to wake up one day in a country that is not your own, with a useless blind man as a husband, responsible for a child you did not bear, trapped in a life that makes you unhappy."

Shay stared at him for a few moments before she summoned the courage to say anything. His doubts worried her. Would that ever happen? She couldn't imagine it. "You're wrong," she said, but her voice lacked conviction. "That would never happen."

He smiled gently. "But you really are not sure."

"I am sure," Shay cried obstinately. "It sounds to me like you're the one who's not sure. You're not sure about me. You probably think an American wife would be too independent or something. And it doesn't sound as though you trust me to know my own mind. Well, if that's the way you want it, then fine."

She turned and fled to the comfort of her room where she threw herself onto her lumpy bed and sobbed as if her heart would break.

The group of demons who had clung to Shay in her wild flight across the courtyard scattered in confusion as a bright light flooded the room at the appearance of Gaius. The angel wrapped the weeping human in his wings, sparks of light jumping like electricity from his form.

One demon, little Festus, who had refused to give up the territory claimed by the demons, hung on tenaciously, even after the arrival of the angel. He realized that a victory now could very well propel him into favor with Lucien, and certainly with Sparn. Now that the cursed old prayer warrior was getting better, their chances for victory looked slim. The demons' only hope lie in making the members at the mission destroy each other and take the mission with them.

"I'm not leaving," Festus screeched. He grabbed hold harder on his prey, causing Shay to cry out in pain.

"Victory is the Lord's," Gaius reminded him. "Loose your hold on her, demon. She is a child of God."

"I won't! I won't!" Festus grabbed her harder and began to pull her toward the group of demons who huddled just out of reach. His flesh crawled where the light from the angel fell on

him, and he whimpered, shrinking from the light as he renewed his determination.

"Oh, Lord," Shay moaned as she thrashed around on the bed. "Help me. I want to do Your will. Help me to accept it."

The instant the words left her lips, a bright light flashed from the angel, blinding the demons present and sending Festus tumbling end over end. He crashed against the opposite wall and sat there dazed for a few moments before trying to rally his friends. "Are we going to take that? Who's with me? They are weak, we are the rulers of earth! Exert your power!"

With shrieks and howls, the band rushed Gaius en masse. The light surrounding the angel became so bright that his outline vanished in it. As if running into a wall of molten lava, the demons scattered with a desperation born of self-preservation.

"This is not over, angel!" Festus screamed as he fled. "There are others here. This one won't even be staying long. You are welcome to her."

Gaius soothed his charge as her tears subsided. "You have a strong will and a strong sense of right and justice. Your persistence and your good work will be rewarded."

Shay felt the tension leave her body. Suddenly, she was sorry about how she had treated Nwibe. "It wasn't right," she whispered against her hand as she wiped the tears from her cheeks. "He's only doing what he feels is best for me. And he's right. I should go back to America. I'll just take up my life where I left off."

Shay rolled over onto her back and stared up at the ceiling. Her heart felt so empty contemplating the thought of returning home. Somehow, it just didn't feel like home anymore. Africa and the mission had captured her heart, and this felt like home. She didn't think she could bear to leave it. A picture of Marcus's sorrowful face came to mind, and her sobbing renewed in earnest.

How could she tell the child she was leaving? What would happen to him after she left? How would Nwibe ever find someone else who would love the two of them the way she did? And why, oh why, did life have to be so hard anyway?

A light, compassionate smile tugged at the lips of the angel. Gaius bent low over Shay, stroking her forehead tenderly with one bronze hand. "My poor child, of suffering you know so little. You are blessed by the Master with health, friends, a ministry, family, so many things that others are denied or lose through sin. I wonder if you have any comprehension of how much the Saviour loves you?"

Gaius kept silent vigil over Shay until she dropped into a fitful sleep. It wasn't until the sun dipped below the horizon that she would wake and go in search of Nwibe to make things right before retiring for the evening.

Lucien paced back and forth anxiously. One eye he kept on the surly demon who brooded like a dark cloud over them all. Sparn had only been back a short time, yet the demons knew enough to avoid him whenever possible. His rage at the failure he had experienced at the bedside of the mighty prayer warrior had left him in the worst mood anyone had yet to see him in.

News of the disaster preceded him. It was said that against the prayers of so many, the demons hadn't even a fighting chance. Of course, some took that for an excuse and didn't hold much hope for Sparn when he met Captain Lucifer in a debriefing meeting later on. The captain wasn't likely to accept excuses, no matter their strength. Rather, if Sparn dared to use them, he was more likely to see it as a sign of weakness.

Lucien himself was barely holding on in the position he'd been given. Now that Sparn was back, he had hoped that some of the burden of leadership would be relieved, but that didn't seem the way things were heading. Instead, Sparn seemed content to attend to his own business and leave the fall of the mission with Lucien. Lucien suspected this was because he was leery of another failure on his record. And sometimes he was sure that their attempt at destroying the mission would indeed fail.

He had succeeded in getting rid of Toby but made the fatal mistake of leaving her in the hands of an incompetent little demon who had botched everything. Now she was back. Things were still tense between her and Don, but even Lucien could sense the attraction between the two of them. In fact, they seemed more oblivious to it than he did, but he didn't count on that to last long unless he could keep up the hostility between the two of them, and that job was getting harder and harder as the days passed.

Today's little victory with Shay was worth a short celebration. He was positive that she would return to the States now. She wouldn't like it, but she'd go. Even if she changed her mind later, as he was afraid she would, because she truly did love Nwibe and Marcus, it would be too late to save the mission by the time she returned. Once she left, they would again be short-staffed. Considering that the two remaining staff members hated each other and had particularly volatile tempers, it didn't take a genius to see that the mission was on a direct course to destruction.

Of course, as Lucien had learned, nothing was certain until

it was accomplished. Now that the prayer warrior was regaining her health, she was bound to start praying for the mission again. So far, she seemed to be the only person who even remembered it existed. Still, she constituted the most persistent threat. It was a direct result of her petitioning that Shay had been encouraged by heavenly agents to join the mission for a term. Who knew who else the miserable old warrior would influence through her prayers next. Certainly, their plans would be greatly hindered by the arrival of more help.

The destruction of the mission could not be counted on through lack of funds alone, although they certainly had an entire task force to increase greed and selfishness in order to prevent the sharing of funds that would provide a life-sustaining supply of food, medicines, and equipment that would make the mission a truly strong and spiritually threatening place. With the institution of materialism, the task force had been singularly successful, and funds at Operation C.A.R.E. were tight at best. Still, they couldn't seem to make any headway with the faithful ones who provided the life-sustaining flow of funds to keep the mission alive.

No, they couldn't count on lack of funds alone. They had to destroy the mission from the inside. Then, hopefully, it couldn't rise again once it had fallen. That Toby had returned was a sad fact Lucien had come to accept. He hadn't been successful in getting rid of her, but he believed he could still use her to take Don Germaine down. In that way, while still irksome, she would remain useful. Once Don was gone, the mission would lack leadership. That would mark the beginning of the end.

Lucien ran his gnarled hand over his face. He felt so tired of all this thinking. The burden of responsibility lay heavy on his shoulders. "You there," he barked to a demon skulking in the periphery of his vision. Little Festus slunk over in obedience, and Lucien's anger burned at the sight of him. "What are you doing here? I thought I told you to get lost?"

Festus shifted uncomfortably. "I have been making myself useful," he bragged. "Just this morning I came quite close to convincing the young one to leave."

Lucien snorted in derision. "She is going to leave. I have seen to that. Now stay away from my work. Instead, I have another job for you."

Festus didn't look pleased at this news, but Lucien ignored him. After all, he wasn't exactly happy about his own increased responsibility. "Keep an eye on the man, Nwibe. Make certain that he does not relent from his position. It should be easy enough, even for you. He is quite sure that the young one will not leave. And I am just as sure that she will. I will see to it personally. And keep the boy from making too much noise about it. I don't want him encouraging his father to waver from his position. Do you understand?"

Festus looked relieved. "Your wish is my command," he assured his leader.

Lucien's eyes narrowed dangerously. "Yes, well, see to it that it is. I can't afford any failures in this assignment. Get some of the other more experienced demons to help you out. You may need the assistance."

"Certainly," Festus agreed, though the distant look behind his eyes made Lucien wonder if the little monster would actually do it. He was half convinced that he should see to it himself. But when he considered the mountain of work before him, he resigned himself to delegation. After all, it appeared that he was in charge. He had to rely on the others at some point.

"I do not want to hear of any failure," he warned Festus. "Or I promise that you'll regret it."

The little demon didn't reply but slunk warily away, leaving Lucien to continue plotting while Sparn brooded.

He came in the door while Toby was busy mixing up a solution to feed to one of the patients who was on a nasogastric tube. He didn't appear to be in any immediate distress, so she didn't pay him any particular attention until she was startled out of her concentration by an exclamation of surprise and greeting from Shay.

"Well, hello there! How is Madina?" The young nurse took the arm of the man and led him toward Nwibe. Toby kept one eye on the little drama as she did her work.

Nwibe repeated the question, and the man set off on a long story that caused Nwibe to become very agitated. As she watched him, Shay became anxious and tugged on his arm. "What's he saying?" she demanded. "Is there something wrong with Madina?"

Nwibe held up a hand to silence her as he continued to listen to the man's story. The native was in no hurry and talked as if he had all afternoon and would in fact enjoy the conversation. Finally, Nwibe cut him off to relate to Shay what he had been saying.

"His wife, the young girl, Madina, is again with child. Only this time, I am afraid she is not yet to her term, but she is having trouble delivering the child. She has been in labor for one night and one day when he came in search of us."

Toby watched Shay do the calculations on her fingers. "But,

that's at least two days," she exclaimed in dismay.

"Yes," Nwibe agreed. "He is certain it must already be too late, but he wanted to try to save her."

Toby thought the man looked awfully cheerful for someone who was about to lose his wife. He waited impatiently while the two continued their conversation. It was clear he wanted to finish the story he had started.

"He left her?" Shay wailed. "How on earth can we treat her if he left her? We've got no good way of getting there. Even the jeep is broken. What are we going to do?"

"Do?" Don interrupted them as he came in and heard the last part of the story. "There's nothing we can do. We don't have wings. We can't fly there."

Toby's heart skipped a beat. "But, we do," she said quietly. All eyes turned on her, and she felt her face get a little red. "I couldn't help but notice that you have an ultralight. I thought it was a little odd. I take it you've never used it?"

"Sure, we use it. Akueke dries the wash on it," Don quipped sarcastically. "What else is it good for?"

"I'm sorry. I was under the impression that ultralights were built to fly from one place to another," Toby shot back. "In this case, someone flying in an ultralight would reach a struggling, pregnant woman very quickly and possibly prevent her untimely death."

Don scrutinized Toby's face. "Let's just say that you're right. We would still need someone who can fly the thing."

"And I just happen to be a pilot," Toby retorted. "Isn't that a coincidence."

"You mean you could fly Don out there to save Madina?" Shay gasped, crossing the room with a leap and attaching herself to Toby's arm.

Toby attempted to shrug her off. "I could, if I had a mind to." She glared at Don. "Or if I was asked nice enough."

"I'm asking," Shay agreed. "I'm begging, if I have to. Please will you help Madina?"

Toby softened a little at the urgency on the young nurse's face. In the amount of time she'd worked with her, she knew that Shay put up with a lot and asked for little. "I'll tell you what, kid," she said. "If you get that stone-hearted doctor to go, I'll fly him."

Don threw up his hands in defeat. "You've got no argument here. Let's go."

Nwibe quickly got directions from Madina's husband, who parted with them under protest. Disgruntled about not getting to complete his story, he assured them that they would be too late but thanked them for trying anyway.

For one instant, as Toby familiarized herself with the controls of the ultralight, panic froze her. "I can't," her mind shrieked as her head filled with visions of Davy and their plane tumbling out of the sky like a dying bird.

"That's right," Lucien echoed fiercely. "You can't. And you don't need to. Why risk your life for some woman you don't even know? What is she to you?"

"Love thy neighbor as thyself," Lileah quoted urgently. "You can do this, Toby. This is the right thing. Do not be afraid. Perfect love casts out all fear. He will be with you."

"Shut up!" screeched Lucien. "You can't win this. Don't you see? She's ours. She doesn't care about these people or their pathetic existence. All she cares about is saving her own miserable hide."

Toby's hand hesitated on the ignition key, the struggle for her will as tangible on the inside of her as on the outside. She felt as though she were being rent in two.

"You see?" hissed Lucien smugly, noting Toby's hesitation. "I told you. This one cares nothing for your self-righteous, pious, goody-two-shoes theology. She'll do anything to save her own skin."

Don cleared his throat impatiently. "Well? Can you fly this

bucket or not? I don't know what possessed that old coot to give it to us in the first place. Medicines, bandages, diagnostic equipment, yes, but this worthless contraption? I'm not even sure it can fly even if you did know what to do with it. Let's just forget the whole thing."

Lucien's eyes gleamed. He barely noticed the humbly bowed head beside him as Lileah prayed fervently. Victory was in his grasp. He chuckled, an evil, hair-raising sound that made Lileah jump as if he had laid a cold hand palm down on her back. This would mean that promotion. He knew it.

"Forget it. Go back home to the States and leave the do-gooders sticking their own necks out," he hissed impatiently. Toby was taking much too long to make up her mind.

A cold sweat broke out on the back of Toby's neck. As though she was in the same room with her, she could hear the pregnant woman's screams of pain, see the filth of the place, smell the hopelessness. Hopeless unless they arrived quickly.

"Losing your nerve, Doctor?" Toby asked calmly, her decision finally made. She turned the ignition key, and the engine sputtered to life.

"It works!" Don exclaimed, then repeated in awe. "It really works."

"Well, we won't be able to say that with certainty until we're actually in the air," Toby replied casually as she nudged the rickety plane down the bumpy lane that would serve as a runway strip. "Cross your fingers, Doc."

Don's hands crept down to grasp the edge of his seat, knuckles white. His eyes flickered nervously from the makeshift runway ahead to the grim line of determination of Toby's jaw. It appeared she planned to get the ultralight into the sky if it meant she had to get out and push it there herself. The plane wobbled and bounced off every little dirt bump in its path. There seemed to be invisible cords tying it to the earth. Don glanced around. Nothing to throw overboard.

"We're never going to make it," he shouted above the shrill roar of the little engine.

Toby gripped the stick so tight that the muscles in her arms stood out in sharply defined cords. Slowly, slowly, one wheel after the other tentatively lifted off the ground. The jarring stopped as the last connection to earth was severed and the little plane, which seemed like a skeleton with the wings of a butterfly, pulled free and bounded up into the sky.

"You were saying, Doctor?" Toby yelled over the hum of the engine and the rush of the wind, a note of triumph in her voice.

Don grinned, too happy to actually be in the air to mind the smug look on Toby's face. The plane tipped neatly to one side and banked away from Niamey.

CHAPTER

16

Marc pulled in the Duffy's driveway and stopped the car, turning off the engine. He made no move to open the door. Cindi retained her seat with equal reluctance to get out. Her eyes were wide and her face pale in the moonlight.

"What if they say No?" Cindi whispered. "I just know I'll start crying."

Marc found her hand in the darkness and squeezed it reassuringly. "Would they have called us here in person if they were going to say No? Why not just call and save everyone a lot of pain and embarrassment?"

Cindi's head jerked in a stiff nod. "You're right," she said, her voice lacking any kind of conviction. "Come on. Let's go inside before they start to wonder what on earth we're doing out here."

They made their way up the driveway until they found the path Russell had shoveled up the walkway to the front door. It was opened before they even reached it, spilling warm, friendly light out onto the sparkling snow.

"Cindi! Marc! Come in, come in," Russell said, smiling broadly. "We've been mulling some cider. Ray, would you get Cindi and Marc mugs of cider? They look like they need something to take the chill off."

Cindi felt detached from her body as she was hustled into the warm living room. In a blur, someone took her coat and handed her a warm mug of cider. She took a tentative sip, enjoying the heat of the liquid as it went down her throat, sending little fingers of warmth threading through her body, which was cold, not from the weather, but from emotion.

Julia was seated on the couch, a book she'd been reading about pregnancy and babies propped up on her stomach as if it were a convenient table made specifically for that purpose. She looked up, her face unreadable, a slight smile on her lips. Cindi shuffled mechanically across the room and sat down next to her.

Julia reached out and took her hand. "Want to feel the baby kicking? He's really going at it." She guided Cindi's hand to a spot on her abdomen where a little foot kicked vigorously. Their eyes met. "Did you feel it?" Julia asked excitedly.

Cindi couldn't stifle a wide smile. "Yes! Yes! Wow, that's really strong! Marc, feel this."

She grabbed his hand in turn and pressed it to Julia's side. He stood a little embarrassed, waiting, but when the feisty little kick tapped his hand, he grinned. "That kid's going to be a football player," he agreed. They continued to feel the baby kick until it stopped suddenly. Silence stretched out awkwardly.

"So," Marc said, struggling to make conversation. "Have you decided on any names?"

"We thought that we'd leave that to the people who will be raising the baby. We think they'd rather choose their own names," Ray replied.

"Yeah," Julia said, turning to them. "So, have you given it any thought?"

Stunned, Cindi couldn't reply. Her eyes flitted from Julia to Ray to Russell and finally rested on Marc, begging him silently to tell her that she wasn't dreaming, that she hadn't heard wrong. His face reflected the shock expressed on hers, and she could get no reassurance from him.

"Do you mean that you're going to allow us to adopt the baby?" she finally asked in a voice that sounded nothing like her own.

Julia nodded. "Yes, we'd like that very much. We know that you and Marc would raise the baby well and provide him with a loving home. He wouldn't want for anything." Ray stepped close to Julia and took her hand.

"We're not sorry about this baby," Julia continued. "We're just sorry for the circumstances. And we can't provide for him, but you can." She clasped Ray's hand tighter and looked up at him before going on. He gave a curt little nod to encourage her. "So, will you accept our baby?"

If there were any words in Cindi's heart, they never made it out her mouth. With a joyful cry, she threw her arms around Julia, sobbing happily. Julia rocked her as if she were a small child, stroking her hair and patting her back. She looked over Cindi's shoulder at Marc, who was weeping too. "I guess this means Yes?"

"Yes," Cindi choked out, pulling away from Julia enough to see her face. "Oh, yes! Thank you so much. You have no idea what this means to us."

Julia's eyes sparkled with tears. "Oh, I think I do."

The joy that filled the little house was only partly observed by the humans occupying it. The angels sharing their space sent out a light so bright it surrounded the house and sent a beam in all directions. The sound of angels singing praises was so loud it nearly rivaled that heard in heaven.

Reissa looked around the living room, closely observing each occupant. Here were five people determined to do what was best for one small unborn child, despite their own personal interests. How happy that made the Master.

Reissa knew that she was again witnessing how the Master, in His supreme love, touched the hearts and lives of the human race, working for the good of His servants and making even the most poisonous darts of the enemy ineffective. It pained her to see how they railed against Him, sometimes working against Him out of selfishness, bullying circumstances to their will and ending up unhappy and alone.

But, every now and then Reissa came across one who was willing to trust the Master ultimately. She had one time asked Him why He allowed trials to come even to these, the most faithful and obedient, when with one word He could protect them from the wiles of the enemy. Just a single word from Him would place a hedge about them that could never be penetrated.

"But, Reissa, would it prove that it is possible to live a life free from sin through My power if they were protected from the sin?" He had asked her. "These, My disciples, prove to the entire universe that I am a God of truth. That those who want to live apart from sin can do it with My help, even in the midst of the enemy's territory. I will not coerce them into doing My will, and I will not separate them from the evil one yet, but if they abide in Me, he will have no real power over them."

Reissa recognized in His words the supreme honesty of God, the clear truth of His character. It would have been so easy to create Adam and Eve without choice or to wipe mankind out following their sin in the garden, but He hadn't done it. And He had paid the price for all of them. Reissa shuddered at the thought of that price, remembering the anguish on the face of the Father as His Son hung from the cruel tree.

Sometimes it seemed to her that she was more keenly aware of the sacrifice, she who had no need of it, than were the humans for whom the sacrifice had been made and who depended on it to spend an eternity with the Master.

"Why so thoughtful?" Shania asked as her lovely face shone with brilliance. "Today is a day for celebrating. You have waited long to observe the fulfillment of the Master's plan for your charge. Shouldn't you be celebrating with us?"

Reissa smiled. "I am celebrating in my heart most of all," she assured the angel. *"The Master is so kind and so good. I won-der, do they realize how much He loves them?"*

Cindi woke the next day with a sense that she hadn't really slept at all the night before. Coursing through her mind were thoughts of babies and plans. There were so many things she had to get—bottles, diapers, a car seat. The list seemed end-less.

She carried a small notebook with her to Ethel's house so she could write down items as they came to her. Of course, her par-ents and Marc's would send some of the bigger items; they were so thrilled about their first grandchild. Cindi wasn't sure if the change she sensed in Ethel's house was due more to the fact that Ethel was getting well or just that it seemed different in her eyes this morning.

The sun's strength melted the icicles collecting on the eaves and caused Ethel to ask to have the shade drawn partially. "I just love to see the sunshine," she apologized, "but it hurts my eyes."

"It's no problem," Cindi assured her, drawing the shade down to her satisfaction.

"You are positively glowing this morning, child," Ethel ob-served, her sparrowlike hands fluttering over the comforter covering her. "You set yourself right down here and tell me what it is that has you so excited."

Cindi settled down with a flush beside Ethel. "I wasn't going to tell you until later. I didn't want to bother you . . ."

"Nonsense," Ethel interrupted. "Nothing that makes you this happy could possibly be a bother."

Cindi smiled. "Do you remember Mr. Duffy, who was having trouble with his daughter Julia?" At Ethel's nod of remembrance, she went on. "Well, Julia is pregnant. She's due in just a few months, in fact. She and her boyfriend, Ray, well, they've be-come Christians, and they told us last night that they want to become nurses and go to Africa as missionaries."

"They're going to help Donny!" Ethel broke in, grinning happily.

Cindi nodded. "Yes, I told them about Operation C.A.R.E., and they are determined to go there just as soon as they graduate and are married. Don could really use the help too. From what I understand, the staff there is not very permanent."

Ethel clasped her hands tightly and raised her eyes toward heaven. "Thank You, Lord, for hearing our prayer." She smiled at Cindi. "I have been praying very hard for your brother's mission. And I keep feeling as though I should be praying even harder. I really think the old devil has taken a stronghold in that place. This certainly is happy news." Ethel leveled a scrutinizing gaze on Cindi. "But it's not the reason for that glow surrounding you. What else has happened?"

Cindi couldn't stop the tears which sprang into her eyes. "Julia and Ray don't feel that they should be raising their baby. They can't give him a good home right now, and they've asked Marc and I to adopt him."

Ethel's hands, which had not come to rest since the beginning of her story, flew immediately to Cindi's and gave them a squeeze. "Oh, my! Praise the Lord and congratulations! Isn't He wonderful?"

Cindi nodded, a sob escaping her lips despite her best efforts to squelch it. "It's the most wonderful thing that's ever happened to me," she said. "But I've got so much planning to do. Now I know why God gives mothers nine months to prepare. Just two isn't nearly enough!"

Ethel squeezed her hand gently. "And I insist you take some time off."

Cindi shook her head stubbornly. "I wouldn't dream of it. I'll manage. Besides, how would you get along without me?" She sighed sadly. "But I guess I will have to think about training someone to replace me before the baby comes, won't I? It's sad, how parts of our lives end when others begin. I always thought I'd never have another sad moment if God would only give me a baby. But I will miss you very much."

"Posh," Ethel teased. "I expect you to bring that baby to see me all the time. It's been years since I had the pleasure of watching a baby grow. And you know," she continued thoughtfully, "you could still help me out with the prayer requests."

All the angels in the room pressed forward to hear Cindi's reply. Did she recognize the opportunity she was being presented with? She had been working with Ethel for several years now and knew the need for sustained, urgent prayer. Would she accept the torch?

Cindi cocked her head as a thought struck her. "You know, you're right. I could. And I was thinking, I'm likely to encounter many other women in my new role as a mother. We'll probably all have similar needs, and I thought I'd like to start a play group. But, what do you think of a play/prayer group? We could hold it right here in your house! You have so much room, and it's a lovely place to gather. On nice days, we could bring the children outside to play."

Cindi stopped short and blushed slightly. "Well, that was my idea, anyway. Marc always says I should think before I go shooting off at the mouth."

Ethel chuckled. "I wouldn't say that. I've always found your ideas fresh and innovative. This one is the best I've heard yet."

"You think so?" Cindi exclaimed with pleasure.

Ethel nodded. "Yes, I do. I think it's a wonderful idea. You have not only my permission and my full cooperation in any way, but also my blessing."

Cindi gave the frail woman a gentle hug. "Thank you. It's been such a pleasure working for you, not like work at all."

"Thank you, my dear. You've been a big help to me also. I appreciate how you kept the prayer chain going when I was ill." Her eyes grew distant as if watching a scene play out in front of her. "When I was sick, I thought about giving up the will to live. I really felt that I had fought a good fight and run my course, and it was time to rest from my labors.

"But one night while I was sleeping, a shining figure appeared before me. He shone so brightly that I couldn't make out his face. And he said to me, 'Ethel, the Master has more work for you. Your race is not yet completed. Go on in the strength of the Master.' And then I slept so soundly I knew nothing until morning."

Cindi's eyes widened. "The night you were anointed," she whispered in awe.

"I was?" Ethel seemed surprised at this news. Then she chuckled slightly. "My, but you must have really thought the old lady was on the way out."

"Well, you *were* sick," Cindi pointed out. "We're very fortunate that you were spared for a time. I don't know what I'd do without you."

Ethel smiled. "Nor I you, deary."

Shelan fluttered around the room trying to keep pace with Lyle, who was in a state of panic. Berniece and Calla would be arriving at any moment, and his fingers were tangled up hopelessly with his tie. Tears in his eyes, he squeezed them shut.

Warg chortled from his corner of the room where he watched the proceedings, so haughty, so sure of himself, that he oozed confidence from every pore. "What are you wasting your time on him for?" he needled the angel. "You know it'll never work out. He's not fit for association with other humans. He's been out of commission for so long he doesn't even know how to relate anymore."

Shelan laid one strong hand on Lyle's head, applying a soothing touch. "Lyle, take it easy. Peace, be still."

Lyle bowed his head beneath the angel's touch. His shoulders heaved from frustration, his breathing labored. Slowly he gained control of himself again. He took one long shuddering breath and let it out with forced determination.

Shelan allowed herself one pleased smile. "The Master will help you, Lyle, if you will just ask."

"Ha!" Warg spit the word out as he clutched his sides. "You have really lost it! Do you have any idea what you just said? As if he's going to pray. That's a good one."

Lyle bowed his head, unaware of the silence that suddenly permeated the room around him. Although he felt a strong urge to pray, it had been a long time, and he didn't know how to approach it. He began awkwardly, "Dear Lord, I know You're there, but I don't know what You can do to help me. All I know is, I need help. This is my first day of work, and I'm so nervous I don't even know if I can make it out the door. I suppose all I've got to do is ask for help, so I'm asking. Thanks a lot."

He took a steadying breath, opened his eyes, and looked around. Nothing seemed particularly different, and for a second, his shoulders drooped with defeat. And then he realized that he felt *calm*. Slowly a smile lifted the corners of his lips. He unknotted the ends of the tie and decided to let Calla mess with it. She could probably do a better job anyway.

"You sneaky, conniving little . . ." Warg shrieked as he fled out the open window. "You haven't seen the last of me. I'll be back. I don't know what you've done to him, but it won't last long, take my word for it!"

If Shelan heard the demon, she showed no sign of it. She stuck close to Lyle as he made his way down the stairs to the kitchen below where he would wait for Calla and her aunt. No doubt Warg would try harder from now on. He had made a fatal mistake thinking it was all over, taking his victory for granted while Shelan worked quietly and steadily on. Yes, he would try again, and he would probably come back in stronger force next time. She would have to be on her guard.

Mrs. Ryan blinked at Lyle, reminding him of a confused owl. A flash of uncertainty stabbed him. Maybe this wasn't such a good idea. His mother wouldn't be able to get along all day without him. Just then, he heard Calla's cheerful toot as she pulled up in the driveway.

She peered in through the screen door before pushing it open and inviting herself in. "Hey, there, Lyle! Wow, you look great! Hello, Mrs. Ryan." She turned toward her Aunt Berniece, who had followed her. "Mrs. Ryan, this is my Aunt Berniece; she'll be checking on you today to make sure you're all right."

Mrs. Ryan smiled. "Why, that's very nice of you, I'm sure. But I can manage fine. Just fine. Besides, Lyle will be here."

"Mom," Lyle sighed deeply. "I've got a job. Remember, I told you? I'm working at the bank now. You be sure to let Mrs. Kendall know if you need anything. She's promised to come check in on you every now and then to be sure you're all right."

Lyle's eyes met Berniece's. For one instant, he felt as if he could read her thoughts. The glance she gave him was full of compassion. Compassion, he told himself firmly, not pity. To him, it was an important distinction. He thought he could detect admiration in her eyes as well. Was she impressed that he had turned his life around? That he had secured a good job? Or just that he had begun to live again? He couldn't be sure.

He wanted to say Thank you. For not kicking him out that first time. For sharing her niece with him. For agreeing to watch his mother, as if it was the most natural thing in the world. For being friendly. For so many things.

But he didn't.

Instead, he offered her a shy smile. Now when he saw her, he didn't think immediately of her husband, Peter, who was responsible for his accident. The first thing that came to mind was how comforting she was, how reassuring. But, at times, he thought he saw pain hiding in her eyes, too, and wondered if she were remembering Peter when she looked at him.

He never asked, but the question was always there. It dawned on him that she had lost more than he had. He was still here, and his life was rocketing off on a grand, unexpected adventure. Peter was gone, and nothing could bring him back. Yes, she had lost more.

"Are you ready?" Calla asked him, checking her watch. "We're going to be late."

Lyle nodded curtly, not trusting his voice.

"Let's get a move on, then." Calla grabbed the handlebars of his wheelchair and forced him into a wheelie as she headed him out the door. "Yahoo!" she shrieked, getting him to laugh in spite of himself.

"You're crazy!" he shouted at her.

"I know, ain't it grand?" she hooted, racing him around the lawn, through the snow once, before heading for the car. She stopped, slightly out of breath. "That settles it. You're going to have to keep up with me yourself, lazybones. I can't wait until you get your first paycheck, and we can start making payments on that new chair."

"We?" Lyle picked up the stray word as if it was the only one she'd uttered.

"Well, no," Calla frowned. "I'm sorry, I didn't mean we, exactly, since I don't have a job. I wish I could help you out though," she added cheerfully. "Tell you what I'll do though. I'll use my superior bargaining skills to get you that chair just as cheap as possible. So, when's the race?"

"What race?" Lyle struggled to get into the car but finally had to accept Calla's help.

"The race around the track when I beat your pants off," she said sweetly, straightening him in the seat and buckling him in.

"Oh, that race," Lyle replied with a glib shake of his head. "That race has been postponed until we run the race where *I* beat *your* pants off."

"You're on, buster," Calla squealed. She bent low over him, fixing his tie as if it were the most natural thing in the world. Lyle closed his eyes and inhaled. A warm, clean, citrusy scent billowed around him from her hair. She finished with a flourish and paused a minute to smile at him, her face only inches from his. "What do you think of that?"

"Thanks," Lyle mumbled. "I couldn't manage to do it without leaving several fingers in the knot."

Calla hopped in the driver's seat, and they backed out of the driveway, waving to Mrs. Ryan and Aunt Berniece. She watched him out of the corner of her eye as they drove into town. "Nervous?"

Lyle nodded stiffly. "Yeah, a little. What if I screw up?"

"You won't," she assured him with a confidence he didn't share.

"That's easy for you to say," he muttered.

"Sure is," she laughed. He laughed with her. It was a new sensation to laugh or hear laughter and not wonder if it was directed at him. It felt good.

She dropped him off at the bank but didn't leave him to fend for himself. "I want to pray with you before I leave," she said.

"Right here?" he asked, bewildered and a little embarrassed.

"Sure, what's wrong with right here?" She bowed her head, her golden hair covering her face like the wings of the cherubim shielding the ark of the covenant. "Lord, we thank You for answering our prayers and leading us to this job for Lyle. We ask You to help him today as he tries to learn it. We also ask that You be with his mom as she copes without him. In Jesus' name we ask it, amen."

"Amen," Lyle echoed, wondering if his face was as red as he

imagined it to be.

"Have a good day," Calla said, bending to give him a light kiss on the cheek. He sat stunned as he watched her hop into her beat-up little car and drive away, honking. His fingertips flew to his cheek. Why had she done that?

And for the first time since they had become friends, he wondered about Brick Brody.

Billie Jo waited impatiently, her nose pressed up to the glass like an excited child. Helen was late, and she was famished to see her children. The ache that began in the pit of her stomach had sent tendrils into all parts of her body, making it seem as though her whole being throbbed with loneliness and anxiety. When finally the twin headlights poked wearily through the accumulating dusk, Billie Jo didn't wait for the car to come to a stop. Throwing open the front door, she bounded out into the snow, coatless, hatless, and barefoot.

Cassidy was out of the car first, and Billie Jo scooped her up with a delighted squeal. "Oh, pumpkin! I missed you!" She buried her face in Cassidy's hair and tried to keep back the tears. Over Cass's shoulder she could see Dallas straining to get out of his car seat, impatient with his grandmother because she moved too slow to suit him. Helen, when she turned around, had deep black circles of fatigue ringing both eyes. Her face seemed much older than Billie Jo remembered, or maybe it was just that she hadn't really looked at Helen for a long time.

Dallas raced over to be held, his arms poking out of his snowsuit and the bulky fabric affecting his gait. "Doesn't he look just like a penguin, Momma?" Cassidy giggled.

"He looks good enough to eat," Billie Jo exclaimed, scooping him up in her arms and showering his face with kisses. Dallas yelped indignantly and tried unsuccessfully to fend her off. Absorbed in the children, Billie Jo missed the look of annoyance on the face of her mother-in-law.

"Well, you are a sight," Helen remarked dryly. "Are you trying to catch your death of cold? A novel approach to suicide, I must say." It was then she caught sight of the open door. "Don't tell me you've left the door wide open to blow cold air on my Jimmy!" she exclaimed in horror.

In a bound, she crossed the space and slammed the door shut. "If you've given him a cold by your carelessness, you'll pay for it," she said, her voice rising in shrillness with every syllable. "I don't know why I trust you to take care of him. You've already proven you're not a fit mother. Now, with even that burden taken from you, you can't cope with taking care of Jimmy. Well, that is simply the last straw. I'm getting tired of traipsing back and forth anyway. I'm bringing Jimmy home with me. You will have him ready to travel by ambulance on Monday morning."

Billie Jo stood by the side of the driveway, snow swirling around her feet, but oblivious to the cold. The only thing she was aware of, besides the children in her arms, was the feeling of rage and anger that welled up inside her.

"This will get you nowhere," Jewel warned. "A soft answer turns away wrath. Careful now." He eyed the flock of demons surrounding Helen warily. They had grown in number and arrogance since he had seen them last. No doubt they were responsible for this new turn of events. They howled and nudged in closer to Helen until they seemed to be propping her up, a puppet to carry out their will. Jewel could smell the peculiar

*odor of fear, anger, and frustration they evoked in Helen. She
seemed totally powerless to separate herself from them, as if
she'd long ago lost the will to be free.*

Billie Jo forced her voice to sound calm. It wouldn't do any
good to start ranting and raving like a lunatic. "No," she said
firmly, quietly. "I won't do it."

Helen's eyes narrowed like a hawk who has spotted a rabbit.
"Maybe you'd rather I contact Social Services and tell them what
a 'good' mother you are? I'm sure they'd be very interested to
know how you let your children play with knives and run
roughshod through your house while you sleep the day away.
Oh, there are lots of things I'd like to say to them." She straightened up with an air of finality. "Of course, you're welcome to
come stay with us, too, but," she shrugged apologetically, "we
simply haven't enough room for all of you. At least, now you'll
only have yourself to look after. Let's hope you can manage *that*."

Billie Jo's mind whirled desperately. There had to be something she could do, some recourse she had. Could this woman,
with one swift stroke, destroy her life? She did not have the
right, but did she really have the means of taking away Billie Jo's
family? One thing she was positive of was that she was no match
against Helen and Social Services. Her mother-in-law was not
above twisting the truth to get what she wanted. She would make
a hundred innocent acts into a criminal indictment.

No, there just had to be some other way to get around this.
Billie Jo's grip tightened on the children as Helen looked hastily
at her watch.

"Well, I don't have time to lollygag around here," she announced. "I've got to get home and make supper for your grandpa.
Let's go. Back into the car, children. You'll see your mommy
again tomorrow."

Cassidy beseeched Billie Jo with her eyes as Helen pulled her
away. Dallas burst into tears, reaching out his little arms toward
her. "Don't worry, bunnies," Billie Jo said with forced cheerful-

ness. "I'll see you tomorrow, and you'll be coming home real soon. You'll see."

"Don't put crazy ideas into their heads," Helen hissed. "You'll only hurt them more later on when it doesn't happen."

But it will happen, Billie Jo said to herself as she watched Helen spin out of the driveway. The last thing she saw was the frantically waving arms of her children. Suddenly she became aware of the fact that she was standing in the snow with bare feet that ached with the cold.

She hobbled inside and collapsed by the side of Jimmy's bed, sobbing. "Jimmy, Jimmy, wake up!" she cried. "I need you. Our kids need you. You've got to be the head of this house again before it's gone."

One of the demons who had come with Helen, stayed behind. He entered the house and assessed the situation. Jewel watched him closely. Slinking around the perimeter of the room, the little demon seemed to be checking out the architecture of the house, but Jewel wasn't fooled by appearances. He moved closer to Billie Jo, and the demon skittered away from them, proving to Jewel that he was as aware of the angel as Jewel was of him.

Finally he settled himself down in a corner and appeared to doze off. Jewel eyed him warily. It could be a ploy, or perhaps he had been assigned to Billie Jo for the weekend, hoping that he could persuade her that prayer was futile and to just accept her situation without fighting it. Whatever it was, he wasn't announcing his mission up front, which meant that he was definitely one to watch. The subtle types were always the most dangerous.

Jewel turned his attention on Billie Jo. She would never make it through the following ordeal without help, strong, spiritual help. She needed a friend. She needed lots of friends. Mostly, she needed the strength of her Best Friend.

"Pray," he urged her. "Pray like you never have before. The Master will answer you. Everything that concerns you, con-

*cerns Him too. He cares for you more than you will ever know."
After a few moments, Billie Jo's sobs subsided, and her lips
began to move. Assured that she was indeed in conversation
with the Master, Jewel hastily winged away, knowing she'd be
safe from provocation from the demon while she prayed.*

*His first stop was Leah's house. He told her that Billie Jo
needed her and didn't leave until she'd gone to the phone with
"the oddest feeling to call Billie Jo." Next, he stopped at Cindi's
house and told her the same thing. Although she was in the
middle of making nightgowns for the baby, she dropped what
she was doing at the first hint of his suggestion and told Marc
that she was going to visit a friend and would be right back.
Later, he knew, she would call Ethel and have Billie Jo put on
the prayer chain.*

*Convinced that he'd done all he could for the moment, Jewel
returned to Billie Jo's house seconds after he'd left. As he settled
down softly beside her, the phone rang. Billie Jo looked up and
hesitated. "Answer it," Jewel said. "You will find some much
needed help on the other end."*

Billie Jo pushed herself up off her knees and went slowly to
the phone. "Hello?" she asked hesitantly, not sure she wanted
to know who was calling.

"Billie Jo? Hey, it's me, Leah. I had the funniest feeling to call
you, and I just couldn't shake it. Something going on? You sound
kinda funny."

Billie Jo's voice caught in her throat. "Le . . . ah," she choked
out. "Something awful . . ."

"You hang tight, Billie. I'll be right there."

Leah and Cindi arrived one behind the other and saved Billie
Jo the necessity of two explanations. Surrounded by their loving
arms, she managed at last to choke out the whole story. "What
am I going to do?" she wailed as she concluded her story. "Can
she do this to me legally? Can she really take away my family?"

Cindi shrugged. "Who knows what character assassinations

she'd be able to support in court or anywhere else, for that matter. From what you've said, she sounds like a ruthless woman who will stop at nothing to get what she wants."

"Then it's hopeless," Billie Jo moaned, clutching her head and rocking back and forth.

"No, no, it's never hopeless," Cindi insisted.

"That's right," Leah agreed. "You're not just going to roll over and play dead, are you? 'Course not. You're gonna fight this, and we're gonna help you. Ain't that right, Cindi?"

Although Leah and Cindi had introduced themselves at the door, they acted like a well-practiced drill team. Billie Jo looked up, a flicker of hope in her eyes. "What do you mean? Fight how?"

"Well, the first line of defense is always prayer," Cindi said firmly.

Leah nodded her head sagely. "Amen."

"If you'll show me to the phone, I'll call Ethel and put you on the prayer chain. After that, we'll all pray together." Billie Jo wordlessly pointed Cindi to the phone and sat staring ahead of her through watery eyes while Cindi placed the call.

Leah rubbed Billie Jo's shoulder. "Don't worry, Billie Jo. God will help you."

Billie Jo nodded without conviction. "Yeah. I know."

Leah detected the lack of confidence and pushed Billie Jo away at an arm's length. "Now, look here," she admonished sharply. "I can understand why you're feeling sorry fer yourself. You're goin' through a mighty awful thing. But, if you expect to go marching up ta the throne of grace asking fer something, you'd better be backing it with some faith. Don't James say, 'If any of you ain't got wisdom he oughtta ask God, who gives bushels full, and he'll get it, but he ought to ask believing, not doubting'? Buck up, now," she commanded.

Billie Jo straightened up a little at that and wiped the tears from her face before Cindi returned.

"Ethel is praying at this very moment," she informed the group. "She says to be of good cheer," Cindi smiled reassuringly, "and not to forget that with God all things are possible."

"Well, what are we waitin' on?" Leah asked. "Let's get to it."

"First," Cindi said, "I think we ought to determine what to pray for. We need a definite target so that we're all agreed."

"Why, we're praying for Jimmy to come out of his coma and save this family, of course!" Billie Jo exclaimed.

"Billie Jo, are you relying on God to save your family or Jimmy?" Cindi asked gently.

Billie Jo flushed and hung her head. "I guess I was thinking about Jimmy doing it."

Cindi laid a hand on her arm. "We need to be asking so that we're closest to the center of God's will. For example, we know that it is always in His will to bring us closer to Him, to help us to discern His will, to obey Him. He's going to honor requests for things that are always in His will, all the time. Now, it may or may not be in God's will to heal Jimmy. We'll certainly pray for that. But, if that's not God's will, we need to find out what His will is and be ready to accept it, whatever it is."

Billie Jo nodded, her head moving up and down as if in slow motion. "You're right."

Happy with the result of his efforts, Jewel moved in close as the women knelt beside Jimmy's bed and began to pray. Angels began arriving, and so caught up were they in prayer that Jewel never noticed the little demon in the corner get up, shake out his tattered wings, and flit away.

CHAPTER 17

Don slumped outside the squalid mud hut and squeezed his eyes shut against the glare of the sun. Every fiber of his being screamed with fatigue. He was unsure how many hours had passed while he and Toby had struggled against death. A fresh wave of grief washed over him as he realized for the hundredth time that they had only won a partial victory.

Toby staggered out of the hut, arms wrapped around a little bundle that, for the moment, was silent. Her face, what wasn't dirty, was pale. For the first time, Don noticed a rivulet of tears, streaked in the mud, caked onto her cheeks. She gulped back a big sob, but her shoulders shook.

Don reached an arm out tentatively and put it around her shoulders, only to have her collapse against his side, sobbing wildly. "I don't understand, I don't understand," she cried.

Don patted her shoulder awkwardly. "These things happen," he said, a hollow ring in his voice.

Toby pulled away from him angrily. "No, that's not it," she spat. "You don't have a clue about what I'm talking about. You have no idea what I've been through, absolutely no idea. What would you know about suffering? Real suffering? A young girl died in there, and you don't feel anything. It means nothing to you. I'll bet you're the pampered son of a wealthy doctor, out here on a whim."

"Yeah, like *you* really care about these people. You're a regular Mother Teresa," Don muttered darkly. But seeing the pain cross her face, he threw up his hands in surrender. "I'm sorry. That was uncalled for."

Toby's finger traced the features of the tiny baby in her arms. "I care. I care a lot. I just didn't realize it until now. Unlike you, I've gone through some hard times in my life. I think . . . I think I've been looking for a home."

"And have you found it?" Don asked with uncharacteristic gentleness.

Toby nodded briefly. "Yes, I think I have. At least, I don't want to leave. It's the strangest thing, but since I got here, I have had the strongest urge to stay. Even when I left that time, I kept feeling like I should go back."

Don sank down into the dirt, his back against the hut. He stretched his legs out in front of him. "Yeah, this place kind of has that pull, doesn't it?"

"Is that why you stay?" Toby asked.

Don let the pause stretch and become uncomfortable before he forced himself to speak. "I used to think that was why I stayed, but I guess the truth is that I don't fit in anywhere else. And I guess I'm looking for answers that must be here somewhere."

Toby sank down cross-legged in the sand beside him, cradling the baby in her lap. "What kinds of answers are you looking for?"

Don squinted up at the sun and then looked directly at Toby, for once meeting her gaze. He was astonished to find that he actually thought she was pretty. He tried to remember the last time he had found a woman attractive and couldn't. "I was in Rwanda before this," he paused and swallowed hard before he went on, his voice as dispassionate as he could make it. "I had a clinic like the one here. When the war began, it was one of the first things to be destroyed. They bombed it . . . along with my patients who were still in the building.

"Some friends hid me. They moved me around from place to place. I treated them, their children, anyone they brought to me. Eventually, there was no one left. I found an abandoned house to hide in. Fortunately, it had a few food supplies. I ate mostly rice and beans every day. At night I would sleep with a mattress over me to block out the sounds of the bombings. And the screams.

"Eventually I was discovered, but it was by someone I knew. He asked me if I would care for some children in an orphanage, which I did until just before the end of the war."

He stopped talking and hung his head.

"What happened to the children?" Toby prompted.

"I went to find them some food one day," Don said, his voice dull. "And when I came back, I found that they had all been herded outside and clubbed to death."

He looked up, his eyes dry and his face expressionless. "Every day I ask myself, why? Why did God let it happen? He let me down, and He let them down. He deserted us."

"*That's right, He deserted you all,*" Merck agreed amiably. "*How many times are we going to go over this, anyway? Why don't you just give in and accept it? Quit fighting me. It's exhausting, and frankly, I don't have time for it.*"

"*Don't ever give up, Don,*" Julian said firmly. "*You will find the answers you seek. But, keep your eyes open, because they may come from the place you least expect to find them.*"

Merck laughed. It was a nasty sound, filled with smug vanity. "Yeah," he chortled, jerking his thumb at Toby. "Like maybe from her. Anything's possible for your dreamer," he sneered at the angel. "How happy I will be when you clear out for good. What will it take? Huh? When are you going to give up on this one?"

"I don't give up," Julian replied softly.

Toby put her arm around Don's shoulders and rested her head on his chest. He felt himself lean into the embrace. "I'm not the right person to ask that question. I don't know much about God myself."

She straightened, and her face took on a dreamy quality. "All I remember about God is a few verses I learned at church. My mom used to be so proud of me! I could recite the Bible for, oh, it seemed like hours. God was my friend, you know? I told Him everything, things I could never tell anyone else."

Toby brushed a wisp of hair back behind her ear. "Somewhere I lost that. Going to college, I got busy, fell in with the wrong crowd. I don't know, somewhere in there I lost that relationship I had with God."

She looked directly at him, seeming to come back from some place. Her face glowed, and he couldn't tear his eyes away from it. "I do know one thing about God though. He hurts more than we do when bad things happen. I questioned that when . . . well, when it felt as though my life ended six months ago.

"I wanted to blame God. I wanted to think He was out to get me or to teach me some lesson. But, the only thing I really know about God for certain is that He loves me. And if He loves me, then He wouldn't do this to me. Not even to teach me a lesson. If I didn't believe that, I couldn't have made it through the last year of my life.

"I've learned something going through it though," she added. "Twice I've asked Him to lead me, and He has. I think . . . I always thought that He left me, but I can see now that it was really I who left Him."

"God had the power to stop what happened in Rwanda," Don pointed out stubbornly.

Toby nodded. "Yeah, and He had the power to keep our plane from going down and to keep this girl from dying while she had a baby. What's your point?"

"My point is that . . . it's . . . why did He let it happen?"

Toby shook her head. "You just don't get it, do you? Why does any bad thing happen? Because of God, or because of sin? Why did this girl die? Probably because she was married too young, worked too hard, had too little to eat, and no prenatal care. Is that God's fault? If I remember my Bible right, we started out in a beautiful garden, which, if you don't mind my saying so, this does not resemble. It was *our* fault that we got kicked out. Not God's. Why blame Him?"

"Because He had the power to stop it, that's why," Don ground out, his jaw tight.

Toby laughed. "You know, I find it amusing that I came to a mission when I didn't want to and here I am teaching *you* about God. My theology is mighty rusty, but isn't that why Jesus died on the cross? To stop sin?"

"Shut up already!" Merck shrieked. His hands flexed angrily, clutching the air. Veins bulged in his neck, and his face became mottled with purple and red. "For someone who claims not to know much about God, you've got an awful lot to say about Him. Just shut your mouth. Nobody wants to hear about it."

A flush of annoyance swept over Don's face. "I thought you didn't know much about God?"

Toby laughed again. "I don't! That's the funny part. You're the great mission doctor, why can't you understand something so simple that even *I* understand?" Her hand flew out, and she gripped his knee, preventing him from hastily scrambling to his feet. "Look, I don't have all the answers. Until this very minute, I wasn't aware that I had any answers at all. It's really helped me to talk to you about this. I guess it's been going through my head for a long time, and I've just had no one to talk to about it."

Lileah smiled, feeling as though she'd somehow come home. The long journey through the accident and across the continent of Africa had led here, and it was a good place. Finally

Toby was listening to her, to the Master. She'd struggled with it for a long time, Lileah knew. And there was still a lot she needed to know. The road ahead of her was long and narrow, but Lileah could sense that at last she had the desire to tread it and find out Who was waiting for her at the other end.

The baby on Toby's lap began to cry, drawing their attention. "What do you want to do about this?"

Don shrugged and stood up slowly, looking around. They had seen no one since they'd arrived. Although there were other huts similar to the one where Madina now rested, finally at peace, they didn't seem to have occupants.

"We'll have to wait for the father to get back. Who knows how long that will be." He bit his bottom lip. "I hate to think of Shay managing the clinic by herself. Maybe you could fly back and see how she's getting along and . . ."

He was interrupted by the smiling face of Madina's husband as he suddenly materialized from the bush beside them. He peered in the blanket and broke into a wide smile, babbling so fast even Don couldn't pick up more than a word or two.

Tripping over his tongue as he tried to form the words he needed, Don struggled to explain that while Madina was dead, she had given him a healthy baby girl. Apparently, enough of the words got through to him because a profound change came over his face. As Toby tried to hand him the baby, he pushed her away.

"*Cadeau,*" he insisted. "*Cadeau.*"

Don snatched the baby from Toby and pushed it toward the man. Madina's husband threw up his hands and walked backward until his back was pressed up against the dirty hut behind him. He shook his head vehemently.

"What's going on?" Toby asked, bewildered.

Don's shoulders sagged. "He doesn't want the baby. Girls are not much valued, I'm afraid."

"What's that word he keeps saying? Is that what he wants to name her?"

"No, he wants to give her to us as a gift. A payment for coming out here."

Toby eyed the man warily. "What will happen to her if we just leave her here?"

Don shrugged. "He'll kill her. Or sell her. Who knows."

Toby reached out and took the baby back, cradling her fiercely. "Tell him thank you," she instructed.

Don whirled around, mouth gaping. "Are you nuts? What are we going to do with a baby? One more mouth to feed and nothing to show for it."

"Well, we can't leave her here," Toby pointed out evenly.

"No," Don agreed slowly. "No, we can't leave her here. Maybe we can find someone who will want to adopt her."

"Maybe," Toby said, but she was paying more attention to the baby than she was to him. "Yes, I'm sure we can find *someone* to adopt her."

The way she said "someone" sounded suspicious to Don, but they had no choice. She was right. They sure couldn't leave the baby here. Whatever happened to her wouldn't be pleasant. He thanked Madina's husband stiffly, without a hint of gratitude in his voice.

The man smiled profusely and began to talk again, his words coming like machine gun fire.

Toby grabbed his arm. "Come on," she was saying. "Let's get out of here."

They found a goat perched on one wing of the ultralight. Don picked it up and set it down. The goats were one of the first things he had noticed when they'd arrived. Goats everywhere. Their choppy bleats echoed constantly. But he quickly concluded that they were like crickets in the States. After awhile you tuned them out and would almost be surprised if anyone brought up the fact that they existed at all.

Toby handed him the baby before taking one wing of the ultralight and turning the plane around to face the barren stretch of land they had used as a runway. As she hopped in and started the engine, Don gripped the baby tighter. Even without the adrenalin rush they'd had coming in, he knew this flight was not going to be enjoyable.

"Ready, Doctor?" Toby asked, giving him a smile.

"As I'll ever be," he agreed, closing his eyes as she gunned the little engine and they began to career down the tiny track of land. He didn't open them again until he felt the weightless feeling of the plane lifting off. At least, he reassured himself, it wouldn't be a long flight.

An unexpected warming swept over the countryside and Ethel Bennington asked Cindi one Saturday morning to open her windows and let a breath of fresh air in.

"Are you sure?" Cindi asked skeptically. "You haven't been well all that long, you know."

"Posh." Ethel brushed the implication away. "A little fresh air never hurt anybody. Besides, ever since I started praying for your friend Billie Jo, the air in this room has seemed rather foul."

Cindi lowered herself to the edge of the bed. "What do you mean . . . foul?"

Ethel waved one hand in front of her face. "Stale, like it's loaded with negative ions. It makes me feel sluggish and sleepy."

"Well, a little rest wouldn't hurt you, you know. I realize Doctor Haskell said you could do whatever you felt up to, but I think you take that as a blanket excuse to overdo it." Cindi moved to the window and opened it a crack. The fresh air blew in, rustling the curtain.

"More," Ethel encouraged, not taking her eyes from Cindi until she was sure that the window had reached the desired height. "And how could you accuse me of overdoing it?" she demanded with a twinkle in her eye. "Why, all I do is sit here and pray, all day long."

"And that takes nothing out of you, I suppose?" Cindi teased obligingly.

"Tell me about this friend of yours," Ethel prompted. "How bad is her husband?"

Cindi sighed. "Well, he's been in a coma for, I guess, maybe a year or so. I've never seen him so much as twitch an eyebrow . . . and yet, somehow I feel as though he's in there somewhere just waiting to be released." She shook her head. "Maybe I'm crazy, or just hopeful. I don't know. But, I can't help thinking that some-day he will snap out of it."

"And this situation she finds herself in?" Ethel asked. "With her mother-in-law?"

"She's ultra-controlling, from what I understand. She's taken Billie Jo's children away, and now she wants to move her son back to her house. It sounds to me like she's a very lonely, unful-filled woman who is looking for ways to be needed in order to patch herself up emotionally."

Ethel's head wagged from side to side. "I can sense the de-ceiver struggling hard in this family. He has a hold on them right now, and he doesn't want to let go." She chuckled shortly. "But, he underestimates the tenacity of this old woman. I'm not going to give up."

As Ethel's head bowed once more in prayer and Cindi slipped quietly from the room, Rafe spun in frenzied circles around the ceiling. The sound that came from his throat was a mixture of hatred, frustration, and downright evil. "I won't give up. I won't give up," he mocked, hissing at the end of each sentence. "We'll just see about that."

Changing his trajectory, he dove suddenly at Ethel, but he was not swift enough to beat Reissa, who intercepted him, sending him spinning across the room and crashing into the wall. He shook himself and sat up, hissing at her.

"Stay out of my way, angel," he warned. "Or you'll regret it."

Reissa adopted a protective stance beside Ethel, crossing her arms and staring at him unflinching. Her wings spread out behind her, making her seem even larger than she was. Rafe picked himself up from the floor and rushed her. His crash sent them tumbling across the room.

Scratching and clawing, Rafe tried to get the upper hand, suddenly disclosing a small black dagger he'd kept hidden in the folds of his tattered cloak. He stabbed wildly, more interested in finding a target than planning one. Reissa fended off his blows with her strong arms but was finally forced to draw her own sword. It gleamed in the shaft of sunlight coming from the open window, and for a moment, the glare blinded Rafe.

He shrieked, and Reissa thought he might retreat. Instead, he shielded his eyes with one arm and rushed at her again, dagger extended. Stepping aside, Reissa parried, knocking aside his arm. Rafe's momentum carried him across the room.

Ethel moaned, drawing the attention of both angel and demon. A triumphant smile flitted across Rafe's face. "She's weakening," he shrieked. "Attack!"

Suddenly, as if waiting for that single word, the room was filled with demons. Reissa began to use her sword in earnest. It was only seconds before an army of angels filled the room. Bodies tangled, sprawling across the room. Light fought darkness, with only the light gladly declaring that it had already won. And in the center of it all, one lone woman sat with her head bowed.

Billie Jo sat beside Jimmy on the cot. She had a clear view of the driveway, though she found herself looking in every direction except that one. Usually she was anxious for Helen to come so she could see the children, this time she dreaded seeing the long, sleek black car drive in, knowing it would be followed by an ambulance. She gripped Jimmy's hand tighter.

"Come on, Jimmy. Wake up!" she pleaded. Then she bowed her head as she had almost constantly since Friday night. "Lord, here we are again. Asking You to help us and trusting that You will. Help us to accept Your will, God. We know that You know what's best for us, even if it don't seem like the best thing to us at the time. And keep our family together, we pray. Thank You. Amen."

As if perfectly timed, Billie Jo lifted her head just as she caught sight of Helen's car pull into the driveway. It was followed closely by an ambulance. Helen and James got out of their car with Cassidy and Dallas as the ambulance attendants pulled a stretcher from the back of the ambulance and followed the little group to the door.

Inside the house the group of angels present took up defensive positions. The decision had already been reached by the Master, but it was well known among the group that the deceiver planned to make an attack defying the ruling through sheer force. Jewel stood beside Billie Jo, the light from his robe enveloping her. She had fought a good fight in prayer, and she had many on her side. He was pleased with her.

Billie Jo felt her hands go icy as she walked across the floor to open the door. Strangely, she felt a peace that she had not experienced in months. It surged through her, and she imagined that she could almost feel it flow out the length of her fingertips. She opened the door and stepped aside to admit Helen and James.

A black swirling mass of demons that had followed the ambulance up the driveway funnelled into the house. Nog was in full battle cry, with Rafe at his side. The two presented a frightful front to the angel guards. No longer fighting with a simple dagger, each demon had a long, black sword and engaged whichever angel was nearest, hacking at random around the room. Although skillfully disguised, it was apparent to Jewel from the very beginning that their target was not Billie Jo or even Helen. They were after Jimmy.

Prayer cover, which was heavy for Billie Jo, provided another whole troop of angels, and Jewel stationed them around Jimmy's cot. They had to keep the way clear for the Master's healing touch, which would be bestowed by Noble himself. If the demons broke their stronghold, Noble would not be able to penetrate their ranks and so could not bring healing to Jimmy.

The sounds of fighting echoed on all sides. Both sides were evenly matched in numbers. Jewel unsheathed his own sword and stood by, ready to help out if necessary.

Cassidy and Dallas hung back, and Billie Jo squatted down in the doorway. "What's the matter?" she asked them.

Cass's eyes were red from crying. "We want to stay here with you and Daddy, but Grandma says that we can't. She says Daddy is going to live at her house and that you have to stay here."

Billie Jo reached out and scooped the children up in her arms. "You know what, pumpkin? Nothing can ever stop us from being a family. I'll always be your mommy and Daddy will always be your father. And you can be sure that I will always try to keep us together, no matter what."

Helen tapped her foot impatiently. "That's a sweet sentiment, Billie Jo, but you're holding up the ambulance attendants, and they aren't exactly cheap."

Billie Jo moved out of the way with the children, keeping them clutched close to her side while the attendants moved toward Jimmy and got set to transfer him from the cot to the stretcher. The only sound in the room besides the scrape of metal against metal was the quiet sniffling of the children.

Helen threw them a dangerous look, warning them to stop their sniveling, but Billie Jo intercepted it and shielded the children from her view. "You know, we'll all be better off this way," Helen was saying solicitously. "You'll see."

Nog sensed that the battle was not going well even before he saw the bright light streak down into the house like a falling star. It was an archangel. If he didn't act fast, it would be too late, and everything he had been working for would be spoiled.

"Arghhh!" he screamed. "I will not be defeated!"

Spiraling down from the ceiling where he had engaged an angel and was attempting to find a hole in his defenses, he held his sword out in front of him as he divebombed at Jimmy. He had to reach the man before the angel did. He had a second. One split second in which his plan could succeed.

He tucked his wings in even closer to his body to lessen the drag of the wind and speed his fall. Both bony hands gripped the hilt of his sword as he fell heavily behind it. His blade, inches from finding its mark, Nog was suddenly blown backward with a force like an exploding bomb.

"THE MASTER HAS CONQUERED DEATH!" Noble exclaimed, his voice so powerful that it sent the demon crashing back more effectively than a ton of dynamite. "He has won!" Reaching out, he touched Jimmy on the forehead. "Rise, and protect your family."

"Ready," one attendant said to the other. "We'll move him

on three. One, two . . ."

He was interrupted as Jimmy's hand shot up and locked onto his forearm. Billie Jo gasped, and the attendant jumped backward as if he'd been bitten by a snake.

"Let me alone," Jimmy said hoarsely. The other attendant, badly shaken, backed up. Jimmy's eyes opened for the first time since the accident, but he didn't seem as though he was seeing anything. Billie Jo shivered at the blank look on his face.

"Daddy's alive!" Cassidy shrieked, a little frightened at the sight of her father moving after so long.

Billie Jo rushed to Jimmy's side, tears streaming down her face. Before Jimmy could focus on her face, he closed his eyes again. If it hadn't been for the shaken ambulance attendant, Billie Jo would have believed she had tricked the whole incident out of her imagination.

"Well?" Helen demanded. "What are you waiting for? It was nothing. Probably a nervous spasm. Let's get a move on."

"Lady, you said this guy was in a coma. Well, it sure looks to me like he's about to come out of it," the attendant said.

"You're not getting paid for a professional diagnosis," Helen snapped. "Just to move my son. Now get to it."

The ambulance attendants exchanged looks but moved in once again to take their positions. "On three. One, two . . ."

Jimmy lurched upwards and grabbed the arm of the attendant nearest him. "Let me alone."

To Billie Jo, he seemed a little more aware of his surroundings. She was sure that his eyes focused for an instant before they closed again.

"I don't have all day," Helen shrieked, refusing to back down, but obviously shaken by what was going on.

"One, two . . ."

Again Jimmy's hand shot up, latching onto the arm of the attendant. He raised himself up slightly. "I ain't going nowhere," he said. "I ain't going." Slowly, as though the effort was taking a lot out of him, his eyes flitted to each face in the room until they rested on Billie Jo's. "Honey, keep our kids," he said, before closing his eyes again.

Helen's mouth gaped open before shutting with a snap. Her face was an open book of pain, frustration, and thwarted purpose. Without a word, she spun on her heel and stalked out the door. James looked at Billie Jo and gave her an apologetic shrug before following his wife. The two ambulance attendants looked at each other before appealing finally to Billie Jo, who seemed to be in a state of shock.

"What are we supposed to do?" they asked.

"Go home," Billie Jo sobbed happily. "We're not going anywhere. None of us is going anywhere."

Bewildered, the men packed up their equipment and followed Helen and James out the door. Billie Jo stood gripping the children as hard as she could without hurting them.

"Momma, is Daddy all better?" Cassidy asked hesitantly.

"Well, Daddy sure has a long way to go, but I'd say that Jesus healed him, and now he's going to get better," Billie Jo said, whispering. A feeling of overwhelming awe flooded through her at the miracle she had just witnessed. "Come here, children."

Billie Jo led Cassidy and Dallas to Jimmy's bedside. "Jimmy?" she whispered, brushing the hair off his forehead. "Jimmy? Can you hear me?"

Jimmy's eyes opened slowly. He smiled tiredly at the sight of her face. "Hello, darlin'. Give me some sugar."

Laughing and crying at the same time, Billie Jo reached down and pressed her lips against his. "Welcome home, Jimmy Raynard," she said.

"It is finished," Noble declared. Ripples of excitement made their way over the group of angels. Quietly the demons seeped out through the walls until only Nog remained. Chest heaving as he lay, still slightly stunned against the brick of the fireplace, he glared at the angel.

"It's not over yet," he gasped. "It won't be over until they are dead or your tardy Master returns to take them away from here. As long as they are on earth, they will be our subjects. We will always have the opportunity to win another victory. It won't be the great battles that win the war. It will be the small skirmishes that are fought every day in hundreds of ways."

With great difficulty, he picked himself up off the floor and limped toward the door. "I'll be back. You can be sure of that."

CHAPTER 18

Spring had come early, and as each new day progressed, Lyle felt as if he were being born all over again. Life seemed to be moving at a rapid clip. Although he quickly mastered his job, he still wished there was some way he could accomplish it without having to deal with customers.

Every time a new person approached his desk to open an account, his palms began to sweat and his heart raced. He considered taking a few banking classes so he could advance to a position in which he would have less contact with new people every day.

This surprised him when he stopped to think about where he was headed. He couldn't remember having a goal since graduation. All of a sudden, he was pursuing a career he'd never thought about. In fact, it was one of several goals. Lately he'd been thinking strongly of getting baptized again, to rededicate his life to Jesus. Pastor Hendricks and Calla had been coming over every week to study with him.

At first, he had to admit, his only motivation was to see Calla more. But as they studied the Bible with him, things he had learned long ago began to come back to him. It was as if, for the first time since the accident, he could hear God's voice clearly asking him where he had been and telling him how much He'd missed his company.

It startled Lyle to realize that God had missed him. He'd considered himself worthless for so long that now he had trouble with the concept. The more they studied, the less he thought about seeing Calla and the more he was drawn to God. Now he was beginning to sense a conviction to get baptized. His main concern was how it could be accomplished. That was something he planned to discuss with Pastor Hendricks the next time he saw him.

"Yoohoo," Calla sang. "You've got to be a million miles away. What are you thinking of?"

Lyle dragged himself back to the present. Calla was sitting cross-legged on the lawn beside him. She had woven a wreath of dandelions, which she was wearing at a jaunty angle in her hair. She looked up at him and smiled frankly, surprising him with her next words.

"I like you," she said, her hands tangling in the long grass, teasing it into short braids. "You're sincere."

"What do you mean, sincere?" he asked.

She told him about Brick then. It was the first time she'd ever spoken of him. She told him how vain Brick had been, how self-absorbed. "Everything had something to do with him, even when it didn't." She giggled. "Mostly, the only reason he liked having me around was to complete the picture. When I met him, he had everything else, except a girlfriend. I think he liked that I was into sports only because he was."

"Do you miss him?" Lyle asked hesitantly, not really sure he wanted to know the answer.

"No," she replied simply. "It was hard when we broke up. But I missed the thought of him more than I ever actually missed him."

"Well, I do, too, you know," Lyle stammered after an uncomfortable pause. "Like you, I mean. A lot, really."

"I know," Calla said quietly, a faint smile tugging at her lips. "I kinda figured you must when I saw your room that time you asked me to get you some clothes." She looked up at him, a sly twinkle in her eyes. "I don't even think my mother has that many pictures of me. It was like a gallery showing, at an art museum. You've really got a lot of talent, you know. Do you draw anything else?"

Lyle blushed with shame as the realization swept over him. She had seen his room! All the pictures he'd drawn of her over the months he'd watched her . . . plastered all over his room like wallpaper.

"Well, do you?" she persisted. "Draw anything else?"

He nodded mutely.

"You don't have to be embarrassed, you know," she told him, reaching up to put one hand on his. "I was flattered. Really."

Lyle squirmed. "I didn't want you to know that I, uh, well, you know. How much I liked you. That's all."

Calla sat back and stared up at him. "Why not?"

Lyle scrambled for an excuse he could explain. How could he explain the strong urge to hide his feelings? To prevent getting hurt? To save face when the inevitable happened and Calla found a new boyfriend?

"I don't know," he mumbled. "I didn't think you'd like it."

Calla threw back her head, her laughter filling the air like the ringing of tiny bells. "Don't you get it? That's one of the things I really like about you. I never wonder if you've got some kind of hidden agenda. I know that if you say some-thing, you really mean it. And I trust you to be honest with me all the time."

Lyle shrugged off her praise. "I can't take any credit for that. My parents raised me to be straightforward."

"Yeah? Well, it's getting to be rare to find anyone like that these days," Calla sighed. "Real rare." She dimpled and flashed him a smile. Lyle was still keenly aware that she hadn't removed her hand from his. "So, when are you getting your new chair? You must have enough money saved now to pay for most of it."

Lyle nodded, finding it hard to contain his excitement at the mention of the racing chair. "As a matter of fact, Russell was supposed to drop it off some time today."

Calla swatted playfully at him. "You goose! You're awfully cool for someone who has been working and sweating for this moment for so long. Why didn't you say anything?"

Lyle groaned. "Why do you think? Because I was afraid you'd force me to go jogging with you or something." In spite of his words, the look on his face implied that he'd like nothing better. "You know I could never keep up."

"I wouldn't expect you to at first," Calla informed him. "What do you think I am? A sadist?" She shook her finger at him. "Don't answer that," she joked. "It's going to take time and practice before you can keep up with me." She bounced to her feet and danced a little jig around his chair. "After all, I plan to be the next Flo Jo."

Hershey, who was stretched out on his side, woke up suddenly when she stepped on his tail. He waved a paw at her as if to say, "Have a care," before falling back to sleep.

"So, is it a date?" Calla asked.

"Is what a date?" Lyle said suspiciously.

"Today, when Russell comes with your chair. You call me and we'll go for a jog."

"Today?" Lyle squeaked. Secretly he'd hoped for some time to practice with the chair and build some endurance before he faced the prospect of keeping up with Calla. "I don't know . . ."

"Hey, the weather's not going to get much better than this," Calla reminded him, gesturing up toward the blue sky studded with fluffy white clouds. "Come on, what do you say?"

Lyle gave up, clearly defeated by her persistence. "OK. I'll call you as soon as Russell leaves."

"Great! Call me," she yelled over her shoulder as she headed for her house at a brisk trot. "Come on, Hersh. We've got some studying to do before we can go running."

Lyle watched her, marveling at her energy and vibrancy. He wasn't sure he knew anyone as outgoing and positive as Calla. "I know marriage is a big step, Lord," he breathed, closing his eyes. "And I want to follow Your will. I also want to marry Calla more than anything I've ever wanted. But it's probably impossible. I know I am priceless in Your sight, Lord, but I've got a serious handicap compared to guys who have both of their legs. If it's not in Your will for me to marry Calla, help me to accept that. Thank You. Amen."

"La-tee-da," Warg chortled. "You've really got a high opinion of yourself these days. What makes you think that having a job makes you any different than you were before? A new haircut, some clean clothes, big deal! You're still the same in here." Warg slapped Lyle on the chest with the back of his curled up hand.

Shelan frowned. "The change that has occurred inside is the only change that matters. All the outside changes, they're only superficial, like a facelift. But, inside, where it really counts, that's what makes the difference, Lyle. That's where you've really changed. You are indeed a child of God now and this demon has no power over you anymore."

"SHUT UP!" Warg shrieked. Veins bulged in his forehead, and spittle drooled out of the corners of his mouth. "You meddling, conniving, worthless do-gooder! This is all your fault. And don't think you won't pay for it. I'm not finished yet."

Lyle opened his eyes, but Calla had disappeared. He felt a cold chill and loneliness settled over him, as if portending the future. He shook the feeling off and made his way into the house to help his mother until Russell arrived.

Shay had watched for the little plane as if it supported her whole future with its fragile wings. Something had gone dreadfully wrong. That wasn't hard to see. She knew what it was as soon as she had seen Toby and Don climb wearily from the plane, Don clutching a tiny bundle to his middle as if carrying the football for a winning touchdown. She remembered the way fear had grabbed her in the pit of her stomach, making it almost impossible to ask the question she didn't want the answer to.

"Madina?" It wasn't Toby's reply so much that made Shay realize she'd changed in the time she'd been gone, but the tone of her voice.

"I'm sorry, Shay. We lost her." Shay had seen the tears in Toby's eyes before she felt herself pulled into a compassionate embrace. Shay had accepted the hug much the same way she had accepted any kindness shown to her after that, with a cool detachment.

"I've seen that look before," Don said to her one day. "In the mirror after I got out of Rwanda. You've got to let it go."

Shay snorted, derision lacing her voice. "You're a good one to be telling me how to let go. You've been hanging on to the past since I got here."

"I know," Don agreed. "And it was eating me up inside, destroying me. It wasn't until I let it go that I was free. That's something that Madina's death taught me. I know that God isn't trying to test us by allowing Madina to die, but do you want her death to be wasted on you? Learn something through it. Make her death mean something."

"It means something, all right," Shay agreed. "It means that I'm glad I smartened up before it was too late. I'm getting outta here just as soon as my time is up. In fact, I wish I could get out sooner."

The sorrowful look on Don's face almost made her repent of her negative words. Instead, she found something to get busy with. She found that when her hands were busy she could zone out in her mind. The time went faster that way, and it didn't hurt if she didn't think.

She hadn't wanted to even see Madina's baby at first. But there was no one to take care of her, and she found herself giving in, unwillingly. She treated the baby with a cool detachment, attending to her needs as if she were any other patient, but not really allowing herself to get too close. She didn't even choose a name for her but referred to her instead as "the baby."

After all, she had reasoned, she'd be leaving soon. No sense getting attached to a baby who would be staying here. Let whoever was going to keep her, name her. It was only right.

Lucien had lost a great battle when the doctor and Toby had at last become friends and allies. The stress it caused forced him to pull hunks of dry, brittle hair from his head until all that remained were ragged tufts here and there. Toby and the doctor had been the cornerstone of his plan, and now it wobbled precariously.

Sparn had not taken the news well either. He sat day after day locked in seclusion, fingers drumming on the arm of a very old, very worn, ornately carved chair. He spoke to no one, not even to Lucien when he appeared each day to give his daily reports. Although it looked suspiciously as if he'd given up, Lucien was sure that he was deep in thought, planning a way in which they could still close the mission.

At least, he hoped so.

For his own part, he thought of little else. But even he was tempted to admit defeat. The old prayer warrior was back on her feet, and rumor had it that not one, but two new nurses were training in the States and intended to come here. Don and Toby, now that they were working together, had designed a training program for local women who wanted to work at the clinic.

Not only was the clinic doing well, but it was expanding. The long-overlooked ultralight had become the basis for a plan to open outreach clinics in outlying areas, to be visited once a week and staffed with locally trained medical personnel. Indeed, the only bright spot that Lucien could see was that Shay Beauregard would soon be leaving. Having been unable to influence her at all until very recently, he considered her merely an annoyance, at any rate. At least now she would be gone, though the loss would hardly affect the mission in light of all the changes.

Still, it would affect three people: Shay, Nwibe, and Marcus, and that was three more victories than he had been able to score in the entire time he'd been in Africa. Surely it was a small battle, but it was better than a completely empty hand. At least, until Sparn came up with something better.

Lucien sighed deeply. He had hoped for a promotion to take him away from all this petty warfare. Now it looked as though it would be a long time before he was able to plan the big battles in which he longed to have a hand. Well, first things first.

As Shay sat in the middle of her packed suitcases and looked around her room at the mission where she'd spent so many wonderful days, she marked the changes. There were nice curtains in the windows, pictures on the walls, a curtain to hide the closet, new paint for the cot. Mostly little changes, she realized, but ones that had said, "I'm here to stay" and "I belong." Now she realized that those statements were a lie.

She wasn't staying, and Nwibe had made it clear that she didn't belong. She packed only a few of the pictures; she didn't have room to carry the rest back. She considered taking down the rest of the things but decided against it. Maybe they would help the next nurse assigned to her quarters to feel more at home.

She picked up her suitcases, heavier than when she'd arrived, gave the room one more quick glance, and then turned on her heel and left without looking back. Shay was surprised to see that most of the staff members were assembled by the old oxcart that was going to take her to Niamey. A few of the children held banners wishing her all the best and saying they would miss her.

Shay felt a lump in her throat that she swallowed with determination. She wouldn't let them see how much she wanted to stay. A sea of arms pulled her forward with a succession of hugs. Toby handed her a few letters to mail when she got back home.

"Make sure you have a scoop of Ben and Jerry's when you get back," Toby smiled, "and think of me while you eat it."

Even Don gave her a tight squeeze. "We'll miss you, kid," he was saying. "You take care, huh? And if you ever want to come back, you just let us know. We'd take you back in a minute."

Shay was barely aware of what he was saying. In front of her stood Nwibe and Marcus. The former stood tall and unemotional, while the latter sobbed broken-heartedly. Shay stepped forward until she was standing in front of him with only inches between them.

Placing her palms on either side of his face, Shay stood on tiptoe to reach his lips with her own. He made no response, his face as hard as stone. As she pushed herself away from him, tears spilled from her eyes. She turned to Marcus, who was sobbing uncontrollably. She took him in her arms and his slender body shuddered violently against her.

"Please do not leave, Madame Shay," he blubbered. "I will do anything if you will stay. I promise I will be a good boy. Please do not leave."

"Oh, Marcus, I wish I could," Shay cried. "I'm not leaving because of you. Please don't ever think that. I'm leaving because I have to. My mission term is up."

"But, I thought you loved us," Marcus sobbed. "If you loved us, you wouldn't leave us." His father's strong warning grip on his shoulder shut him up, but he continued to weep.

Shay shut her eyes tightly, blocking out everything around her but the boy in her arms. "I'm sorry, Marcus. I'm truly sorry." Pushing him away, she staggered blindly to the oxcart, feeling gentle hands help her inside. The sea of faces in front of her was a blur as the cart lurched away, carrying her from the mission forever.

Shay waved half-heartedly for a moment before burying her face in her hands and giving herself up to the emotions that flooded through her. Every fiber in her being screamed at her to go back.

"Are you totally stupid?" Lucien screeched. "Go back? You're nuts! The man doesn't want you. He made that plain. What do you want to do? Make a complete fool of yourself? HE DOESN'T WANT YOU! Live with it."

Gaius smoothed a large hand over Shay's forehead. "You know in your heart that is the right thing to do. You know Nwibe. Do you think he would say what he did for your own good? Or for his own? He is lonely. Your company has been like sunlight to him. He is an unselfish man. Whose good do you suppose he had in mind when he rejected your offer of marriage?"

Shay sat up, suddenly amazed at the thoughts that were crashing through her head. It hadn't occurred to her before that Nwibe might have a hidden agenda behind what he had said to her. Had he really said it only to discourage her? To make her go back for what he thought was her own good? She flushed with anger at the thought. How dare he try to manipulate her, even if it was for her own good!

Lucien took one look at the resolve on Shay's face and de-

cided it was time to haul out the big guns. "Look here," he said in his most intimidating tone of voice. "Wise up. You don't want to go back. Take my word for it. That place is nothing but trouble. Why, you'd have to take care of the baby, Madina's baby. You don't want to do that, do you? Every time you look at that child, you'll remember her mother and how you practically sent her to her death.

"Just look at the opportunities that are ahead of you! You're young, healthy, even pretty. There are hordes of eligible young men back in the States who will be fighting over you. You'll have plenty of money for luxuries. And baths, don't forget baths. As many and as often as you want. And food, everything you've been craving since you got here. Don't be foolish. Forget about this place. Embrace your future."

Gaius frowned at the demon's rhetoric. "More is not necessarily better," he told Shay. "You have gained wisdom, maturity, and a true compassion for others while you have lived here. The gains far outweigh the inconveniences. Pray." he urged her. "And hear the Master's will for you."

Shay watched the crowd in front of the mission grow smaller and smaller until it all but disappeared from the horizon. Silently she bowed her head and poured out her heart in prayer, feeling free for the first time of the weight of Madina's death. It was a burden she had carried without cause, she realized now. As it slid from her shoulders, she could see the path she must take set clearly out in front of her.

Marcus continued to stand beside his father, even when everyone else returned to their business. He stared after the cart until it became a speck in the distance, blurring with the heat until it no longer even resembled a cart.

"She is gone, Father," Marcus said finally, trying to speak around the lump in his throat. He felt totally empty inside, as if someone had poured him out onto the ground at his feet. The feeling seemed as bad as when his mother had died.

Nwibe reached down and put his arms around his son. Marcus choked back sobs he didn't want his father to hear.

"Why are you crying, my son?" Nwibe asked gently.

Marcus caught his breath. "Because Madame Shay is gone, and I will miss her," he answered reluctantly. "I . . . I love her. When she is here, I am happy, and I don't miss my mother so much. She makes up fun things to do. Who will by my teacher now?"

"Madame Shay is not gone," Nwibe replied confidently. "She will always be with us."

Marcus cocked his head trying to comprehend this bit of news. "You mean like when someone dies and their memory stays with us always?"

"No," replied his father. "Like when someone is with you always because they love you and they can't leave. Marcus, look up the road and tell me what you see."

Obediently, Marcus turned and looked up the road. A lone figure, burdened with luggage, was walking toward the mission. Marcus caught his breath in a quick gasp. It couldn't be! It had to be! Dropping his end of the stick that attached him to his father, he ran toward the figure, which grew larger by the moment. When he reached her, he was panting so hard he couldn't speak. Shay looked at him, laughing and crying at the same time. Dropping her luggage, she gathered him up in her arms, swinging him around and around.

"You came back! You came back!" Marcus repeated over and

over as if to help himself absorb the wonderful truth of it. Shay set him down.

"Yes, I came back."

"Why?" Marcus asked curiously. "You said that you had to leave."

"Maybe someday," Shay agreed, "but not right now. Right now my life is here. There are people who need me."

"I need you," Marcus said simply, picking up one end of her heavy suitcase and dragging it along after him. "I need you most of all."

Shay laughed. "Yes, you need me. Who else would take you on picnics? Who would play flashlight tag with you? Who would play touch football with you?"

"Yes, who else?" Nwibe asked, as they walked up to him still smiling. Shay immediately became sober.

"Now look here," she began, after taking a deep breath. "I know you don't think I belong here and that I need to go out and live my life before I really know what I want to do with the rest of it, but I've been doing a lot of thinking and praying and . . . I'm staying." She said the last almost as if it were a challenge.

"I know I'm young, but I'm going to grow up no matter where I am, and I think what I'm doing here is the most important thing I can do right now." She lifted her chin belligerently. "Besides, I have a baby to take care of."

Nwibe's eyebrows arched in surprise. "Madame Madina's baby?"

"Yes," Shay said in a tone that dared him to disagree with her. "I couldn't help her mother, but I can sure help her. I'm . . . I'm going to ask Don if I can adopt her." She eyed him warily. "And nothing you can say will talk me out of staying. Nothing at all. I've made up my mind."

Nwibe shook his head as if the thought hadn't occurred to him. He made a little bow in her direction. "Far be it for me, Madame, to attempt to sway you in your decision. Indeed, you seem to have your mind set on it. Tell me, is it your intention also to give this boy a mother?" He indicated Marcus with a tip of his head.

Shay's eyes widened and a little of the fight left her face. Marcus held his breath waiting for her reply. So far, he had been able to make nothing of the conversation except that she was staying. The rest of what they said seemed to be cloaked in double meanings.

"I, well, you said, that is, I thought you didn't want to marry me?"

Nwibe smiled. "Now, I never said that. I said that I believed you should go back to America to get an education in living before you decided to spend the rest of your life here in a country which is not your own." He spread his arms wide and shrugged. "And yet, here you are. Do you intend to stay for more than one more term?"

"Yes," Shay replied guardedly, as if she was afraid he wouldn't take her seriously or would try to talk her out of it. "I intend to make Africa my home until Jesus comes back."

"And you plan to adopt a baby?" he persisted.

Shay winked at Marcus. "Actually, I plan to adopt two children eventually and probably have a few of my own."

"You two needn't think you are putting anything over on me," Nwibe said archly. "I know what you are up to."

Shay grabbed Marcus's hand and swung it back and forth. "Uh-oh, Marcus. He's on to us. We're going to have to figure out some way to get around that, or we'll never have any secrets."

Marcus grinned. "I know a way, Madame Shay."

"Good. And you can tell me all about it later. Right now I need you to go run and tell Doctor Germaine that I'm back and I'm staying. Will you do that for me? Oh, and on your way back, would you find Madina and bring her to me?"

"Madina?" Marcus knew of no one on the compound by that name.

"Yes, Baby Madina. I'm going to name her after her mother."

"Yes, Madame Shay!" Marcus started off at a brisk trot, but he stopped at a respectful distance long enough to see his father and Madame Shay embrace. What a wonderful day! A new mother and sister all at the same time!

Lucien looked at the pair with disgust. This was the last straw, the very last straw. He'd tried everything, and nothing seemed to have any effect on these people. It was those cursed angels!

He looked around at the bustle of celestial activity. Where once demons had partied like whiling dervishes, now sedate angels guided, instructed, and helped everywhere. And he knew beyond a shadow of a doubt it was all because of that cursed prayer warrior in the States. At least, he was thankful that he wasn't personally responsible for that horrific blunder.

That had been Sparn's responsibility.

Lucien looked around once more. His skin shrank in loathing at what he saw. It was time to pay Sparn a visit and find out what the great leader had hatched up to retake command of the post. Lucien found himself fresh out of ideas.

He located Sparn in the same defeated position he'd occupied for the past few months, hunched over, wings drooping listlessly behind him. Jezeel, Merck, and a few of the minor demons tormented each other near him, but they were the only ones still left at the mission besides Lucien and Sparn.

"Commander Sparn?" Lucien asked. Sparn looked up sluggishly, his eyes red-rimmed and vacant.

"Lucien. Yes. What is it?"

"Sir, I'm afraid that the little Cajun girl came back. I tried everything, but the angels have gotten so much power that it's really hard to get through to these humans. They just aren't listening to me. And I'm the only one out there, sir. I'm the only one left fighting. I'm afraid it's a losing battle."

"Yes, Lucien, I'm afraid it is." He slammed his fist onto the arm of his chair with some semblance of the old fight in his face. "These cursed angels. They make our work so hard."

Lucien cleared his throat. "So, what I was wondering, sir, is what plan you have to take back the mission? Is it to be a fierce battle? Should I call in reinforcements? Or maybe sabotage? Or should we attempt to take someone out? Doctor Germaine, perhaps? What is it to be?"

Sparn waved him into silence. "Nothing, it is to be nothing. Don't you see, Lucien? I have no reinforcements, because I have failed. I've been demoted. We're to stay here, you and I, with this petty troupe of demons. With this paltry force, we are to harass and torment the humans as best we can until the old prayer warrior finally dies and people forget to pray about this place. Until the prayer cover is lessened, we have no real hope of winning here. We are severely outnumbered."

Lucien's jaw dropped and an angry flush turned his face a mottled purple. "Do you mean to tell me that I'm stuck here? You promised me a promotion!"

Sparn frowned. "We didn't win, did we? So you get to share my demotion. Look on the bright side, Lucien. We're in this together." His hollow laughter filled the air, and Lucien found himself wondering about the demented look in his eyes. Maybe the old demon was losing his mental capacities.

Lucien stumbled out into the bright sunshine. It was unconscionable to think that he would have to stay in this miserable place for an unspecified length of time. What was he supposed to do? Play petty tricks in an attempt to lower morale? Why, he had a military mind. He was being wasted in this post. Couldn't anyone see that?

He raised his fist in the direction of the States. "You can't last forever," he shouted. "And when you die and everyone forgets about this place, I am the one who will reclaim it. I! Lucien! And then I will receive a promotion, and I will not have to eat the dust of this place ever again. And we will rule forever! Forever!"

His last shriek died into the wind as a sudden dust storm kicked up, surrounding him in a cloud of dirt and blotting his figure out of the landscape for a moment.

CHAPTER 19

Cindi was going over the menus with her replacement when the call came in. "It just rings like this all day," she explained to Pam. "Most of the time it's a prayer request, and we write those in here." She grabbed a green notebook and headed for the phone.

"Bennington residence," she said cheerfully.

"Cindi?" It was Marc's voice, but she barely recognized it. "Julia's in the hospital. It's time!"

The phone fell out of her hand, and she scrambled to pick it up again. "Marc? Right now? You mean it's time right now?"

"Yes," he laughed. "Right now. Hurry up!"

She hung up the phone without even saying goodbye and stared blankly at Pam.

"What's going on?" the woman asked. "Are you OK?"

"I'm having a baby!" she cried. "I mean, Julia is. My baby! I have to leave. Can you take over?"

"Certainly. You've gone over everything with me. I'll be fine. You go."

Cindi fled, the door slamming behind her. She returned sheepishly once for her purse and a second time for her jacket. The spring air was warm but tended to get chilly toward evening.

Although the trees were sporting a brand new set of leaves, Cindi didn't even take a moment to admire them.

The maternity ward at the hospital never seemed so far away. The parking lot was full, forcing her to park in one of the back lots. She sprinted cross-lots to reach the hospital, only to remember that she'd entered the opposite side. By the time she stumbled off the elevator on the correct floor, she was so breathless she felt lightheaded. She found Marc pacing back and forth in the lobby.

"Where have you been?" he asked excitedly.

"The traffic was heavy, and I had to park way in the back," Cindi tried to explain, panting. "But what's the rush? First babies take forever."

"Not this one," Marc said proudly. "A nurse just came out and told me it would only be about another fifteen minutes."

"Fifteen minutes?" Cindi squeaked, turning pale. "I . . . I have to sit down."

Marc laughed. "Why? You're not having a baby!"

"I feel as if I am," Cindi retorted. "Oh, Marc, can you believe it? In fifteen minutes I'll be holding my baby."

"Or sooner," Marc pointed out, nodding toward the nurse who just entered the lobby.

"Mr. and Mrs. Trahan?" she asked quietly. "The baby is crowning, and Miss Duffy asked me to come and get you. She would like you to take the baby as soon as it's born."

"She doesn't want to hold it first?" Cindi asked, worriedly.

The nurse shook her head. "No, she feels it would be best if you take the baby right away."

Cindi dug her fingers into Marc's arm as they followed the nurse down the hall. She led them into an anteroom to the nursery. "You can stay right here. We'll clean the baby up a little in the room. As soon as it is ready, we'll bring it in here for you to hold." She handed them both gowns. "Put these on, and then you may go into the nursery."

White-faced, Cindi and Marc put the scrubs on and went into the nursery, trying to ignore the babies lined up by the window. A young nurse was making rounds, taking the babies temperatures and heartbeats. She gave them a smile and continued on with her work.

Although it was only about ten minutes, it seemed like years before the first nurse returned with a tiny bundle in her arms. She smiled as she handed the baby into Cindi's waiting arms. "It's a girl," she replied to the question in their eyes.

Tears streaked Cindi's face as she looked with wonder at the tiny baby in her arms. "A girl," she whispered. "Did you hear that, Marc? A girl."

Marc reached out a tentative finger and stroked the baby's face. "Then she is Esther Julia Trahan. Hello, little Esther."

"Esther," Cindi echoed the name they had chosen long ago for the daughter they had always dreamed of. "Hello, Esther. You're such a beautiful baby." She looked up and found the nurse close to tears herself. "When can we see Julia?"

"They're getting her cleaned up right now, but in about fifteen minutes you could see her. Why don't you sit in the rocker, and I'll come get you when she's ready for visitors."

Cindi sat down in the rocker and Marc sat beside her. Her eyes were on the tiny face of her new daughter, but her thoughts were soaring with prayers of praise and thanksgiving.

Although Reissa knew that Cindi and Marc weren't aware of their presence, she knew they could feel the heavenly host surrounding them. A chorus of "Holy, Holy, Holy" had been started, and the angel voices added notes to the melody that had never been heard by human ears. It was as if an avalanche of snowflakes, each with a different pitch, were cascading down the side of a mountain, each in perfect tune with the others.

A soft knock on the nursery room door caught Cindi's attention. She looked up quickly, expecting a nurse, but instead found Russell. He had on a scrub suit.

"Mind if I take a look at my new granddaughter?" he asked.

Cindi smiled through her tears. "Of course not. Come in. Sit down." She gently handed him the baby and watched as his face crumpled and tears streamed down his face.

"Isn't she beautiful?" he sobbed. "I only wish I could watch her grow up." He looked up quickly. "Don't get me wrong. I'm glad you're adopting her, but it's hard to part with someone you are just getting to know."

A strangled little cry escaped Cindi's throat. "What do you mean? You're her grandfather. You'll always be her grandfather. Nothing will ever change that. I think Esther is fortunate that she has so many people to love her."

"We expect you to come and visit whenever you want," Marc insisted. "In fact, we're the fortunate ones, since we'll gain an extra babysitter."

Russell laughed. "You're both very kind. I know Julia didn't want to see, Esther, is it? She was afraid she'd become attached to her. Esther, that's a pretty name."

"Esther Julia Trahan," Cindi elaborated, putting emphasis on the Julia.

Russell looked up in surprise. "Esther Julia? How wonderful! Be sure to mention that to Julia. I think she'll like that."

A nurse interrupted them. "Julia may have visitors now," she said. "I think she'd like to see the adoptive parents."

Russell nodded his head. "Go on. I'll watch Esther until you get back."

Julia took Marc's hand, and they followed the nurse to Julia's room. She lay back against the pillows, pale and tired looking. She gave them both a faint smile when they walked in. Her red eyes betrayed that she'd been crying. Ray, sitting beside her, looked miserable too. For one crazy instant, Cindi was afraid they would decide not to go through with the adoption.

"How is she?" Julia asked weakly.

"She's beautiful," Cindi said, swallowing past the lump in her throat. "Your father is holding her right now. He's quite a proud grandparent."

Julia smiled. "I'll bet. He would have liked us to keep her." She exchanged a look with Ray. "But we still feel that this is better. You both can offer her a much better life than we can. There will be more children for us later. I feel sure that this is God's will for this baby."

Cindi found herself smiling as relief washed through her. "Esther," she said suddenly. "We named her Esther Julia."

Julia laughed softly. "Really? Esther Julia. I like that. Now she'll always have a part of me."

"She will anyway," Cindi assured her. "We intend to tell her all about you and Ray when she's old enough. I'm sure that she will respect you as much as we do for the decision you've made. I know it can't be an easy one."

Julia sniffed, and her eyes filled with tears. "No, no it hasn't been easy. But I don't want to be a second mother to her. She's your daughter. I don't want her to get confused. I want her to know about me, about us, but I want to follow her kind of at a distance, if that's all right."

Cindi nodded. "Whatever you feel comfortable with. I'm sure you'll hear of her progress through my brother Don when you get to Africa too. I'll be sure to write him long, newsy letters and tell him to pass them on."

Julia sank back a little onto the pillows. "That sounds good. If you don't mind, I'd like to get some sleep. It's been a rough day."

"Sure." Cindi gave Julia a quick hug before they left the room. "And thank you again."

They found Russell exactly where they'd left him. Esther, on the other hand, had woken up and wanted a bottle. One of the nurses was trying to show Russell how to feed her, but she wasn't having much luck.

"Here, Mommy," Russell said, giving up in disgust and handing the bottle and the baby to Cindi. "You do it. I'm all thumbs."

Cindi laughed and took his place, looking up helplessly at the nurse. "I'm afraid I don't know much more than he does."

After a quick lesson, Cindi was relieved to watch Esther settle down to her bottle. She sucked contentedly, eyes half closed.

"When can we bring her home?" Marc was asking the nurse.

"Miss Duffy will be released tomorrow, sometime before noon, so I expect that's when the baby will be released also, unless there are complications."

"Complications?" Marc was quick to ask.

"Nothing to worry about, I'm sure," the nurse assured him. "But sometimes babies develop jaundice and so have to stay longer. But it's really nothing to worry about."

That night Cindi went over everything in the nursery a hundred times, trying to assure herself that all was in readiness to receive Esther the next morning. Marc found her at one o'clock in the morning, sleeping in the rocking chair, cradling a stuffed rabbit.

The next day they arrived at the hospital before the patients had even been served their breakfast trays. Occupied with a rush of women in labor, the nurses were only too happy to turn over care of Esther to Cindi. The pediatrician arrived just before noon to check her out of the hospital.

"You mean we can go now?" Cindi asked nervously, half expecting some hidden reason why they must stay.

"Yes, you can go home now," the pediatrician echoed. "You've got one healthy baby there, Mrs. Trahan, but give me a call if you run into any problems."

"Marc, did you hear that? We can go home."

Marc grinned tolerantly. "Yes, honey, I heard. Let's go."

"Oh, we can't go yet," Cindi insisted, paling. "You've got to go check the car seat, and I have to talk to one of the nurses about formula and . . ."

Marc took her arm. "I've already checked the car seat a dozen times. And you've got formula that the nurses gave you. You can call them if you have any other questions. Come on. Let's go."

The ride home seemed to take an eternity, with Marc slowing at Cindi's insistence before every bump and pothole in the road. When finally they pulled up into the driveway of their home, Cindi breathed a sigh of relief before taking Esther gingerly out of the car. Marc took her arm and together, with baby paraphernalia hanging off every appendage, they made their way into the house.

Cindi set everything on the floor by her feet. She held Esther up slightly so the baby could see the house. Tears filled Cindi's eyes, and her throat choked up.

"Welcome home, Esther," she said simply.

Shania wrapped her golden wings around the trio. "God bless this house until He returns," she added.

As she prepared lunch, Billie Jo listened to the sounds coming from the other room. Cassidy and Dallas's childish voices mingled with Jimmy's deep one. They were asking him questions again. What did it feel like to sleep that long? Did he remember anything? Did he have any dreams? How did he know they needed him to wake up?

Ever since the day he'd begun to come out of the coma, they hadn't left his side. Somehow sensing that he needed rest, they played quietly. During the brief times when he woke up, they plied him with questions or told him stories. Gradually, the periods of time when he was awake began to outnumber the times when he slept.

Helen had come over several times, not saying much to Billie Jo; she confined her conversation to Jimmy. She told him how glad she was that he was awake, but wouldn't it be a good idea for them all to move in with her so she could help more? Jimmy continued to tell her that was unnecessary, but it didn't stop Helen from badgering him with the question every time she came.

Billie Jo held her tongue. She had won. There was no sense rubbing it in, even though she felt like it sometimes. She continued to be awed by what had happened and, almost as if afraid that gloating might somehow nullify all the good, she contented herself with pitying Helen. After all, she only continued on in this vein because she was lonely and wanted to be needed again. Understanding her motivation helped Billie Jo to cope with her mother-in-law.

Hearing Jimmy's deep laugh, she peeked around the corner of the half wall that divided the kitchen from the living room. Dallas was on Jimmy's lap as he sat reclining in the new recliner Helen had brought a week ago when she learned that he was strong enough to sit up. The child looked up adoringly into his father's face, hungrily observing his every expression.

"He thinks the world of you," Billie Jo said softly, coming up behind him.

Jimmy looked up at her, his face still thin by comparison to before the accident, but beautiful just the same. His warm brown eyes held her face as hungrily as Dallas's held his. They crinkled around the edges as he grinned. "Where you been hiding yourself, darlin'?"

He reached out one long arm and pulled her in close. "Look what Cassidy can do," he told her. Together they watched Cass as she recited the twenty-third Psalm. When she finished, Jimmy became sober.

"That was the closest I ever want to come to walking in the

valley of the shadow of death," he said quietly. "But you know, I don't remember the accident much, just Bubba screaming at me to get outta the way, but I remember the angels."

"Angels?" Billie Jo asked excitedly.

Jimmy nodded slowly, his eyes focused on something far away. "Yeah. I was in this dark place. It was comfortable and all, but I was missin' y'all terrible. Still, I didn't really want to leave it. Every now and then, though, I thought I hear'd you callin' at me. But then one day, this bright, shiny person, I dunno, I guess it must have been an angel, came and told me that y'all was in trouble and that I had to come quick."

Cassidy had crept in so close to her father that her breath blew gently on his cheek. "Don't stop, Daddy. Then what happened?" she begged.

Jimmy shook himself a little. "Well, I tried to come, but shoot! It was hard work. Sometimes I felt like I got outta that dark place for just a couple seconds when something pulled me right back, like quicksand. I could tell it didn't want to let me go." He smiled up at Billie Jo. "But when I opened my eyes and I saw your Momma's smilin' face, I knew I was back for good."

Cassidy and Dallas squealed with delight as Billie Jo bent down and kissed Jimmy fiercely.

"And don't you ever go away from us no more, Jimmy Raynard," she said passionately.

Jimmy chuckled. "Not a chance, darlin'."

The children climbed down off his lap and began to stack blocks. Jimmy leaned his head back against the chair and closed his eyes for a moment. Billie Jo reached out and stroked the hair back off his forehead as she had done so many times while he had been in the coma. He smiled.

"I remember that. You done that often?"

She nodded.

"So, darlin', do you think it was angels what brung me back to y'all?" he asked suddenly, his forehead wrinkling in doubt.

"Oh yes!" Billie Jo exclaimed. "Why, Jimmy, you have no idea how I prayed for you while you were in the coma. Me and so many other people. We put you on the prayer chain and everything. And I could feel them here. The angels, I mean. They were here. I'm sure of it."

"It's a funny thing," Jimmy reflected. "You know, I never was too much of a religious man, left that mostly up to you. But now I feel like the hand of God touched me. And I want to know more about Him. I want to know why He cared enough to help me. And I want to know what He done it for, my accident. Was it really an accident? Or did He have some purpose in it?" He laughed shortly. "I'm starting to sound like them kids asking me questions about being asleep. But I feel like a kid, in a way. Like a baby, starting all over again."

"And you are," Billie Jo said softly. "You're a baby Christian. I'm so glad, Jimmy. I've become a lot closer to the Lord myself through all this. Sometimes I couldn't see how I was going to make it or if it was even worth getting through. I was so tempted to give up, especially when the kids were gone. But God showed me that He cares for us at all times, not just in good times, but in bad times too."

"That He does, darlin'. That He does," Jimmy agreed. "And just as soon as I get onto my feet again, we're going to start going to church. As a family. My staying home days are through. We'll all go together."

Jewel smiled as she listened to them talk. It had been a long, dark journey for all of them, but one that ultimately brought them closer to the Light. This next part of her job, watching them grow in spiritual maturity, was her favorite. Oh, she expected to see Nog now and again, but the demon could have no real hold on these people unless they allowed him to. No, they were listening to the voice of the Master now, and she was His obedient servant.

Lyle popped a wheelie at the end of the driveway in his new racing chair while he waited patiently for Calla and Hershey. They were going to go jogging together as they did every day. At first, Lyle hadn't been able to keep up with Calla for more than a quarter of a mile or so. Now he could easily keep pace with her during her shorter route of four miles. He chafed with impatience, wondering if he'd ever be able to go the eight miles of her longer route.

"Come on, slowpoke," he yelled as he sighted her coming out of her house. She waved at him and did a few stretches before bounding down the road with as much energy as the dog next to her. Lyle spun out easily to her side as she ran past him.

"Ha, ha!" she laughed. "Who are you calling a slowpoke?"

"You," he teased, pulling ahead of her for a few strides to prove that if he had to, he could win a race against her any time. In truth, if it were short enough, he could. Calla had admitted that she was not fast at shorter distances.

"Slow and steady wins the race," she always reminded him. "Or at least that's what they tell me. But fast and steady probably wins more often."

Lyle got into a rhythm, propelling the racing chair along evenly beside her. Calla jogged easily, jabbering about being glad to be out of school and what she intended to do during summer vacation.

"Aunt Berniece wants me to take the summer off, but I don't think I will. I can't, actually. I need some money for books and things for next semester, and I'm not likely to get it loafing around in the backyard soaking up the sun. Although the glare might scare the ravens out of Aunt Bernie's garden," she said, laughing at her own joke.

"What kind of job are you going to get?" Lyle asked without taking his eyes off the road ahead of him.

"Oh, I don't know," Calla replied casually. "I thought about being a teller at a bank."

Lyle's hands slipped off the wheel, and for a second, he veered out into the road before he could correct himself. "You mean you're going to come work at the bank?" he asked incredulously.

"Why not?" Calla asked. "Know anyone who could give me a good reference?"

Lyle laughed. "That's funny. That's very funny." He feigned seriousness. "It's too bad. We have an opening for a data entry clerk. It's a temporary spot too. Only for a few months, because the woman who has the job is out on maternity leave. But you said you wanted to be a teller. Nope. Wouldn't work."

"What?" Calla shrieked. "You're pulling my leg, aren't you? Get out! Are you serious?"

Lyle grinned. "About which part?"

Calla swatted at him, but Lyle managed to duck. "Are you saying that you wouldn't mind being a data entry clerk for the summer?" he asked solicitously.

"Of course I wouldn't mind it, you goose!"

"Even if you had to work under me?" he persisted slyly. "I can be a pretty hard boss, you know. I have high standards for my employees."

"Oooooh," Calla teased. "Getting pretty high and mighty at the bank already, are we? Well, I think I can manage to work for you without one of us killing the other one. What exactly is your position at the bank, Sir Boss?"

"I'm in the Trust Department right now," Lyle said. He'd actually just been transferred, but it sounded good anyway. "I handle Cash Management."

"I'm impressed," Calla said. "Very impressed. Why didn't you tell me you had been promoted?"

"Wellll, it's not a promotion, exactly," Lyle admitted. "More of a transfer. But now I don't have to work with the customers. I'm a lot more comfortable behind the scenes."

They jogged along in silence for a moment before Lyle finally broke it.

"You know, I was wondering about something," he ventured, puffing a little from exertion.

"Oh, yeah? What's that?" Calla asked.

"Would you marry me?"

Calla stopped abruptly as if she'd run into a brick wall. Her mouth, which was hanging open, closed with a snap. "Did you say what I think you said?" she asked incredulously.

Lyle turned his chair and wheeled back to her, panting slightly. "That depends on what you think I said," he replied nervously.

"Say it again," she instructed.

"Would you marry me?" he repeated obligingly.

"That's what I thought you said." Calla jogged past him.

Lyle stared after her for a few minutes before pushing his chair hard to catch up. "Well?" he asked, pulling alongside her. "Are you going to answer the question?"

"Yes," she said simply.

Lyle glanced at her suspiciously. "Yes you're going to answer the question? Or Yes you'll marry me?" he asked.

"Both," she said. "But . . ."

The surge of joy Lyle felt at her answer died and a sense of dread took its place. "But, what?"

"Only if you can beat me to that tree," she finished.

Lyle nodded at the large elm that hung halfway across the road at the top. "That one?"

"Yup," Calla said. "Ready, set, go!" She sprinted ahead of him before he even realized what was happening.

"Cheater!" he yelled, applying himself fiercely to the wheels of his chair. The road slipped quickly beneath him as he drew up closer to Calla. Ten feet. Five feet. He slipped past her right at the finish line and let his chair careen to a stop on the grass beneath the old tree.

Calla came up to him out of breath. "Congratulations, you won," she smiled.

"You cheated," he accused her playfully. "I also think you let me win there at the end."

"Well," she said frankly. "I didn't think the chances of getting you to ask again were very good, so I stacked the deck. But, like you said, I did have a head start. Should we run two out of three?"

Lyle laughed. "Not a chance. I don't want to risk losing."

Calla flopped beside him on the grass, accompanied by Hershey, who panted like a runaway locomotive. "You know we can't get married until after I graduate from college, don't you?"

Lyle nodded. "Right now I'm just so happy that we're going to be married at all that time is no obstacle. Besides, I was thinking about going to college myself."

"Really? To do what?"

"I don't know yet, but I have finally realized that my life didn't end with the accident; I just opted out of it. It was my decision all along. Now that I have my whole life ahead of me again, I don't really know what I want to do with it yet. I'll pray about it, and I know that God will tell me what He wants me to do."

"Did you pray about us?" Calla asked.

Lyle nodded. "Fervently."

"Me, too," she admitted. "Ever since that day when Hershey found you under that tree. I knew then that I really liked you."

"Despite my handicap?" Lyle asked.

"No," Calla corrected him, "I think because of it. You were different. Angry at first but more focused and less vain than the guys I was used to. They were so hung up on looks. You didn't care."

"That's because I didn't have any to be hung up on," Lyle joked.

Calla swatted at him. "None that you knew of, maybe, hiding in the guise of an old man before your time. At least I know what you'll look like when you're old. But I saw the real you hidden inside right from the beginning."

"Must be that X-ray vision you've got," Lyle teased.

Calla sniffed. "Now you're making fun of me, but it's true. I was right, wasn't I?"

"I don't know," Lyle asked, fishing for a compliment. "Were you?"

Calla got up on her knees, crawled jerkily to the side of his chair, and kissed him hard on the mouth. "Yes, I was. I'm always right. Now, let's get going before we cool off. We've still got two miles to go."

Lyle continued to sit in the shade of the tree, still stunned by the kiss, until she yelled at him. "If you don't get moving, I *will* make it two out of three," she threatened.

Shelan followed behind the two of them as they made their way back home. Noble suddenly appeared beside her.

"You've done a wonderful job," he said. His voice filled the air like the haunting melody of panpipes, lingering long after he had finished speaking. "It was a tough assignment, with little hope at the beginning. You have managed well. The two of them will be very happy together too."

Shelan watched Calla and Lyle kidding with each other. "Yes, I believe you're right."

"This is Ali," Noble said, indicating an angel on his other side. "She is Calla's guardian angel. You have probably seen her before. The two of you can work together now. But," he looked around as if gauging the sky for storm clouds. "I think you'll have relatively little trouble from here on in. Still, be diligent, you never know when the enemy will strike."

Prayer Warriors

He laid a hand on each of their shoulders. "Goodbye, my children. You don't need my help anymore. I am returning to the Master. I look forward to the day when we will once again all be together." With those words he vanished, leaving only the imprint of his bright light.

A cool summer breeze brought the laughter of children and the murmur of voices fluttering into the room where Ethel Bennington sat with her head bowed in prayer. A slight smile crossed her face as she leaned forward so she could see out of her bedroom window.

Spread out on the manicured lawn beneath her, like so many colorful squares in a patchwork quilt, were mothers and their children. Some of the babies lay on blankets beside their mothers, others were being rocked or nursed. Small children played silly games of tag and other things they made up. Clustered in little groups, mothers were talking softly and praying.

Ethel caught sight of Cindi, leaning over little Esther. The baby was six months old now and trying to sit up. Just when Cindi thought Esther had her balance, she would pitch to one side or the other, smiling and giggling as if she thought it was a terribly interesting game.

Cindi's dream of a mother's prayer group had been accomplished, and Ethel wondered idly if Cindi realized that what she had started was much more than simply a time for mothers to get together and encourage one another. These women, whether they realized it or not, were on the front lines of battle against the enemy. Their prayers were strengthening ministers, staffing missions, restoring marriages, bolstering teachers, and nurturing children. Each thrust of the enemy was met by their parry of diligent prayer.

Their members included the battle-scarred and weary. Among them, Ethel could see the faces of Billie Jo and her friend Leah. Their children played with the others, but even in their carefree play, she knew they were not free from the effects of fallout.

From the trauma of being separated from his mother, little Dallas had been slow to speak, and when he did talk, it was with halts and slurred words. Billie Jo was quick to say that he would soon grow out of it now that he was safe, but fear and pain lingered in her eyes whenever the boy attempted to speak. Cassidy was a quiet girl whose outgoing nature had been curbed prematurely. When approached by strangers, she was quick to hide behind her mother. These scars would last a long time, but they would also serve as a reminder that evil would never permanently win.

Ethel drew away from the window with a sigh. As hurtful as it was to see the effects of sin in the world, she always reminded herself to look up. Soon Jesus would come back home. Though the victory was already won, the battle would soon be over. Then and only then could she rest in the joy of the Lord. Ethel bowed her head and took up her prayer where she'd left off.

Around her, angels busily came and went. Only Reissa stood quietly by Ethel's side, one strong hand on her shoulder. Her great strength filled the frail, old woman by her side, giving her both peace and persistence. It would be long after nightfall before Ethel would finish praying and seek any rest. Quietly, firmly, she led the assault against the enemy.